"A stunning, wonderfully tense thriller about deceit, grief, fame and perfection, and the secrets we carry beneath our skin. A magnificent, knockout thriller."
—Christina McDonald, *USA Today* bestselling author of *Do No Harm*

"Shocking twists, whip-smart turns, and a deep dive into the dark side of celebrity. I devoured it."
—Robyn Harding, bestselling author of *The Swap*

"As suspenseful as it is fast-paced and exquisitely thrilling . . . *Her Perfect Life* needs to be on your to-be-read list immediately. It's genius!"
—Hannah Mary McKinnon, bestselling author of *Sister Dear*

"I loved this book! My nerves were shredded by the time I reached the last chapter of this big-hearted page-turner."
—Rachel Howzell Hall, author of *And Now She's Gone*

"Yet another knockout novel by Ryan . . . A spectacular read!"
—Samantha M. Bailey, *USA Today* bestselling author of *Woman on the Edge*

"Ryan has a sure hand with her page-turning, twisty plotting and complex, multifaceted characters. Readers looking for a fast, thrilling read will love this one."
—*Library Journal*

HER
PERFECT
LIFE

HANK PHILLIPPI RYAN

A TOM DOHERTY ASSOCIATES BOOK
NEW YORK

This is a work of fiction. All of the characters, organizations, and events portrayed in this novel are either products of the author's imagination or are used fictitiously.

HER PERFECT LIFE

Copyright © 2021 by Hank Phillippi Ryan

All rights reserved.

A Forge Book
Published by Tom Doherty Associates
120 Broadway
New York, NY 10271

www.tor-forge.com

Forge® is a registered trademark of Macmillan Publishing Group, LLC.

ISBN 978-1-250-25884-7

Our books may be purchased in bulk for promotional, educational, or business use. Please contact your local bookseller or the Macmillan Corporate and Premium Sales Department at 1-800-221-7945, extension 5442, or by email at MacmillanSpecialMarkets@macmillan.com.

First Edition: September 2021
First Mass Market Edition: July 2022

Printed in the United States of America

0 9 8 7 6 5 4 3 2 1

For Jonathan, as always.
For my dear readers.
And for all of us—to honor and
remember those we lost.

HER
PERFECT
LIFE

PROLOGUE

They say you can't choose your family, but if you could, I would still have chosen Cassie.

She was my big sister, and everything she did was perfect. Her perfect dark hair, which curled or didn't depending on what Cassie wanted. She had perfect friends, and perfect dates, and whispered phone calls, and boys came to pick her up in their cars. She got to wear lipstick. Once when I sneaked hers and tried it, she caught me. She didn't even laugh. Or yell. Or tell on me.

When Cassie went away to college that year, something changed. She came home for winter break, but she stayed in her room. My mother and I couldn't figure out what she was doing. Cassie would come out only to make cups of coffee, then stare out the window at our snow-dappled backyard, at the pond where she'd tried to teach me to ice-skate, and at the big sycamore tree where we once found a huge hornets' nest that fell in a summer wind. I'd picked it up, and wanted to save it for show-and-tell, but Cassie screamed and told me it was full of bugs. She grabbed it from me, and one stung her. She didn't even cry.

We had a dog, too, a dear and dopey rescue named

Pooch. Cassie never liked the name, but our dad did. And then Dad died, and Cassie never wanted to change Pooch's name again.

When she left for college, Mumma kept her room just the way it was, with all her stuffed animals and souvenirs and photographs, and didn't let me move out of my little bedroom into her bigger one. Cassie was always the favorite, and I always thought of it as her right.

That first college winter vacation, my mother found a notebook, one of those black ones with white dots on the cover. She opened it to the first page. I saw her face change. Without a word, Mumma turned the notebook to show me. Cassie had drawn a calendar, with carefully ruled pencil lines spaced equally apart. November. Then December. She'd crossed off the days, each one, with an X in black marker.

"Poor Cassie," Mumma said to me. I remember how soft her voice was, carrying an undercurrent of worry or sorrow. "I wonder what day she's waiting for. This is not the work of a happy person."

"I know," I'd agreed, nodding sagely, though at age seven, I didn't really know. And it was almost as if Mumma wasn't talking to me, but just to herself. I do remember how I felt then, even remember my eyes widening in fear of things, dark things or scary things, under the bed or in the closet—things that kids' imaginations, if they're lucky, conjure as murky vanishing faraway nothings. Things that come in the night. Visitors. My mother's worry was contagious, too, a chronic disease I have yet to conquer. "Mumma? What do you think is wrong with Cassie?"

And then Cassie was gone.

The police said they looked and looked for her, even said they'd tried to make sense of the calendar she'd left behind. My mother got sicker and sicker waiting for her.

Years later, I went off to college myself. By then, Pooch had died.

Mumma eventually died, too, never knowing.

And then there was only me.

What happened to Cassie? I imagined her dead, of course. I'd imagined her kidnapped, imprisoned, hidden, brainwashed, indentured, enslaved, made into a princess, transported by aliens to their faraway planet. I saw her in grocery stores, on book covers, in the backgrounds of movies, a lifted shoulder or sunlight on a cheekbone, that little dance she did when she was happy. Once I saw the back of her head three rows in front of me on a plane from Boston to New Orleans and leaped out of my seat with the seat belt sign still on, but it wasn't her dark hair and not her thin shoulders, not her quizzical smile after my lame *Oh, I thought I knew you* excuse.

We were too far apart in age, I guess, to have that sister connection some people talk about, the sense of knowing where the other is, or when they're upset. Sure, she was my only big sister. But she was already wrapped up in her own concerns, and I was a goofy little kid, and my sibling worship didn't have the time to evolve into mystical bonding. Was she still alive?

I still have a picture of her and Pooch, the one Dad took with his camera that wasn't a phone. The almost-sepia rectangle of daughter and dog is faded now, and cracking, with old-fashioned wavy once-white edges. The original one is in my apartment, and the copy thumbtacked to the bulletin board over my desk at Channel 6.

At some point you have to stop looking, I told myself. But still. If she did something truly bad, how much did I want to know? How would that knowledge change my life? My career? Maybe it's better for me to pretend she never existed.

But I know she did exist.

Sometimes it feels like she still comes to me in my dreams, this time asking me to find her. So I couldn't help but imagine that; approaching her, confronting her, gently, gingerly, or standing in her line of sight to see if there was a glimmer.

Would I even recognize my big sister after all this time? I was seven when she vanished, and Cassie was eighteen, so . . . maybe.

Maybe not.

Or maybe she'll recognize me. She'll find *me*.

CHAPTER 1
LILY

Standing center stage at the spotlighted podium, a newly won Emmy in hand and a glitteringly bejeweled audience applauding her, Lily knew she was being ridiculous. But she examined each face, quickly as she could, from the big shots in the front row to the smaller-market wannabes in the back of the Boston Convention Center auditorium to the randoms scurrying the periphery—the latecomers, the technicians, the bustling event staff and black-uniformed security. Was that one Cassie? Was *that* one?

It was absurd. Foolish. Delusional. There was no way Cassie would be in this audience, but that would not stop Lily from looking, scanning, wondering. Not just tonight, but everywhere she went. Her brain had developed its own facial recognition software, grown adept at comparing and analyzing. And always rejecting. *So far.*

But tonight it wasn't only Cassie she was looking for. And that made Lily's scrutiny all the more intense.

The applause quieted, most upturned faces now expectant. Lily saw a few glance at their watches. Ten fifteen on a Saturday night. Losers yearned to go home.

"I'm so thrilled to accept this on behalf of all the

Lily Atwood team . . ." She knew that sounded glib, but rules allowed only one recipient at the podium, necessary to prevent rambling wine-fueled acceptance speeches. "We all work so hard, and let me especially thank my darling producer, Greer Whitfield, without whom—stand up, Greer!"

She pointed to a front table, and saw her gesture magnified, becoming gigantic in the huge TV monitors flanking her, the white sequins of her body-hugging gown shimmering. Greer stood for a fraction of a second, and Lily could see her colleague's discomfort at being the center of attention even for that long. Lily blew her a sincere kiss, then went on.

"And thank you to all who have contributed to our success—including my confidential sources." She winked and got a murmur of laughter in return. "This is a shared honor." She heard the wrap-it-up music, spoke more quickly. "It's an inspiration, and a promise to continue to protect the public from . . ."

She finished her speech, did one last crowd check as her colleagues applauded again, then accepted the arm of the tuxedoed host who escorted her backstage to the professional makeup person they'd hired to make sure the winners looked even more perfect in their triumphant photos.

The makeup artist in her white apron—*Too young, not Cassie*—and hairstylist in a black smock—*Too old, not Cassie*—and the officious pompadoured photographer with his too-tight black shirt and too-tight black jeans. *Not Cassie.*

"Congratulations," the photographer said. He eyed her up and down. "I'm Trent. I'll make you look more gorgeous than you already do. Big, *big* fan."

Lily smiled, accustomed—and inured—to the scrutiny. Leering men, brash and brazenly familiar, were part of her life. She'd dealt with it too long to be unnerved by it, most of it at least, and the ones who pushed too hard got pushed right back.

As long as none of the ugliness touched Rowen.

Rowen was safe, Lily knew, safe with nanny Petra, probably deep into one of Rowe's beloved spy-kid novels. Since Rowe had started on chapter books, she'd insisted she wanted to be a spy, "Just like you, Mumma." No matter how often Lily explained investigative journalism, Rowe, with the stubborn wisdom of a seven-year-old, would have none of it. Lily's cell phone was set to vibrate at a call from Petra, and Petra had learned to be just as vigilant as Lily. Not on the lookout for Cassie, of course, but for the unknown.

Fame, Lily knew, had two conflicting sides. The glory. And the danger. The power. And the spotlight. The raging relentless spotlight.

"Smile, Lily." The photographer—Trent—had used her first name as if they were the best of pals. Familiarity was permanently attached to fame. The smiles of recognition. Selfies-on-demand with people in grocery stores and on the T, people at airports and the dry cleaners. Lily's face was in their living rooms and bedrooms and on their cell phones via streaming video. They saw her, close up and constantly. No wonder they felt like they knew her. But Lily, on the opposite side of the TV camera, could never see whose eyes were on her. What strangers heard her every word.

"Lily? Hon? Turn your body this way now." Trent demonstrated, angling his own shoulders, tilting his chin, eyes looking up from under his lashes as if Lily didn't know exactly how to arrange her face for its best angle. A black-shirted assistant adjusted a battery of lights on metal stands, fumbling with clanking flaps that softened the high-wattage bulbs.

"Give us that famous Lily smile," Trent ordered. "*Love* the camera."

As his flashbulbs popped and bloomed, Lily heard more applause from inside the auditorium, other winners and more losers. Was her source here? Somewhere? Tonight, Cassie wasn't the only person she was looking for. Lily was also searching for *him*. Her new and unerringly knowledgeable source. The one who had, in just the past few weeks, given her a couple of amazing stories. Lily couldn't help but wonder if he—or she?—would be here tonight. To share Lily's success? Or maybe, although disturbing to consider, with some other agenda. A motive.

Lily had to laugh at herself. That worry—her chronic assessing worry—helped make her a good reporter. If whatever she feared didn't happen, all the better. If it did, she'd be prepared.

Trent fussed with his lights, instructed his assistant, demonstrated yet another pose. One particular security guard wearing a black cap and starched black shirt seemed to eye her with more than ordinary curiosity. Was *he* the source? A vested waiter, carrying a tray of empty wineglasses. Why had he stopped to adjust the linen-covered high-top table directly across from her? *Everything isn't about me,* she reminded herself. But it was difficult to ignore the spotlight when it followed you everywhere.

"Two more, Lily," Trent announced. He'd tilted his head the other direction now, motioning her to copy him. She remembered the first time she'd heard her source's voice. To this day, she and Greer debated whether the caller was really a man.

But he'd told them to call him Mr. Smith. And the caller's tips had turned out to be true.

The stories were nothing Lily and Greer couldn't have found on their own if they'd thought to look. But they were dead-on accurate. Lily and Greer had begun to trust him. To look forward to his calls.

Last week, he'd blown the whistle on the local health inspector's school cafeteria reports. Dozens of them, he'd revealed, were signed and dated the same day.

"It's impossible," Mr. Smith had whispered. "How can they properly do all those inspections in one day? I fear they are faking them. And it is putting kids at risk."

Lily, imagining her own first-grader Rowen with food poisoning or salmonella or some hideous virus, had tracked down the documents. Mr. Smith was correct. The health inspector—facing Lily and her photographer's video camera and barricaded behind his institutional wooden desk—had denied, made excuses, stalled, misdirected, and then outright lied.

"We have no evidence of foodborne illness," the man said.

That's when Lily knew she had the goods. "Have you ever *looked* for evidence?" she asked.

"That's absurd. Of course we've looked."

"I see. Let me put it another way." Lily had pulled the stack of questionable reports from the manila files she held on her lap. "How do you explain this, then? You did *all* these inspections the same day?"

She'd placed the incriminating paperwork on the desk in front of the inspector, at which point he stood, yanked off his lapel microphone, and ordered her out of the room. They'd caught it all on camera.

The inspector's wife—enraged—had called Lily after the damning story aired. And her husband got fired. "How could you do this to him?" the woman demanded.

"I didn't do it to him," Lily had gently reminded her. "He did it to himself."

Now she looked again at her newest Emmy. People had gone to prison as a result of the story the shiny statue honored. Lily's victories, in the strange calculus of television news, were someone else's disasters.

"Got it, Lily," Trent said as a final flash came from his camera. "You're—"

A burst of applause came from the auditorium as the double doors clanked open. Three tuxedoed men, arms draped across each other's shoulders, barreled out, hooting self-congratulations and brandishing their trophies.

"Take our photo!" one demanded. "Move it, Lil! Our turn!"

"Thanks, Ms. Atwood," Trent's pink-haired assistant whispered as Lily stepped away from the backdrop. *Too young, not Cassie,* Lily's brain registered as the young woman went on. "You're so awesome. I wish I could be just like you."

Lily's cell phone, tucked into the black satin evening bag hanging on a thin chain over her shoulder, vibrated against her thigh.

She grabbed it, clicked it. "Thank you so much," she said to the assistant, but her mind was racing. Petra was only supposed to text if something—

It wasn't Petra. *Sender unknown.*

Congratulations, the text read. *The white sequins are perfect.*

Lily gasped. Her eyes darted to the left, to the right, to closing doors, and winding corridors, to the marble-floored lobby filled with celebrants milling about clinking glasses and laughing and posing for selfies. He—or she?—was here. Had to be. No other way for him to know about her dress.

Who is this? she typed back. *Where are you?*

You know who it is. The words appeared, dramatic in their time delay. She could almost hear his—her?— voice saying them.

Lily began to type, but the next words came up before she could send.

I'll call you Monday. The words seemed to glow, and the hubbub around Lily faded into the background as another message appeared. *And I'll give you the best story ever.*

CHAPTER 2

GREER

Did I want to be Lily Atwood? Well, sure, I suppose. But a whole lot would have to change for that to happen. Like everything. Right now I was too mismatched, too awkward-faced, too curly-haired, too exactly not what a TV star looked like. So I learned to be the smart one. Greer Whitfield, the smart one.

I'd watched Lily, same as everyone else, as she accepted her Emmy—ours, really—in front of the worshipping crowd in the convention center. She'd thanked me, extravagantly and elegantly, with a toss of her Lily hair and a sincere smile on her Armani lips and those white sequins glittering her personal starlight. I'd stood, briefly, as she'd ordered me to, the audience murmuring their approval. They weren't approving me, though, but Lily's effortless generosity, her understanding of team spirit, their longing to be just like her. Approval is such a sister to envy.

Lily's now-empty chair was next to me at the banquet table Channel 6 purchased, the white damask tablecloth littered with shards of baguette crusts and the purple blotch of someone's spilled cabernet, but Lily's napkin was folded artfully by her dessert plate, not even a lipstick smudge on her white china coffee cup. I worry that I sound envious when I describe this, but I'm not. It's not me who creates the food chain, it's the rest of the world. I am smart enough to know how that works. And where my place is.

But being the smart one can take you a long way in television. The smart one is not your rival, the smart one is not your adversary or challenger. The smart one, if they're smart *enough*, is the team player who'll make you more famous, be the brains and the messenger and the organizer. And have the confidence—or pragmatism—to let you take the compliments and applause. Or, on the days things don't go your way, the blame. It was fine for me to take the blame; blame rolled off me like whatever cliché you choose. And I honestly didn't care, that's another critical element. I was the one you're not *supposed* to like. The tough one, the rule-enforcer, the keeper of deadlines. The protector of Lily's flame. Her fame.

Other women in the Emmy audience—the ones not captivated by Lily—sneaked a moment to check their own reflections in fancy compacts, comparing the lift of their eyebrows to Lily's carefully natural ones, the color of Lily's lipstick to their own, wishing their hair were better or different or more like Lily's; wondering how long their faces would last and how Lily, at only thirty-three, an age she'll reveal instantly if asked, can look so young and so chic and so wise at the same time. *So Lily,* as I have actually heard people say. Now they've clicked their compacts shut, given themselves a personal score that only counts in the mathematics of fame.

I was seriously not jealous of her, that's what people didn't understand. I honestly admired her. I wanted her to succeed. If she succeeds, I succeed, and the station succeeds, and everyone is happy. Especially me, since as long as she has a job, I have a job. Television only works if the hierarchy is respected, each person does their designated job to the best of their ability and understands no matter what, it's the "talent" who gets the credit.

Lily was the definition of talent. And it's not that she doesn't work hard, and it's not that she isn't sincere, and she's definitely not a diva.

Just ask her, ha ha.

No, truly, she's terrific.

She's so super-terrific that last year she turned down a New York network job—a job they'd offered us as a team—so she could stay in Boston and not have to make her daughter, Rowen, change schools. "I'm so sorry," she'd told me, tears in her eyes.

"Forget it," I'd assured her. And it was true, I was perfectly fine staying here. It was just me, no family, no life. No pets, because how could you be fair to an animal when work is 24–7? The way I looked at it, and really there's no other way to look at it, I was married to television. I didn't need to be a bigger fish in a bigger pond. I didn't need friends.

In the tumult of the and-the-winner-is applause, Lily had urged me to join her onstage, even though she knew it was against the rules, because Lily doesn't care about rules. Plus she knew I'd refuse, as I have for the past almost-two years we've worked together and the past two times she's—*we've*—won Emmys. We're a good team, she's told me, Lily-and-Greer, and she's right. She has the fame, and all that comes with it. I don't need that. I have other skills.

CHAPTER 3

LILY

"Did you win, Mumma?"

Rowen's sleep-thickened little voice came from under the white down comforter. Her daughter, somehow, always sensed when Lily had come to her bedroom door to check on her, even if only to watch her sleep. Petra had been dozing on the living room couch when Lily got home, head on one of the fringed butterscotch suede pillows. Valentina, fidgeting in some cocker spaniel dream, curled on the carpet beside her. Val opened her eyes as Lily came in, then closed them again.

"Did you?" Rowe persisted. "I'm not going to sleep 'til you tell me."

"I did, sweetie," Lily whispered. "I just came to make sure you're still perfect. And you are. Go back to sleep. It's very late."

"Yay. Told you. I knew you would win." One thin arm flopped the comforter away. Rowen, head still on her penguin pillowcase and clutching her plush black-and-white Penny to her chest, opened one eye, then the other, then abruptly sat up in the top bunk, her penguin night-light glowing on the wall beside her, and spread her arms wide, entreating. "Did you bring it? Can I have it?"

"Yes and yes, honey," Lily said, holding up the

statue. "We'll talk tomorrow. Night-night, love and penguins."

"Night-night, love and penguins, Mumma. But I'm not one bit sleepy," Rowen insisted, but her eyes fluttered, struggling to stay open. "And we get to be on TV still, right? Me and you?"

"We'll see, honey. We're not quite sure yet, okay?" Lily put her Emmy on Rowen's lace-topped dresser, the figure's raised globe and pointed wings reflected in the mirror. She'd hoped Rowen would forget about Monday's TV taping. Lily had tried to get out of it, and, so far, failed. "I'll leave Emmy for you, though. And she can keep you company."

Lily crossed to Rowen, the hem of her white dress dragging on the carpeted floor, too long now after she'd yanked off her strappy high-heeled silver sandals. "And Emmy will make sure you have sweet dreams. Kisses?"

But Rowen had slung her legs over the side of her bed, her bare feet dangling into the airspace over the bunk below. "You're so pretty, Mumma. Can I have that dress someday?"

"Sure, honey. You can have everything you want. Someday." She swung her daughter's legs back under the covers and tucked the puffy comforter around her thin shoulders, making sure the raggedy stuffed penguin, one eye missing and once-black wings thinning, was in place in the crook of Rowen's arm. "Is it maybe about time for your dear old Penny to get a gentle ride in the washing machine?"

"You're so pretty, Mumma . . ." Rowen's voice trailed off, and her long eyelashes fluttered gently, then closed against her soft cheeks. Lily watched her little chest rise and fall, memorizing her, absorbing the fragile innocence of her seven-year-old. The time seemed to go by so quickly, every day so fleetingly precious, with Lily constantly battling to prevent her own celebrity from coloring Rowe's view of the world. And increasing her vulnerability.

They'd gone through a rough patch, two years ago, when Rowe had started asking about her father. Lily hadn't been ready to discuss it, and, stalling, had successfully skirted the issue. But an insistently curious woman in the produce section of the grocery store had stolen Lily's control over that.

"And this must be Rowen," the woman had said, reaching out to the little girl, almost touching her, until Lily had inched the shopping cart between them.

The woman—black yoga pants and a shabby-chic leather jacket, stylish crimped hair, and careful lip gloss—had looked Rowen up and down, assessing. "I've heard all about you on Facebook, Rowen," she said. She'd started digging into a black leather tote bag, and Lily had felt her own heart constrict when the woman pulled out a cell phone. "I love penguins, too. Do you and your mother visit them at the aquarium? Can I take a selfie with you two? Right here by all these beautiful apples?"

No, no, no, Lily thought. She never put Rowe's photo on social media, not a recognizable one at least, but once used a shot from behind showing Rowe's sandy hair in a penguin-ribboned ponytail. *BG loves penguins,* Lily had captioned. She called Rowen *BG* online, for baby girl, and never used her name. How did this woman know it? Easy enough, Lily supposed. It was impossible to keep anything secret.

Lily had wanted to yank the penguin ribbon out of Rowe's hair, right there in front of the Granny Smiths and the Honeycrisps, and spin her cart away. But the public Lily had to be approachable, relatable, engaging. One wrong word in the Star Market and the internet could turn Lily from beloved icon to full-of-herself bitch. Social media loved a falling star.

"Oh, I'm so flattered, thank you, but how about

you and me? Just the two of us?" Lily had stopped the selfie train in its tracks. "But not my—"

"Of course," the woman said, the warmth leaving her voice in just those two words. She stashed her phone away with an unnecessarily dramatic gesture. "Far be it from *me* to intrude on your precious—"

"So kind of you, I so appreciate it," Lily had said, as sincerely as she could, then turned her cart deliberately, telegraphing her intention to continue down the aisle. "Happy shopping!"

"Why do we never hear about Rowen's father, Lily?"

In the beat of silence that followed, Rowen had curled a finger into a belt loop of Lily's jeans and tucked herself in behind her mother. Rowen, then not even four feet tall, had left no space between the two of them.

"Oh, gosh, I beg your pardon?" Lily tried not to react, tried not to grab a Winesap and lob it at the woman's smug face. "I'm not sure why you'd ask me that."

"You *media*," the woman had sneered, suddenly a viper. "You think you're above it all." She pivoted her cart, then pivoted it back. "Better ask your mother about him, *Rowen*," she'd said. And then, the wheels of her cart rattling, had bustled away.

"Attention shoppers," a fuzzy voice on the public address system had boomed through the store. "In our famous cheese section right now, a demonstration of all the different kinds of Parmesan . . ."

Rowen had not budged. Around them, shoppers pushed their rackety metal carts, a display of Meyer lemons tumbled to the ground as a toddler wailed, the fragrance of fresh cilantro and parsley, of ripening cantaloupes and pungent spring onions surrounding them, just another Saturday in the grocery. Except for Rowen and Lily, now side by side at a moment in their lives that Lily had planned for. She *had*. But not now, not today. Not in the grocery store.

Rowen had asked, of course, since about the time she'd turned four: *Why don't I have a daddy?* And Lily had been ready for that. *You do have a daddy,* she'd assured the little girl, *and I love him very much, but he lives far away, and I love you enough for both of us.* That had satisfied Rowen; or seemed to. But then the grocery store viper struck.

"Mumma?" The girl's almost-green eyes had welled, widening, as they looked into Lily's matching ones. Lily had stooped, dropping herself to Rowe's height.

"What, honey?" Lily knew Rowen would ask—her daughter was whip smart, with a memory like a computer. Lily had learned not to make promises she couldn't keep. And negotiation was less and less successful.

"Why did the lady ask about my father?" Rowen whispered.

Lily felt like bursting into tears. "Why do *you* think, honey?"

A shopping cart or two rolled by them, impossible for the shoppers pushing them to know a life-changing moment was occurring in the fruit department.

"Does she know him?"

"No, honey, I'm sure she doesn't." Which wasn't quite true. The woman was probably just a toxic gossip-monger. But Lily couldn't be sure of anything, especially not about Sam Prescott. Not about what he wanted or where he was or why he'd made the decisions he'd made. It was her fault, too, a massive error in judgment for both of them that had resulted in the most adorable child imaginable. Lily would never have decided otherwise. Sam knew that, and had agreed, never tried to stop her, left her to it. And soon after, left both of them entirely.

She alternately cursed Sam Prescott and longed for him. He'd told her his wife, enraged, had found out about them. Demanded he cut all ties. As a result, he was missing out on his own daughter; either exactly what the bastard deserved, or unendingly sad. Lily had resisted googling him as much as she could. But she knew Sam was still practicing law, and divorced, and then married again, to some Isabel DeSoto, la dee dah, who was rumored to be running for Congress or something in Colorado. Big money, big family, big power. Big boobs. No kids. Ticked all the necessary Sam boxes, apparently.

But difficult for Lily to be angry when she was as much to blame. And maybe it wasn't about blame, but more about trust and hope and passion. Glorious ridiculous reality-twisting passion. Twenty-seven days. She'd trusted Sam so much, she'd even told him about Cassie. So much for that idea. So much for trust.

Rowen's lower lip began to pooch out, the sign that she was thinking, and not happy thoughts. *Pout-face,* Lily called it. Lily glanced at each shopper who went by, making sure she wasn't about to be criticized by some meddling busybody.

"What are you thinking about, kiddo?" Lily asked.

"Did my daddy not like me?"

"He loves you, baby girl," Lily whispered as shoppers steered around them, probably thinking little Rowen was being stubborn or demanding. Lily hoped they weren't analyzing her parenting, and tried to adopt a pleasant, unworried expression. If Rowen melted down in public, it would instantly magnify, multiply onto social, her personal life as fodder to be dissected and criticized. #badmother, she could picture it. Setting the internet on fire. "We just decided to live far away from each other, honey. And I love you double much."

"Double much?" Rowen's head tilted as they walked, as if calculating.

"Triple much, super much, the most muchness there could be." Lily leaned down, kissed her daughter's forehead. "Now. Your choice. Should we keep talking, or should we look for peaches?"

"Peaches!"

Two years had gone by, Lily thought now, looking at her daughter's sleeping face. Rowen had accepted, Lily hoped, that her father lived far away, and had "issues," a word Lily used to explain reality while glossing over specifics. Rowen didn't need to know about their first weekend in Aspen, or what happened in the days after, or Sam Prescott's manipulative first wife, or his ambitious new one, or the single most impetuously bad decision Lily had made in her adult life. Rowen had been the result, and Lily was fine with that. When she was a little older, Lily might tell her more of the story. The rest of the story. A better story.

A better story. Why did those words remind her of—oh. Her source. Who'd promised to call Monday. Lily's newest Emmy glowed in the soft night-light as she tiptoed toward the door of her daughter's bedroom.

If Rowen didn't exist, Lily thought, it would be as if she herself didn't exist. How had her own mother dealt with Cassie's disappearance? How could she have let it happen? She hadn't understood the intensity of the connection, not really, not until Rowen appeared in her world. But she'd never let anything happen to her daughter. Never. She touched the wooden doorframe, just to make sure.

"Night-night, love and penguins," she whispered. But Rowen was fast asleep.

CHAPTER 4
GREER

I knew Lily didn't want to do this, and I knew she'd freak when she saw me and the camera crew marching up the begonia-lined bluestone front walk of her home at nine o'clock on a Monday morning, but she certainly understands TV news isn't only about journalism. It's about the people who watch TV, and the need to keep them watching. And how we do that is by making our TV reporters be endearing, adorable, appealing. Just like you, only luckier, prettier, smarter. With gorgeous homes and designer kitchens and fresh-cut flowers year-round. In sales meetings we called it *aspirational,* as in "to make viewers aspire to having everything the talent has."

If viewers knew what "having everything the talent has" meant, they'd rethink their position.

Wade and Warren, the photographer and the light guy, had parked the white Channel 6 news van in Lily's asphalt driveway, and now were arguing over who had to carry what and why they had to shoot a lame feature instead of real run-and-gun news. They'd rather shoot someone getting killed, or already dead, or at least something burning. Today, they had Lily. Lily and her daughter, Rowen, who calls Lily "Mumma." As if they're royalty.

I poked the black doorbell button on the front of Lily's white Victorian, one of those uniquely quirky Wellesley homes with manicured suburban lawns and ancestral trees. Her mailbox was already full, with white and brown envelopes sticking out the top of the black metal container, so I grabbed them as a good teammate does. The graceful pale green branches of Lily's ancient weeping willow fluttered in the soft May breeze.

The bell chimed inside, and I readied myself to win this impending battle. Channel 6's up-close-and-personal "Summer on Six" series was an annual command performance. Even for Lily Atwood. Especially for Lily.

"You know how much I hate this, Greer," she said, even before she got the front door all the way open.

"Here's your mail," I said, handing her the pile of assorted paperwork. "Can we leave the door open for Wade and Warren? They've got the gear."

"Don't try to distract me with the mail." Lily took the envelopes and tossed them on a glossy wooden side table as I followed her into the living room. I knew she neglected her mail, as if the world should magically pay her bills or schedule her appointments. Fan mail came to the station, as well I knew. Since I answered it. Her cell phone was stuck into a back pocket of her jeans. "You're truly going to make us do this?"

I almost laughed at the fresh pink-and-white lilies cascading from a crystal vase on the coffee table, and nubby green containers of massed paperwhites blooming fragrantly along the front bay window. Equally aspirational—her long white couch, mounded with white and butterscotch pillows, and the pale butterscotch side chairs bringing springtime to Lily's living room year-round. A *white couch,* for god's sake. With a seven-year-old.

"Is there no way out of it?" Lily, hands on hips,

stopped under the white archway leading to her dining room and then to the kitchen. Our destination, if
all went the way I'd planned. The backyard was my
plan B.

Her hair was still twisted up on top of her head, and
she was still barefoot, a simple white tee tucked into
her beltless jeans. But I could tell by the fresh eyeliner
that she'd begun to put on makeup, so I figured she
understood there was no avoiding the shoot. I simply
needed to let her think the decision to proceed was
her idea. Even though Wade was already lugging the
awkward steel tripod and clanking aluminum light
stands into the front hallway, with Warren behind
him, trundling the black metal roller case of lights.

"It's not *me* making us do it," I semi-lied, saying "us"
so she'd understand how little influence I had. "It's the
powers that be. You're Lily Atwood, right? And your
viewers can't get enough of you."

"But I hate that I have to—" Lily was shaking her
head, crossing her arms in front of the Ralph Lauren
logo on her shirt. "What if we just—"

"Listen, kiddo, there are reporters who they're not
using in this feature. That's when you've gotta worry,
right? Being wanted is a good thing. Look on the
bright side."

"Mumma! Greer!" Lily's daughter Rowen had the
nanny by one hand and was dragging the poor young
woman into the living room, Lily's carefully adorable
dog prancing at their heels. Petra went to Wellesley
College, nannied while she figured out her next career. She'd contemplated moving home to Sweden or
Denmark, someplace like that. Of course Lily had a
cover-girl nanny, all engaging accent and a tumult of
blond hair.

"I'll take the puppy," Petra said. "Unless? You need
me?"

"He's fine here," Lily said as the dog snuffled at her blue-jeaned legs. "See you later, Petra. Have fun."

"Wow, do you get bigger every day, Rowey?" I gave in to Rowen's running hug as her nanny left us, the little girl's head coming just above to my waist. She was such a mini-Lily, the same sandy hair and wiry shape, even her forest-green eyes. She smelled of almonds and vanilla, same as her mother, and even wore the same jeans and white tee.

"I'm almost eight. In three months. Are we doing our TV today?"

"We sure are, kiddo," I said before Lily could answer. "And here's Wade and Warren. You remember them?" I flinched as Wade's tripod narrowly missed knocking into the vase of lilies.

"Hey, Rowen," they said at the same time. "Hey, Lily."

Warren hefted his camera. "Where do you want us, Greer?"

"Outta here," Lily answered, but she was smiling.

Of course, Lily knew enough to be congenial with her crews. Rowen had slipped her hand into Lily's, looking at her with joy and anticipation. It was tempting to shoot them right there in the light of the late-morning sunshine, oh-so-casual mother-daughter celebrity peas in a pod.

"Kitchen?" I suggested. "Viewers love that. How you've decorated, and whether you have the fancy pots and pans. This is supposed to be a welcome-to-summer feature, what the news team stars do in their spare time. Maybe you two can make ice cream, something summery like that."

"Make ice cream." Lily's tone dismissed that idea.

"Ice cream!" Rowen, at least, was on board.

Lily's phone rang, a three-note trill. Her face went white. The phone trilled again.

"Lil?" I asked. "What?"

She was clearly expecting a phone call, or news of some kind. She'd reacted, instantly and dramatically, to the sound. A thousand possibilities crossed my mind—doctors, lovers, relatives. Not that I knew any of those people. I'd tried to find out, casually, as most work colleagues do, but Lily was a vault about her personal life. She wasn't closing me out, she truly wasn't, she was like that to everyone.

"Rowe? Honey? Will you take Wade and Warren to the backyard? We'll shoot out there. Just like we talked about?" Lily's voice seemed tense. "In a minute, sweetie."

The three had barely taken a few steps when Lily turned her back on them, put the phone to her ear. "Mr. Smith," she silently mouthed to me. "Hello?" she said into her cell.

Mr. Smith. No two words could have made me happier. Whoever he was—or she, I still wasn't convinced—had given us a couple of slam-dunk stories, and if our new source was about to lay another one on us, all good.

"Hello?" Lily said again. "Hello?"

I eased closer to her.

"Nothing," she said, and looked at the phone again.

"Damn," I said. I saw her expression. "What? You suddenly down on our hero?"

Lily blew out a breath, plopped down on her pristine white couch. She stretched out her legs, her pale blue toenails perfect, of course, and stared at her feet.

"So Saturday night," she said, not looking at me.

"Congrats again," I began, then felt the tension. "Saturday night what?"

Lily leaned her head back against the couch, closed her eyes. "When I was getting my photo taken, after? When you wouldn't come with me?"

"Yeah." I perched on the arm of the couch. "You know how I feel about photos."

"Smith texted me."

"Great," I said.

"And told me my dress was perfect."

It took a beat for that to register. "He was there? It wasn't televised, was it?"

Lily shook her head, still not looking at me. Then she did. "Nope. I suppose someone could have livestreamed it to him. But that means someone else there was communicating with him."

"Someone could have done an Instagram live," I reassured her. "Or anything live. It's impossible to keep stuff off social media."

"You could come up with a billion explanations, Greer, but so what. He was watching me. *Me.* And somehow saw me in that dress. He made sure I knew he had. He called me before the photos were even done."

"Weird," I had to admit. "Verging on creepy. But not necessarily. You know sources. They're nuts. That's why they're sources."

Lily shook her head. "He also texted that he'd call me today. 'With an even better story,' those were his words."

"Lil? And that's bad because?"

I slid down off the arm of the couch, and Lily scooted over to make room. I stuck my legs out alongside hers, and her perfect toes made me wish I'd worn my newer sneakers. But then I wasn't the one on the air. Not the one in the spotlight. *I* didn't have to be perfect.

"Well, he just hung up."

"You're overthinking," I tried to convince her. "Maybe he—"

"I know, got cold feet. Changed his mind. Got disconnected. Got interrupted. Lost his cell phone signal. I know, I know. But . . ."

Lily stood, brushed down her jeans. Pressed her lips together. Chin down. Her thinking pose.

From outside, we could hear Rowen and the crew laughing.

"About today's shoot," she said. She took a few strides toward the kitchen, then seemed to change her mind. She turned, pointed at me. "I have some requirements."

"Require—?" *Requirements,* I thought. *Talent. Give me a break.* "Lily, hey, this is not a negotiation, I'm afraid. The powers want you, and—"

"Fine. They can have me. But not Rowen." She waved toward the backyard. "She's been on TV before, when she was little, but she's older now. Recognizable. I'm serious. *She* didn't sign up for this."

I rolled my eyes, rolled my whole head, then tried to rein in my frustration. "Lily, come on. This is the deal. The viewers love you, they want you, they can't get enough of you. And Rowen is part of the package. The Lily package. The single-mom, career-woman, gorgeous, smart, having-it-all perfect package. Perfection is in the perception. It's a good thing."

"Nope. Nope, nope, nope. It's an impossible thing."

"It's not my call, Lily." I saw my producer life flashing before my eyes. " 'Summer on Six' is their baby, you know?"

"And Rowen is *my* baby," she said. "I'll quit, really will. There's nothing more important to me than Rowen. Rowen's safety."

"And keeping her fed," I reminded her. "And cared for in the manner—" I made a grand gesture, encompassing the lilies, the Italian-tiled fireplace, the expansive bay window. "To which she has become accustomed. Ha ha. But I mean, come on, you already kept her out of school this morning to shoot this, right? So *maybe*? Possibly? Come *on,* Lily. You might be overreacting to . . . to I don't even know what."

We faced off, Lily and I. Standing, I was taller than Lily, especially now that her feet were bare. The fragrance of the pink-and-white lilies on the coffee table sweetened the air, and outside, I heard Rowen's crowing little laugh again. Lily turned at the sound, physically straining toward it, and then she turned back to me.

I could see her brain calculating her leverage, how far she'd really go. She'd told me about some encounter with a viper woman, as she'd called her, a year or so ago in a grocery store, which seemed to push her over some edge. Lily'd never told me about her past, much less her family; even who Rowen's father was or how that had happened. I knew she was from the Midwest, went to J-school in Missouri, never been married. That's about the gist. We're colleagues, but I'm five years older than she is, and we're not what one would term "friends." It's a job. She doesn't know about my family either, such as it isn't. Anything about me, in fact. She's never asked, not beyond the shallow "have a good weekend" niceties. She has no idea what a weekend might even include for me. I was the producer-researcher-administrator-fixer, she was the talent. The balance of power was precarious.

"We can do back-of-heads, long shots, see her from far away." She nodded, deciding, pursed her plumpy lips. "But no close-ups. She's a *child*. My child."

When Lily's cell phone rang again, we both flinched.

CHAPTER 5

LILY

Sender unknown, Lily's caller ID read. Mr. Smith. Lily couldn't shake the trepidation about Saturday's messages. "Mr. Smith" had never said anything personal before, commented on what she'd worn, or what she looked like. Maybe that was what unnerved her. Something was changing their equilibrium.

"Answer it." Greer moved closer. "It's him."

"How would I exist without you telling me what to do?" Lily whispered.

Greer had moved even closer, obviously wanting to hear the call for herself. *Why not?* Lily thought. *Might as well have an earwitness.*

She hit the green circle on the phone screen before the end of the second ring. "Hello?"

"Hello, Lily," the voice said. "I hope you like the flowers."

Lily's eyes widened. The fragrance of the lilies seemed to intensify, the sweet scent, so enticing when she'd thought they'd come from someone else, now seemed sinister. Almost suffocating.

"The flowers are from you?" Lily asked. She should have suspected it. The flowers—*lilies*—had arrived without a card. Something Sam used to do, back when he was still trying to keep them "together," even though he was also together with his wife. The first one. It had crossed her mind, more than once, that Sam was Mr. Smith. That he'd taken up this pretense to be able to stay connected with her. And Rowen. But again, that fairy-tale thinking made no sense.

She saw Greer wince.

"Oh, no, no," Mr. Smith's voice laughed through the speaker. "Not from me."

"Okay, not from you. Then how did you—?" She stopped, interrupted herself. People who called reporters were often eccentric. Rule-breakers. Whistleblowers. Coddling sources, reassuring them, was part of the deal. You didn't have to like someone to get a good story from them. The flower thing was strange, but she wouldn't take that bait. He might be guessing, or fishing. She'd stay on the opposite side of that fence. "So nice to hear from you. How can I help you?"

Greer gave a quick thumbs-up, seemed to agree with her tactics.

"As I said the other night," the caller went on, "I may have a good story for you."

"Terrific," Lily said. Remembered her manners. "And thank you again for your guidance." Maybe she could try a little test. "I thanked you, as much as I could, in my acceptance speech."

"I know," the caller said.

He *had* been there. She'd bet anything on that.

"And yes," he went on. "I am working on another investigation for you. But I have hit a bit of a roadblock. I wanted to let you know not to expect anything until tomorrow. I will call you then, if that fits your schedule."

A noise came from behind them. Lily turned to see Rowen, green-banded croquet mallet in hand, followed by Wade holding the blue mallet and Warren the black one. They stopped in the dining room, two talls and a small in the middle, a threesome in the carved wooden archway.

"Mumma?"

Lily held up her forefinger. Mouthed the words, "One minute," pointed to the phone, then swirled her finger, directing them back outside. She somehow didn't want Mr. Smith—or whatever his damn name was—to know Rowen was even in the room.

"Of course," Lily said as she heard the back door close again. "You choose the timing. We're eager to hear." She stuck out her tongue at Greer, pretending to gag on her own possibly too-obvious flattery.

"Until then," the caller said. And hung up.

"Weird." Greer plunked her hands on top of her head.

Lily looked at the blank phone screen. "Yeah. You've got to wonder if it's worth it, Greer. My—I don't know—accessibility. He has my cell number and knows where I live, because—"

"Does he, though?" Greer asked.

They both looked at the flowers. Gorgeous, voluptuous, expensive.

"Someone sent them, but he said it wasn't him." Greer pursed her lips, thinking. "Have you gotten flowers without a card before?"

So there was a question that was more complicated than it sounded. She had. But long ago. A different Lily ago. But she couldn't let—didn't want to let—Greer in on any part of her private life. She didn't mean it to be unfriendly, but she'd recognized, as she'd stepped deeper into TV world, what happened when people mixed business with friendship. People meddled. Asked questions. Tried to help. Crossed lines. She would be a good reporter pal, but a producer, even a reliable, knowledgeable one like Greer, didn't need to know Lily's personal business. And definitely not her past.

"Oh, I suppose so." Lily waved off the inquiry as if anonymous flowers were part of her TV life, like clothing allowances and autographs. But if it wasn't Mr. Smith, maybe—maybe?—the lilies were from Sam. Would that be a good thing or a bad thing? What would he have meant by them?

"You should call the florist," Greer suggested.

"Like I didn't think of that," Lily said. "Sorry, I don't mean to be brusque, but Rowen accepted them." She took a deep breath, spooled it out, stared at the flowers. "She's not even supposed to answer the door. Stupid me, I was in the shower. And Petra was out. If I'd been doing my regular job instead of this dumb shoot, she'd have been at school. Or at least I would have answered the door, and I would have known—I mean, what if—"

Lily pictured it. Those home surveillance cameras were so hackable, she hated them, but now she longed for one. "What if he was Mr. Smith himself? At my *house*? What if—"

"Stop. Lily. There are no what-ifs," Greer interrupted. "Sometimes flowers are just flowers."

"He was at. The. Emmys!" Lily felt her eyes well. "He was there. And that formal voice, you know? Nobody talks like that."

"Maybe." Greer shook her head. "But he could have easily seen your dress on social—someone probably Instagrammed it. You have, like, a billion followers. You're cranky now and making something out of nothing. He's a good source. He has nothing to do with the flowers. He was guessing."

"I should toss these into the trash." Lily frowned. "Or am I overreacting?"

"Mumma?" Rowen's voice again, from the other room, coming closer. "Come *out*! We *need* you!"

"You, overreacting? Imagine." Greer raised an eyebrow at her. "Let's do this thing, Lily. We'll keep Rowen safe, and you'll be even more adored."

CHAPTER 6

GREER

I knew enough about Lily to understand she's one of those women who thinks they can have it all, and if her life isn't perfect, then there's something wrong that someone else ought to fix. She had no idea how often it was me fixing it. And she didn't need to know. All part of the job.

When we got to her backyard—an expanse of green lined with fading yellow daffodils and an ocean of white tulips, the grass elegantly short, where weeds dare not even attempt to grow—Rowen and Wade and Warren were clustered around a croquet wicket in the far corner, protected from curious neighbors by a high white fence.

I mean, *croquet*. How retro is croquet?

But "Summer on Six" required showing our talent engaged in a summer activity, and playing in the backyard was perfectly acceptable. Lily and Rowen— the fence was two feet taller than the little girl—in an adorable mother-daughter croquet match. Cute, shootable, endearing. Aspirational, if you aspired to the 1950s. More cinematic than playing video games, I rationalized. With all the arm-twisting I'd had to do to convince Lily to do this at all, I'd take what I could get. And then maybe the two of them reading in the redwood lounge chairs under the leafed-out sugar maple. Walking hand in hand. Picking flowers. For this, I went to journalism school. But then, Lily had, too.

What did she want me to do, call the police because someone had sent her flowers? I considered attempting to track down the sender, maybe that would make her happy, make her realize how much she needed me, but apart from calling every florist in Boston, that would be impossible. And who lets a little kid answer the door?

"Wade? Warren?" I called out as the screen door closed behind us. "You wanna set up your gear? If I could lure you from this crucial match?"

"Bummer." Wade lofted his mallet, his blue Channel 6 shirt untucking from his jeans. "I was about to achieve world domination."

"No way." Rowen leaned down, clonked her green ball through a wire wicket, then held her mallet in triumph. "You lose, Wade."

"Sorry, guys." Lily had reached her daughter, draped an arm across Rowen's shoulders. "Did this one warn you she's Olympics material?"

"I could tell she was letting us win." Warren replaced his mallet in the rack, then started opening his tripod, flapping down the latches that held the three legs in place.

"Got that right," Rowen said. "Mumma, can we . . ."

As Rowen chattered, I noticed Lily scanning the tops of the fence, left to right, then behind them. Keeping her daughter close.

It took two hours, once we got started, to shoot the whole piece. Every angle imaginable of the two of them walking and talking and hitting croquet balls, Lily's laughter sounding completely genuine. She eagle-eyed the camera, standing in front of her daughter whenever she could.

"You're getting Rowe," she'd whispered to me once. "You think I don't see?"

"We'll fix it in post," I kept reassuring her. "I'll be in the edit booth, you can look at the finished story before it airs. Give me a break, Lil, we had a deal. We won't—" I stopped, not wanting to complicate things with Rowen. If she knew we were avoiding her face, it might spook her, so might as well avoid the whole 'we're protecting you from bad guys' topic. "Don't worry, Lily," I said.

We interviewed them both, looking forward to summer, blah blah, reading in the backyard, school field trips to the aquarium to see Rowen's beloved penguins. I had a few doubts about exactly how well this was going to work, not showing Rowen's face. And worried about the extent I'd have to throw our star under the bus to explain my way out of it. Out of self-preservation, I'd allowed the crew to shoot Rowe's face anyway, and might still be able to convince her to let us use the video. I could always say we'd gotten it by mistake—those darn photographers—but since we had it . . .

I'd cross that bridge when we came to it.

CHAPTER 7
LILY

Lily had watched Rowen walking all the way up the wide cobblestones to the imposing front doors of the Graydon School, regretting, for the millionth time, that she couldn't allow her daughter the real-life experience of public school. Lily herself had been just fine at Hamilton Elementary, even with the fragrance of chalk dust puffing through the classrooms and those awkward molded wood desks, impossible for a left-hander. But Rowen needed more protection than Lily's parents could ever have imagined. More than Lily, back then at least, could have imagined.

Until Cassie, of course. But maybe no one and nothing could have protected her. Sometimes, in the twisted memories of Lily's brain, two of the most important people in her life merged into one.

"Bye, Mumma!" Rowen, waving goodbye, was almost too far away to hear. Lily waved back from the front seat of her black BMW—an indulgence, but she needed Rowe to ride in a safe car—as Graydon's doors closed, her daughter securely inside. Petra would pick her up at four, as usual, when Lily had to be at work.

Such a juggle, Lily thought, pulling onto Channel 6's chain-link-fenced back parking lot. Kind of a first-world juggle, though, she had to admit. The heavy metal gate lifted open as she inserted her key card into the slot, and she aimed her car at the parking place marked with her name. Was that a good idea? Anyone who came into the lot would know exactly whose car this was and could find her license plate number. Another example of celebrity's pitfalls.

"First-world problem, kiddo," she told herself again, this time out loud. She took a sip from the insulated coffee mug in the console cupholder, feeling more relaxed in the fenced-in lot. She'd talked to a therapist about her constant suspicions, her hyper-assessment of every situation, but it hadn't taken too many sessions for the professorial Dr. Hrones to latch onto the Cassie story.

"You don't like surprises, I can understand," the psychologist had told her, looking over his wire rims. He'd made a note on a yellow pad with a fancy black fountain pen. "Perhaps that's why you became a reporter. You always need to know the answers. But sometimes fear can be channeled, and quite successfully, into curiosity. And as a reporter, Lily, you're allowed to question. Required to. As such, you've made a prudent life choice." He'd pointed his pen at her. "What do you think?"

She'd actually thought, *Get me out of here*. Respected doctor or not, he knew who she was, and where she worked, and one even inadvertent word to a tabloid reporter could give Lily another hashtag. #PsychoLily, maybe. Or #CrazyLily. She had to be careful who she talked to. Even perfectly trustworthy doctors. Nobody was perfectly trustworthy.

"Could be, Stephen," she'd told Dr. Hrones. And then, even though he was probably right, she canceled her future appointments. She didn't need some wavy-haired guy in a tweed blazer to tell her how the loss of Cassie—the yearning to know what had happened—had changed her life.

Still. She didn't want to infect Rowen with her own persistent fear that the world was a dangerous place, even though it was. Being in a newsroom made it all the worse. The news was always bad, that's what made it news. But kids should be happy and free. Feel safe. She'd protect Rowen from it all, as long as she could.

Lily switched her mind to the day to come. She'd tried to forget about those lilies. Finally, she'd given them to Petra, who had swooped them up, vase and all, to take to her over-the-garage apartment.

Out of sight, out of mind. Maybe she could make that philosophy work. For flowers, at least.

The green numbers on the dashboard clock changed to 10:15. She'd be late for work, but Greer'd have to live with it. Lily was still unhappy about her producer's pushy attitude at the taping yesterday. She was well aware the crew had taped Rowen's face, but she'd deal with that later. *Greer would be nowhere without me,* the thought crossed her mind. Lily always got the feeling Greer was vaguely critical of everything Lily had or did. Or said. Or wore. Greer was always pushing her to be more careful, more special, more perfect. *Perfection is in the perception,* Greer constantly reminded her. *You need to keep people loving you.* She supposed Greer was right. Television was infinitely fickle.

Replacing Greer would be a major pain. And if Greer insisted on trying to produce Lily's entire life— what did it matter? As long as they kept succeeding. She looked at the cell phone, still in its holder on the BMW's dash. Still stubbornly silent.

Smith was the more important concern. He'd said he'd call.

Coffee in hand, she began to gather her laptop and tote bag and, not even looking, reached out for her cell. When it buzzed, she flinched, and grabbed it so fast it flipped and dropped onto the carpeted floor.

She twisted down to retrieve the buzzing thing, hitting the lid of her coffee on the center console, which dumped milky liquid onto the seat beside her.

"Damn it!" she muttered.

The phone buzzed again. Ignoring the spreading coffee, she dived for the cell, through a scattering of cookie crumbs and dog hair, finally scrabbling her fingertips around it, and pushed the green circle.

"Hello?" The murky coffee on the black leather seat next to her began to seep into the decorative white stitching.

"I hope I have not caught you at an inopportune time," the voice said.

Smith.

"Not at all." Lily scanned the parking lot, couldn't help it. How'd he know to call *after* she'd parked and turned off the car? He might even be in the unfenced visitors' lot in front of the station, ducked down in his seat. Maybe he'd waited for her to drive in. Watched for her. Would he have her in his sights when she got out? When she went into the building? It wouldn't take a genius. She arrived at the same time, give or take, most days. Left at the same time, too.

"So pleased to hear from you." Lily kept her voice calm and congenial, but focused out the car's windshield. No one in the driveway. No one on the redwood bench under the three rangy Norfolk pines. No one on the wide sidewalk that led to the low yellow-brick Channel 6 building. "You said you'd hit a roadblock yesterday."

"Indeed," Smith said. "But before we get to that. I'm hearing there appears to be a—situation? Shall we say? At the Graydon School?"

"A situation?" Lily tucked the phone against her

shoulder, yanked on her seat belt, punched the ignition. Shifted into reverse. Gunned it. "At Graydon? What kind of a situation?" Lily pulled up to the metal gate. The striped bar now closed her in.

"I cannot be sure," the voice said. "Shall I call and check for you? Let you know?"

She jammed her key card into the slot. Missed. The card hit the outside of the metal card reader, then spun to the pavement. "Damn it!"

"Lily?"

She slammed the phone into her holder on the dash, pushed open her door to retrieve the card.

"Can you hold on, please?" Lily yelled, making sure he could hear her. "I'm just—can you tell me what's going on?" she asked, keeping her voice loud enough for him to hear. "Do I need to call 911?"

She scraped the card from the asphalt, slammed the car door closed, tried again to get the card into the reader. Smith knew, he must know, her daughter was at Graydon. This wasn't a coincidence, and whatever the hell was happening there was not a coincidence either. This was exactly what she feared, *exactly,* the fragile boundaries of her life disintegrating, with no key cards needed to invade her space. Or Rowen's.

"Nothing like that," Smith told her. "I merely thought—"

With a clank and a wheeze, the gate finally opened. Lily hit the accelerator.

"—you might be grateful to be contacted. I am calling to assure you there is no need to worry."

She couldn't decide if she loved his voice or hated it, wanted to hear it or wanted not to. Without him, she'd be inside Channel 6, oblivious to Graydon. Where her daughter was. And all the other children and teachers and—

"What situation?" She heard her tone go harsh. He

was toying with her. She couldn't allow that. She would not be manipulated. "Mr. Smith? What situation?"

"I assume you are on your way?" Smith said. "I need to go now, but I will be in touch."

She checked the rearview. Was he following her? He *knew* Rowen was at Graydon, there was no doubt about that. Lily herself had watched her daughter go inside. Maybe Smith had watched, too, maybe from the school's parking lot. Just like he might have been watching Lily herself from the Channel 6 lot. From now on, she would never leave, never *budge,* until she saw those heavy doors close her child safely inside.

"Wait, Mr. Smith? Thank you *so* much," Lily said, trying to soften the edge out of her voice. "I would be so grateful if you would just tell me—" She'd accelerated through an almost-red light. Graydon was fifteen minutes away. Fifteen minutes of highway, then eternal suburban stoplights and crosswalks and who knew what other obstacles. Was she hearing a siren? She buzzed down her window. No. Yes? No.

"Hello?" She hated, *hated,* the power he had over her. With the click of a cell phone button he could help her or hurt her. Tell her something true or not true. She hated him. She loved him. She needed him. And right now, so did Rowen.

"Can you hear me?" she asked. She needed to call Headmistress Glover. *Now.* Rowen didn't have a phone, of course; none of the students her age did. There was no way to contact Rowe, except through Maryrose Glover. Or by hurtling through the front door, which Lily was ready to do.

She heard a dial tone. He'd hung up.

"What?" Lily didn't have time to be annoyed. She engaged the Bluetooth. "Call Graydon," she said, keeping her eyes on the road. She sped onto a rotary, careened out the other side. She heard the phone connect. Heard someone pick up.

"This is Lily Atwood," she began. "I need—"

"This is the Graydon School," the recorded message talked over her. "Your call is important to us. Please leave a—"

CHAPTER 8

GREER

It wasn't like Lily to be late, I thought, looking at the clock on my computer screen. But then Lily could do what Lily wanted to do. Maybe she was still angry with me about yesterday's taping. She's not good at hiding her emotions, even though she thinks she is. I could never confront her about that counterfeit serenity. The minute I did, she'd work even harder at pretending. But I didn't make the rules. I just followed them.

And this morning, I, at least, had work to do. I sneaked my coffee into the "no liquids or food allowed" edit booth and logged in to the video screener. I searched for Lily House SOS—the unfortunate acronym for "Summer on Six"—which brought up the footage from the backyard. The sky pristinely blue, the clouds storybook puffy. The already-lush maple, with the morning sunshine filtering through its variegated leaves, made a soft rustle as the breeze trembled them. It was postcard-worthy in real life, but made for crappy video. That intermittent light dappled splotches on Lily's face—and Rowen's, too.

"Not that it matters," I muttered.

It was crappy all around, I decided as I scrolled through the video, since Lily, totally savvy about where the camera was pointing, had done her best to keep Rowen's face out of the shots. We had Lily and Rowen hand in hand, from behind, naturally. Their dumb dog bounding through the shot, Valentina, her name was, since the fluffy cocker spaniel had been Rowen's Valentine's gift. Which could be cute for the story. Lily had a photo of the puppy wearing heart-shaped deely-boppers tacked to her bulletin board. She'd pinned it next to a photo—a vintage one, with scalloped edges—of a little girl and a scraggly border collie. Once, I'd made the mistake of asking Lily who that girl was. "Is it you?" I'd inquired, trying to be friendly slash conversational. She shut that down, damn fast. I scrolled through the backyard video again.

We had a close-up of Rowen's croquet shot, with the thwack of the mallet hitting the ball. We did a few takes as she attempted to get the ball through a wicket. We'd only use the successful ones, of course. *Everything Lily and her family does is perfect,* that's the message we send. Preposterously, a butterfly danced into the shot, flittering its white wings above mother and daughter. Only Lily's universe could make that kind of moment happen, a gentle Snow White comes to contemporary Massachusetts, her adoring forest creatures surrounding her.

I double speeded through it all, as usual. Cute, cuter, even cuter. I could see things just as clearly twice as fast—real-life speed seemed agonizingly slow. The light changed on the video, a burst of snow and then black, and then out of focus/into focus on Lily's face.

We'd slipped the mic cord up Lily's shirt to hide it, and clipped the tiny mic to one side of the ribbed collar. She'd draped her hair over one shoulder so her glossy curls wouldn't interfere with the sound.

"This is absurd," she said. "I'm in my backyard with full makeup and three extra lights. Very natural."

"You look great," I assured her. "It's TV."

"Don't I know it," Lily said, as Wade zoomed in then out again. "Sound check, sound check."

"Sound check!" Rowen crowed.

"What're you seeing in the background?" I heard my own voice on tape, since I'd stood behind Wade to make sure the camera placement didn't include a tree sticking up behind Lily's head, or stark slashes of light, or reveal the shiny green garden hose that coiled like a serpent in the back corner of the lawn.

"Rolling," Wade said. Warren had tilted the fill light to soften any darkness that dared mar Lily's face. Rowen sat next to her mother, her little legs barely reaching the grass below her white wooden chair, her white Mary Jane sandals grazing the green tips of the manicured lawn. Valentina, at the beginning of the interview at least, had plunked at their feet, head on oversize paws.

"Ready?" I asked. Viewers would not hear my questions on camera, but it was more conversational, more engaging, to have Lily responding. Lily nodded, fussed with her hair. She didn't look happy. But I knew she would change that as soon as the interview started.

"So, Lily," I began, and as expected, her face bloomed into a soft openness. *So happy to see you all,* her expression seemed to say. *So thrilled to know you.* "Let's talk first about why we're not seeing Rowe—I mean, your daughter."

"Welcome to our home, everyone," Lily said, not answering my question. So Lily. "My daughter and I are so pleased to share some of our summer plans with you. But I—and I know you parents will all agree." Big Lily smile. "Privacy is so important these days, and although I'd absolutely adore for you to meet my daughter and get to know her, she's a little shy, and I'm proud of her for being confident enough to tell me. And, of course, I respect her wishes."

I almost burst out laughing, and I could see the consternation cross Rowen's face. What her mother had said on camera was completely untrue. And I'd been baffled at the time—we'd discussed that Lily would offer a plea for family privacy, make it stem from her own maternal concerns. Make it a thing. Lily *adores* hashtags, she's obsessed with them, and we'd talked about creating a special one for this, #FamilyOffLimits. Maybe #ProtectRowen. Or #OurSpace. This was a detour.

"I see," I'd told her, making it clear from my tone that I didn't. I could have signaled Wade to stop rolling, but Lily was looking at me, bright-eyed and ingenuous, and I thought, *What the hell.*

"Great," I chirped, again making it obvious it wasn't. "Sounds like you're raising a very wise little girl." #SaveRowen? "Tell us about your summer plans, though. Are you two doing the same kinds of things you did as a child? Were you a onesie like your daughter? Or did you have siblings?"

For such a seemingly innocent question, Lily's face—even in her confident on-air mode—betrayed some sort of shadow. Sorrow, I decided, after all my years as an interviewer. Then—anger? Then the placid Lily face. Then a tinkle of laughter. "Oh, you bring back so many wonderful memories. Yes, absolutely, we played croquet on our big front lawn—it probably wasn't as big as I remember, since I was my daughter's age back then. And we played Statue, and Duck-Duck-Goose—and summer seemed like it would last forever. But now I'm so happy to have our summers in Boston, and we do plan to try to get to the Cape. Of course. And maybe a trip to the beautiful north shore."

She crossed her slim legs, the effortless white tee moving with her body, her shoulders tilting at a practiced and flattering angle, her hair obedient.

This summer, they'd have their personal book club,

Lily went on, blah blah, play soccer, go for ice cream, and bicycle together. "We're both still beginners." Lily laughed. "But we love mother-daughter biking."

Whatever her faults, Lily always put mothering first. Sometimes, in my opinion, when she didn't need to. Maybe Lily had spoken with her daughter earlier that morning and explained about privacy. Because why bother to tell *me* about it, right? I leaned back in the rickety swivel-chair and took a sip of my contraband coffee, making sure no drink police were looking through the window in the edit booth door.

The useful thing about a taped interview—you can look at it again. Hear it again. In real-life conversation, someone says something, with a tone or an attitude maybe, but then it's gone. Did you interpret it correctly? You'll never know, because it's vanished, leaving only your possibly incorrect decoding and potentially destructive conclusion. I leaned forward as the tape rolled on, listening for one specific exchange I wanted to hear—and watch—at real speed.

"So, *did* you have siblings?" I'm still not sure why I asked again; maybe subconsciously I wanted to see if Lily would react again, maybe it was unworthy of me. But hey, it was only tape.

"Not sure that matters for this, Greer." Lily scratched her forehead and rolled her neck, fidgety movements she knew full well would land this section on the cutting room floor. "Let's move on."

"Mumma?" Rowen touched her mother on the arm.

"What, honey?" Lily made a slashing motion across her throat with one finger, signaling Wade to stop rolling. Too bad Wade and I had a standing secret deal that no one but me—not even Lily Atwood—could tell him when to cut the camera. He'd MacGyvered the red On light to do what he wanted.

"We have Aunt Cassie," Rowen said. "Don't forget Aunt Cassie."

I waited. Cassie? Aunt Cassie? A sister—maybe?—
Lily had never mentioned. I thought about that pic-
ture of the little girl with the border collie. The one
Lily hadn't wanted to talk about.

"That's right, sweetheart," Lily said on the tape. If
I'd closed my eyes and only heard her tone, I'd have
thought it was a moment of loving approval. But I'd
seen her face. She'd meant exactly the opposite. Lily
then looked at the camera, dead center. "Shall we
move on?"

CHAPTER 9

LILY

Hands clenched on the steering wheel and ignoring two yellow lights, Lily finally made it to Graydon's long gravel driveway. She buzzed down her window. No smell of smoke. No sirens, she thought, no orange flames leaping high in the distance. No people running to their cars in the adjacent parking lot. No racing ambulances spitting gravel and speeding ahead of her, no swirling blue lights slashing across the shoulder-high hedge of flowering yellow forsythia. No SWAT teams in black suits stalking the campus for an active shooter.

She made the final curve up to the circular driveway, pulling closer.

Her phone trilled. Greer.

Beyond the soft rise of lawn and landscape, the imposing gray edifice of the weathered stone building stood there as always. Not on fire. A parade of white blouses and navy pleated skirts was spilling out the wide-open front doors.

Two by two, some holding hands, the students trooped onto the wide entryway sidewalk where earlier Lily had waved goodbye to Rowen. No girls were running. No one was crying, from what she could tell. Two tall female figures stood sentinel on either side of the front doors, clipboards in hand. Their posture seemed attentive, but calm.

Her phone trilled again. She clicked Accept. Kept her foot on the accelerator.

"Lily?"

"Yeah, yeah, I'm sorry, Greer, I know I'm late, but—" Lily began. She tried to make her point as she focused on the bobbing navy and white. Where was Rowen? "Smith called to say—"

"What's wrong?" the voice interrupted through the tinny speakers. "Where are you?"

Lily scanned the sea of lookalikes, focusing, squinting, trying to spot the penguin-beribboned ponytail or the outrageously chunky white tennis shoes Rowe insisted on. She pulled over to the side of the driveway.

"Graydon." The girls coming out now seemed older than Rowe, but who knew. "Listen, Greer, can you call the school? Or someone? See if you can find out what's going on?"

"On it. But while I do—"

One thing about Greer. She'd act first, ask questions second.

"Smith called, said there was a situation at Graydon," Lily went on. "Then he hung up." Still no Rowen. Had she already come out? Was she still inside? It looked like a fire drill—or an active-shooter drill? If it was a drill, Lily didn't care what kind it was.

"Answering machine at the school," Greer reported.

"Damn. Me, too. I'm sure it's—" What *was* she sure of?

"I'll try the newsroom assignment desk," Greer said.

"Great. Let me know. I'm getting out of the car. No. Wait. They're . . . leaving? Or something." The girls seemed to be headed toward the octagonal bandstand in the middle of what they called "the Meadow," an expanse of lawn used for commencements and concerts and festivals, and once, that Lily remembered at least, a memorial service. "I'm going to go see."

"Lily. Be careful."

Lily watched the last of the emerging students. Had to be a drill of some kind. If it were an emergency, wouldn't they have reversed-911'ed the parents? Like they did on snow days? But there had been no call. "Careful of what? Hang on, I'm switching off the Bluetooth."

"Seriously? What if he's there?" Greer persisted.

"He?" Lily had the phone in her hand now, clenched. "Have you actually seen Rowen?"

"Seen? Why? Why wouldn't I have seen her? Greer? Do you—"

"I'm at the assignment desk now, hang on."

Lily felt the tiny bits of gravel through the delicate soles of her black flats as she trotted toward the students. Seemed as if nothing was deeply wrong. Adults stationed strategically between the school and the bandstand seemed to be guiding the students to a planned destination. Some of the girls who'd clasped hands were swinging them now, playful and carefree in the morning sun. She still hadn't seen Rowen, but maybe—was Rowen still inside? And *that* was the emergency? And they were getting the other girls away? From what? The back of her neck clenched, she could feel the tears in her eyes.

But no one had called her. If something had happened to Rowen, someone would have called.

"It's nothing." Greer was back. And her voice had taken an odd tone. "And kinda ridiculous, but it's kinda our fault. Since we did that story—from Smith, remember?—about how schools aren't fulfilling their fire drill requirements, Graydon's doing one a month. A pop drill, they're calling them. Like a pop quiz. Unscheduled, spur of the moment, only the headmistress knows. *Et voilà.* This morning's situation."

"A fire drill." Lily hadn't realized how fast her heart was racing until she felt it slow. It looked so peaceful now, seeing it through this "no problem" lens. Some of the girls now ran free on the Meadow, apparently released from the drill routine, their skirts fluttering, ponytails and braids dancing, even a peal of laughter floating across the greensward. She didn't want to be a frantic hovering parent, she told herself, no reason to race up there like some hysterical mom. The sun warmed on the top of her head, and she wished for sunglasses. Heard the caw of a faraway crow. Why would Smith call her about a fire drill? How would he have known about it? Maybe he was connected with the school department—he'd given them the lunch thing, the fire drills. Now this.

For a moment, Lily inhabited a separate world—an observer, invisible to the students and the teachers. She felt her forehead furrow at her own question. *Why would Smith call her about a fire drill?*

A squirrel scrabbled up a nearby tree, startling her. The row of elegant cedars screened the faculty parking lot from the driveway. Sort of.

"You there?" Greer's voice over the phone.

"Why'd you say be careful?" Lily asked.

"Because—why would Smith call you about that? Something that's nothing?"

"Exactly." Lily stopped. "Oh. Because he knew I'd come here."

"Yeah," Greer agreed.

"Or to get everyone outside." Lily started walking toward the school. She wasn't leaving without seeing Rowen. Helicopter mom or not. "Including Rowen."

"Yeah."

Her footsteps crunched on the gravel now, determined. Ridiculous how she could laser focus on taking down some miscreant, but her brain turned to butter when it came to Rowen.

"Greer? You said, 'Pop drill'?"

"Yeah, you know," she replied. "Unannounced. The principal—"

"Headmistress." Lily strode ahead, squinted against the sun, watched the closed front door. Wondered who was still inside, and why. "Maryrose Glover?"

"Yeah. Apparently, she sets them up personally. So they're a surprise to everyone. Makes it feel more real."

"How'd Smith know, then?" Now Lily could see the weathered board of the arched oak main entrance, the wrought iron flowers—iron roses, sometimes they called the students that, too—garlanded around the door's perimeter. The heavy black door latch, also rose-decorated, had supposedly been there for more than a hundred years. The inner locks were state of the art, though, Lily had been told when Rowen enrolled. *Our tradition is unchanged,* Headmistress Glover had explained. *But our futures must be financially secure.* "How'd he know about the drill?"

Lily could almost hear her producer thinking. "Good question."

"And, listen, Greer?" One of the teachers at the end of the sidewalk bordering the Meadow was coming her way. Caralynn Treece, one of Rowen's favorites. The one who'd told her she might grow up to be an artist, and the reason Lily's fridge was covered with drawings of Valentina and ponies and rainbows. Lily had to talk faster. "Remember he told us yesterday he had a story for us? But he'd hit a 'roadblock'?"

"Yeah, so?"

"Remember, Rowen wasn't at school yesterday. I'd kept her out at the last minute for the taping. But how could he have known? Maybe he'd waited for us to arrive at Graydon, but we didn't. So this happened *today,* because he needed her to be here."

The line was silent for a beat. "He or she," Greer said.

"Because he'd know I'd race here as fast as I could." More silence.

"That I wouldn't be at the station. And I wouldn't be home."

"Ms. Atwood?" Caralynn Treece had lifted a hand in greeting, then gestured back toward the girls congregating on the Meadow. "Were we expecting you? We're in the midst of a fire drill, so—"

"But that's dumb, Lily," Greer was saying. "It's like the boy who cried wolf. The next time he tells you something, you'll ignore it. He's undermining his own credibility. Why would he do that?"

"Is everything all right?" Caralynn tilted her head, concerned, the multicolored beads in her graying dreads clattering. She pulled an airy green cardigan closer around her.

Lily, trying to look reassuring, put up a forefinger, stalling Caralynn. *One second.*

"Right?" Greer's voice persisted. "Like the boy who cried wolf."

"I hear you," Lily said. "But in the end the wolf was there."

BEFORE

CHAPTER 10

CASSIE

Cassie felt the warm midmorning sun wrap her in its October glow as she hurried up the cobblestone walk to Wharton Hall, a classically imposing gray stone behemoth at the edge of the Green. Okay, so, like, she was wrong, she'd been wrong to worry that being a college freshman was going to suck. Berwick College was actually kind of great. Even when she had a meeting with a professor on a Saturday. Especially when.

She missed her family, sure. Dumb scraggly Pooch, who snuffled and whuffled and nudged her bare skin with his cold nose and loved her unconditionally. Even Mumma, complaining about Cassie's too-tight jeans and too-short crop tops—*It's the style, Mumma,* she'd argue. But Mumma, too, did it from love. *You're a special girl,* Mumma always told her. And little Lily, who spent every moment with her face in a book. She was a cutie, for a little kid. And so annoying/not annoying, how she copied Cassie's every move. They were "nice," and "predictable," and now she'd outgrown them. *Roots and wings,* her mother had told her. Now, flying on her own, or trying to, she understood what that meant. Family mattered. But she'd see them at Christmas.

And now she could wear her Docs, with *no* tights,

and her coolest, shortest pleated plaid skirt, and no one could tell her to change. She adjusted her backpack strap, making sure it didn't drag at the shoulder of her sapphire-blue cropped cardigan.

"Hey, Cassie! On the way to Wharton, too? How's it going?"

She looked up at the woman's lilty voice. A cascade of hair, plaid skirt, and cardigan, coming down the steps of Wharton Hall, walking toward her. Cassie thought she recognized her from—the dorm?

"Great." Cassie smiled, trying to make her expression welcoming. She could *not* remember this girl's name. She kept walking. "Sorry, so late! Gotta go," she said over her shoulder.

Carillon bells chimed from the tower across campus, classical something, Handel or Haydn. But the chimes meant ten minutes until her session with Professor Shaw. Professor Zachary Shaw. She got a little chill, thinking of him, but dismissed it. *So* inappropriate. She was eighteen. He was a professor. End of story. But still.

The sun vanished behind her as she entered the subdued lighting of Wharton's mahogany-paneled hallway, lined with money-heavy oil paintings of benefactors and patrons, wire-rimmed glasses and high collars, the earliest painted with thick glossy strokes and matted in velvet and framed in elaborate carved wood, then down the hall to the almost photographic black and whites of the silver-framed newer graduates; two with close-cropped hair and iconic black turtlenecks, a current governor wearing obligatory pearls, a Pulitzer winner, a confident blonde in a lab coat and stethoscope necklace. Cassie would be a success, too. Her life was only beginning. It would be perfect. She'd make it so.

She wrapped her fingers around the curved brass handle of Professor Shaw's office and pulled open the heavy wooden door. Then let it close again. She resisted the urge to check her cheeks and lip gloss and bangs one last time. She looked fine, all good, no reason to push it.

"You going in?" A guy reached for the same door, backpack slung over one shoulder, his flannel shirt open over a black tee. "Or are you just playing with the door?"

She felt his eyes on her, noticing. She ignored it, or pretended to. He seemed older than her, however that mattered. That girl she'd seen outside walked by.

"Whatever." Cassie gestured for the guy to go ahead. "All yours. Do you have an appointment now? I thought I was the ten."

But he didn't move toward the door. "You Professor Shaw's student, too? I'm Jem Duggan. I haven't noticed you before."

"Well, thank you," she said, edging her voice with teasing sarcasm. She put a twinkle in her eyes, knowing the blue of her cardigan matched them exactly. "I'm Cassie Atwood. Maybe I was invisible before?"

He raised an eyebrow, seemed to consider her sanity. "If you say so," he said. With one smooth motion, he pulled the door open again and disappeared inside.

Cassie felt her eyes go wide. He'd ignored her? "Nice to meet you, too," she muttered. She had to admit it took her a beat to pull herself together, get her confidence back, stash the older guy, maybe a senior even, in her "never mind" drawer. Because now it was five minutes until time for her meeting. With Professor Zachary Shaw. Who taught *biology,* she thought with a silent giggle.

Smoothing her skirt under her, she sat on the one straight-backed wooden chair in the hallway outside the office door. Plopped her backpack on the hardwood floor. The bio lab was down the hall, where she had classes Tuesdays and Thursdays. It was the weekend now, and the place rang hollow, no students sharing notes, no bells or buzzers, no latecomers' footsteps racing, no buzz of gossip or peals of laughter. The numbered wood-and-glass classroom doors, as well as the more basic ones labeled Supplies and Utility, were all closed. The place even smelled empty.

Except for the office behind her. She had to wonder, had to, what would happen after that door opened.

Now if only that Jim or Jem or whoever would leave. Invisible, huh? She totally suspected—in fact, she totally knew from how he'd looked at her and kind of everything—that she, Cassandra Blair Atwood, was not invisible to Professor Shaw.

NOW

CHAPTER 11

LILY

"Mumma!"

Lily hadn't understood how on edge she was, how close to tears, until she heard her daughter's voice, Rowe's perfect little voice, carrying across the manicured front lawn. The wolf had not arrived. Every nightmare vanished with Rowen's voice—the chemical spill, the fire, the abduction, the horrifying, unthinkable, unimaginable disaster. Rowe was safe, smiling, holding hands with Headmistress Maryrose Glover, coming toward her. To Rowen, Mr. Smith did not exist.

"Gotta go, Greer," Lily said into her cell. "Rowe's here, I see her, and all is fine."

"So what happened? I still don't get why Smith called. A fire drill?"

"I don't get it either. But yeah, a fire drill. Now I need to deal with this." Lily squinted toward the headmistress and her charge, but they telegraphed nothing but peaceful serenity.

She clicked off her call, then raised a hand in greeting, trying to recompose her face to signal nothing was wrong.

"Hello, Headmistress," Lily said. "I'm just here to—"

"Ms. Atwood? Hello. To what do we owe this

visit? And—Ms. Treece?" Maryrose Glover, Gray-don's headmistress for as long as Lily could remember, spoke as she strode toward them, regal and elegantly postured, escorting the blithely carefree Rowe, who stopped to pick a feathery white dandelion from the otherwise pristine grass. The little girl puffed the weightless seedpods into the sunlit space ahead of her.

"Fairy dust, Mumma!" Rowe detached her hand from the headmistress's and dashed toward her. "Did you come to see me? Is it a special day? Hello, Ms. Treece!"

"It's always a special day when I see you, honey," Lily said, returning Rowe's hug. The girl stayed next to her, arms wrapped around Lily's waist as Mary-rose Glover watched.

"Everything all right?" the headmistress asked. Her black-rimmed glasses made a headband on her signa-ture platinum bob; the popped collar of a white cot-ton shirt set off her high cheekbones and discreet pale lipstick. "Rowen saw you, insisted it was you, and I was a bit confused. Have I made a mistake on my calendar?" She eyed Lily and Caralynn up and down, still wary, assessing. "I hope it's not a problem that I brought her with me—she did insist."

"Not a problem at all." Lily bent quickly and kissed the top of her daughter's head. She glanced at Caralynn, improvising. "Just hoping for a quick chat with you, in fact, Headmistress."

"Ready to get back to class, Rowen?" Caralynn seemed to understand the impromptu script. "Your mum's here on school business. Aren't you clever to have spotted her? But now, spit-spot, back to class."

"That's what Mary Poppins says! You're not Mary Poppins." Rowen pointed at her teacher. "Is she, Mumma?"

"Who knows, kiddo," Lily said, teasing. "And we don't point." She pretended not to be reluctant as she unwrapped herself from her daughter's hug. She wished they could just go home. Go home, and stay there.

The specter of Smith's call still hung in the air, and pretending it was an ordinary day was by definition a lie. On an ordinary day, she wouldn't be here. She couldn't help but steal a few darting glances. Bushes, hedges, driveway, parking lot, trees.

The boy who cried wolf, Lily thought again. But again, there was no wolf. Not here, at least.

But the wolf had called her on the phone. "Warned" her. Was he hiding now, to see what she would do? Bushes, hedges, driveway, parking lot, trees. Nothing. She felt like a bug on a pin. Under an invisible microscope. "You two could talk about Mary Poppins on the way to class, Rowe, and then when I come to pick you up, you tell me what you discovered."

"Like an interview. Like you do." Rowen, enthusiastic, took the bait.

"Exactly," Lily said. "See you at four, kiddo. I'll pick you up. Petra's got an errand to run." She didn't, actually, but Lily herself needed to pick up Rowe today. Make sure she got home safely.

Like Mumma hadn't done for Cassie, her unrelenting memory whispered. But she was the mumma now, and she would not fail her daughter.

The two women stayed quiet as teacher and student walked back to the school building, deep in conversation, Rowen gesturing, braids bouncing as she trotted to keep up with her teacher's longer steps.

"What can I do for you, Lily?" the headmistress finally said, returning to first names as she did when it was only the two of them. "You keep looking around—may I ask, are you looking for something in particular?"

Yes, Lily thought.

The headmistress stayed silent. Another one of her skills, Lily knew.

Lily watched her daughter finally disappear behind Graydon's imposing front doors. *She's safe now,* Lily reassured herself. And she'd have to make sure Rowe didn't grow up to be as skittish as she herself was. The world was not dangerous, not every minute of every day. It just felt that way.

"I got a phone call at Channel 6," Lily began. She'd tell the truth, as much as she could, from the most benignly unthreatening point of view. She moved a tiny pebble with one toe of her shoe. "The caller said something was happening at Graydon."

Glover frowned. "Happening? That concerns me, Lily, on behalf of every child at the school. If there's the slightest possibility of a problem, I need to call the police. Report it. It's my responsibility. What is 'happening'?"

"The caller didn't say." Which was true. "I tried to call here first, but it went straight to voice mail. Which made me all the more suspicious. But the caller had mentioned Graydon, and since Rowen—"

"Of course." Glover crossed her arms over her chest, red fingernails against white shirt, then turned to look back over the grass to the wide front doors of Graydon's main building and the Meadow lawn. The students were still outside, some with heads close together in clumps and groups, making long shadows in the manicured grass.

The headmistress turned back to her. "Is there something I need to know?"

Glover had softened her voice, maybe because her subordinate and her student were no longer in earshot, or to make Lily feel as if she were chatting to a friend. Glover's manner, her ability to read a room, her relentless and incessant fundraising, all that was legendary at Graydon. *How much would you spend to protect your child's future?* Lily remembered Glover, black suited and bespoke, asking a select group of parents that unanswerable question. How much would she pay to protect Rowen? There was no financial answer. The moon, the stars, the universe.

"I'm a reporter," she felt she had to explain. "I get endless phone calls, warning of this or that, or predicting calamity or disaster, and I'd say—a vast majority of them are nothing. But it's the rest of them, the few tips that are true, that's why I have the job I do. So—"

"Exactly what did the caller say?"

Lily imagined this was the patient tone the head-mistress took with dawdling students. Or parents late with tuition.

"He just said—"

"He."

Lily nodded. "He said there was a situation at Gray-don." She tilted her head, remembering. "Did anyone else know you were having the drill today? And let me ask you—was it originally planned for yesterday?"

CHAPTER 12

GREER

I put down the phone and leaned back in my desk chair, staring at the graying drop-tiled ceiling, wondering what Lily would do without me. I'd spent the rest of the day doing my job as assigned, responsibly doing what they pay me for, researching and organizing and digging up new stories, while Lily swanned around who knows where doing who knows what. It had been hours since Lily had hung up on me at the school. Where, of course, everything was fine.

If you ask me, her parenting verges on suffocation, and she must be wearing herself out, escalating every single damn thing into a Lily-centered crisis. She'd called back, finally, all breathless, saying she had "appointments," where she "had to be" and would pick up Rowe at four and bring her here to the station so we could catch up before day's end.

I clanked myself back upright, the chair wheels squeaking in complaint. This whole division of duties—ha—is a joke. You'd think Lily would be embarrassed. Yet I'm convinced she actually thinks she's pulling equal weight. Maybe, in the skewed physics of television, fame weighs more than actual work.

The wooden top of her desk is so polished I can smell the lemon-scented cleaner the cleaning people use on hers but somehow not on mine. A stack of bright red file folders is centered in the middle, but the tabs are unlabeled, and it's easy to tell they're empty. There's actually a sleek porcelain container holding a curving white orchid plant in the upper-right-hand corner. It's almost—Instagram ready. Like, #BeautifulPerson. It should be more like #WhoWatersThatThing?

If I kept a flower on my desk it would be knocked over by coffee cups and file folders that actually are full. Of work. But what was I supposed to do? Criticize her for being too perfect? Not that she *is* all that perfect, but she looks it. Which, again, is all that matters in TV.

Still, even Lily can't totally avoid coming to work for a whole day. I've covered for her, which is better for the both of us. I'm predicting she'll come in and take a stroll through the newsroom, acting all purposeful and focused as if she'd been around all day. Like setting up an absence alibi—to convince people she'd been here, diligently on the job the whole time, but people just hadn't seen her.

I had to admit, out on an actual interview she was all business, a quick study and an expert questioner. So maybe she was only super-neurotic about her personal life.

Aunt Cassie. Rowe had definitely let something slip there. I'd never worked with anyone so protective of her personal history. People have to chat, right? Make small talk in the car, or having coffee? It's called *sharing*. Conversation. It's how the world works. Not Lily's world, apparently.

Still. Even with Lily's storied privacy, seemed like I'd hit a nerve with this Cassie person.

I winced at myself, once again half-regretting my curiosity. Like Lily's instant charisma, curiosity is what made me what I am. I wish she liked me more, though. Noticed me. It doesn't matter, it doesn't, but it would be nice.

I'm honestly not being creepy sinister about this. She's famous, she's a big deal, so therefore, she's interesting. That's just how the world is. She's a celebrity, so everyone wants to know everything about her. Her clothes, her ideas. Her perfect life and how she got it.

With the inalterably present subtext of *I want that, too.*

Did I want that? I shook my head, answering myself. Hell, no. Not at all.

Aunt Cassie. I looked again at the photograph on the wall, the scalloped, yellowing edges, the fading image of a little girl and a dog. Was this a picture of the elusive Cassie?

If Lily kept this photo, it must have meaning, I thought, staring at it. It must have power. There were no other truly personal things on Lily's bulletin board. Press passes, a few fan letters, the cover of *Boston* magazine showing her in glamorous makeup and wearing a black tulle ball gown and white sneakers. SO LILY, the headline read. Boston's glam go-getter. She believed her own publicity, which drove me crazy. We *all* made her who she is. The photographers, the lighting people. The producers. We did the work. She had the fun. She got the rewards.

"Shut up," I muttered to myself. My brain just went places, made up its own stories. Even I got tired of them sometimes. Wished my brain would turn off. If Lily were here, where she was supposed to be, my mind would be otherwise occupied. So this was really her fault. I wouldn't be able to track down Aunt Cassie if Lily were sitting here at her lemony desk, so yeah. Her fault. What would I know if I found Cassie?

I carefully removed the photo, checking the back of it. No date, no inscription, no fading imprint of blue numbers. Nothing. I pinned it back, ever so carefully, exactly where it had been before.

No other clues in the photo. No street signs, or numbers on a mailbox, or something that would make it easy, like a big sign saying "Welcome to Lincolnwood" or "Cohasset." No license plates. Impossible to tell whether this was Lily's older sister, or her younger sister. If it was her sister at all. Maybe a family friend, one of those people you call *aunt* for want of an easy specific?

Without a conscious thought, I stood and yanked open the top file drawer in the metal cabinet next to Lily's desk. I glanced at the clock. Just enough time. I hoped.

Parallel metal bars held green hanging file pockets, each one with a few tabbed file folders. None was marked *Personal*. I took a deep breath, gave myself producer absolution, and removed the one marked *Paystubs*. I found what I needed. Memorized the first three numbers and put everything back. I couldn't unknow it now. Not to mention also knowing Lily's plump salary. But again, she was talent.

Lily's Social Security number started with 159. Since Social Security numbers—for people Lily's age, at least—indicated the state where the card was issued, 159 might mean . . . I clicked into Google. Searched. Got the answer. Pennsylvania.

Which meant exactly zero. There were so many variables. Maybe her sister—I'd decided it was her sister, just to make thinking about it easier—had been born someplace else. Maybe—there was a whole list of maybes. *Where are you, Aunt Cassie? And why is Lily trying to hide you?*

"Greer?" Lily's voice from down the hall. I flinched, startled, and stepped away from her file cabinet. How could she arrive just in time—almost—to catch me snooping? A flitter of a guilt-worry caught in my throat, and I dropped into my own desk chair, eyeing Lily's file cabinet, then pushing it with my toe to make sure the drawer I'd opened was completely closed. At least I was a good burglar.

"Hey, Lil." I reopened my emails, pretended to be diligently reading them like a good, hardworking producer. I swiveled to face the voice. "What's up? Oh, hey, Rowen."

"Hey, Auntie Greer, I'm here to visit Mumma's newsroom again." Rowen's hand linked with her mother's, their matching eyes ridiculously genetic. Even their cheekbones matched. "And maybe be on TV."

"Silly girl," Lily said. "You don't give up, do you?"

I knew enough not to get into that one.

"Anything . . . new?" I tried to add subtext to my question, hoping Lily would know I was referring to Smith's call, and interested in what happened at Graydon.

"Tell Greer what happened at school today, Rowe." Lily stashed her tote bag under her desk. "You can sit in my seat, right here, while I go check on something in the newsroom. You two chat, and maybe later, I'll bring you downstairs. But the four o'clock news is on now, honey. That means only reporters can be in the newsroom. Okay, Gree? Two minutes."

I hoped Lily thought I was smiling at being relegated to hang out with a seven-year-old and not smiling at her transparent—and expected—alibi ruse. Or at the manipulative nickname. *Gree*. Kidding me?

"So what happened at school?" I began as instructed. "Your mom tells me you write poems. Did you bring any with you?"

Fire drill, lots of bells, they got to go outside, no new poems. I listened, with an enthusiastic expression on my face, as Rowen chattered about the events of the day. "Then Mumma came, and it was a surprise, and then I went in, and then Mumma talked to Headmaster Glover, and there was a butterfly that almost came into the school with me!"

"Whoa." I nodded as if imagining such a thing.

I had to make sure this conversation, if related to Lily, was spotlessly innocent. I pointed to the sepia photo. "Isn't that a cute photo?"

Rowen nodded. "It's Pooch."

"Pooch?"

"Pooch," Rowen said. "Mumma's dog when she was little. My age. We have Val, and Val is bigger and funnier. Pooch is in dog heaven, Mumma told me."

I nodded, sympathetic. "That must have been a long time ago."

"Before I was born," Rowe said.

She began to roll pencils across the desk, watching them plop onto the floor. Time was running out. *Mumma, why did Greer ask about Aunt Cassie?* All I need.

"So, um, and that's your mumma in the photo with Pooch, right?" Old journalism trick. People love to correct you, no matter how old they are. And when they correct you, you get the answer you wanted in the first place.

"No, silly." Rowen did an expert eye roll.

"No?" I frowned, the perplexed adult. "I thought it was."

"It's not Mumma." Rowe's voice carried a twinge of Lily-like disdain. "It's Aunt Cassie."

"Rowen?" Lily was framed in the doorway, her eyes darting back and forth between us.

Her hair had that effortless aura of salon visit, and I could still see tiny red dots along her forehead. Appointments, huh? Blow-dry and Botox, no question. But then, she had to be perfect.

I stood, making a big show of gathering the yellow pencils from the floor.

"Rowen's been racing pencils," I explained. "She's an expert." I felt bad trying to weasel information from a child, but curious me wanted to know more. And it wasn't going to come from Lily, that was for sure. To distract her, I planted a worry. "What's the scoop from the newsroom? Anyone notice you were gone today?"

"Huh?" Lily seemed truly baffled. She's convinced even *herself* she doesn't have to play by the real rules. "You think they noticed I wasn't here?"

"Probably not," I said. "I'm sure it's fine."

"Your phone is ringing," Lily said, pointing. "Rowey? Say goodbye to Aunt Greer."

CHAPTER 13

GREER

I couldn't decide how to answer Smith's opening question—"Do you know who this is?"—because if I said yes or if I said no, it meant the same thing. I did know the name we used, but I didn't know who he or she really was. I clamped the phone to my ear as if somehow that could get me closer to the truth. I'd recognized my caller's voice as I watched Lily and Rowen stroll down the hall away from our office. Hand in hand, little and big, perfect and more perfect.

The girl in the sepia photograph, the mysterious Cassie, seemed to stare at me from Lily's bulletin board.

"Yes," I quickly said, "I know who this is—not your name of course, but yes."

"I knew you would."

Smith's voice seemed like a man's today, I decided, but maybe there was something on the phone that distorts or alters the EQ, like we did in editing to disguise an interviewee's voice. Why was he suddenly calling me? He—or she—had only contacted Lily in the past. I wondered if this was some sort of end run around her. Or fishing for information.

"Did Lily tell you I called earlier today?"

"This morning, yes, of course she did." I pretended

Lily always told me everything. "That's why she went to Graydon."

Silence on the other end. "Yes, this morning," Smith finally said.

Another pause, and I sat back in my chair, phone to my ear, staring at the floor. Drying crumbs from my afternoon snack of potato chips had not quite buried themselves in the carpet's thin gray pile, and one of Rowe's pencils had rolled under Lily's desk.

"So, Ms. Whitfield," he said. "Can we keep this off the record?"

"Sure," I said, lying yet again. I plucked a potato chip crumb from the carpet, tossed it toward my metal wastebasket, and almost made it. I hate off the record; it's journalistic quicksand. So I always say yes and then renegotiate when the time comes if need be.

"I mean just between us." Smith's voice had lowered, insistent. "I mean off the record even to Lily. Agreed?"

"Agreed," I said. Whatever.

"So you will not tell her about this call, or anything that comes from it."

"Mr. Smith?" Why did he want me to keep something from Lily? That made me eager to know it. "I agreed to off the record, and my word is my word. I've been in television for a long time, and my reliability is why I am where I am. So what can I do for you?"

"Why don't we discuss it in person?"

In person? "Tell me more."

Smith began to speak, and I began to calculate. I stared down the empty corridor outside my office door—a strip of grimy carpeting, other office doors, and finally the doorway with the red Exit sign. The newscast, sound muted, flickered from a tiny monitor on Lily's desk, and a bigger (and older) one on mine. I was alone, with a bit of breaking news of my own. I was going to meet face-to-face with our secret source.

"I know it's already close of business," Smith was saying, "but if you can fit it into your schedule, I am free later this evening. I have a major story for you. I know you are the brains behind Lily's beauty, Ms. Whitfield."

I had to admit, the guy knew how to flatter. And how TV worked. And psychology.

"Sounds good. Is there anything I can research in the meantime? So I can come in up to speed?" Old producer trick. See if the source will give some hints of what's to come.

I heard him breathing on the other end of the phone, so I knew he hadn't hung up. I waited. He was deciding, while I was having a mental debate of my own.

Would I tell Lily I was meeting Smith?

"Let us say nine? The lounge at Lido. The theater crowd won't return until after the final curtain, so it will be public, but not crowded. Does that work for you?"

"Okay." I nodded, even though Smith couldn't see me. And, sadly, he hadn't risen to the "research" bait. But a good story is the grail, and it'd be gratifying—I grimaced at my selfish motives—to know something that Lily didn't.

"Ms. Whitfield?"

"Yes?"

"You mentioned research. Did you know Lily has a sister?"

And he takes the bait. Of course I knew. Thanks to Rowen. But that was the last thing I imagined he'd say. "Sure," I said.

"You'll want to look into that," Smith said. "So. Lido. At nine."

"Lido at nine." I wrote the place and time on my notepad. *Lido, 9PM.* "What name?"

He—definitely *he* now—laughed out loud. "Smith,

of course. But that's hardly a problem. I'll recognize you."

And I heard the sound of the phone disconnecting.

So that gave me a moment of pause. Recognize me? How?

CHAPTER 14

LILY

"Petra?" The moment Lily opened her front door, key still in the lock, she sensed a shift in the atmosphere, a disturbance, a fragrance of something unusual. "Are you home?"

"Mumma?" Rowen stood beside her on the front porch, yanking on the strap of Lily's shoulder bag. "We have a package! Can I open it?"

"Petra?" Lily took another step inside, saw the butterscotch chairs, empty, the white couch, pristine, the lilies on the coffee table. *The lilies on the coffee table?* That was the fragrance.

"Petra?" she called out again. Petra must have put them back for some reason. Wait. They were *different* lilies. More lilies?

"Mumma? This was on the mail bench."

Lily turned. Rowen had a shoebox-size cardboard box in her hands, professionally labeled, but no store logo. Lily often got packages—books, and hair stuff, clothing, and makeup from Saks and Neiman's, toys for Rowen. And now she was making ordinary into sinister. Again.

"Can I open it? What is it?" Holding it to her ear, Rowen gave the box a little shake, then another. "Is it for me?"

"Let's wait, sweetie. Can you not shake it? And put that down for one little second?"

Rowen put the package back on the bench. "One thousand one." Picked it up again. "Mumma? Now can I open it?"

"Honey?" Lily heard the edge in her own voice.

"O-kay." Rowen apparently heard it, too.

Where was Petra? Maybe cooking, maybe in the bathroom, maybe Lily was just too damn tired from trying to analyze every little thing that ever happened, figure it out whether it was scary, or threatening, or dangerous. Plus her head hurt, and she was completely starving, and though Rowen had eaten a waxed-paper packet of graham crackers in the car, they were too carby for Lily to have any herself.

"Petra?" Then she recognized what else was off. "Val?" She patted her hands together. "Here, girl!"

I'm losing it, Lily thought. *Low blood sugar strikes again.* But—more flowers?

"Maybe Val and Petra are in the back," Lily said, brushing her hair from her face. "Why don't you run to the back fence and see? You could surprise them."

Maybe she should go back to Dr. Hrones. No one could go through life—not happily, at least—when every little thing turned into a worry. *Cassie's fault,* if you thought of it that way. Things that happen to someone else could topple the dominoes for everyone around them.

She watched her daughter trot to the back fence. Rowe wouldn't be able to see over it, because it was deliberately tall enough to block casual curiosity. But it gave Lily a minute to regroup. Bring herself back to reality.

It had been a long day. With the phone call from Smith, and the heart-twisting drive to Graydon. Then the perplexing fire drill—the timing of which, Maryrose Glover had insisted, was known only to her. And that might be true. Maybe Smith had one of those scanners set to the fire department frequency and heard the call to Graydon. Fire departments had to know about drills. Didn't they?

"Mumma, I can't *see* over the fence." Rowen, returning, had put on poutface, but that lasted all of two seconds. "But I heard Val barking! She's out there."

She scooted past Lily and dashed into the house.

"Rowe!" Lily called, following after her. "Wait, honey!"

"What, Mumma?" Rowen had turned to face her, and like a little mirror image, stood in the entryway with impatient fists planted on her hips. "Come *on*!"

The dog was in the backyard. Lily felt her heart pounding. She put her hand over it, felt the air go out of her lungs.

"Vallie!" Rowen called out.

Lily heard another sound from the back of the house. A different one. A human one.

"Hey, Lily. Hey, little one." Petra, wooden spoon in hand and wearing one of Lily's French aprons, came out of the kitchen, pale hair twisted into a messy bun, a swath of what looked like flour on one cheekbone. Lily heard dance music buzzing from Petra's now-dangling earbuds.

"Oh, you're home. Fresh ravioli for dinner." She raised the spoon, victorious. "I made sauce, too, and now everything smells of garlic. I'm a mess, and so is the kitchen. Val's been out back, playing with the squirrels."

Val bounded into the room, tail at top speed, as if she hadn't seen them in months. She first headed for Lily, then veered to Rowen. The two clattered out of the room, laughing and barking. Lily heard the back door open and slam closed. Nothing was wrong. Except.

"Where did the lilies come from?" Lily hadn't

meant it to sound like that, accusatory and critical. Her emotions were getting the better of her today. Everything out of proportion.

Petra furrowed her forehead, perplexed. Lowered her triumphant spoon. "Where? They were delivered today, is that what you mean? When you were gone." She took a deep breath, wiped a strand of hair from her face.

Lily saw her staring at the flowers.

"Oh. They're like the ones you gave me." Petra pointed her spoon at them. "Should I not have accepted them? Did I make a problem?"

Lily waved her off, stopping her. "No, no, Petra, it's fine, it's—"

Petra's shoulders dropped. "I should have understood."

"No, don't worry, Pet, nothing to understand. It's complicated." Lily tried to smile. "I'll deal. You cook. All fine. Flowers are always good. I was just surprised to see them. Go. All fine."

"Cool." Petra saluted with her spoon again, then headed back for the kitchen.

Good. Lily wanted her out of there. She walked toward the faceted vase, eyes on the green plastic stick poked among the pink-and-white blooms. Between two flat prongs, it held a white envelope, edged with a garland of Willaby's trademark yellow roses. She removed the envelope. Flipped it.

Sealed.

She took a deep breath. Sat on the couch, turning the card over and over. The sealed flap taunted her.

"Get a grip, woman," she muttered. It would reveal something or it wouldn't. But how did whoever sent this second bouquet know she'd given away the first one?

"Mumma?" Rowe's voice from the kitchen archway.

"Yes, honey?" Lily turned to see her. Rowe's hair had come out of its pigtails, and she'd lost another penguin bow.

"Petra wants to know what time for dinner? And I wanna know how many raviolis we each get. Petra says eight."

"Eight sounds just right," Lily said. "Then see if you're still hungry. And how about—we'll have dinner two minutes *after* you put your bow back on and wash your hands and set the table? Then come get me."

"It's in the back, I bet," Rowen said. "It must've fell."

"Fallen," Lily said. "They'll do that. Now scoot."

The second she was alone again, Lily slid one fingernail under a corner of the envelope and peeled back the sealed flap. She heard the paper rip, and pull, and release. She heard Petra and Rowe laughing from the kitchen. She saw the yellow garland bordering the card's edge.

Using thumb and forefinger, she drew out the card.

There was just one word, in script, written in black fountain pen.

Cassie.

BEFORE

CHAPTER 15

CASSIE

She'd tried to keep her mind on what Professor Shaw was saying, something about creating a plan for the rest of the year, something about lab practicums, something about extra credit. There was no need, she knew it, for them to have this meeting here and now. This could have been decided by a memo or two, or in the fifteen minutes between classes. He'd left his office door only half-open, she noticed, and a few people, some students and some teachers, maybe, walked past. He hadn't acknowledged them. Wharton Hall was open, but Berwick had no classes on weekends.

"As midterms draw nearer," he was saying, "I like to assess the progress of students I feel have some—shall we say—aptitude. Are you enjoying class, Ms. Atwood? Do you feel you're acclimating to campus life?"

He was asking a question, Cassie told herself, like regular adults do. He wasn't coming on to her, he *wasn't,* this was how adults talked.

"Yes, of course." She could feel his eyes on her, on her bare legs, but maybe she was making it up. She dearly wanted to smooth her skirt, but that might make it worse, calling attention to it. She wished she'd worn tights.

"Let me show you some of the textbooks we'll be using the next semester. You can see whether you're interested in some independent study."

He turned his back to her, ran a finger along the row of books on a shelf behind him. His black turtleneck was probably cashmere, and without a speck of lint, and his dark hair curled, just the tiniest of bits, over the collar. The shelves contained a few slim books of poetry. Tucked among the textbooks, she saw Whitman and Frost and Yeats.

She sneaked a glance around his windowless office. Posters from the Barnes Museum, both still lifes, both framed in black metal. A Picasso and a Cézanne, she recognized. Both apples, but so very different. *Apples to apples,* she might say, commenting on them to show she understood art and was witty. Maybe.

There were no family photos. No wedding photos. No little kids. A framed degree from Penn.

She tried to think of what Frost poem she might casually drop into the conversation. *Two roads diverged in a yellow wood,* she recited to herself. *I took the one less traveled by . . .*

He pulled a brown leather volume from the shelf. He turned to her, looking down at her, and held the book out to her with an expression she could not decode.

She lifted a hand to reach for it. Took it.

The sound of a buzzer—so sudden and so surprising—startled her so completely that she dropped the book on his desk, where it tipped over the pencil holder. She stood, wanted to fix it, as the buzzers grew louder and louder. Lights flashed, strobing blue, the spell of their shared silence shattered and vanished.

"Ms. Atwood?" He left the book where it was. Righted the pencil holder. He took a leather briefcase from behind his desk and stuffed a sheaf of papers inside. Then the book, too. "That's the fire warning. I know it's always a false alarm, but we're required to treat every one as real. You have your belongings?"

Fire alarms in this old building were set on a hair trigger—even this early in the semester, the buzzers and lights had already interrupted Cassie's classes several times. They'd been told such an iconic building, and all the history it held, could never be replaced. Not to mention the people inside.

The week before, Cassie'd had to raise her voice as she and her roommate left class and dutifully trooped outside, the buzzers incessant and unrelenting.

"When it's a real fire, no one will care," she'd predicted. "We'll all just assume it's another drill, and sit there, and poof. Toast. Up in smoke." She'd mimed her prediction with a wave of her arm. "They're, like, setting us up to ignore them. What're they thinking?"

"I know, so dumb. Has there ever actually *been* a fire?" Marianne had shifted the stack of books in her arms as they walked back toward the dorm that day. "Or is this them all freaking out?"

Now Professor Shaw paused, his hand on the handle of his briefcase. He shook his head as if amused. "This old building, right? All those nooks and crannies? No matter what they do . . ." His expression seemed to change. Harden. "You need to go, Miss Atwood," he said. "Out the door, turn right, up the stairs, and exit the building. Keep walking. Away from the building."

Cassie gathered her belongings again, pretending she was hurrying, but watching him from under her lashes. She knew it. He was stalling, too, opening a drawer and closing it, taking a pencil from a jar on the desk and sliding it into his jacket pocket. He was waiting for her, watching her. Maybe he'd decided to ignore the alarm, knowing how often they were meaningless. They would be alone in the building, just the two of them.

Is that what he wanted?

Cassie lowered her head to zip up her backpack and peeked at him through her curtain of hair. What if they just . . . stayed here? Who would know, since everyone else would be gone? It was a false alarm, anyway. The perfect cover. Everyone else would think they'd gone their separate ways. No one would ever think they were together.

"Ms. Atwood." He'd picked up his briefcase and gestured toward the door. "We need to go."

We need to go, he'd said.

What if there was *a fire,* the thought raced through her mind, *and I was trapped inside, and he saved me? Or, what if . . .* She twisted the story. *What if I saved* him? *And*—

"I need to lock the door after I leave," he went on, raising his voice over the buzzing alarm. "So, Ms. Atwood?"

What was he signaling her? She had no choice now, she had to go. And see if he came after her.

"Of course. Just making sure I have all my notes from today." She tried out a smile, but he'd walked to the door. He held it all the way open for her.

"See you another time," he said.

"In your office? Here?"

She could tell by his emerald eyes that he was pretending to be surprised. "My office hours are posted on my door here." He gestured her out into the hall. "And now you need to go."

She could feel those eyes on her back as she walked toward the open office door and up the blue-railed concrete stairs to the main exit. She couldn't help it, and risked a glance behind her. A few stragglers, a student or two, a teacher, hurrying or not, toward the exit. Not Professor Shaw. Where had he gone?

She turned back, kept walking the corridor, the blue alarm lights strobing, the buzzers, their volume rising and falling, but unceasing. A few more steps to the open door. She could see daylight outside, the sun, and in the distance the grove of maple trees where students would gather with clandestine wine and occasional weed. Silly, silly, *silly* people, still kids, really, and she was feeling just the opposite. She was an adult, she was eighteen and could make her own decisions. This was a false alarm. They could go back inside when it was over.

She and Professor Shaw could laugh, she could almost imagine it, and then they could talk about biology. And maybe poetry. And art. She felt a tiny smile. How was she acclimating to college life? he'd asked her. Very, very nicely.

Or maybe she was imagining things.

"Get a grip, Cass," she muttered. But she didn't listen to herself. All kinds of wonderful things might happen. A false alarm was almost like . . . a tease.

"Ms. Atwood?" A voice from behind her. "Cassie?"

NOW

CHAPTER 16

GREER

Cassie Atwood. For someone I'd never heard of until yesterday, thanks to Rowen and our Mr. Smith, now I was beginning to know a lot about her. Weirdly unsettling that our tipster source was giving us—me—information on Lily herself. The flickering images on my TV monitor showed the closing graphics of the seven o'clock news. I did feel guilty; Lily would freak if she knew what I was doing. Then again, she would never know. Plus, Smith asked me to do it. Like a research assignment.

Cassie Atwood Pennsylvania, I typed. The cursor blinked as I thought. Why would someone be loath to discuss a member of their family? Lily could have just said, *Oh, yeah, my sister Cassie. She's an artist in Paris. A survivalist in Utah. She's a hotshot investment banker; we never hear from her. I love her. I hate her. She's dead.*

Police, I typed after *Pennsylvania*. Then *investigation*. If something were wrong, some kind of a mystery or a situation, that would pull up the news coverage. I was looking for a good story, I knew. *Cassie Atwood, person with normal happy life* wouldn't be that interesting.

Cassie Atwood Pennsylvania police investigation. Five words.

Nothing is ever what we predict; the universe can come up with complexities the human brain is incapable of inventing. Soon, I'd know.

It gave me a chill. In ninety minutes, if all went as planned, I'd finally meet Smith. Mystery solved. And I'd find out why he'd asked me about Lily's sister. I'd wait for him to bring that part up, of course.

Out my window, Boston was edging into dusk, the streetlights lining the sidewalks with the glow of powerful blue-white halogens. There was even an ice cream truck on the street, a harbinger of the coming summer. Maybe I'd walk to Lido, in fact, take in the spring evening, see if I could hear the tinkling of the truck's ragtime jingle. I remembered Mom buying one orange Popsicle that she'd split in half, and we'd share it, down to the sticks, as our mouths deepened to bright orange. I can't hear ragtime like that without thinking of it, and of her. Lily and Rowen must be home now, making their own memories.

When I go home, there's no one. Relationships, that's for later. Family, all gone. It's not fair to a pet that I work this much, so I haven't even a solitary goldfish. Or maybe I'm the solitary goldfish, swimming and swimming and getting nowhere. But I have time.

Thirty-eight isn't old, it is just what I am. Thirty-eight is the new thirty. Thirty-eight is old enough to have experience, some control, to be in charge. It also means I have time, plenty of time, to do whatever I want to do and be whatever I decide to be. Blah-dee-blah. I didn't even know what that is. My life is far from storybook perfect. But for now, it's fine. At least my life—my work—is real. My life *is* my work. Perfect enough for me.

Back to my search. I hit Enter.

I stared at my computer screen, at her name in indigo-purple on the main search page. *Cassandra Blair (Cassie) Atwood, B. 1981.* No date of death. An "Images" sidebar box, with two tiny photos, showed a classic '90s college student, flannel shirt over a crop top, hair in a scrunchy, brown lipstick. She looked happy, but that's how people looked in posed photos, the ones where you knew you were supposed to plaster a happy expression on your face. No matter what the fashion or circumstance, though, Cassie was an attractive eighteen-year-old.

But she'd never gotten any older. Not that anyone knew of, at least.

Links to several TV news stories from back then popped up, the headlines recording the increasing— and then lessening—emphasis on the story.

Hamilton girl reported missing, said an early one. *Family asks for help.* When I clicked on that story, a quick thirty-second voice-over showed what looked like a high school graduation photo. The sound on the next story, a longer one, was full of annoying glitches and audio dropouts, but it was clear from watching the video that Cassie graduated from Hamilton High, and had lived in a modestly landscaped two-story home. Was it the one in the sepia photo? She'd attended the private and pricey Berwick University— must have been a smart girl—and that was the last anyone had seen her. I wrote *Berwick* on my scratch pad. There seemed to be no father, I'd noticed as I watched the stories. Police officers, very Midwest, with mustaches and broad shoulders, said she'd likely come back on her own.

"College students," said a local police lieutenant chyroned Walter B. Kirkhalter, Berwick Police Department, "tend to be immature and unreliable. Away from home for the first time, on their own." He stood behind a too-short bouquet of microphones duct-taped to a

metal stand. Seemed to be tiptoeing for a way to blame
the missing girl for her own absence and not blame her
at the same time. He leaned down into the mics again.
"We are looking for her with all our assets and asking
everyone to help us find her. But we are hoping she'll
appear on her own."

Nice, I thought. I wrote *Kirkhalter* on my scratch
pad. The headlines grew pessimistically darker as the
coverage continued. A roommate with red-rimmed
eyes, *Marianne* was all they called her, showed
Cassie's perfectly made bed, and a row of flannel
shirts hanging in "her half" of the closet.

"There's nothing *missing.*" Marianne seemed as if
she could barely get the words out. Her blond hair
was supposed to pouf in a Princess Di look, but one
side was flat. Her eyeliner had melted into fear lines
on her cheekbones. Princess Di was already dead, I
calculated. But everyone knew what had happened to
her. Killed by fame and celebrity.

"Did she have a boyfriend?" a reporter in a red tie
and navy suit jacket asked as he flipped a network-
logoed mic toward her. "Did she seem upset about
anything?"

Typical, I thought. Upset. Boyfriend. Years pass,
reporter's questions never change. Watching old TV
stories like this was like reading a book where you
knew the ending. Knowing the end, it's easier to decide what's prescient and what's peripheral. What's
relevant and what isn't.

The headlines devolved into WHERE'S CASSIE? as
if, like Cher, it took only her first name for everyone
to understand who she was. One story was titled "Up
and Disappeared," a reference, as it turned out, to
what Cassie's maternal grandmother, tight white curls
and ice-blue eyes, had told one reporter. I'd gasped
when I saw her grandmother's name. It made me realize what I'd forgotten.

"That girl always did what she wanted," Lily Horgan had told the reporter with a twinge of a Southern accent. "From day one, moment one, I swear she was in charge. If she up and disappeared, I do believe she did it of her own choice. And if she doesn't want us to find her, well, we won't."

Lily. That's who I'd forgotten in all this. My Lily must have been named for her grandmother. I did a calculation in pencil on a yellow stickie. Lily would have been seven back then, maybe. Old enough to know her sister was missing and definitely old enough to be terrified and sad. But where was she in all this coverage? We'd seen Cassie's mother—Lily's mother—whose obituary was later included in an anniversary story about the still-missing Cassie. We'd even had a quick glimpse of the flop-eared pet I knew to be Pooch. But they'd kept Lily off the screen. I wondered if that was on purpose, to keep her from the spotlight. To keep the little girl private. Or safe.

The grandmother, Lily Horgan, must be dead.

Marianne, roommate with no last name. Could be anywhere. She could have been helping Cassie, maybe, covering for her.

Which gave me another idea. I looked at the clock. I could do this search really fast. I hovered my fingers over the keyboard, considering. *Missing* . . . I shrugged, giving myself permission to type. *Missing persons who walked away on their own.*

The results popped up as varied and diverse as a *Law & Order* show, lists of them, terrifyingly long lists, from a two-year-old who'd been in the back seat of a van in a dry cleaners parking lot to a nineteen-year-old college student who was last seen on her way to class, to a forty-six-year-old who apparently dumped all her belongings, from jewelry to stuffed animals to a blender and a wedding dress, into a trash bin before she vanished. Or maybe someone else dumped them, I frowned as I read the story, second-guessing the investigation.

My mind cataloged and sorted the individual stories as I viewed them, searching for similarities and differences. So many situations, but all the descriptions ended with some version of "They were never seen or heard from again," like the refrain of some disturbing tale told around the campfire, designed to frighten teenagers into being careful and staying aware.

Lots of white vans in these stories, I noticed. I felt like a human database, organizing and shuffling and looking for patterns. Women and girls. Mostly women and girls. Men were rarely kidnapped. Men did not "disappear." Women did.

Many of them were later found, of course, dead. But. I felt my eyes narrow as I looked at the screen, scanning only for the ones who were still unaccounted for. There was a pattern there, too.

Many of them seemed to have set up their impending absence. Prepared for it. They gave away possessions. Made nonchalant-sounding phone calls to relatives about how they had exams or were taking a week off to take a break. Told professors they'd been called home for an emergency. They'd plotted to delay the moment someone would miss them, or wonder about them, or start worrying. They'd strategized to give themselves a head start.

Cassie hadn't left any notes, or warnings, or plans. Unless, of course, she had sworn people to secrecy. That would be a difficult secret to keep, knowing the heartbreak it would cause.

It must be a terrible juggle, I thought as I stared at my screen, to decide to leave your family and friends, knowing they'd be in anguish forever. What would make a person do that? Love, money, fear, anger, temptation? Again and again, by far, most of the never-seen-agains were women.

It was either breathtakingly self-centered or a method of self-preservation.

Grandmother Lily Horgan had said, "If she doesn't want us to find her . . ."

Grandmother. I wrote that on my scratch pad. I couldn't believe the reporter hadn't pushed her. "Would Cassie have left you all?" That's what I would have asked. "Her loved ones? Was there something she was running away from? Or running to?"

Grandmother Lily might have had a clue. Even roommate Marianne. *Marianne.* I added her name under *Grandmother.*

But the reporters hadn't pursued it, not what was used on camera at least, and now it was too late.

"Late!" I yelped the word as I stood, pushing back my desk chair. No time for makeup or hair or preparations. Outside, dusk had fallen in earnest, that May color of the sky that's pink and purple and unphotographable—seemingly new colors of nature in wild, reckless abandon, taking the atmospheric stage for the last moments of their life, until the darkness again falls. Smith, here I come.

I'd get there just in time.

CHAPTER 17

LILY

If she hurried, she could make it. Lily followed Petra and Rowen into the kitchen, each carrying their dinner plate to the sink, and tried to come up with a reasonable excuse. Thank goodness for Mother's Day, the second Sunday in May. That meant that today, the second Tuesday, florists were probably going nuts with orders. And open late. Willaby's, according to her quick internet search, was open until nine. She could get there just in time.

"So, guys?" Lily said over the sound of the water running in the kitchen sink. Rowen had put on the yellow dishwashing gloves, a million times too big for her, but she loved them. Loved squirting the dish soap into a pan of water and watching the bubbles. She'd outgrow that, Lily knew, but it was sweet while it lasted.

"Watch out, Mumma!" Rowen had turned, and in one motion puffed a billow of soap bubbles in Lily's direction. They floated over the pale wood floor, then plopped to the ground, popping in defeat. "I'm bubble girl!"

"Right. Bubble girl. And now you're clean-up-the-floor girl." Lily smiled, though, reassured that Rowen could enjoy anything. That was the Sam Prescott gene, Lily had to admit. He could be the most—

anyway. "While you're cleaning up, you two, I'll pick up ice cream." She'd finally come up with an unrefusable offer. Then remembered how late it was in Rowen world. Recalculated. "For tomorrow."

"Jamaica Jamoca!" Rowen scooped up another handful of bubbles. At Lily's expression, she blew them into the sink. "And I can stay up 'til you get home!"

"Any flavor is fine." Petra eyed Lily as if questioning the sudden shift in agenda. "About how long . . . ?"

"Forty-five, tops," Lily said. "You two maybe . . . have a story? And no staying up, kiddo. I'll come in for penguins."

She was trying not to bolt, but it was all she could do to measure her steps until she got to the front door, opened it, and stepped outside. A waft of lilacs from the garden next door floated across a soft puff of breeze, and the new leaves on her white birch rustled, whispering in their own soft voices.

She had to stop for a moment, taking it in. She was always so crazed, moving so fast, not noticing her surroundings. Here, on her very own porch, and her dear daughter inside playing with bubbles, she tried to remember to—

The box. The box still on the porch bench. The one Rowen had rattled. The one that held the thing she didn't remember ordering. She stared at it, the seconds ticking by. In the time she'd waited, she could have opened it.

She scooped it up to take it with her in the car. Or—why would she take it in the car?

"Lily!" she admonished herself out loud. "You have to go!"

Leaving the box, she raced to her car. The florist had to tell her, *had* to, where those flowers came from. They could dodge her on a phone call. But not in person. She was Lily Atwood.

As she opened the door of Willaby's, a tinkling

from bells announced her arrival. Two women, identical in tight black tees, black jeans, and cropped curls, looked up, then smiled at her.

Felicia and Arnelle Hunneman owned Willaby's, named for their activist great-aunt who'd started the first minority-owned florist in this neighborhood so many years ago. Each wore canvas garden gloves and flower snips on orange lanyards around their necks. Long-stemmed roses and lilies and peonies and greens piled precariously on the counter in front of them, black plastic containers of baby's breath holding them in place, and a lazy Susan of enclosure cards sat in front of a cash register. The bells tinkled again as the door clicked itself closed. The fragrance of rose and spicy eucalyptus surrounded her, intense as if she'd entered a secret garden.

"Lily!" Felicia greeted her, saluting with a graceful pink rose. "Welcome to our annual Mother's Day chaos. It you want to place an order, do it now, sister. We're stripping the last of the roses here. After this, it's carnation city."

"We don't do carnations." Arnelle shook her head. She picked up another rose, snipped off the lower stems. "But we may be down to daisies. Anyway—hey. You got here just in time. What can we do for you?"

"The lilies you sent?" Lily began.

"They're okay, right?" Felicia peeled off her gloves, stuffed them in a back jeans pocket, came out from behind the counter.

Lily nodded. "Yes, perfect. As always. But did you . . . deliver two? Two bouquets?"

"Ah, yeah." She tilted her head. "And?"

Arnelle had joined her twin in front of the counter. "Is there a problem?"

Was there a problem. Exactly the question Lily knew she'd be asked and still hadn't decided how to answer.

"Oh, no, of course not." She waved off their concerns, trying to look like she was telling the truth. "But so silly—two bouquets. Same lilies, exactly. That's what I get for being named Lily, I suppose, right?" She tried to keep it light, and talked faster to cover her unease. "The *first* bouquet—there was no card. But the one that came today, with your store's card—the vases were the same." She made the globe shape with her hands. "So—"

Felicia stepped back behind the counter, leaned down, and came up with an empty fishbowl vase. "Like this?"

"Yeah." Lily recognized it, nodded. "Exactly."

"We have those made special," Arnelle said. "So it must have come from here."

"Hey. That means *those* were the other lilies." Felicia pointed at her sister.

"Must be," Arnelle answered, nodding.

"We named that particular bouquet after you, actually," Felicia interrupted. "The Perfect Lily. Because you helped us get the loan that time and—"

"And we're grateful." Arnelle finished the sentence. "So—"

"Felicia? Arnelle? Thanks." Their ping-pong conversation was making her headache return. "Can you look up the transactions?"

She stopped, mid-sentence, seeing the same perplexed expression pass over each woman's face.

"I'm just trying to find out—" she went on.

Arnelle had taken a step forward. "Lily? Sure. We can look it up for you."

"Arn, those were Venmos, right?" Felicia tapped on the computer. "Huh. It's just a weird—it's just 'at flowers.' No name."

The bells tinkled again, and Lily moved aside as a young man in a white button-down shirt and jeans entered. "'Scuse me," he said. He looked at his watch, then at each of them in turn. "Ah, it's kind of an emergency." He shrugged, sheepish. "A sorry-for-being-late emergency, if you know what I mean."

"It's fine, I'll wait," Lily said.

Felicia laughed. "A red-rose-level emergency?" she asked. "Or daisy level?"

Lily tried to stay patient, though she could almost hear the time ticking away. But this poor guy, fighting on some emotional battlefield, his emergencies so ephemeral they could be solved by flowers. She thought of the lilies on her coffee table, flowers someone—*someone*—had sent to her, actively turning beauty into a sinister message, a false intimacy, an intrusion into her home. And into Rowen's. And that name on the card. Cassie. How many people even knew that name?

Cassie knew about Cassie, though. But if Cassie were still alive, and had found her, why didn't she come out and say so?

The bells tinkled again. The young man left carrying a sheaf of long-stemmed red roses in pale green tissue paper and walking with a newfound confidence. The cash register drawer clicked closed.

"Lily?" Arnelle came out from behind the counter. "Poor guy. Totally in red-rose territory. Flowers will do the trick, though. Flowers always work."

Lily tried to retrieve her last thought—a wisp of an idea that now eluded her. But she was here to find out about those flowers. Flowers that were not flowers, but a message. Or a threat.

"Here's the problem," Lily said. "I don't know who to thank for the flowers."

"But the second bouquet was *signed,*" Felicia said. "Maybe that's why they sent two. Because they forgot to put a card in the first one?"

The women exchanged glances. Lily got the feeling they thought she was unnecessarily concerned—they ran a flower shop, people bought flowers. And here was Lily interrogating them. But she had no choice.

"Was it a man who called?"

"I just don't remember," Felicia said. "It was on speaker; we do that so we can work and talk. We get so many calls."

"But they said to sign it from Cassie?"

"From Cassie." Arnelle nodded, seemed to be remembering. "Yeah."

"No, Arn," Felicia interrupted. "Just Cassie. Just the name. Not 'from.'"

"That's the same thing."

"It isn't, though." Lily felt tears come to her eyes. The name *Cassie,* written, solitary on the card, was like an incantation or a threat. A menacing whisper.

She'd dreamed about Cassie. She remembered feeling an emptiness, the change of the light with Cassie's bedroom door closed, and TV people always outside and her mother's tears seeming never to stop. Gramma Lily had been there, too, had lived with them after that, even while Lily was in college.

At some point, she'd rationalized that they were trying to protect her. But Cassie was gone, so Lily'd never understood what she was being protected from. From sorrow? Or from a continuing threat? Cassie might be alive now. She might not be.

All Lily knew was that things could be taken away from you, any second of any moment of any day. Things—and people you loved—could disappear. The world was not reliable, not any second of any moment of any day.

"Signed 'From Cassie' isn't the same as just the word *Cassie.*" Lily yanked herself back to the present. "'From Cassie' means the flowers were *from* Cassie. That a Cassie had sent them." Or sent by someone else pretending to be Cassie. Or by someone trying to thoroughly spook Lily. "But writing just *Cassie*—"

The sisters had both moved closer to her, and she saw them silently communicating their concern.

"Oh, I am so sorry, you two," she said. "I'm on TV, is the thing. I've got to be careful. And if someone has my home address, it's just, I wish I knew who it was."

"Oh. Right." Felicia nodded. "Never thought about that."

"Yeah," her sister added. "Me either."

"So—are you saying you don't know a Cassie?" Felicia asked.

And there was that question again. That dilemma. She knew a Cassie, of course. But the question was, who else did?

CHAPTER 18
GREER

Of course I wondered, as I rounded the final corner, why Smith had escalated to meeting in person. Why he'd brought up the sister, Cassie. But what did it matter? If I could nail down a good story, Lily'd be thrilled. One more thing she didn't have to do, right?

"Right," I answered myself out loud. The couple walking past me on the wide sidewalk, arm in arm, floaty skirt and dumb fedora under the orange glow of the streetlight, didn't glance at me, even though I was talking to no one. People are used to that now; they assume cell phones and earbuds.

I smiled, remembering. Rowen calls them *earbugs*, no matter how many times Lily corrects her. They do seem to have a sweet relationship, and Rowen adores her. Got to give her props for that. Although yeah, Petra the nanny makes that so much easier. Lily only has to be adorable and motherly when she needs to be, while Petra does the heavy lifting. And Lily has her housework person, and the gardener, and her famously flexible work hours. But again, I remind myself, we all do the best we can. If Lily couldn't hire that household staff to allow her to work, then I wouldn't be able to work with her. I'm well aware that what happens to

Lily happens to me. Just ask Lily. She has a job, I have a job.

Again, all the more reason to keep her happy.

The door of Lido looks like a bank vault. Steel, maybe, or aluminum, with that burnished leaden texture that's both elegant and protective. Like they want to keep some people in and some people out. And they should be well aware of which they are.

The door opened as I approached, letting out a shaft of amber light and a burst of jazz and conversation. I stopped, waiting to see who would emerge. Smith had said he'd recognize me, which was either disturbing or not. It's not as if I hide. But it was only two women, laughing, in jeans and black blazers and matching tousled hair. They didn't give me a second look. That never happens when I'm with Lily.

Deep breath.

The warmth of Lido surrounded me from my first step inside. The light levels, all softened pink and indirect, were designed to make everyone look rosy and desirable. As Smith had predicted, some of the white-tableclothed squares were empty, some with four chairs, and others with two. There was no table with just one person. And no one at the host station. I knew Aiden, had seen him at that post several times. But not tonight.

I looked at my watch. Five after nine, so I was politely on time. The diners hummed with private conversations, glasses clinked. "La Vie en Rose," sinuous and sleek, played from hidden speakers. The walls were papered in red velvet, so ridiculously over-the-top opulent that they were hip. Each table had two flickering candles looped inside stands of ivy that fell luxuriously over the tablecloths and onto the hardwood floor. I wondered how the waitstaff didn't trip over the tendrils or tip over the lighted candles.

"Are you the Smith party?" The voice came from behind me.

I turned and saw—no less shallow way to say it—an incredibly handsome guy in a navy blazer. Maybe Aiden was on vacation or something.

"Yes," I said. I was still baffled by this guy, who, for some reason—too confident? Too relaxed?—seemed an unlikely employee. "Is he—"

"Private room," the man said. "Follow me, Ms. Whitfield."

Whoa, I thought. Elaborate. I dutifully followed him through the restaurant, avoiding the ivy, and we arrived at a carved wooden door with a glass door-knob. And no windows. I'd seen it before of course, but assumed it was an office.

"Please," he said.

The door opened to reveal what might have been a library, floor-to-ceiling bookcases filled with leather volumes. In the center of the room, a long rectangular table, covered in a textured white cloth. At the head of it, taking the power position, a man stood, finger-tips on the white damask. A crystal pitcher of ice water and four glasses waited on a silver platter in front of him. A tall glass chiller, festooned with silvered glass grapes, held an uncorked bottle of white wine. Smith's stemmed glass—the man must be Smith—was half-full. Another beside it was empty.

Did I recognize him? I took a beat, processing. Tall, clean-shaven, fortysomething. White button-down shirt and black jeans. I'd never seen him before, pretty sure of that. I heard the door close behind me. And we were alone.

"Ms. Whitfield." The man gestured me to the seat beside him. "Right on time."

So. In for a penny, in for a pound, as my grand-mother used to say. I could hardly yank open the heavy door and bolt. As I stepped toward the offered red-velvet upholstered chair, I realized *Lily* had done this to me, planting seeds of uncertainty. Otherwise, I'd be fine meeting a source in a perfectly safe restaurant.

"I'm Mr. Smith," he was saying, "and I'm grateful you could spare the time. Wine?"

"Water would be great," I said as I took my seat, and decided not to mention that this was my job, no matter what time it was. And time was pretty much all I had. I thought about straight-out asking who he was, but decided to see how this unfolded. Plus, if he thought I *would* recognize him, like tonight was some big reveal, it would be embarrassing not to.

I tried a sip from the heavy crystal glass he handed me, figuring there was no need to be wary of the water since he'd poured it from the pitcher.

"Cutting to the chase," Smith said. "I've done a lot for you—you and Lily Atwood. Wouldn't you agree?"

I lifted an eyebrow. Wary now, not of the water, but of what felt like the beginning of a negotiation. "Sure. Thanks," I said.

"As always, this is off the record, correct? Just between us?"

I twisted the water glass on the lavish tablecloth, leaving a tiny ring of damp on a white-on-white woven rose. "Sure."

"Has she told you much about herself?" he asked. "Lily?"

"Lily?" I frowned, trying to play out where he might be going with this. "Like about what?"

"For instance, I mentioned the sister. Had you known about her before?"

This had moved instantly into creepy-stalky. "What does Lily's sister have to do with anything?"

"Fine, forget about that." He put up a hand as if to ward off my imminent criticism. "You know about her daughter, certainly. Rowen."

I felt my back stiffen. It was all I could do not to head for the door. Or call 911.

"Who are you?" I stood, knowing it looked aggressive, but maybe that was for the best.

"Look. Ms. Whitfield. I mean no harm, I assure you of that. Sit back down." He paused. "You can leave whenever you want, but—"

"Damn right I can," I said. "What's this about?" I sat, but perched on the edge of my chair, poised for flight. I took my phone from my jacket pocket. Held it in plain sight, like a weapon. "And who are you?"

"Look. I'm a private detective." He slid me a white business card. "Which is why I can feed you those stories, right? But I have a client—and again, this needs to be off the record." He left the challenge hanging in the air.

I could still hear the music, faint and French, from the dining room behind us. Which meant this room wasn't soundproof. I nodded. "Go on."

He took a sip of his wine and leaned back in his chair, putting his hands together as if in prayer, touching under his chin. "I have a client," he said, "who misses his daughter."

My eyes narrowed as I tried to decipher that.

"Rowen Blair Atwood." He paused. "Is his daughter. He adores her, he misses her, and he is not allowed to see her. Did Lily ever tell you about this? Are you confidantes? Friends? Does she trust you enough to have told you about this?"

I felt my chin go up, and my defenses along with it.

"Ah. I see. No. Well, of course, I understand if she needs to keep her employees at a distance. Her staff. She's Lily Atwood, after all."

I refused to engage with this. I indicated as much with my expression.

"To go on." He lifted the bottle, and rivulets of condensation slid down its sleek green glass. "Are you sure you don't want wine? It's a terrific New Zealand pinot gris."

I was biting the inside of my cheek. I needed to relax. Let go of my ego. Maybe the wine would help. A sip. "Sure," I said.

The pinot gurgled into the glass, pale as the moon. He handed it to me, holding the stem. The icy wine chilled my fingers, startling in the warmth of the room. He was right. It was perfect.

He almost smiled, watching me drink it. "I have a client, as I said. He's a good guy. I wouldn't be telling you this if he weren't. I know Rowen is safe and happy, happy as a little girl can be with one parent, and I am well aware . . ." He tilted his head. "Speaking of which. Sorry for the awkward voices on the phone. And the formal construction. One cannot be too careful," he continued, using the recognizable Smith voice.

"Your client," I said, "is Rowen's father?"

Smith nodded. "He showed me her birth certificate, and I checked it out. Happy to provide it for you." He leaned down, lifted a cordovan leather briefcase. "It's all in here. And the very cooperative ski lodge where Ms. Atwood and Mr.—my client—ah, *met,* confirmed they were together on a March weekend eight years ago. Spring skiing. And Rowen was born the next—"

I knew Rowen's birthday. December 30. I said nothing.

"December 30. Here's the situation. My client is full of remorse. He's her father. And although he's spent so many years offering to help, trying to connect, wanting to be family, your Lily won't allow it. Won't let him."

A stream of words raced through my mind. *Paternity, custody, court filings, child support.* I'd let him fill in the blanks.

"Why?" I asked. *She's not* my *Lily,* I wanted to say.

But I might as well let him think it worked that way. That I had influence.

Smith took another sip of wine. Finished the glass. Poured another. I wondered if this whole story was even true. I had wondered, of course, about Rowen's father. Lily had never alluded to it. Lily had green eyes, though, and so did Rowen. The green-eye thing would be telling, but not a deal-breaker. And if Smith could find the birth certificate, so could I.

"Why? I assume there's a whole list of whys." He shook his head. "She's embarrassed, I suppose. My client was married when they . . . got together. Lily was already on the track to stardom, and I suppose she didn't want to risk the . . ." He shrugged. "This is delicate, and I'm sure you can fill in the blanks. But, to put it in PG terms, home-wrecking party girl is probably not the image Lily is going for. Or the one her employer—and yours—would approve of. I also assume there's a moral turpitude clause in her contract. If she trusts you enough to have told you about that."

"They're standard." I couldn't help saying what I knew. Every major talent contract builds in protections for the employer, which meant, in this case, if Lily ran naked through Boston Common, or spat on the mayor or shoplifted or got nailed for drunk driving, she could be deemed in breach. And could instantly be fired. No severance, no pension, no recommendations. An adulterous affair with the accompanying lurid details Smith seemed to have uncovered would be devastating.

I shook my head. Imagining it. "They'd cut her off immediately. Her whole persona is pretty much #PerfectLily. She'd be . . . toast." And so would I. Which I didn't say out loud. "Toast."

"Exactly." He pointed a forefinger at me, approving. "And that's why I need your help."

CHAPTER 19

GREER

The door behind us clicked. Creaked open. I flinched, spooked by the smothery red velvet and incessant purr of seductive music and the growing apprehension about what Smith was telling me, and turned to see who'd arrived. The door only opened partway, and it blocked my direct line of sight. I could make out a sliver of a person, body obscured by the candlelight and dim restaurant behind, but I guessed it was a man.

"We're fine." Smith raised his glass at him. "All good."

A waiter, I deduced, duh, this being a restaurant. The door clicked shut. I wished I could have more wine, but I had to keep my wits about me. Smith had said his client, Rowen's father, needed my help. This whole rabbit-hole conversation in this unsettlingly private room had taken all of twenty minutes, but it represented a lifetime-long tangle of a situation.

"You need my help? I wouldn't feel comfortable doing anything that might make Lily unhappy," I began.

I nodded at myself, warming to my own refusal. This guy was pretending to be amiable, but he was nuts. Whatever he wanted, there was no way I was gonna do it. And the second I got out of here, which had better be soon, I'd call Lily, or better, go straight to her house. Who knew what this "client" person had in mind? This guy was cutting me out of the herd, trying to separate me from Lily.

"Her life is perfect," I said. "And it needs to stay that way. Rowen's, too."

"Oh, I understand." Smith radiated agreement. "And well put, Ms. Whitfield. But if you don't help me, well . . ." He seemed to be considering his next words. Almost regrouping. "Here's the thing. And I know it's worrisome. Because if there's no longer a need for, as you say, perfect Lily, there's no need for perfect Lily's producer. Correct? If she's fired, you're expendable?"

I risked another sip of wine. If I finished the glass, he'd try to refill it, and that might be too tempting.

"And in truth," he went on, "what I'm proposing couldn't make Ms. Atwood unhappy, because there'd be no way for her to find out about it." He shrugged. "Unless you can't keep a secret. And I know you can."

"Who's your client?" I asked. I'd begun to wonder if maybe I could *protect* Lily from something. If Rowen's father—if that were even true—was after Rowen, whatever that meant, it would be best if Lily were aware of that.

Smith blinked at me, as if maybe deconstructing my tactics. Then he nodded, once, as if he'd finished a discussion with himself. "Okay, sure. You could find the birth certificate as easily as I did. But let me show you a notarized copy, stamped and dated. Then you won't have to go to all that trouble." He reached into his briefcase again, pulled out a manila file folder, flapped it open. The black-and-white document, with the promised raised notary seal over the signature, looked authentic, though I was always skeptical.

"See?" He point to the name above the line *maternal name*. Lily Blair Atwood.

"Blair is Rowen's middle name," I said out loud.

"Family thing." He pointed with a forefinger, tapping the paper. "And here, under paternal name. Samuel Reed Prescott."

"I don't know that name," I said.

"No reason you should, Greer—may I call you Greer? Unless Lily confided it to you. No? But here's the thing. You might hear of it, and soon. Is the name Isabel DeSoto Prescott familiar?"

That name I recognized. Running for Congress out west somewhere. Tough, strong, admirable. "He was married to *her*? When he and Lily—" I stopped, realizing I was buying this story by repeating that. "When you *claim* he and Lily—"

"No. No." Smith closed the file. Put his phone on top of it. "First wife, big mess, total disaster. Back then, she threatened to make an unholy stink about it. He actually told her about his affair with Lily. And then about Rowen. Not sure what he was thinking, but he did. So Lily agreed to keep it quiet—frankly, I think she and my client loved each other. But you know. Impossible. So long story short, Lily keeps Rowen, my client stays married. Time passes. And then, a couple of years or so ago, they get divorced, first wife moves who knows where. My client eventually remarries, and wife number two is eager to bring Rowen into the family. Bygones, no judgment, all one modern happy family."

"Sounds good," I said, picturing it. "I guess good. If handled properly."

"I agree. But Ms. Atwood . . . doesn't."

I tried to see this through Lily's perspective. "Huh. Because it's still the same tabloid backstory."

Smith nodded. "Home-wrecker, party girl, secret past, hidden daughter, and now, dismissive to the poor good guy who just wants to see his daughter. Keeping that adorable little girl away from her devoted but scorned father. Making her own celebrity image

more important than her daughter's well-being and
personal emotional growth. Not a good look, I fear.
That's why—"

"No, no, wait." I waved away his words. "It's not
the same story if we present it as a *different* story. Still
true, but with our spin. We get out in front of it, embrace it. All good, everyone happy, life goes on, Rowen
has a cool dad. It's adorable, it's relatable, it's all for
Rowen, her perfect daughter, and hurray for the greater
good. Love and logic conquer all."

I celebrated my idea with the last sip of wine and
allowed Smith to refill my glass. Lily would be thrilled.
I'd solved her problem, and in only half an hour. It's
my job to keep Lily perfect, and I'd done it again. As
I always tell her, perfection is in the perception. "It all
works. See?"

"I do indeed. And my client does, too." He replaced
the wine bottle in the cooler. "And we offered the ex-
act same opportunity. But Ms. Atwood refused."

"She did?" I stopped, wineglass midair.

"Remember, Greer. She's Lily Atwood, public figure, but private mom. She's made a big deal of keeping her daughter out of the spotlight. No pictures on
social media, no interviews with her on TV."

I winced, thinking about how I'd tried to weasel
Rowen's face on camera. I'd only been thinking of my
story, not how it might affect the little girl. Much less
how it would impact Lily's life. I closed my eyes for a
brief second, regretting. But it was Lily's fault, actually. She should have trusted me. Should have told
me. *I produce her.* I took a sip of wine.

"But for my client," Smith went on, "it's all about
being a dad. For years, his first wife held this transgression, this betrayal, this unforgivable sin—over his
head. But now he's free and happy and eager to move
forward. Lily—is not. And poor Rowen is the victim."

Outside the room, the music had changed. Softer

now, less recognizable, like a subtle heartbeat, an undercurrent to dinner table tête-à-têtes that had passed main courses, and finished dessert, and were winding toward the rest of the evening. Deciding who'd be going home with who, and what would happen after that. Emotional chess games.

"You're not asking me to convince her, are you?" I twisted the stem of my wineglass. "I mean, that's impossible. The whole . . ." I waved a hand, encompassing everything. "I'd have to tell her I knew about this. She'd be furious, and accuse me of meddling, and she's already iffy about—"

I stopped. He didn't need to know about our relationship, or lack thereof.

"No." I changed my tone. "Hard no. Full stop. Thanks for the wine."

"No, Greer, that's not it, not at all, and you are so right. I'd never ask you to persuade her." Smith leaned forward, fingers laced, elbows on the table. "But look. This is delicate. In so many ways. I get Lily's obsession with privacy."

"It's not an obsession, it's realistic."

"*And* with her celebrity." Smith went on, ignoring me. "Her reputation. It's all fragile. But my client— he's not interested in his reputation. He's interested in his daughter. She's part of him, and Lily's taken that from him. But." He spread his palms. "Against my best judgment, he's willing to compromise."

"How?"

"He just wants to talk to Rowen."

I looked at him, skeptical. "Talk to her."

He nodded. "In person."

I almost laughed, but it was more baffling than funny. "I'm not saying I will, but how am I supposed to *get* Rowen to have him 'talk to her'?"

"Aren't you Lily's emergency contact? If the school can't contact Petra?"

"Yeah. So?" It crossed my mind to wonder how he knew that, and about Petra. But he's a detective.

"So, easy. The school—Graydon—is planning an outing to the aquarium tomorrow. They have a new exhibit of some kind. Fish. So all you have to do is be at the aquarium when—"

"At the aquarium." This was almost entertaining now. "A place I have never been. Or mentioned."

"It's by that hotel, right? You can be in the parking lot. Meeting a source, you'll think of something. A friend. A business acquaintance, I don't know, maybe your old college professor. I mean, does Lily *always* have to know where you are? She keeps *that* short a leash?"

He looked into his wine. Then back at me. "You'll see Rowen as she gets off the bus. The headmistress will be aware. Maryrose Glover knows you, I assume?"

"Yeah." Who knows if she'll remember me, though. I'm only the flunky who keeps Lily's life perfect by shepherding her daughter when Lily's doing some personal thing and Petra's unavailable. Just me, your ever-helpful Greer.

"Good. You'll tell Glover you'll bring her in shortly. You'll take full responsibility. You and your friend/source/professor chat with Rowen. Rowen tells her mom she's seen you, all fine. If she mentions a man, who cares. You'll think of something."

I know my face must have looked like I smelled bad cheese.

"There's no risk, Greer. Except the continued sorrow of an innocent man who happened to listen to his heart instead of his head. He could stalk her, or shadow her, or follow her, but that's not his style. I got them to set up a fire drill at Graydon so he could see her. He watched her from the parking lot. But he made me call Lily. So she wouldn't worry."

"That was *you*? But she *did* worry." *In the end, the wolf was there,* Lily had said. "Hey. Did you get them to move the drill because Rowen stayed home that day?"

He shrugged, admitting it. "What can I say. Things don't always go as planned. Bottom-lining it here. Now that he's seen her, he's even more determined. I'll never understand how it feels to be a father, but this is my client's dearest wish. And your Lily will not allow it. Rowen has never met him. Never seen him. If she even mentions this encounter, Lily will never connect it. It's a gift. A gift only you can give."

A gift. I took a sip of wine. My defenses were lowering, and I was having a hard time coming up with a reason why this wasn't fine. And I had to admit he'd hit a nerve. A short leash? *Huh*. Why should I tell Lily where I am all the time? *She* doesn't bother to tell *me*.

Almost ten o'clock now. And honestly, thinking about it, Smith had a point about his client. He must not be that bad a guy if he's married to Isabel DeSoto. It wasn't difficult to imagine how horrible it would be, through no fault of your own, to be kept from seeing your own daughter. To have the women in your life whipsawing your little girl back and forth. I sneaked a look at Smith, but he seemed busy with his briefcase.

Plus, he was right about Lily. She was good at that, getting the world to be how she wanted it to be. All she did was protect herself, while pretending it was best for Rowen. Keeping that perfect exterior, while her daughter was—well, without a father. And Smith was right, the meet-cute scenario *could* sound perfectly reasonable. Couldn't it?

"No. I don't think so," I said before my brain caught up. "It's too—it seems wrong."

Smith nodded. Clicked his briefcase closed. "How?"

"I can't put my finger on it," I had to admit, "but it's manipulative. It might be reasonable in the short run, but something could happen, and Lily would find out, and she'd never speak to me again."

Smith raised his eyebrows. "And that's the most important thing about this? *You?* How Lily feels about *you?*"

"No. I mean, I just don't want to lie."

"Look. Ms. Whitfield. I get how you feel about Lily. You're projecting that with everything you say. Lily is not the most—well, from my research, she's standoffish. Protective. Almost obsessed with her celebrity. Her image. Right? To her, you're a cog. Not a person. A means to her ends."

I tried to keep my expression noncommittal. That was a nasty way to put it, though not totally wrong. Still, I was used to it. I was her producer. It was my job to make everything work.

"What if you could make her really happy? I mean, so happy that she'd be indebted to you forever?"

I couldn't have been more confused. And probably showed it.

"Lily's sister. Cassie. As I mentioned before. She's never talked about her to you, I bet. Right?"

Right. "So?"

"She disappeared."

"Twenty-some years ago," I said before I could help it. *Damn.*

"I see. So you did your homework. Good. But Lily has no idea where her beloved sister is. Probably thinks she's dead."

I felt my eyes getting bigger.

"Exactly," Smith said. "She's not dead. And I think I can help Lily find her. Think what a story that might be. You're the producer. You could do a reunion. On live TV."

With those words, I could actually see it. I could envision it, the gorgeous Lily, the moment Cassie entered, cameras rolling. The tears of joy and gratitude.

The ratings. She'd be—well, who knew what she'd be, but it was the story of the century.

Or a shit show of infinite dimensions. Risky as hell.

"No way," I said. "What if, I don't know. Her sister hates her, or doesn't want to be found? Or a million other land mines."

"Greer. Don't you get it? This is why I've been giving you all those stories. To prove to you that I know my stuff. That you can trust me. It's all been leading to this. The possibility that we—you—could find Cassie for Lily. And reunite them."

"Why do you care?" I'd suddenly grasped the missing piece.

Smith nodded. Tried to refill his glass, but the wine bottle was empty. He returned it to the chiller, placing it upside down.

"I knew Cassie, too," he finally said. "I know what happened. And I need to make it right. You can help. But first, my client needs to see his daughter."

For some reason I felt like crying. Families were so complicated. It almost—not quite—made me relieved I had no siblings and that my parents were gone. Poor Rowen and Lily. And Cassie, whoever and wherever she was. And some pitiful guy, who'd fallen in love with the irresistible Lily, and now just wanted to see his daughter, a little girl who was stolen from him by fame and celebrity. I took my last sip of wine, too. Watched Smith watching me. *Wait a minute.*

"Are *you* Rowen's father?" I had to ask.

Smith laughed, a short bark of what seemed like genuine amusement. "And that's why you're the producer. You know a good story. But I assure you, I am not Rowen's father."

"If you say so," I said.

"But I am your Mr. Smith." He tapped the white business card on the table. "And first, my client needs to see his daughter. And I'll help you produce that.

Then, we'll talk about the big reunion, the one that's certain to be your next Emmy-winning story. I'm a detective, right? I can find out anything."

"Well . . ." I pictured that scallop-edged photo. Had to be Cassie. Lily must care; otherwise, she wouldn't have kept it. She'd told Rowen about Aunt Cassie. So she must hope for her return.

If I didn't arrange the meeting, the whole sordid story of Rowen's father and Lily's home-wrecking would fill the front pages. Lily would be unemployed and humiliated and canceled.

And so would I.

Plus, it wasn't like this guy would give up—he'd just find another way. In fact, Lily was lucky he'd come to me. If I arranged this, I could control it. Like he said, produce it. And if we got a huge story out of it, that'd be perfect.

"Okay," I said. "I'll do it."

BEFORE

CHAPTER 20

CASSIE

"Cassie?" The voice behind her came closer. The alarm bells inside Wharton Hall were still blaring, the klaxons earsplitting.

She turned, her heart in her throat. She'd read that expression in some book, but never thought it could be true. But no. It was not Professor Shaw calling her name.

Flannel shirt—Jem? Or something?—had come up beside her. They'd reached the front door, and he pushed it open.

She rolled her eyes at him, couldn't help it. Invisible, huh? He fell in step beside her, matching her stride for stride as they left the building, as if they were together.

"What?" She had to yell over the alarm noise. And then, as they got farther outside, she couldn't resist. She stopped on the front walk and turned to look at him, hoping her expression was sufficiently dismissive. "Did I somehow become visible? Suddenly?"

"Hurry," he said, not answering her. He pointed to the green in front of them, to the students clumped and mingling, some ambling away. "*Go.*"

"What?"

"Get away from the building. Now." He grabbed

her arm, actually pulled her along the front sidewalk, with such strength and determination that she stumbled, almost fell, but he'd steadied her and propelled her forward.

"There's smoke inside," he said, moving forward, taking longer and longer strides. "Come on. Come *on*."

She followed him, only because he was an idiot and she wanted to tell him so as he trotted away from her across the lawn. She hurried toward him, trying to catch up, her Doc Martens boots tramping the clipped green grass.

"Hey!" she called out. Smoke? She turned back to the building. She didn't see any stupid smoke.

The alarms blaring from inside the building grew softer as she moved away. Flannel shirt was still a few steps ahead of her.

"Listen, dude—"

He turned. "Jem."

"Jem, whatever."

A wild whoosh shook her, almost took her breath away, as she stumbled at the sound and the noise and the surprise. Jem caught her, and as he lifted her back to her feet, she saw what had caused it, and the noise, and the collective gasp of the students on the green who witnessed it, too.

Plumes of black smoke billowed from the historic building with a rumble and a thunder, almost stealing the oxygen from the very air they breathed. Glass shattered, and tiny flakes of ash billowed through the air like angry confetti. Someone screamed, screamed so loud, and then someone else, and the footsteps of the people running away mixed with the calls for help and the sirens, too far away now, *too far*, and Jem grabbed her arm again.

"We need to go." He grabbed her arm so hard she could never have escaped.

"Zachary!" she cried out.

"I told you it's Jem," he said, and he was pulling her away.

She ran, almost backward, with Jem propelling her, never taking her eyes off the pluming black, what looked like—flames?—reflecting from the inside, bringing the stained glass windows to life with their destructive light. She imagined those faces in the hallway, the ancestors, their portraits singed and crisped and finally gone as if they had never existed, erased by the fire and never to return.

"He's inside, he's in*side*." Her voice came out a whisper, and she clenched at Jem's arms, digging in her heels, trying to get him to stop.

"Who?" Jem stopped, turned to her, focused on her. "Who's inside? No one's inside, everyone's out, they—"

"Professor Shaw." She pointed pointed *pointed* toward Wharton Hall, jabbing the smoky air. She could hear crackling now, a simmer of flames, and saw orange tongues of fire licking against the gray stone. "He was still inside when I—we—left, and I never saw him come out."

Jem stared at her. The sirens screamed closer.

"You're sure?" he said.

She watched his chest rise and fall under his black tee. She could almost hear him thinking.

"Yes. I'm sure," she whispered. "I would have seen him. I was—watching for him."

With one last hard look into her eyes, Jem broke free from her and ran toward the fire. She saw his slim figure outlined by the green grass, then surrounded, blurred by gray smoke, then swallowed by the black. He was as gone as if he'd never been there.

"No!" she called out before she knew what she was saying. "No!"

NOW

CHAPTER 21

LILY

"Greer?" Lily laughed at herself as she questioned her empty office. Clearly, Greer was not there. Which was odd, since after yesterday's not-so-subtle cracks about Lily's absence, she'd made a big deal about getting to the station on time. And now, it seemed, she'd even arrived before Greer herself. Tiny victories. From all the closed doors, she could tell no one was in her neighboring offices, either coming in later to work an afternoon shift or already heading out to their day's assignment. A newsroom gets quiet midmorning—the early shows over, and street reporters seeking their next story.

She put her half-empty thermal coffee mug on her desk. Out of habit, she clicked on her TV monitor, but kept the sound off. She'd dressed for a research day, a black tee under a black blazer. A necklace from the stash in her bottom file drawer would make her air-worthy, but as of now there were no shoots on their schedule.

When her desk phone rang, she decided not to answer. She hadn't finished her first coffee, hadn't settled in. It wasn't Smith, because he always used her cell, and that was the only call she cared about. The phone rang again. "Hey! Forget it!" she ordered it out loud. She let it go to voice mail and popped open her computer.

The phone stopped ringing.

"Thank you," she told it, and put in her email password. The phone rang again.

"Kidding me?" She glared at it, grabbed the receiver. "Lily Atwood."

She cradled the phone against her shoulder. The receptionist downstairs, Audrey, was telling her someone was in the lobby to see her, which meant she'd lost this episode of telephone roulette. People were always showing up, wanting to talk to her, *needing* to, they'd plead. Sometimes with their personal tales of woe and disaster, but sometimes hoping to see her without the television screen between them. Sometimes they brought gifts, even flowers—her heart twisted, remembering what she still didn't know. Maybe this visitor was Smith?

"Who is it?" she asked. "What about?"

She stood as she heard Audrey's responses. A detective? Looking for Greer? "No, she's not here yet," she went on, her mind racing. "Send him up. But, Audrey? Just yes or no. Did he say anything else?"

She hung up, glanced in the wall mirror as Audrey said no, saw her own worried face looking back at her. Nothing was wrong with Rowen, at least; Maryrose Glover had her cell number and would have called her for that.

The elevator door down the hall clanged open. She fingered her hair away from her face, trying to understand why a cop was here looking for Greer. If the police wanted to talk to her, they would have called her. Unless Greer had done something wrong. If Greer was working on a story and had requested something sensitive, maybe this guy was a source. Or a suitor? Maybe Greer had met a cop in a bar and they'd hit it off.

She planted herself in the doorway, wanting to assess him before she let him enter their office.

Youngish, but not too young, she saw as he walked toward her. Audrey had called him *detective,* so he couldn't be that young. Fortysomething, maybe. Navy jacket, white tee, jeans. Leather backpack slung over one shoulder. Standard-issue tough guy. But tall, slender, wiry. Maybe she was right about the cop-in-a-bar scenario. She could picture Greer and this dark-haired police detective, two workaholic information junkies, heads together to solve crimes. Greer seemed to have no personal life—not that she'd mentioned, anyway—so this might be a good thing.

Not a cop she'd met before, but she wasn't on that beat. She watched the recognition on his face, though, saw that dawning expression that she'd seen so often—*Oh, it's Lily Atwood.* Lily always attempted to mentally fill in the blanks of their assessment. *She looks different than on TV. She's older younger smaller bigger taller shorter—more attractive or not—than I thought.* The detective's unreadable expression lasted a millisecond, then vanished.

"You're Lily Atwood?"

He pretended to ask it as a question, as if he truly didn't know, and she didn't call him on it. "Yes. I'm Lily Atwood. What can I do for you, Detective?"

"Walt Banning." He flapped open a badge wallet, flapped it closed. "Ms. Atwood? You work with Greer Whitfield?"

"Is she okay?"

The detective took a breath. Lily frowned, watching him mask his reaction.

Before he could reply, she picked up the receiver on her desk phone. Dialed Greer's cell. No answer. No answer. Voice mail. "Greer? It's me. Where are you? Call me."

The detective shifted the backpack strap on his shoulder.

"When was the last time you talked to Ms. Whitfield?" Behind him, images flickered on her TV monitor, the crimson headline graphics fronting the midmorning newscast.

"Is Greer okay? What's wrong?" Lily hung up, trying to read the detective's expression. He had high cheekbones, dark eyes, and a thin scar beside one eyebrow, though it might have been shadow from the overhead lights.

"This hers?" The detective reached up and took down a laminated press pass that had been pinned to the bulletin board above Greer's desk. He stabbed the pushpin back into the cork and dangled the pass from its red lanyard. "She still recognizable from this photo, if we show it around?"

"Yes, it looks like her, but stop." Lily pointed to it. "Show it around? Who to? You said—last night? Is she okay?"

"Can we do this my way, Ms. Atwood?"

"No," Lily said.

"That wasn't an actual question," he said. "But this is. When was the last time you saw her? Greer Whitfield?" He held up the press pass again. "You can tell me that, certainly. Did she tell you where she was going? What her plans were for last night? Who she was with?"

This guy was off, totally off. He didn't act like a cop, even an incompetent cop. She flipped over the cell phone in her hand. Flipped it again. Saw his eyes on it, watching her motions.

"Are you really a police detective?" She half smiled as she asked him, to show she was kidding. "If something's happened to Greer, tell me what information you're looking for. And I'll do anything I can to help."

The detective tapped his pen against his notebook. It made a pocking sound, like a clock ticking out his thoughts.

"She's missing, Ms. Atwood."

CHAPTER 22

LILY

Lily put one hand on her desk, then lowered herself into her chair. "Detective? You're not with homicide, are you? You're not saying she's—"

"Hang on," he said, holding up his cell. He stepped into the empty corridor, turned his back.

Her brain revved into overload. She looked at Greer's desk, stacked with files and spiral notebooks. A mug of pens. Her computer screen saver generating a maze of white tubing, over and over and over. Greer's empty chair. Missing? What did that even mean? *Missing* had to mean *dead*.

And Lily would have to somehow explain this to Rowen. She loved Greer. She'd be inconsolable. In Rowen's world, people didn't just go missing. In Lily's, they did.

She had a memory, a wispy-edged, sepia-toned memory of a tall gray-haired man, a man in a black parka with a wintry dusting of snowflakes on his shoulders, standing in the entryway of their house in Hamilton. Lily'd been cross-legged on the living room carpet, cutting out dresses for her Buffy paper dolls. Her mother had called the man *detective*. Mumma had scooted Lily out of the room as she brought the man inside, leaving scraps of colorful paper scattered over the blue-carpeted floor. Lily had clutched her paper Buffy and run all the way upstairs; then tiptoed down again, step by silent step, and parked herself on the third step from the bottom, trying to hear what her mother and the detective were saying. It must be about Cassie, she knew it was about Cassie, and for one blossoming moment of hope, she thought maybe they'd found her, found Cassie. Or that she'd changed her mind. Decided to come home.

Lily waited, with fingers crossed on both hands, crossed tight as she could. It seemed like time had stopped. Finally she'd heard the front door close again.

When she tiptoed back into the living room, she'd seen her mother crying. Head in hands, her shoulders shaking under her thin gray sweater, Pooch snuffling up against her lap. Pooch's tail had been wagging, hard, as if he were trying to reassure her everything would be fine. Lily, transfixed and frozen, had felt her last reserves of hope float up to heaven.

Mumma had cried every day after that. The police had come back a couple of times, too, and she'd even tried to talk to them, but she was little, and they wouldn't listen. That's when Gramma Lily had come to stay with them. Making sure Mumma got the rest she needed. They'd sit on the edge of Lily's bed, side by side, Gramma smelling of what she called *mew-gay*. Lily had looked it up. *Muguet,* it turned out to be. Lilies of the valley.

"She's my little girl again," Gramma had told her. "We need to take care of your mumma, my little Lil. It's only the three of us now."

"Will Cassie come home?" Lily had dared to ask.

"We can always hope so," Gramma had told her.

Now this Detective Banning had arrived at her door. She was no longer the child, waiting and powerless. Cops don't come by themselves to tell a reporter that their producer is missing. It wasn't how the system worked. Not at all.

"Detective? What was that phone call? Was that about Greer? Have you gone to her apartment? How did she—have you asked her family? Is anyone else investigating? Do you want us to put something on the air? Is that why you're here?"

"All good questions." Banning had stashed his notebook in his jacket pocket, checked his watch, and turned to look behind him down the hall.

She looked over his shoulder, too. The hallway was empty.

"Detective . . . Banning? Are you expecting someone?" Maybe he was hoping Greer would arrive. Checking his watch to calculate how long she'd been gone. "Was Greer supposed to show up someplace and didn't arrive? Where? With who? Did she not come home last night? Who told you that? When? How do you know she's not at maybe Starbucks, or at a friend's house, or out running? What do you mean, *missing*?"

She knew she was talking too fast, cross-examining, but this guy had not told her one tangible fact. "What happened to Greer?"

Banning checked his watch again, an oversize black plastic runner's contraption with an array of readouts, chunky against his sinewy wrist. "I know it's upsetting, Ms. Atwood," he said. "But—"

Lily's cell phone rang, vibrating in her hand like a living thing. Ten thirty now. The detective cocked his head at the phone.

"Do it," he said.

She did not take her eyes off of him as she accepted the call. "Lily Atwood."

"I thought you were ignoring me," the voice said. "You usually answer more quickly."

Smith. No matter what story he—or she, it sounded like today—had for her, Lily had to keep the line open for Greer.

"So don't say anything, but is the detective there with you now?" he—or she—asked.

She remembered what Greer herself had said, just yesterday, about the Graydon alarm. *The next time he tells you something, you'll ignore it. It's like the boy who cried wolf.*

"What?" she whispered into the phone.

Smith ignored her question. "Please. Don't say anything about me. Do what he says. I am sure Ms. Whitfield will be just fine."

And then he hung up.

What Smith had said—*I am sure she'll be fine*—was a threat, a flat-out threat. Because it proved he—or she—knew about Greer. And where she was. He'd asked about the detective, too. That meant Smith knew Banning.

Still, all she'd said out loud was her own name, and "What?" Simple to explain. If she lied.

"Wrong number," she said. "Of all times."

"Happens," Banning said.

"Yeah." Lily stared at her phone. Willing it to ring again.

Willing it to be Greer. Willing her to be safe, telling Lily not to worry, that she was running late. She'd laugh and laugh when she heard the story of the mysterious detective arriving at their office, having concocted this story that she was missing. These days, if you couldn't reach someone instantly on their cell, Lily reassured herself, everyone decided it must be a disaster. But it rarely was.

In thirty minutes, the afternoon shift would be arriving, and this hall would buzz with activity. Their privacy was about to end.

"Detective? Why are you here, where Greer obviously isn't—instead of out looking to find out where she is?"

She classified his expression as patronizing.

"We know what we're doing, Ms. Atwood. It's not just me. So listen."

He looked at his watch again, then gestured toward Greer's desk. "I need to—we need to—look through her computer and notebooks. See if there's a calendar, or a schedule, some clue as to her whereabouts."

"So you think she was planning to go somewhere, or to meet someone."

"Ms. Atwood? I'm trying to be polite here, and hey, I'm not trying to be a jerk. But the sooner we get the show on the road, the sooner we may find your friend. How about her computer password?"

"I don't have the authority to let you look through her property." Lily was blocking the cop's path, but didn't move. "I'm so worried about Greer, but we need to ask someone who can legally say yes. I can't." She shook her head, perplexed. "Don't you need a warrant?"

Banning put up a palm and advanced toward her, taking just one step as if he were trying to calm a wary animal.

"Ms. Atwood? Are you a lawyer? No, correct? I'm not required to explain this to you, but I will, and then we're done." He took another step toward her. "It's called the safekeeping exception. Ms. Whitfield is not a suspect. She is a potential victim. She may be in danger. She may not. Anything I find is not to be used as evidence against her, but to help find her."

He took a deep breath. Lily imagined him trying to control his anger.

"And now, Ms. Atwood. It's time to either help me or get the hell out of the way. Apologize for the language. What if you were the missing one and I'd asked your colleague to help find you? Or listen—has there ever been anyone in *your* life who went missing? Then you'd know how desperate their loved ones feel."

Lily felt tears come to her eyes. This guy's random sarcasm landed harder than he could have imagined.

He took a step closer to her. "You're part of the solution or part of the problem." He swiveled to the stack of notebooks on Greer's desk, a multicolored pile of book-size spirals. Took the one from the top.

"I have to get the news director," Lily said again.

"Sure." Banning licked a finger, flipped through the pages of the notebook. Put it back. Picked up another one. Lily watched as he turned the pages. If she left and ran to the news director's office, the guy would be alone in here. She checked the hallway. Still empty. Where was Greer?

She turned, deciding to call the news director. But Banning was looking at a Channel 6 scratch pad, glue-topped, the size of a paperback book.

She took a step closer, trying to see the words, but Banning now held the pad with its cardboard back to her, so she couldn't.

"This was between the notebooks," he said. "It's a list, and dated yesterday."

"What's it say?"

"At the top, it says *Lido, 9PM.*" Banning gestured with the pad. "You know that place?"

She did. "So that's where she was last night."

"It's a start," he said. "But then—any of these other words mean anything to you?"

He held the list so she could read it. The air between them stayed so silent that Lily could hear the fluorescent lights buzzing.

There'd be no reason, Lily thought as she read the list, no reason she could imagine, for Greer to have a list like that. Those words, just four words, could only be put together to mean one thing.

Kirkhalter, Grandmother, Marianne, Berwick. In four words, the chilling story of her own past. For some reason, but unquestionably, Greer Whitfield had decided to investigate the missing Cassie. Now Greer was missing, too.

BEFORE

CHAPTER 23
CASSIE

Cassie knew what her mother would tell her. Gramma Lily, too. *You're only eighteen. Leave it alone.* But she *had to* sit in this creepy, clammy waiting room at Penn General Hospital. Had to know. Professor Shaw had been rescued from the Wharton Hall fire. But would he live?

She'd understood, in the flash of an instant thought last night, understood what had really happened last Saturday morning.

It had been her fault.

Her. Fault. She had stalled. *Kept* Professor Shaw there. Tried to read his body language, wondering why he'd arranged to meet her when the building was mostly empty. If she'd only followed the fire alarm's directions and left, the professor would have, too.

Then he wouldn't have been inside when the explosion happened. It had been her complete fault, the whole thing. And *he* knew it, too. If he didn't die and he could still think, that would be what he'd remember. That she had delayed him from leaving. If not for her, he would not be here in intensive care. It was her fault. *Her* fault. Her *fault.* She could almost hear the words, as if a jury were passing judgment on her.

Nurses in scrubs and flowered tunics bustled past.

Men dressed in white clattered empty stretchers to an emergency, or away from one. The soft gurgle of a massive tank of tropical fish, a moving rainbow of placid obliviousness against the beige cinder block wall, almost taunted Cassie with its serenity. She'd been unable to concentrate on classes, or her roommate, or her responsibilities at Berwick. The smell of the fire—it was still in her nose, even all these days later. She could still hear the sound, the explosion, her own cry.

If she closed her eyes—but she wouldn't, she couldn't—she'd see Jem Duggan engulfed in all that black. No, she'd told him, *Stop*. But he hadn't listened.

That day, as soon as she could, Cassie had ripped off her soot-infused clothing and thrown it all away, stuffed all the evidence of disaster into a metal trash can and smashed down the top, made it gone forever, erased and nonexistent and so she'd never have to wear those things, not ever again, they were bad luck and now she knew it. Even her Doc Martens, they had to go. They were sacrifices, sacrifices to the fire. *Make him be okay*, she begged the universe. *I'll do anything*.

Now she fidgeted in the uncomfortably unyielding white plastic chair. Cassie pulled a flyer from her purse, a printed memo that the provost had sent to parents. Someone had slid two copies under each dorm room door. She unfolded it, and read it again. *Investigators suspect a gas leak in one of the aging pipes under Wharton Hall*, it explained. They theorized the leak had gone undetected in a rarely used room in the building's basement, the leaking gas had built up in the enclosed space, and "met an as-yet unexplained ignition source."

Police tell us they see no ongoing threat to any building on the Berwick campus or to any citizen of the Berwick community, the memo went on. It assured parents and students that each and every building on campus had been exhaustively and comprehensively tested to make sure no additional leaks existed.

Everyone was discussing it, speculating. Marianne had told her some kid had told *her* that Berwick had done it on purpose to get insurance money.

"Blow up a building? Their own famous building?" Cassie had never heard anything stupider. "With people inside?"

"They thought everyone was out, I guess. It was a Saturday, right? Maybe they didn't mean to blow it *up*, you know? Just like—have a fire, and then have damage and then insurance would pay for everything." Marianne had added another textbook to the stack in her arms as she talked. "I mean, how do I know? I'm just telling you what everybody's saying."

"Everybody's an idiot," Cassie said.

"You were in there," Marianne replied. "Did you smell gas?"

"What are you, police?" Cassie was sick of it, and didn't want to talk about it, and every time Marianne insisted on it, which was like all the time, it made Cassie sadder and angrier and more heartsick. "And no, I didn't smell the freaking *gas*."

Which she hadn't. But maybe you didn't. She'd only smelled fire. And that was after. She still smelled it.

Police cars were parked everywhere on campus. Big trucks emblazoned with the green-and-blue PENNGas logo were stationed at each building.

Wharton Hall was now surrounded with a hastily erected temporary chain-link fence, the building's historic windows boarded with thin plywood, its iconic stone façade blackened and charred. Across the front door, a barricade of yellow plastic tape draped from a series of orange cones. Classes were reassigned to other buildings, and things were supposed to be back to normal.

But how could Cassie concentrate on Baudelaire

or quadratic equations when her entire brain was filled with something else? The hospital's aggressive fluorescents buzzed and glared above her, a muted television mounted to the wall flickered sports scores. Each breath she took smelled like disinfectant. And death. Would he *die*?

Gray double doors marked NO ADMITTANCE barricaded her from the patients' rooms behind. With a clang and a lurch, one of the doors banged open. A white-coated doctor, her gray-streaked hair in an efficient ponytail and glasses dangling on a loopy chain beside her stethoscope necklace, consulted the clipboard she held and walked toward her. Cassie's heart beat with hope, beat so hard she had to stand up.

"Are you—" The doctor looked at her, then at her notes again. "Beresford?"

Cassie's shoulders sank. "No. But is it about Professor Shaw? I'm his—"

The doctor, with a wan smile, kept walking. Headed, as Cassie watched, toward a frazzle-haired woman and a pink-cheeked little girl, a grieving Madonna and child holding hands in the corner. Family, Cassie knew. You had to be family to find out.

Cassie lowered herself into the chair again and stared at the grass-stained toes of her white sneakers, trying to look into the future. But she couldn't make it feel real.

"Are you family?" the receptionist had asked when Cassie first arrived.

"No," she had to admit. "I'm his—"

"I'm sorry, hon," the woman had said before Cassie could finish. Her name tag said *Sarita M*. A vase of white carnations and a mug of red ballpoint pens made a barrier on the tall slate counter between them. "Family only. I'm sure they'll make it public when the time comes."

Cassie couldn't stand it. "Is he okay, though?"

At the receptionist's withering expression, she realized what a stupid question that was. "I mean, I know he's not, and that's why he's here, but I mean, will he *be* okay?"

A tall, thin woman, with a cascade of dark hair and holding a narrow spiral notebook, had stepped up to join Cassie at the reception desk. "Sarita? I'm Tosca Manukian. From *The Journal*?" the woman said. "Working on the Berwick story, and I wondered about Professor Shaw."

Cassie had eyed her up and down, curious.

"You need to call public information, Tosca. You know that," Sarita interrupted.

"Yeah, but—" Tosca went on.

"No buts, Tosca. Just rules." Sarita swiveled, putting her back to the two of them.

"You were asking about Zachary Shaw, I couldn't help but hear." The reporter had turned her attention to Cassie. Flipped a page in her notebook. "Might I ask—are you Professor Shaw's—"

Cassie could feel the woman assessing her.

"Student? Were you there at the Wharton Hall explosion?" The reporter clicked her ballpoint open. Poised it over the pad. "Can you tell me your name? What you heard and saw? I know the police are on campus. Did they talk to you?"

No. No. No. She could never say a word about it. Not to this reporter, not to anyone.

"No," she said out loud.

She tried to calculate how big a lie she could get away with. The other people, there hadn't been many, but still, had all marched out, obedient. No one could have known Professor Shaw had stayed behind. Except for her.

Oh. And Jem Duggan. He'd been inside, too. He

must have stayed around the office—she hadn't noticed—and then followed her out.

"No to what?" The reporter clicked her pen open, then closed, then open again. The clicks sounded like Cassie's brain trying to get into gear.

"No to anything. Everything." Cassie needed to end this conversation, now, and decide what to do.

She turned and walked back to her seat, felt the reporter's eyes on her, tried to ignore it.

As the reporter moved out of her line of vision, she felt that part of the pressure relent. Plenty of other students for her to interview. She'd never remember Cassie. Cassie'd never even said her name.

Bells pinged, and something buzzed, the murmur of conversation wrapped her in a blanket of soft sound. Cassie put her head in her hands, defeated. She needed to talk to him. To make sure he didn't blame her. Tendrils of guilt began to creep up her arms, wind around her shoulders, twist around her throat. If he died, was it her fault?

She felt a presence. An arrival. She looked up, her eyes welling with hope. But it was not a nurse. Or a doctor. Or the police.

"Jem?"

NOW

CHAPTER 24

LILY

Lily stood on the sidewalk outside the smoked glass street-side window of Lido Bistro, watching as Banning tried the restaurant's front door. According to the chic black lettering on the burnished aluminum, the place was closed. "Cocktails at 5," the sign said. "Post-theater supper at 10." She'd insisted on coming with him, though he'd initially tried to dissuade her.

"Let's give them a minute," Banning said, giving the curved door handle a last rattle. "I know they're inside, maybe they're back in the kitchen. Owner already told us this morning he knew Ms. Whitfield. But didn't see her last night. There's a maître d', though." He flipped open a notebook. "Aiden? Cowley? Aiden Cowley ring a bell? No?" At her shrug, he flapped the notebook closed. "He's off today, apparently. He might have seen her last night. We'll find him."

The two of them, side by side on the cracking gray concrete, had parted the flow of the ear-budded college students who attended classes in the midcentury stone office buildings along the block. Once a mecca for insurance companies and law firms, a performing arts college had scooped up the city block at the edge of the theater district and created a makeshift urban campus, bordered on one side by the historic green expanse of the Boston Common and on the other by the asphalt and nonstop traffic of the Mass Turnpike.

She and Banning had arrived here a few minutes earlier in his unmarked beige four-door. Unmarked and undercover, Lily figured, since the car didn't have a police radio or computer console or wigwag lights.

But why Lido? Someone might have chosen it, she decided, specifically because of its proximity to departure. They could swoop a someone—Greer—down the clammy rabbit hole of the crowded Boylston T stop, or hustle her into a car and straight onto the Pike. It could have happened so quickly. So seamlessly.

"Detective?" Lily'd asked as they drove closer, trying not to picture that. "You're sure she's not home?"

"That's why we're looking for her," Banning began. "You know the people who live next door to her?"

She didn't. Lily almost blushed, thinking of how she'd never been to Greer's house. Or apartment. Wherever. But they weren't friends. They were colleagues. That was Greer's personal life.

"No," she said.

"They said they hadn't heard Ms. Whitfield come home last night. Said that's never happened before. They went to her door, and it was wide open. They went in, looked for her, but nothing. So, yeah." He'd shrugged, stopped at a stoplight.

"Does she come to Lido often?" he went on. "You ever been here with her?"

"No," Lily said. Greer did her job, Lily did hers, and they went home to separate lives. It was true, but embarrassing to articulate it.

"You've worked together how long?"

"Greer and I—we're not really *friend* friends. We work together, but we're not much for girl talk." Explaining it made her sound so indifferent. "I have a daughter, maybe is the reason, and she doesn't."

"And your daughter's father? Your husband?"

"Single mom," she'd told him. Then worried. "Does that matter?"

"Just asking," he'd said.

They'd arrived at Lido, and his questions stopped as he'd maneuvered the car into a tow-zone space across the street.

"Look around." Banning gestured at the squatty gray office buildings, the neon marquee of the Emerson Colonial Theatre, the trendy façades of tiny, hip restaurants. "You know anyone else around here who might know her? Someone who works in one of these buildings, for instance?" He looked at her, expectant.

"Isn't there surveillance?" Lily peered up at the front of Lido, then at the other businesses, scouting for the telltale fishbowl lenses of video cameras.

He'd actually rolled his eyes.

"Ms. Atwood? Surveillance isn't going to tell us whether there's someone Ms. Whitfield knows who works in one of these offices. Someone who might have asked her to meet him? Her? Here. Anyone?"

She shook her head, slowly, trying to think. A police car, blue lights swirling and siren blaring, screamed by, careening up Boylston Street. Banning glanced at it as it passed but seemed unconcerned, even paging through his spiral notebook.

She wondered what the two of them would look like to someone watching from above. Or from across the street. Or from behind the smoky Lido window. A couple in navy blazers and jeans. Lily always expected to be recognized, but so far, not a glimmer from passersby. College kids, she figured, reassuring herself, weren't much for watching local news on TV.

College. Berwick. Where Cassie had disappeared.

"Detective?" Lily couldn't keep this from him. Greer's list. But the door to Lido had opened. She took a step toward it.

"No," he said. "Stay here."

He disappeared inside, leaving Lily in the noon sunshine, hearing the final fading notes of the police siren and the *tick-tick-tick* of the crosswalk timer at the corner. *Tick-tick-tick,* she thought. Was time running out for Greer?

Greer's notes had meant she was researching Cassie, and now Greer herself was missing. That had to be connected. Or it didn't. Lily stared at the sidewalk.

Problem was, there was no way for Lily to investigate on her own. She didn't trust this Detective Banning, and he clearly didn't trust her. And it could very well be that Greer's curiosity about Lily's past was not connected to wherever Greer was now. Which might be the dentist, or the gym, or in someone's bed, Lily tried to reassure herself. Still, Banning was looking for her, so there was something serious he hadn't deigned to tell her yet.

But the moment she brought up the list, it could send the detective down a dead-end path and not help find Greer at all. Even make this situation worse. She yearned to keep the past in the past, but discussing the list would force her to tell Banning exactly what those words meant. And the past meant gossip, and drama, and publicity, and pity. *Perfection is in the perception,* how many times had Greer said that to her? *Screw up, and your viewers will never look at you the same way.* Lily might even be fired. They'd couch it, in some phony way, but she'd know why. Perfect Lily had to stay perfect.

But Greer. Finding her was the most important thing right now. And what if . . . Lily stared into nowhere, seeing only the blur of the lunch hour crowd and the hard stairstep architecture of the Boston skyline and her own uncertain future. What if Greer had found a link to Cassie? And had gone off on a hunt of her own?

Would that be wonderful? Or a disaster?

The door to Lido opened. Banning came out, squinting into the sunshine.

"She was there at nine fifteen last night," he reported. "One of the waitstaff recognized her from that press pass."

"Was she with someone?" Which would be either the good news or the bad news. "Did they know who? Did they pay with a credit card?"

"Oh, I didn't ask that." Banning blinked slowly. "No, there's no record of that, Ms. Atwood. And they'd never seen the guy before."

"A man, though," Lily said.

"Yup. Totally narrows it down."

She could do without the sarcasm. "Wait. Is that why you had me stay outside? Did you tell them to look at me through the front window? Are you, like, parading me?" she persisted. "Were you trying to see if they recognized me from last night or something?"

"You're Lily Atwood, ma'am." Banning raised an eyebrow. "I don't need you to be here in person for people to know who you are. All I had to do was say your name."

Lily frowned. "Why wouldn't you let me go in, then?"

"It's not my job to tell you things, Ms. Atwood. And I needed to see how you'd react."

The ticking of the crosswalk timer started again, depositing a new group of chitchatting students on their side of the street. College kids always reminded her of Cassie. Two young women, arms draped over each other's shoulders and sharing a pair of earbuds, ambled up the sidewalk, all sunglasses, ripped jeans, and beach hair. Like life was everlasting, their time on earth incalculably infinite. The last time she'd seen Cassie, back that last Christmas vacation, she'd been about this age, just turned eighteen, her image indelible in Lily's mind. Memories didn't age, but people did, so Lily'd once put Cassie's photo into an online age-progression program, trying to embed a new mental photograph of her sister.

She'd burst into tears at the result. Cassie looked exactly like their mother, a crushing emotional combination that had sent Lily to Rowen's bedroom, needing to watch her sleeping, to make sure she was still there, penguin in arms and comforter kicked aside. She'd drawn the downy white covering back up over her little girl's shoulders, breathing a grateful prayer. Had her own mother prayed for Cassie?

The blast of a car's horn brought Lily back to the Boston street.

Banning was taking his cell from his pocket. "Banning," he said into the phone. He held it up, looked at her. "Gotta take this," he said. "Give me a sec." He walked a few steps away.

Maybe it was news about Greer. She watched him, trying to overhear. Then Lily's phone, in the back pocket of her jeans, vibrated, too. Maybe *this* was Greer. She put it to her ear, hope filling her heart. "This is Lily Atwood."

"I see you," the voice said. "I see you both."

Smith.

"And getting along so nicely, you two."

Lily looked up, scanning the endless expanse of office windows around her—shades, blinds, curtains. Lights on, lights off. Precariously rusting fire escapes zigzagging up the sides of the gray stone and red brick. Every parking place on the street was full, car windows rolled up. Where was he? How was he seeing them? He'd helped her, her and Greer, given them stories and inside tips. He'd never misled them or steered them wrong, never been anything but courteous and respectful.

But yesterday at Graydon, she'd worried he was

watching, too. He was the boy who cried wolf, Greer had said. And now Greer was gone.

"Where are you?" She felt if she kept scanning, she'd see him—her?—a silhouette behind a window or a figure in a doorway. But she couldn't look everywhere, and if he could see her, he'd know when to hide. "How can you see me?"

Banning had looked up from his call, maybe concerned by the tone of her voice, and had turned to watch her, concerned.

"There a problem?" he mouthed.

She shook her head, put up one forefinger, waved him off. This time, she turned away from him. Hunched her shoulders, trying for privacy.

"Watch it, lady!"

A kid on a scooter zoomed past her, ball cap turned backward and a brown paper carryout bag looped to his handlebars, leaving a wake of marijuana and french fries. She made herself even smaller.

"Smith?" she whispered.

"You want to find your friend?" the voice said. "Tell the nice detective about Cassie."

BEFORE

CHAPTER 25

CASSIE

Cassie had been in hospital rooms before. heard the incessant alarms and beeping monitors. She'd watched her father struggle for breath in his too-small bed under the too-tight sheets, the bars raised on either side of him like he was a child in danger of tumbling out. She'd never forgiven him for dying. For leaving her.

Now, five years later, sitting in the Penn General waiting room with herself five years older and her life truly just beginning, there was barely a sound. Silence mostly, or the papery rustle of magazine pages, quiet murmurings. No one here was happy. The happy ones got to go home, she thought, leaving only the grieving hopefuls, cloaked in their gray sorrow.

Professor Shaw *couldn't* blame her, she told herself. How could she have known it was a real fire? She needed to cut that worry out of her brain. Discard it. Move on.

She'd looked up to see Jem Duggan, lankier than she'd remembered, paler. Taller. Older. He had a bandaged right arm, a square gauze pad taped to the right side of his face, and a patch of his dark hair shaved away to allow a row of crisscrossed stitches high on his temple, scabbed now with browning red.

That macho confidence he'd had in the Wharton hallway, coming on to her, calling her invisible, seemed as
far away as her own happiness.

"Yeah, it's me," Jem said. "I saw you through that
big window—" He gestured toward the hallway. "And
I was headed ho—well, back. What're you doing here?
You weren't hurt somehow, were you?" He scanned
the room. "Oh. Intensive care. Professor Shaw. Are
they telling you anything?"

Cassie couldn't decide what to say. She'd asked
around about Jem, of course, the idiot guy who'd
raced back into Wharton as the fire got worse. Marianne had told her she'd heard that Jem Duggan hadn't
actually gotten into Wharton Hall before he was overcome by smoke. Firefighters had found him on the
concrete front steps of the building, his head bleeding, one arm kind of burned. So everyone was saying.
He was just a random guy to Cassie, the snarky one
who'd called her invisible, so no reason to check any
further.

"How are you?" She had to ask, and plus, thinking about it, if not for him, really, she might have
lingered in the building, too. Might have wound up
behind those ICU doors, maybe hooked to a machine.
"Thanks for. . . ." She shrugged. "Getting me out. I
thought it was another one of those false alarms, you
know? How'd you know it wasn't?"

The more she thought about it, the more grateful
she was. She'd been so focused on Professor Shaw that
she hadn't even imagined what might have happened if
Jem hadn't come along, urging her to hurry. He wasn't
really an idiot to go back in there. More like brave.
He'd saved her life, if you looked at it that way.

"Coincidence," he said. "Lucky guess."

"Lucky for me." She frowned, picturing it again.
"Really, though, how'd you know there was a real

fire? And why'd you go back? It was so awful by then, when it, like, exploded. You were so—"

"Dumb?"

"I was going to say courageous." Jem was kind of pitiful now, bandaged and bedraggled. "But yeah. Dumb."

"I didn't get very far," he said, looking down at her. "That's why I have this bandage. And my hair got all singed, see? They told me I tripped on the steps and fell on my head."

"Good thing, right?" Cassie pictured it again, Jem disappearing into the blackness. "You were totally invisible in all that smoke. Like you'd vanished. You'd have died, maybe, if you'd gotten inside. Did they tell you anything about Professor Shaw?"

He sat down beside her, smoothed the dark denim of his jeans. "Some nurse washed my clothes for me. Can you believe it?" He didn't look at her, just at his outstretched legs. The laces of his boots looked new, stark against the battered tan leather. "Funny how the world works."

She watched him, wondering how it would feel to have a narrow escape. To be brave enough to risk your life to save someone else's. Did she care about anyone enough to do that? She tried to imagine it— her mom, or Lily. Would she save her sister from a burning building? Of course she would. But she'd never have to.

"What made you do that, anyway? How do you know Professor Shaw?"

"My teacher. Like you. I took a gap year, two really, almost three, after high school."

Cassie nodded. She'd thought he'd seemed older. Which would make him maybe twenty-one. Old for a freshman, but lots of kids took time off before college.

"What'd you do?" she asked Jem. "In those years?"

He shrugged again. "Bummed around. So, you and Professor Shaw . . ."

The way he was looking at her now, she felt something different in his appraisal, but it vanished so quickly, maybe she was wrong. She waited for him to finish his sentence.

He smiled. A soft, fast smile. He straightened in his seat and turned to face her. He was one white plastic chair away, and she felt his energy filling the space between them. She almost wanted to move farther away.

"Is it a thing?" he asked. "You and Professor Shaw?"

"Are you kidding me?" She answered too loudly, in her surprise, and quickly covered her mouth. Sarita, at the reception desk, gave her a death stare. "Well, that's rude." She whispered now, leaning closer to him so people would stop looking at them.

"Not really." Jem's voice was quiet now, too. "You're here, right? See any other students? I don't." He crossed his legs, leaned back, draped his left arm over the back of the chair between them. "Makes sense to wonder what's up between you."

"Nothing is up." She shook her head to make it sound truer. Closed her eyes briefly to illustrate her scorn. "At all."

"Fine. Forget I asked."

"Fine. I will," she lied. But there had to be a reason he'd brought it up. "How about you? Are *you* friends with him?"

"So, guess I'll head out." He flapped back the right cuff of his plaid flannel shirt, revealing a stretchy beige bandage. "They gave me pills, which I don't really need. They kept me all this time to be sure I didn't have a brain thing. Now I just have to change all this twice a day, which is a pain, but it'll heal."

"Does it hurt?" She winced, looking at the thick bandage. The firefighters had rescued Professor Shaw, too, the newspaper said, who'd collapsed a few yards from the front door. Everyone else had made it out. Including her. Because of Jem. It almost brought tears to her eyes. She needed to take care of him, the same way he'd done for her. "Brain thing?"

"It's fine. Ibuprofen, rest, and I'm all set. I'm supposed to call if I get a headache."

"Headache? Like a concussion? Listen, do you have a roommate or someone to help you? Or, like, parents?" He seemed too old, and too cool, to be living with parents. Twenty-one was a total adult, but concussions were bad. "Are you supposed to be alone?"

Jem smiled in a way she couldn't quite decipher. "Is that an offer?"

NOW

CHAPTER 26

LILY

"Cassie?" Lily kept her voice low, her phone clamped to her ear, urging Smith to talk faster. "Tell the detective about *Cassie*?"

Banning had gone back into Lido, signaling her with a pantomimed tip of an imaginary cup that he was getting coffee. That left Lily on the sidewalk, trying to bargain.

Her mind raced through the possibilities. Had Greer told Smith about Cassie? Or had Smith told Greer about her?

"How do you know about Cassie? Do you know where she is? Where Greer is? Do you have her? You say you can see me, so you know I'm alone. If you have Greer, or know where she is, then you have to—"

His chuckle, interrupting, shocked her into silence. "Do I? *Have* Greer?" Smith's voice sounded authentically amused.

She kept scanning the office windows, couldn't help it, felt scrutinized. Toyed with. "You just said—if I tell the detective about Cassie, that might lead to Greer. How do you even *know* about Cassie? And as for Greer—yes, that you have her. Or how else do you know about this?"

In his silence, the world around her seemed exactly

the same; the same blue sky, and the same flapping, complaining pigeons, the same snippets of music from wafting open car windows as drivers waited, engines idling, at the corner stoplights.

She'd worked on a jigsaw puzzle once, with Cassie. Her mother had suggested it, and Cassie agreed to be parked at the living room coffee table with her little sister and two hundred pieces of Van Gogh's *Sunflowers*. At one point, with the puzzle half done, Cassie had unintentionally knocked the board with one elbow, sending the tiny, interlocked puzzle sections falling to the floor, ruining the slowly materializing picture. Lily, age maybe six, had burst into disappointed tears. She'd wanted to see the finished flowers, longed to see the final painting.

"Oh, Lillow!" Cassie had exclaimed. "I'm so sorry! But don't worry, we can try again."

Lily felt like that now. The puzzle of Greer had been forming, Lily's mind putting the pieces together. And now, with the addition of Cassie, they had fallen apart.

"Ms. Atwood. Lily," Smith finally replied. "Haven't I always been on your side?"

"Yes, that's why—and we may not have much time, so—"

"I can warn you when he's coming out of Lido," Smith said.

"How would you know?" Noontime in Boston, the sun straight overhead. The heat crept up her neck and under her hair. Where was Greer?

"Lily? What if I told you Ms. Whitfield is perfectly fine? That yes, she was at Lido last night. And I know because I was there with her."

Lily leaned against the restaurant's stone exterior, grateful it was there to steady her. Puzzle pieces, puzzle pieces. Where did they fit?

"But if she was meeting with you here last night . . ." *Why hadn't she told me?* And that's when they must have talked about Cassie. "So that means this detective is actually looking—for *you*."

Smith did not reply, and this time, in the silence on the other end, Lily did hear a noise inside. The buzz of an intercom, maybe, or some sort of electronic alert. Or not.

"He's coming out," Smith said. "Thirty seconds."

Lily took a step onto the sidewalk, eyes on the still-closed door. "Thirty seconds is long enough. You're the big source. The anonymous caller. If you know so much, tell me where Greer is."

"Here's what matters," Smith said. "Banning is a private investigator. But it's *Cassie* he's looking for. Ms. Whitfield is involved in the search, too."

"What? Why?" Lily felt the seconds ticking away. Smith had always told her the truth before. But maybe it was the reverse of the boy who cried wolf. Tell the truth, over and over—and thereby train your victim to believe it when you tell the big lie.

"Do what he says," Smith instructed. "Be patient. If you're patient, you'll be fine. Because trust me. Greer's not in danger. Cassie is."

BEFORE

CHAPTER 27

CASSIE

"Wine?" Jem had closed the door behind them after gesturing her inside. Floor-to-ceiling windows overlooked the vast Berwick Forest, now a chaos of burnt orange and flaming red. This wasn't a dorm room, not even close, and hadn't he told her it was? Cassie tried to replay their waiting room conversation as she took in the long tweedy couch, two black leather chairs, the built-in bookshelves, and the desk by the window, stacked with what looked like textbooks—she recognized one Professor Shaw had assigned—and a pile of spiral notebooks.

The place looked expensive. Curtains, and carpeting. Plus, it was a real apartment, not like the dorky room in Alcott Hall she shared with Marianne. Who, it crossed her mind, might be wondering where she was. Not that she had plans with her clingy roommate, but it was pushing six o'clock.

Cassie had been second-guessing herself from the moment she and Jem walked out of the hospital together, crossing the too-bright lobby lined with gurgling tropical fish tanks and slumped weary visitors, and then revolving out the thick glass doors into the autumn evening. They continued along Mountville Street, orange flags for Berwick's upcoming Fall Festival fluttering from every streetlight, more bicycles than cars in this college town. At first, Jem's long strides covered more ground than her shorter ones, and she'd trotted to keep up. But he'd noticed and slowed his pace to keep them side by side.

She honestly did owe it to him to make sure he got to his dorm safely, she reassured herself as they passed the intentional graffiti on the front of Whole Latte Love and the wrought iron gargoyles of the Voltaire Bookstore. It meant absolutely nothing, except it was what a thoughtful person would do. After all, he—a total stranger—had hustled her out of danger at Wharton Hall. So today, her turn to be the good guy. She'd walk him home, then leave. Her debt would be paid, the balance even.

And it was safe, because you had to sign into dorms if you didn't live there, and everyone was supposed to leave the door open. She wasn't going *inside*, anyway. She was dropping him off.

At first, they walked in silence. He seemed to check on her from time to time, observing her, stepping off the curb first when they crossed each narrow side street. Mountville Street was all businesses, but some older students had apartments above the too-expensive clothing stores and Berwick souvenir shops. The side streets had mostly houses for the real people who lived in the town of Berwick. *Townies*, they were called.

"We're close, right?" she asked. "I didn't know there were any dorms this far off campus."

"Late admission," he said. "You know."

She didn't, but whatever. "Sure."

"Cassie?"

The crosswalk beeps started, and she stepped into the street. "Yeah?"

"Since we're here?" Jem pointed past the zebra-striped crosswalk to Outpost, the corner restaurant where a few cast-iron tables, set with baskets of paper napkins and IPA bottles as vases, waited for the Friday night beer-and-burgers crowd. The bass line from "La Vida Loca"—*as always*—thumped from inside, and Cassie heard a riff of laughter. She'd been in this place, couple of times.

"Since cafeteria food sucks, we could get dinner," Jem went on. "Hospital food sucks, too, so I'm pretty hungry. How about it? You up for the Post?"

She was, she was starving, and Post burgers were awesome, and food in the caf totally did suck.

"Well . . ." She stalled, considering. The Post had booths. Dim lights. A din of talk and music. Plus. If Jem was twenty-one, he could drink. Maybe if he had a beer, or two, she could get him to tell her why he'd thought she had a thing with Professor Shaw.

"I guess . . ." She weighed her options as they stood on the corner in front of the restaurant. Friday in Berwick, no classes tomorrow. Mountville Street was getting a TGIF vibe, the loosening energy of the impending weekend, the relaxing of responsibility. The promise of the unexpected encounter, or a memory-making event. Thing was, this Jem had a way of throwing her off balance. Like he wasn't really asking what he was asking. It had been her idea to make sure he got home—hadn't it? Or maybe not.

"No, thanks," she said.

"Thought I'd ask." He gestured at an empty round table as they approached. "They have room, though, see?"

"Let's get you back to the dorm." She walked purposefully past the restaurant, reinforcing her decision, putting it behind her.

But she needed to know about Zachary Shaw. And Jem had brought him up. She chewed her bottom lip as they walked. That reporter who'd shown up. Tosca? Something? But she didn't seem to know anything.

It was driving her crazy that Professor Shaw might

blame Cassie herself for delaying him. What if he died, blaming her? Things should be easier than this, less complicated. How could anyone have known there'd be a gas leak? Mumma had always warned her—life could pull the rug out from under you.

"Here we are," Jem said.

"Wait. You said *dorm.*" Cassie stopped as Jem approached the boxy yellow-brick building. Four stories, she quickly counted, each front window white-shuttered. A carved granite sign mortared just under the flat roofline said "One Mountville" in old-fashioned scripty letters. She turned her head to look at him, baffled. But he was walking toward the building.

"Jem?" She stayed on the sidewalk, didn't follow him as he continued past the potted copper chrysanthemums and up the three front stone steps. "This is a regular apartment building."

Jem pulled a loop of keys from his jeans pocket, stabbed one into the metal latch that flapped over the edge of the black metal front door. Clicked it. Kept his hand on the key as he looked down at her. "Yeah, so? It's cool, right? None of that ridiculous dorm stuff. I mean, we're not kids."

Two motorcycles roared past, speeding away down Mountville. Cassie saw a woman on the back of one of them, blond hair flying under her helmet, her arms wrapped around the driver. Friday night, Cassie thought, fun night in a college town, and was she suddenly the doofus freshman, terrified to go into an older guy's apartment? This was what life was all about, adventure, new experiences, and if she didn't take control of her life, right now, she'd forever be a small-town girl with a small-time life. Jem was right, they were not kids. The whole point of college was to get out on your own. Make your own decisions. Be in the world without someone else's rules. And maybe Jem knew stuff about Professor Shaw.

Why not see if he'd tell her?

She'd tossed her hair to prove she was in charge, and followed Jem Duggan up the steps and through the front door. When the elevator doors slid open, he'd gestured her in first. She'd chosen the left wall. He'd walked toward her, and she felt her heart race, apprehensive and wary, but then he'd reached past her and pushed the lighted button marked four. He'd moved to the opposite side of the elevator, as far from her as he could get. Silence, until the doors slid open, revealing a carpeted hallway, soft twilight shimmering through a four-paned window at the end of the corridor.

And now he was asking if she wanted wine.

NOW

CHAPTER 28

LILY

Cassie is.

Never before had two single words so pivoted Lily's world on its axis. Ten seconds until Banning came out of Lido, Lily figured. She stood in the middle of the sidewalk as if nothing had changed. She had ten seconds to get her knees and brain to work again. To regain her equilibrium. To plan her next moves.

Greer's not in danger, Smith had just told her. *Cassie is.*

Cassie. Meant Smith knew her name.

Is. Meant Cassie was not dead. It meant Smith knew that. And Banning, too, whoever he was. Cassie lived, existed, somewhere. As Lily had always, she had to admit, believed.

Five seconds. Not a sound from within the restaurant, not a motion from the glossy front door. Maybe Smith had been wrong about the timing. Maybe something had changed. Maybe Smith had been guessing. Three seconds.

Greer's not in danger, Cassie is. Danger. What danger? And with that phone call, Smith had given her the upper hand. She now knew that Banning knew about Cassie, but he didn't know she did.

The opening front door caught the sunlight, and

flared for an instant as Banning walked out, as if he were being announced by personal lightning. He carried two blue-and-white paper cups, and reached one toward her.

"Skim milk and Splenda," he said. "Just guessing."

Lily accepted it and almost took a sip. Then stopped. Silly to worry, she knew, but if Smith wasn't lying, Cassie—*Cassie!*—was in danger and Greer wasn't (where *was* she?) and Banning wasn't who he said he was. And now she was supposed to drink something from a stranger? But if she didn't, he'd know she was suspicious. She felt the warmth of the beverage through the thick paper. Felt the weight of her own concern.

"Hot," she said. "But thanks."

"Was I right? About the Splenda?"

Maybe she could get rid of the coffee by throwing it on the sidewalk in frustration. With him, for asking such an idiot question. And frustration with herself, for ignoring her instincts that this guy was a phony. But maybe this was a good thing. Maybe now that she had some new puzzle pieces, she could use them for ammunition. Get closer to him. Find Greer. And find Cassie.

"Sure, Splenda, thanks," she began as if he were so clever and intuitive. As if she trusted him. She'd start by asking the question he expected. She managed a brief smile. "Did you find out anything about Greer?"

Banning nodded. Saluted her with his cup. "I did, in fact. Not from the Lido people, they're worthless, nobody saw anything or knows anything, typical, no one ever does. And the vacationing maître d' is apparently at the beach with no internet. Who does that? But my research team got back to me with some info."

"Great," Lily said. His research team? "So? What'd they find?"

She pretended to try her coffee again, pretended it

was still too hot. She'd find a trash can at some point. Banning sipped from his own drink, watching her. She looked at her cardboard cup again. At the plastic lid. At the perforated flap. *Wait.* He'd gone in for coffee? Why on earth would he take the time to do that?

"Detective? I have to say you don't seem very—" She pursed her lips, tried to find the right word. "Concerned?"

"Whoa. Wait. Are you *serious*?" Two young women with matching dark hair, glinting sunglasses, ripped jeans, dangly earrings, and what looked like textbooks in arms were striding up the sidewalk toward Lily and Banning. The one who had spoken, or more like shrieked, Lily thought, was pointing at them. Then conferring with her friend. "I mean, am I right, or what?"

Lily glanced at Banning, who shrugged, looking amused. The students—they must be students—took a few more steps, approached, and stopped in front of them. Staring at them. At Lily.

"I am *so* sorry to bother you," the student said. "But you're Lily Atwood, right? I am such a fan!"

Lily put on her public face, serene and welcoming. Focused on her reality. These were viewers, and viewers protected her job, and her paycheck, and Rowen's school and Rowen's future. She couldn't say, *I'm busy,* or *I'm talking to the police,* or explain what she was doing. If she was anything but congenial, these two might whip out their phones and snap her photo. They might tap open their super-followed Instas and go to payback work on her. Later she'd get the tag—and get linked to #LilyTooBusy or #LilySoCanceled.

Even now, with her life swirling ominously around her, she had no choice. There was a routine that came next, and she would play it out. Acknowledge, connect, then disengage.

She put up a forefinger at Banning. *One moment.*

"Well, yes, I am," she said out loud, smiling appreciatively. And it was sincere, she did appreciate them. They had no way of knowing what an unfortunate time it was. How worried she was. How much she needed them to get the hell away from her. "How wonderful of you, and lovely to meet you. And you are?"

"I'm Iris-Colleen Walters," the student said. "Call me Colleen. And this is my roommate."

"Soraya Barbash," the other student said.

"And, oh, Ms. Atwood, you are incredible. We watch you all the time. Don't we, Sor? I mean ... wait." Colleen reached into her backpack, pulled out a phone. Tapped the screen. "Ms. Atwood, let's do selfies!"

No, Lily thought.

"My pleasure," she said. "But really *really* quickly. And I'm Lily. But then I need to—you know." She looked at Banning, but he'd taken a step or two away and seemed deep into his phone. It was all she could do not to scream. But the show must go on.

She'd give these two fans the shorthand version. Get herself off the hook by letting them feel as if they were getting inside information. Then get them out of here. She looked at them conspiratorially, as if she were sharing some unspoken secret. "It's a work thing."

Colleen and Soraya had plopped their books and backpacks on the sidewalk and, in what seemed like practiced choreography, stationed themselves on either side of her, wrapping their arms across her shoulders as if they were old friends. Lily was used to it, the touching, to people assuming she'd be fine having strangers drape themselves over her. She understood that viewers felt they actually knew her. They'd seen her from their living rooms and bedrooms, heard her finding answers and giving advice with authority and enthusiasm.

Wasn't that what it meant to be a friend? Lily encouraged it, the bond of trust and connection. It was part of the job. She sincerely loved it, the recognition, but now she had to move this along. She had to find Greer. And Cassie.

"Me first, okay?" Colleen held her cell phone arm's length high above her head.

Lily saw the three of them in the screen, all expertly looking toward the lens as Colleen framed the shot.

"Lily, ready? Look over here. You ready? Doing it."

Lily smiled her happy-Lily smile, open and comfortable. *Click click click,* Lily heard the snaps from the phone.

"Now this way, Lily." Soraya's white-cased camera was now up in front of the three, and Lily saw the picture about to be captured in the second photo. *Click click click,* Lily heard again.

"Let's see." Colleen used two fingers to spread her screen, narrowing her eyes to assess the quality. "Perfect," she announced.

Lily stole a look at Banning, who'd now turned his back on them.

"Aw, so nice to meet you both." Lily held out her hand for Colleen's phone. "May I see?"

"You probably have to make sure it's a good photo." Colleen nodded sagely as she handed over her phone. "I *totally* get it. Once on social media, always on social media."

Lily smiled, conspiratorial again, then flipped through the photos, stopped on one of them, tapped the screen. Handed the phone back. "Thanks. They're great. You're students at—Emerson College, I'm guessing?"

"Freshmen," Colleen said.

"For another couple of weeks, at least," Soraya added.

"You are so perfect, Lily." Colleen held her phone to her chest as if she were hugging Lily herself. "I'm a journalism student, totally because of you. You do so much good."

"Plus, you're totally kick-ass," Soraya added.

"Aw, just doing my job." Lily remembered this age, Cassie's age, and how much promise the world held when you were a freshman. If you survived it. Only one Atwood sister had. Or, she realized with a start, maybe not. "Let me know if you'd be interested in an internship. When you're juniors, of course."

"So cool!" they said, almost in unison.

"Terrific. Have a great summer," Lily said. She clicked Accept when the AirDrop she'd sent came through. Now she had the selfies, too. "Anyway, now I've got to—"

"We know, you're *working*," Colleen whispered as she gathered her backpack. She slung it over one shoulder, wincing with the weight. "Good luck with that guy."

BEFORE

CHAPTER 29

CASSIE

Cassie did not know where to put herself. If she took a seat on Jem Duggan's couch, then she was on the couch. That might not be the safest. If she stood where she was, just inside the door of this not-dorm, this actual apartment—which, unlike the Berwick student housing, had no resident assistant and no sign-in sheet and no record of who came and went—then she looked like a total lame juvenile dork.

She took one step onto the wall-to-wall carpet, a soft chocolate-colored expanse that went from the front door and across the living room and stopped at the kitchen. Where Jem stood, under a light that hung from the ceiling like an upside-down funnel, with a bottle of pink wine in one hand and a half-full stemmed glass in the other.

"It's rosé," he went on, gesturing at her with the bottle. "Hardly even wine."

She knew what rosé was, and his patronizing explanation kind of made her mad. He *did* think she was a kid, and that was annoying. She'd come here in good faith, pretty much at least, and now it felt like if she refused him, he'd think she was even more immature. Inexperienced. She stood taller and with a confidence she didn't quite feel, placed her black canvas tote bag on a side table by the door. A scatter of mail had been left under the silver-framed poster of a pale moon coming up behind a dark mountain. She could read the address on one stamped letter, and it said Jeremy Duggan. Jeremy, she thought, tucking that away as if it mattered.

"I adore rosé," she said. She remembered an ad she'd seen in *InStyle*. "Perfect for an autumn evening."

"You gonna stand there by the door?" Jem asked. "Come in, have a seat. Or check out the woods. I have a pretty cool view. You ever see Berwick Forest?"

She took a few steps toward him, almost to the couch, and then halfway past the couch. She stopped at the center of the sleek glass coffee table. A *Time* and a *Newsweek,* she saw. The newest ones. He was smart, she decided.

"Should *you* be having wine, though?" Now she was remembering a show she'd seen on TV. Some guy with a concussion, and he'd started to have a drink, and his girlfriend stopped him. "Isn't that bad for a concussion?"

"Yup. Absolutely," he said as he poured more liquid into the glass. "You see there's only one of these, right?"

She watched the pink go almost all the way up.

"This is for you." In three steps, he was an arm's length from her, and held out the glass, his hand encircling the curved bowl.

She took it by the stem, but was unable to avoid touching his fingertips as she did. The glass felt shivery cold, the liquid inside looked gorgeously pink. She moved one step away from him, and the backs of her calves hit the metal rim of the glass coffee table.

"Ow," she said. The wine sloshed, but didn't spill. *Pull it together, Cass,* she thought.

"You haven't even had one sip." Jem laughed. "But that table, you know. It has a mind of its own. You want the couch or a chair? Or you know, it's almost sunset. The view is kind of great. Come see, out on the balcony."

She looked toward the window, then at the big leather chair, then at the couch. Then at her glass. It wasn't like she'd never had wine before, everybody had, and beer, too, and it was no big deal. And fun, until someone had too much and turned into a jerk. Or threw up. But this was a guy she barely knew, and there was too much stuff that could possibly happen. She tried to predict what Marianne would say when Cassie told her about this. Her roommate might call her an idiot. Or she might be jealous.

"Or, you know, don't. All good. And you don't have to drink that if you don't like it." Jem had stuffed his hands into the back pockets of his jeans. "Anyway. Thanks so much, Cassie, for walking me home."

He stood, motionless, looking at her.

"Sure." She toasted him with the glass. "Thanks for making me get out of Wharton. And I'm glad you're okay."

She saw him take a deep breath, saw his chest rise and fall, saw his expression change. She took one sip of the wine, a tiny one, and it tasted like pink. Nice pink. Something moved outside, on the balcony, caught her eye, a shape going past the sliding glass doors. She laughed when a red bird landed on the narrow balcony railing. The bird cocked his head at her, seemed to be curious about what was going on inside.

"So cute," she said, smiling. "See that car—" But when she turned back to Jem, his eyes were still on her. "What?" She couldn't read his expression. "There's just a funny bird on your—Jem? What?"

"Nothing," he said.

In one motion, faster than Cassie could do anything, Jem seemed to crumple. His face disappeared from her line of sight, so fast she was almost confused, and then she saw his body, stretched long and dark against the dark carpeting, one leg tucked under the other and arms at his sides, his face pointed to the ceiling. She actually looked up, like, *What was he looking at?* His eyes were closed.

She felt the blood drain from her face. What the— what was she supposed to do? Should she call 911? Yes? No? She put the stupid wineglass on the coffee table, right on top of the *Newsweek,* and knelt on the carpet. Her hair fell in front of her face as she bent over him, and she twisted it away with a frustrated gesture.

"Jem?" She patted his cheek with the soft flat of her hand, tentative, and worried. What was she supposed to do—she had no training for this, she needed to call 911, she needed to call *someone,* what did people do? She saw his eyes flutter—*See? Not dead not dead*— and bent closer to him, her hair resting on his chest. She put one of her hands on each of his shoulders.

His eyes opened. He looked at her, his face inches away from hers now, and blinked, half smiling, like a sleepy cat awakening from a contented nap.

"Whoa," he whispered.

His eyes closed again, and that terrified her, because maybe he was getting worse, and then what would she do? Then they opened again.

"Whoa." It sounded like he was almost talking to himself. "That was kinda strange."

She sat up, now on her knees beside him, hands on her thighs, her eyes focused on his. "Are you okay?" was all she could think of to say.

He puffed out a breath, blinking at the stucco ceiling as if trying to clear his thoughts. He touched the bandage on the side of his head. "What happened?"

"What—well, you collapsed." She felt worried, and guilty for some reason. And a little glad she was here, because what if she hadn't been and this had happened? Although she never would have known about it. "Did you hit that same place? D'you think you're having a concussion thing? A reaction?"

She frowned as she watched him, reading confusion on his face, and tried to think of concussion things. Someone had gotten a concussion on one of those TV survivor shows, she remembered that. She held the first two fingers of her right hand. "How many—"

"Peace," Jem said. He shifted his shoulders, straightened his legs. His feet were under the coffee table, and he was so tall his tan boots almost reached the couch. Jem looked bigger to her now, splayed on the floor in front of her. Heavier. She hoped she wouldn't have to pick him up. She would never be able to lift him.

"Come on, Jem. Be serious." She held up the fingers again, three this time.

"Three," he said. "Boy Scouts."

She adjusted her body to sit flat on the floor, legs akimbo, leaning toward him. At least he was talking. And the color seemed to be coming back to his face. Were you supposed to give someone like this water? Or no water? How was she supposed to know?

"Do you have a headache? How d'you feel? Does anything hurt? Where's your doctor's phone number? You have to go back to the hospital."

He closed his eyes again and put up a palm to stop her. "I'm okay, Nurse Cassie. Just let me be a sec." Another deep breath. "Probably dehydration. Or low blood sugar. Or both. You know?" He opened his eyes and turned to her. His face had softened as if he were embarrassed. "I told you the hospital food sucked, and I—maybe I didn't have enough water. No biggie. I'm fine. Here." He held out a hand. "Help me up."

She used the coffee table to launch herself to her

feet. "No way," she said. She brushed down her jeans, her knees now dotted with carpet lint. "Stay there. I'm getting you water. If you stand up, you might fall over again. And, like, hit your head again. Don't go to sleep." She pointed at him, remembering another concussion thing. "You're not supposed to go to sleep."

"Yes, Nurse Cassie," he said.

Where would glasses be? She opened the kitchen cabinet closest to the sink, but there were no glasses.

She stared at the stacks of plastic baggies, each stuffed full of pale green oval pills. Each bag was sealed with clear tape, and they were piled like cordwood, filling the top and middle shelf. On the lowest shelf, one baggie was open, green ovals from inside it scattered across the bottom. She frowned at them as if they were alien creatures. Why would Jem have so many pills? And in the kitchen?

She stood, motionless, one hand on the hard white cabinet knob. Her knees went soft with fear and horror. She knew what the pills were. She'd seen the "Watch Your Drink!" posters plastered all over the school. With photos of pills that looked just like this.

She closed the cabinet. Found the one with the blue glasses. Her heart beat so hard it almost hurt.

That wine. That chilled rosé. She'd only taken one sip. One. The glass, with its pink and pretty contents, was still on the *Newsweek,* and had even caught a bit of the sunset light and glowed, for a fraction of a second, as if it were radioactive. Or she might have imagined that.

Had Jem put one of those pills in it? *One of the bags was open.* She put a hand to her chest. She was lucky. She was. She'd leave the rest of the wine alone. And she felt fine. Didn't she?

"You all right in there?" Jem's voice from the living room. Oh. No. She was taking too long. Maybe he'd remembered if she'd looked for a glass, she'd find his . . . things? And then he'd know she knew.

"All good!" She turned on the water, calling out over the noise. "Waiting 'til the water gets cold." She could probably go to jail for a million years, she thought as the water ran. Probably just for *seeing* those things. And she'd totally be expelled. Berwick had a totally strict honor code, and drugs were like— she had to get out of here. She hoped Jem didn't ask her about them. She'd have to pretend none of this happened.

Her eyes rested on the now-closed cabinet. Her mind buzzed with fear. How many women had been hurt by drugs like the ones it held? Oh, holy crap, and what if she'd had more of that wine?

Trying to act like nothing had changed, she knelt again by Jem's side, glass in hand. He'd crossed his arms over his chest and watched her as she came toward him. Maybe he was too out of it to remember she might have seen his illegal stuff. She had to leave. Had. To. Leave.

"I see you found the glasses," he said. "Any trouble with that?"

She felt the blood drain from her face. Almost dropped the water. "In the first cabinet I opened," she said, trying to look normal and smiley and not like a person who had just seen like a whole cabinet full of dangerous hideous illegal drugs that could put him— and her—in prison for the total rest of their lives.

"Great," he said. "Got to admit, I've been lying here wondering what would have happened if you hadn't been here."

"Drink this," she said.

NOW

CHAPTER 30

LILY

"If you're ready, Ms. Atwood?" Banning was leaning against the front window of Lido, legs outstretched on the paved gray sidewalk. He pantomimed smoking a languid cigarette. "If your fans are satisfied?"

Lily tucked her phone back into her tote bag. "That took all of thirty seconds," she said. "And if I remember correctly, you're the one who decided to get coffee. So, let's move forward. What did you find from your research guys?" She kept every trace of suspicion out of her voice. Smith had told her to do what he said.

That didn't seem so dangerous, out here in the safety of broad daylight. She'd go for it. As long as it seemed prudent. Greer was somewhere—safe? And Cassie was somewhere, too. Alive? Which sent her heart hammering. But maybe not safe.

And she, Lily Atwood, was one hundred percent in the middle of it. And one hundred percent confused.

Banning gestured to his car. "We'll discuss it on the way."

"The way to where?" Getting in the car with this guy was a big step away from safe. But again, she argued with herself, Smith had said to trust him. She took out her phone, kept it in her hand. Smith had said Banning was a private investigator looking for Cassie. She needed to know who had hired him. And she was increasingly skeptical that Greer was actually gone. But where was she?

"Calling someone?" he asked.

"I need to tell my nanny where I am," she lied. Although calling Petra and checking in about Rowen was actually a good idea. She wished there were a way not to be apart from her daughter so often. But she wanted Rowen to grow up confident, and self-reliant, not needy, not demanding her mother's attention at every turn. To have a perfect life, and not worry about everything that *might* happen, the way Lily did. "She's on a—" Lily stopped her own sentence. Banning did not need to know that level of personal detail. "Anyway. You were about to tell me about the research guys."

Banning had stepped off the curb, glanced both ways, and began to jaywalk, striding diagonally across the four lanes of Boylston Street. Lily followed, not having much choice, and trotted after him, hoping no renegade Boston drivers decided to turn right on red and plow into them before they got to Banning's car.

Which, Lily realized as they approached, was probably unmarked because it wasn't actually a police car. Which also explained the lack of law enforcement equipment inside. Still, if she suddenly refused to accompany him, he'd know that she'd been clued in about something. And no matter who he was, he was on the trail of Greer. And Cassie. And so was she. She had to risk it.

The locks on the passenger side disengaged with a click as Banning pointed his key. She opened the sun-warmed passenger door herself, yanked on her seat belt, cradled her tote bag on her lap, and kept her phone in her hand.

"So? The research guys?" she persisted over the

rumble of the ignition. She buzzed down her window, giving herself more space. "And where are we going?"

"Yeah. Hang on." Banning had placed his back-pack on the back seat and then turned to look over his shoulder as he eased out of the parking place. The stoplight must have turned green since their jaywalk-ing. Car after car buzzed by, even as Banning chal-lenged them, inching into the nearest lane. "Gimme a break," he muttered. "Jerks."

Lily watched out the window, too, eyeing the still-dark façade of Lido. She imagined Greer opening that silvery door last night, knowing she was about to meet Smith. And wondered, again, why Greer hadn't told her.

Banning steered the car into a lull in the traffic, headed them away from the city and toward the Mass Pike, a pin-straight eight-lane highway that stretched from Boston all the way to the New York border. Once you were driving the Pike, Lily knew, there was no stopping, no slowing down, no getting out. Even the toll booths were electronic, no gates or guards.

"The Pike?" Lily tried not to sound concerned as she imagined being trapped in a speeding car on an inescapable highway.

"Yeah," Banning said again. He slowed for a yel-low light, infinitesimally, then turned right, setting off a chaos of horn honking from startled drivers.

"Banning? You're doing this on purpose, I under-stand that." Lily twisted back her hair with one hand to stop it from blowing into her face as the car picked up speed. "You're stalling," Lily went on. "Deliber-ately. And apparently with some amusement. My pro-ducer is 'missing.' You came to my office and made a big dramatic deal about that. So if that's true—"

There. She'd said it. And now his veracity was on the line. "If that's true, who's looking for her? And where are they looking?"

She imagined Greer sitting at her desk at Channel 6 right now, drinking coffee and being annoyed that Lily was late again. Since Banning hadn't tried to hide his search of her belongings, Greer would also be wondering who'd ransacked her desk. Lily pictured that list. The list Greer had made.

And if Greer *was* at her desk—or at the hairdresser or the doctor or the dry cleaners or any number of quotidian places that seemed increasingly more logically true than "missing"—then it was Lily herself who was in trouble. *But Banning knew about Cassie.*

Banning drove onto the turnpike's entrance ramp like the car was part of him, his left wrist draped over the steering wheel at twelve o'clock, his other hand at six. Foot steadily on the accelerator. He glanced at her, seemed to be assessing.

Cars whooshed by on both sides, taunting and dodging the mammoth eighteen-wheelers that took up more than their share of pavement. Anyone who honored the speed limit was soon far behind them. Banning reached up, unsnapped a pouch on his sun visor, and took out a pair of dark-lensed Ray-Bans. He slid them on.

"Banning?" Lily refused to just sit here.

"Remember the list on Ms. Whitfield's desk?" Banning turned to her, his expression now annoyingly unreadable.

She signaled him with her phone. "You know? I'm going to try calling her again," she said. "Maybe she's back."

Banning moved the sunglasses to the top of his head. Veered into the fast lane. "Sure," he said. "So that means you don't want to talk about her research?"

"Of course I do," she said. "But I'll just try."

"Gotcha," he said. "But while you're waiting for her to answer." He paused, apparently allowing his sarcasm to take effect. "Let me tell you about the list."

One ring. *Be there,* she willed it.

"They seem like random words," Banning began. "Don't they? But you recognized them. I'm a professional. Like you are. I know when people are lying. And you're lying."

Two rings. "Huh," she said.

He nodded. "So. One by one. The first item on Ms. Whitfield's list was *Berwick.*"

Three rings. "Berwick, yes," Lily said.

"You're from Pennsylvania." Banning kept talking, didn't wait for her to answer. "So you've gotta know Berwick is one of those fancy liberal arts colleges in the western part of the state, all stone buildings and independent study."

Still no answer. It was silly, she knew, to keep up the calling charade. She didn't really believe Greer would answer, but she was grateful for somewhere to pretend to focus her attention. Somewhere other than Berwick.

"Sure," she said. "Everyone knows that. Maybe Greer went there? Did you check that? Does she have a grandmother or something who—"

"I see you remember the second word, *grandmother.*" Banning nodded, an approving professor. The traffic slowed, almost stopped, as they approached the endless construction that collapsed four lanes into one. They crept along in the shadow of a dingy overpass, the afternoon sun obliterated by the cracked concrete and exposed steel above them.

Lily buzzed up her window against the accumulating dust and exhaust. Four rings. On six it would go to voice mail. If Greer had left her phone on her desk, gone to the bathroom or to someone else's office, or the vending machine room downstairs, she might not hear it. Magical thinking, Lily thought. *Hang up.* But she couldn't do it.

It felt like admitting defeat. Like accepting that

Greer was gone. She'd never not told Lily where she was during the workday. In the past, Lily had sometimes been annoyed with Greer's neediness, as if she were trying too hard to prove herself to Lily. But Greer always texted. After Banning's arrival, Lily had checked her messages. But there'd been nothing from her. Five rings.

"But skip the grandmother," Banning said. "And go on to Marianne." In the gloom of the underpass, a series of red brake lights flashed on in front of them. Banning brought the car to a complete stop, then draped his forearm over the steering wheel. "Know any Mariannes?"

Banning was playing with her like a cat teasing a vulnerable mouse. But for now, she had to pretend she didn't know that. Maybe he was honestly asking her, maybe he had no idea how those words fit together, and her own personal baggage was making this into an inquisition.

"Doesn't everyone?"

"Sure." Banning checked his rearview. "And then finally, Kirkhalter. A fine Pennsylvania name. Know any Kirkhalters?"

Lily shook her head silently, stared through the windshield into the line of cars in front of them, motionless on a road that was meant for travel. Stalled, like she was. Held captive in a story of her own creation. The perfect-Lily story.

The story that was never true.

She tilted her head back against the seat. Might as well find out what he knew. And with that, it felt as if a chapter of her life was ending. The part where she'd successfully hidden her too-tabloid past from a voracious and fascinated public.

Greer had been researching Cassie. And this Banning—or whoever—was on the same trail. Were they working together? Bigger question: did she want to protect herself more than she wanted to find Cassie? Now she had to face that choice.

"Are you leading up to something?" Lily turned to Banning, surprised, then, to see he was looking at her, too. "Can we just cut to that?"

Someone behind them honked, then someone else, and the traffic lurched ahead again, merging like a massive deck of cards. They moved forward into daylight, the revealed sky bluer than it had been before.

BEFORE

CHAPTER 31

CASSIE

Jem now sat with his back against the coffee table, knees bent, feet on the carpeted floor. "Thanks," he said. "Sorry about that. I had a concussion a while ago, from football. Guess I wasn't as fine as I thought. Then, you know. Wharton."

"You sure you don't want me to call a doctor?" Cassie, sitting beside him with her arms wrapped around her knees, watched him take careful sips from the water she'd brought him. Watched the color come back to his face. She'd played out various terrible outcomes in the moments before he'd come back to life, how she'd have to call 911, how an ambulance would arrive, how she'd have to explain—but that hadn't happened. He was fine. Now her problem was those green pills. If she called for help and people swarmed in, like police, even, and they found the pills, and she was here . . . No. She had to leave. "Maybe call the hospital, see if there's anything you should do? Does your head hurt?"

Jem drained the last of the water, then took a deep breath. "Not really." He touched two fingers to the side of his face. "The bandage is still all right?"

"Looks fine to me," she said. What she'd seen in

the kitchen cabinet meant nothing but disaster. She *had* to leave.

"You got more than you bargained for tonight, I guess." Jem set the glass down between them. "But I'm fine. You should go." He cocked his head toward the sliding glass doors leading to the tiny balcony. "Kind of gloomy out there now, though. The sun goes down fast this time of year."

The woods beyond the glass were draped in total darkness, only the silhouette of the trees visible against the purple-blue sky. The edges of their top leaves looked like a painting, or like fabric, Cassie thought, lace against a starlit canvas. When she and Jem left the hospital, it was sunny. Now, even the living room had gone gray, the sunset over, their only light filtering in from the kitchen. It made her almost sleepy, and it felt much later than it really was.

"I'll be fine," she said, deciding that was true. "I'll go out to Mountville, get the campus jitney. It'll be good."

Jem nodded. "Right. Great. That works. But—" He picked up his glass with the paper towel. Held it toward her. "Before you go, could you get me more water?"

She got to her feet, took the glass. "Um, sure, but does that mean you can't get up?"

He grimaced, touched his bandage again. "I can, yeah, definitely. But I'm gonna be happier sitting here. But it's cool, you go. Catch the jitney. I got this."

"But what if—" She couldn't help but worry. And was annoyed with herself for getting involved. She'd thought that walking Jem home was the least she could do to repay him for hustling her out of Wharton Hall. She couldn't just leave the guy. But he was completely toxic. "Listen, after I get the water. Is there someone I can call? Or you can? To come be with you?"

Jem closed his eyes.

"Jem?" She bent over him, her face close to his, worrying.

"Oh," he said as his eyes opened again. "I was thinking. About who to call."

His eyes were intensely dark brown, and she'd put herself closer to him than she'd planned. "Let me bring you the water."

She flipped a light switch on the wall, and two round spotlights on the balcony came on, making the forest outside even darker. The second switch turned on a tall gooseneck lamp in the corner. At least they could see better now. She heard a sound from the living room. Was Jem talking to someone? She stood, motionless, listening. But she only heard murmurs.

"All good," Jem called out after a moment. "A buddy's coming to hang out with me, he says he'll be here pretty soon."

"Great!" she called back.

"He could take you back to the dorm."

"Great." *No way,* she thought.

She turned on the faucet. She yawned, then shook her head to clear it. She wasn't tired. She was simply— whatever she was. In a strange guy's apartment, like a drug dealer, even, and alone. But he might be really hurt. She puffed out a breath. How many people had *he* hurt? The water rushed out of the faucet, hit the metal sink below, swirled down the drain.

She stared at that cabinet again. She'd touched one of the bags. Hadn't she? If her fingerprints were on the bag . . .

She grabbed a striped dish towel, wrapped her hand in it. No, she'd need two. One to open the cabinet, one to wipe off her prints. She lifted one padded hand. Touched the white knob. Began to pull open the door. Should she do this? *Hurry,* she thought.

"Cassie?"

Cassie gasped at Jem's voice, flinched, and the cabinet door swung open.

"Ow! Damn it." Jem stumbled backward as the wood hit his eye. He clamped one hand over it, and bent down in pain. "What the—*shit,* Cassie."

"Jem! I'm so—"

He lurched backward as she stepped toward him, one line of blood now visible below his left eye. The water gushed from the faucet. She yanked it off, dropped the towels in the sink.

"I didn't mean to—" She took a step to help him, but he'd turned away, hit one shin on the coffee table, stumbled again. And fell.

Had his head hit the coffee table?

His eyes were closed. A bandage on one cheek, blood on the other. One arm flopped out beside him.

"Jem?" She took a tentative step closer to him. Another step. She saw his chest rise and fall. She felt tears come to her eyes, tears of uncertainty and apprehension and fear, of having no idea what to do.

"Jem?" She'd made her voice louder, but he did not respond. She stepped between the couch and the coffee table and, holding her breath, leaned down and gently, carefully, touched his shoulder with her fingertips. She felt the hard bone beneath his flannel shirt.

He was breathing. He was.

She fell to her knees, terrified, and as she did, her back bumped the coffee table, and the blue glass tipped over and hit her wineglass, and pink wine and clear water spilled onto her jeans and onto her shoes and onto the carpet.

"Jem!" She grabbed Jem's shoulder, moved it, shook it, and Jem's head turned toward her, startling her, and she jerked back, and hit the stupid coffee table again. The two empty glasses rolled off and hit the floor on opposite sides of the table, then stopped in the carpet's thick pile. "Jem?"

But Jem did not move. His eyelashes, long and dark, rested on his cheeks, and one curl of dark hair had fallen across his forehead. The bleeding had stopped, it really looked like it had stopped. The room smelled like pink wine. But Jem was breathing. Was this her chance to escape?

Almost without thinking, she used one finger to move the hair off his forehead, his skin still warm to the touch. Alive. *Go, Cassie,* she commanded herself.

She felt the tears begin, felt their dampness on her face, and she wiped them away with the back of her hand, furious, and terrified. She wanted her mother, she wanted her father, she wanted someone, anyone, to come help her and fix this and take care of her and tell her what to do. She pressed her palms to her face, trying to hold it all in and make it go away and when she opened her eyes, Jem would be laughing at her. And she'd be so mad. Then she'd storm out of here and never see this idiot again.

She stared at him, ignoring her own tears now, willing him to be joking with her, some stupid insane boy joke, and she'd laugh, she promised she would. But Jem's face, serene and still, *and blood on his cheek,* seemed to taunt her.

There could be no more wishful thinking. She had to do something.

She took a deep shuddering breath.

Okay. She knew what to do. First, stop being hysterical. Then, call 911. She reached for the receiver of the black phone on the end table, the one that Jem had probably used to call his friend. She stopped, hand in midair, halfway to the phone.

Jem had called his friend. Who was on his way here. She felt her heart racing, constricting, making it difficult to breathe. Whoever showed up here—Jem's friend or the ambulance people, or whoever—would find her here in this apartment.

What if he even *died*?

They'd question her. They'd blame her. It would be horrible, it would be—had she killed him by giving him the water? Or by hitting him with the cabinet? It was a *mistake*! How was she supposed to know what to do? She hadn't *killed* him, of course she hadn't, but what would she say? She imagined it, how she'd tell what had happened. She envisioned it all, the pictures racing through her mind like a terrible dumb movie where the woman was guilty and everyone knew it, and she got tripped up and trapped by her own pitiful answers.

The truth would sound like a lie. They'd never believe her.

It would first be all in the papers; that she had been here, a freshman, and they'd try to interview her, and how she'd been the one who'd *kept* Professor Shaw in the building and it had led to him almost dying, and now she was here—*here*—in the apartment of the *other* person who'd been hurt in the Wharton fire and that was so, so—*impossible* that they'd never believe it was a coincidence.

And he was a drug dealer. And she had seen the drugs. Knew they were there. Might have even touched one of the bags. And too late now.

Should she get rid of them? Toss them out the window into the woods?

She cried out, a soft whimper of terror, covering her mouth with both hands to stop herself from sobbing with fear. She was in trouble.

She stared out into the dark maw of the Berwick Forest, thinking about whether *she* could disappear into the dark, like the entire vast forest of trees in front of her, disappear in the night and never have to ever—wait. She didn't have to do that. She didn't have to hide drugs, or dump them. She didn't have to disappear, or do anything except have her regular life. Because no one knew she'd been in this apartment.

Cassie bent down and picked up the glasses from the floor, replaced them on the table. One water glass. One wineglass. One person on the floor.

She used the tail of her flannel shirt to wipe off the stem of the wineglass, and put it back on the *Newsweek*. The paper towel she'd used to wrap the water glass was still on the coffee table. She'd only touched that glass directly when she filled it—and the towel would smudge her fingerprints. She hoped it worked that way. Even if they found someone's fingerprints, she didn't think they could tell when they were from. Plus hers weren't on file anywhere. She couldn't believe she was thinking like this. But she was.

She could use her shirt when she touched the doorknob. And the elevator buttons. Or she could run down the back steps, there must be some. Make sure no one saw her leave.

Her heart lifted with possibility. With freedom. No one would know.

Unless Jem had told his friend she was here.

NOW

CHAPTER 32

LILY

"Tell me about your sister Cassie," Banning said as he accelerated onto the open highway. "Why do you think Greer was researching her? Do you know anything about what happened to her? Where she is?"

"I . . . Why are you asking about Cassie?" Lily paused, calculating. Banning had steered into the fast lane with scarcely a look into his mirrors, and the speedometer was now topping seventy. She wasn't afraid of him, not exactly. If Cassie was in trouble, Lily needed to understand whose side Banning was on. And where the maybe-not-missing Greer fit into it. Lily didn't know anything about Cassie. Question was, what did *Banning* know?

"Lily? Skip the phony bafflement." Banning had turned to her, slicing the space between them with a forget-about-it gesture before he looked at the traffic again. "You know as well as I do. Those four words on the list only go together to mean one thing, and that's your sister, Cassie Atwood. Everyone in law enforcement knows her. The great cop failure. The beautiful missing college girl. Missing, or hiding, or . . . wherever she is."

"But that was a long time ago. She might be dead."

"Maybe." Banning nodded. "But let's come back

to that. Cassie went to Berwick, spent most of a semester there, and then she was gone. *Marianne* was next on the list. Cassie's roommate was Marianne Dawe. Now deceased. *Kirkhalter* is Walter Kirkhalter, the cop who headed the investigation."

"Who is also dead." Lily heard the bitterness in her own voice. The dismissive Detective Kirkhalter, who'd given the impression from the start he thought Cassie would turn up someday. That she was pulling some con, or prank, or cover-up. A couple of years ago, Lily'd gone to interview him, reminding him she'd been just a little girl the last time they'd met, even reminded him of the paper dolls. And of what she'd tried to tell him back then. What he'd dismissed as fantasy.

But she knew, knew when she was seven and now that she was so much older, what had really happened. She remembered the thick night, remembered it as if it were yesterday, and the glow of her penguin night-light, the one Cassie herself had outgrown.

Cassie hadn't awakened her, just stood over her little twin bed in the darkness. Somehow Lily had felt her presence, opened her eyes, and squinted into the gloom.

"Cassie!" she'd whispered. And felt her eyes widen.

"Shhhh." Cassie was holding her Penny, the stuffed penguin she'd left perched on the ruffled pillow shams of her bed when she went off to college. "Whisper. Promise me you won't tell."

"I promise," Lily said, and whispered, too, because she wanted to make Cassie happy.

"I've done a bad thing, Lillow," Cassie had said softly. "And I have to go."

Lily had tried to understand. She knew what "bad thing" meant, and she'd done bad things, too—sneaked extra cookies, or lied about brushing her teeth. She'd struggled to see her sister in the dark.

"What bad thing? Just say you're sorry, and it will all go away."

Her eyes had adjusted to the darkness, and she saw her sister wipe a finger under one eye. "I *am* sorry, Lillow, I am. But this one time, saying sorry is not enough, and I have to go. I just wanted to say—"

"Mom's not gonna let you," Lily had argued. "You have college."

"You have to not tell Mom, not tell her anything, hear me, Lillow? You're my Lillow, and you're my best friend, and I am counting on you to act like a big girl. You *are* a big girl. And you have to promise promise promise."

"Is this a dream?" Lily remembered even now, wondering that.

"Maybe," Cassie said. "If that's easier. But you take Penny, and every time you see her, she'll remind you of your promise. And remind you of me. I'll always try to watch out for you, best I can. I'll try to know where you are. But I've done a bad thing, a very bad thing. Still, my Lillow, you *remember* me, and that I love you."

Lily had reached out for the fuzzy penguin and hugged it to her, closing her eyes as she did.

And when she opened them, Cassie was gone.

Then Lily had done a bad thing, too. She'd broken her promise. And told the police. She missed Cassie so much, and if Cassie apologized, no one could be mad at her anymore. That's how it worked. And she held out Penny, *showed* him, to prove Cassie had really been there.

But the tall police officer in the black parka had told her it was a dream. He'd told her not to repeat dreams. And that she was never to speak of it again.

All those years later, Kirkhalter, aging and vague in his living room recliner, had seemed to need to scour his memory for even a vestige of the case.

When she'd traveled to Berwick to see him, she'd expected he'd look different, everyone did after twenty-five years. But sixty-something Kirkhalter seemed to have allowed gravity and power to claim him. In their so-called interview, Lily saw spidery veins in his thickened nose, the planes of his face pudged out, his skin loose and dappled.

And he'd refused to own up to his failure. Since he'd retired, he'd told her without a seeming trace of regret, his files were long gone.

"Did you at least regret that the search didn't continue?" Lily had tried to ask it gently.

He'd stared her down. "You'd be happier if we'd found your sister's body, miss?"

Lily had gasped at the harsh and heartless question.

"So you gave up?" Lily'd retaliated, snapped at him, had to, couldn't help it.

"And we're done here, miss." Kirkhalter had yanked a lever to tip his recliner chair back to upright. Cocked his chin toward his front door. "You can show yourself out."

She'd cried for hours afterward.

When Lily'd read Kirkhalter had died in a car accident, she was authentically sad. With him gone, more of Cassie's history was gone, and Lily's, too. Soon there would be no one who knew anything firsthand. No files, no investigations, no evidence, no direct knowledge. Just the memory of a girl who once existed, captured in a photo with her dog.

"Kirkhalter died in a car accident, yeah," Banning said, interrupting her thoughts. "The final word, *grandmother*. Cassie's grandmother—your grandmother."

Lily spooled out a breath, wondering, for the millionth time, if Cassie had sworn Gramma to secrecy, too. "She's dead now, too."

"I know."

"You do? How?" Lily pushed him, harder than it probably warranted, annoyed with herself for having this too-personal conversation, annoyed with herself for being so open with him while trying to get some leverage. "Did you get my grandmother's obituary from your research guys?"

"*Cassie's* grandmother. Yup."

Banning's answer hung in the air. In the silence, Lily heard the low rumble of the air conditioner, and the grumbling sound as the tires traveled over imperfections in the pavement. This was the part of the Mass Pike where Boston couldn't decide whether to be beautiful or tough, industrial or commercial; out one window, an abandoned train yard, out the other, a scaffolded soon-to-be-chic hotel development.

Lily felt equally torn as the multicolored landscape blurred by. Here she was, literally carried along on someone else's mission. Someone who had tried to convince her—by lying—that their mission was shared. He might be on the hunt for Greer, but she believed Smith. Banning's goal was Cassie.

"And that's enough answers from me." Lily adjusted the tote bag in her lap. Her phone felt warm, she'd been clutching it so long. "I took your little 'list quiz,' although obviously, you already knew what the words meant. Now it's your turn. I have a list of questions of my own. Like—where are we going? Where is Greer? How do you know about Cassie? And why do you care? You can answer in any order you like." She crossed her arms over the black canvas bag and shifted position in the black leather seat, challenging him. "Ready? Go."

"Hang on." He glanced at his rearview mirror. "Gotta pass this guy."

He accelerated, hard, zooming around a rackety exhaust-spewing landscape truck, and then veered back into the fast lane, swerving so precariously that

Lily almost lost her balance, the truck receding behind them like a vanishing rusty splotch.

"Whoa," Lily said.

"Jerk. Some people don't belong in the fast lane. Anyway. One more thing. You've looked for her, right? You must have. On the other hand, you're hardly tough to locate. She could've easily contacted you if she wanted to. Ever consider that maybe she doesn't want to?"

"No," Lily lied.

Banning stared straight ahead.

As if he knows I'm lying, Lily thought.

"Look," she went on. "I was seven when she—left, disappeared, was kidnapped, whatever she was. She had a calendar, I remember, drawn on her notebook. She'd crossed off the days. My mother and I saw it the last time she was home. It seemed as if, day by day, Cassie was marking time until something. Waiting for something. We never knew what."

She pictured that notebook, the X-marks Cassie had made. All Cassie's belongings had been boxed up after seven years, the day the "presumed dead" ruling came. Mumma had made a ritual of it, calling Lily home from college to see the packing and taping and the final discarding. Lily was still heartbroken by the memory of her grieving mother, thinner than ever and brittle around the edges, eyes permanently red-rimmed and bereft. Mumma always seemed to blame herself, which was still a puzzle. And then she died, too. Lily had kept only the one scallop-edged photo, the one she now pinned to her bulletin board.

"If she's alive—" She said the words again, then assessed Banning's reaction for some flicker of confirmation or denial. His eyes stayed stolidly on the road. "If she's alive, why hasn't she contacted me? If she's dead . . ."

A reality came over her, a dawning, a vision of

two puzzle pieces fitting together. Lily put one finger to her lips as if to stop herself from talking, making sure she was right. She nodded, agreeing with herself. Took her finger away. "If she's dead, there'd be no reason for you to be making this big deal about it."

She lifted her chin as her mind raced ahead. "You know what happened," she said. "Don't you?"

She stared at him, waited for him to reply. Waited as they passed a highway marker, waited as she watched the flash of a purple-striped commuter train speed by on the roadside tracks.

"Did you hear my question?" she asked.

Banning nodded, focused on the road ahead of them, a straight gray strip heading west. "Yup. I heard it."

Lily slapped the dashboard with an open palm. "Banning!"

He flinched, surprised, and looked at her, quizzical.

"Banning," she said again. "Where the hell are we going and what the hell are you doing?" She tapped open her phone, brandished it at him. Tapped the number nine. "I'm calling the police. You're kidnapping me, you know?" She tapped one. "So answer me. All I have to do is hit the one, just one more time. And believe me, I will."

A state police car sped by them, navy and silver, blue wigwag lights glaring in the sun, siren at full blast. Other cars slowed, moved over to let it pass. Banning slowed, too. The police car wailed out of sight, the sound diminishing, leaving them with only the hum of the air conditioner and the buzz of tension between them.

"Well?" She held up the phone at him, her finger poised.

"I'm a private detective," he said. "As I'm sure your friend told you on the phone."

"Are you even kidding me?" Lily's eyes widened,

then narrowed at him. "You came to my office under false pretenses," she hissed. "You lied up one side and down the other, basically impersonated a police officer—" Lily stopped herself, recognizing her vulnerability, and knowing Banning, or whoever he was, had the physical upper hand with her. Especially now that she'd made him confess his deception. She put up both palms, pretending to calm herself. "Look, Banning. Is it really Banning?"

He nodded.

"I'm sorry," she said. "But hey. I need to know where Greer is. That she's not in trouble. And why she's gone."

"She's fine." Banning steered to the right, moving across one middle lane, then the next. "At least, she was when we met last night at Lido."

BEFORE

CHAPTER 33

CASSIE

"Nothing," Cassie said. She'd hoped Marianne would be out of their dorm room, somewhere, anywhere, like any reasonable college student on a Friday night. But no, when she got back from Jem's—*Jem's!*—her roommate was sitting cross-legged on her ridiculous apple-green comforter, leaning against the pink pillows stacked behind her back against the twin bed's headboard, reading a thick hardcover textbook.

The minute Cassie arrived, Marianne had taken a yellow highlighter out of her mouth and asked what she'd been doing. Cassie had hoped "nothing" would be an acceptable answer.

"Right." Marianne tapped the highlighter against her lips, her eyes full of mischief. "Nothing inside at a bar? Or nothing in someone's dorm room?" She wrinkled her nose, sniffing. "You don't usually smell like wine."

"Wine?" Cassie tried to sound baffled. She hadn't noticed, maybe she was used to it, or too afraid, or too distracted. Now she had to scramble for an answer. "I've been at the hospital, if you must know." Cassie made herself look sad, which wasn't hard to do, and began to unbutton her flannel shirt. Their door was open a sliver, because the heating system in the dorm was so gross, it was always too hot.

Cassie moved behind the door, so in case anyone walked by, they couldn't see her. Three buttons open, and she pulled the shirt over her head. She kept talking as she unzipped her jeans, pulling them off, too, feeling the damp splotches all down one side. You couldn't see them on the dark denim, but Marianne was right. You could smell the wine. It made her want to throw up, not the wine itself, but the memory of the wine, and everything that went with it, and what might be, must be, going on in that apartment right now. But now she was here, and alcohol was alcohol. And this hospital excuse might work. Plus, it was partly true. People would have seen her there, for better or for worse. Her mind raced ahead, imagining the obstacles to come. Might as well own as much of it as she safely could. "I agree, I stink," Cassie said. "Hospital smells are the worst."

"Yeah, but, Cass." Marianne looked skeptical, pursing her lips. "Gotta tell you, that really smells li—"

Cassie interrupted, looking even sadder, staring over Marianne's shoulder as if deep in memory. "I remember from my dad. My mother and I were there all the time. When he died. That smell of alcohol, and death, always makes me incredibly depressed."

"Oh, stupid me." Marianne was frowning now. Cassie hoped in embarrassment, in regret of her wrong conclusion and inappropriate teasing. "Hospitals. Are so grim."

Cassie wadded her clothing into a ball, kept on her camisole tank and her underwear. "I'm gonna take a shower." She'd take the winey clothes into the shower with her, rinse them out at least, not make a big deal out of going all the way down to the washing machines in the basement. She could do that when

Marianne was gone and wouldn't notice. "Hospitals. I hate them."

Marianne nodded. Felt guilty, Cassie hoped. She and Marianne had been matched—however that worked—by the college and were only just beginning to understand each other's quirks and living habits. Now she wished her roommate would stop asking questions, for once in her life. Cassie needed to think.

What had Jem said to his friend on the phone? Her name? Had he even said she was there? She willed the memory back, thinking about the timing. *Hi, it's Jem,* he might have said. *I'm* . . . Then he would have given some explanation of what happened, and he would have described his situation, not her.

Cassie clutched her damp clothing closer to her chest, felt her shoulders drop in defeat. She could make up rationalizing stories all she wanted, but bottom line, she had no idea. And if Jem had said her name, distinctly enough so that whoever it was would remember it, she'd know soon enough. If they—whoever *they* was, police or detectives or doctors or family or Jem's friend on the phone—started looking for her, it wouldn't take long to find her. Like, two seconds.

She took a scrunchie from her dresser top, wrapped her hair into a ponytail. Saw her own face in the dresser mirror, pale and drawn around the edges. Her lip gloss was all worn off, her lips pale and ghostly, and her eyelashes glommed together from mascara and tears. After the shower, she'd pull herself together. Marianne was not the brightest bulb. Maybe Cassie could escape to the library or something.

The thought of it made her so weary, though. Seeing people, other kids, wondering if they were looking at her. Gossip was the engine of this school, she'd learned that, the buzz and whispers and sidelong glances, who was pledged to sororities, and who was blackballed, and who had a stash of diet pills or Ecstasy in their backpack. And they probably got that stuff from Jem, too. What else might have been in that horrible apartment?

What if the police came or something? Here? And questioned her? All she wanted was to go to sleep. For, like, ever.

She startled herself with that dark thought. Tried to brighten her face as she turned back to Marianne. She had to find a normal, and be normal, and pretend everything was normal. There were no secrets. She had no secrets. She was just Cassie, who went to the hospital, and then came home.

"So I'll just—"

"Wait. A. Minute." Marianne drew out the words as if she were figuring out a complicated problem. "The hospital? Why? Were you checking on Professor *Shaw*? You were, weren't you?" Marianne had tucked her highlighter into the textbook to mark her place. Focused on Cassie.

Cassie's head was starting to hurt again, bursting with fear and possibilities. She felt trapped, like, on the inside, and on the outside. What gnawed at her, what thickened her brain as if someone was filling her head with sand, was that she should have done something about Jem, but she hadn't, and now it was too late because she already didn't do the right thing, and now there was no way out of it. If she killed a drug dealer, or even if she left him to die . . . how in the name of everything could that have happened to her?

She wished Marianne would just shut up. If everyone would mind their own business, everything would be fine. But everyone wouldn't.

"I—" Now Cassie had to say something. Give some reason why she was at the hospital. It's not like people just hung around there. "I—"

"Oh, Cassie, you are so thoughtful," Marianne interrupted. "I mean, that is so great of you. We're all so worried about him, but only you actually went to check on him. Did they tell you anything? I mean, do we know why he stayed in the building so long? Oh. Wait. No. I just thought of something."

Marianne grabbed the pillow with the pink peonies, held it to her chest.

Cassie waited, almost seeing her roommate's mind at work.

"You know *what*?" Marianne leaned forward, eyes wide, engaging her. "I bet? He stayed to make sure everyone was out. Don't you agree?"

One thing about Marianne, if you didn't answer her, she'd just keep talking. For better or worse.

As Marianne elaborated on her theory, Cassie had to admit it wasn't actually a bad explanation. Maybe? It wasn't her fault Professor Shaw had been inside so long. It was *his*. She played out the scenario, the one where he'd hung back to protect whoever might still in the building. To leave no child behind. He was brave, and selfless, and devoted, and—wait. No.

It was a terrible thought. That would mean her. That he'd waited for *her*. Her face felt cold, suddenly, icicles up her neck. She pretended to listen to her prattling roommate, and standing there, in the stupid dorm in the stupid school holding her stupid clothes, which she should just *burn,* she started to hate Professor Shaw. With that smarmy turtleneck, and that hair, too long for a person his age. He'd been eyeing her, she knew it. And that was wrong. And actually, now that she remembered it again, he'd delayed *her* from leaving the building.

Shifting the wadded clothing in her arms from one side to the other, she chewed the inside of her cheek.

She could feel her body moving into the position of telling that version, hear the tone of her voice saying it, felt her chin go up, and her face arrange in an earnest and half-unwilling disclosure. Who would they believe, the poor college freshman or the predatory professor?

She adjusted the dankly incriminating clothing in her arms again, felt her expression change to sorrow and regret.

I wouldn't want to hurt his reputation, she could hear herself whispering to whoever it was, but—

"Cass? Hey, sister. What're you doing? Are you listening to me?" Marianne was waving at her. "I was asking you, did you hear anything about that other guy, Jim? No, Jem. Jem. Who tried to go in to save him." Marianne pursed her lips as if trying to retrieve a memory. "*You* were there, I remember. But did you see him going in? Was he at the hospital, too?"

"I don't know." Cassie tried to answer everything with that phrase. There was no reason that she, Cassie, an innocent bystander, a *freshman,* should know anything about anything. Only problem was, people would have seen her at the hospital. She needed to bring that up herself and create the perfect story to go with it.

"Yeah, I wanted to drop off some flowers for Professor Shaw." She concocted the explanation on the fly. "He was—is—my prof, of course. But dumb me, he's in ICU . . ." She hesitated. Was she offering too many details? "But they wouldn't let me, so I left them at the front desk. Lilies, they were." She shrugged, naming the first flower that came to her mind. "I didn't put a card, because he's a teacher, so I didn't want anyone to get the wrong idea. I'd just meant to cheer him up, like a surprise." She was talking too fast, but she was into it now. "They'll probably give them to someone else. It's fine. And then I just walked up Mountville Street a little. You know. To clear my head," she added, laying the groundwork in case anyone had seen her there. "Then I came home."

"Cassie, you are the best. The nicest." Marianne was shaking her head in what seemed like profound approval. "It's all so amazingly awful."

"Yeah, it *is* awful." Cassie ignored the undeserved praise, hoping it would be taken as modesty. She was anything but the best, and it made her stomach hurt to hear this stuff. Marianne's innocent questions, though, were proof that she was going to have to prepare to juggle. To not look guilty, or even *feel* guilty when she answered people. That was the way to create a perfect lie. To really believe you were telling the truth. Not to tell too much, and then change the subject. "But more important. Have you heard anything new about how the fire started?"

Cassie heard footsteps in the hallway, then a murmur of conversation. Doors opening, and the undercurrent getting louder. The footsteps came closer to their room. She took the few short steps to the bathroom, tossed her winey clothes into the bathtub, and grabbed her fleece robe from a hook on the door, tying the thick white belt around her waist.

Marianne cocked her head toward the hallway. "What's all *that* about, you think?" she said. "Maybe a party or something?"

"Friday," Cassie told herself as much as Marianne. "They're probably already buzzed. We should close the door."

"You guys?" Someone rapped on their doorjamb. More than one person in the hall, Cassie heard. Voices. Low and intense. Not partiers. "You in there?"

"Hang on. What's up?" Marianne trotted toward the door, then turned to Cassie. "You decent?" she whispered. "It's, like, Rajit. One of the voices at least."

"Pretend I'm not here," Cassie said. Rajit. The head resident assistant. That could not be good.

"But you *are* here," Marianne whispered.

"Marianne? Cassie?" The voice came through the

cracked door, which seemed to be opening, slowly, by the sheer force of whoever wanted them to answer.

"I'm in the shower, then." Cassie pointed to the bathroom. "Just tell her—"

"You guys!" The door opened, halfway, and Rajit had curled her head and shoulders into the opening. "I know you're in there, the door's open. Come on, you two. You know you're supposed to answer me."

"Oh, hey, Raj." Marianne stretched, then yawned. She pulled the door all the way open. "Must have fallen asleep. What's up?"

Cassie tried to ease back toward the bathroom. And the safety of the shower. One step closer. Two.

Rajit, in her uniform of black jeans, Berwick tee, and aggressive red lipstick, stepped into their room and seemed to be checking in each of the four corners as if she suspected the roommates had been trying to hide something.

NOW

CHAPTER 34

LILY

Lily jabbed a finger at the lighted neon sign displaying a giant crimson horse just off the turnpike exit. She and Banning had stopped at the red light that swayed above Exit 217, a tangled skein of streets Lily'd always thought had been designed by a particularly sadistic civil engineer.

"Banning," she said. "Pull into that gas station. Now."

"Why?"

The light stayed red.

"*Banning.* If you don't, I'm opening this damn car door and getting out. And I am calling the real police. And listen." She recited three letters and three numbers. "I know your license plate, and I know there's surveillance video of you coming into Channel 6, and in one phone call, the cops will be on you faster than you can say *impersonating an officer.*"

The light stayed red. She swore she saw Banning smile, his eyes still obscured by those sunglasses.

"So Greer met with *you*?" she asked. "Last night? At Lido?" Not half an hour before, while Banning was inside Lido, Smith had told her Greer had met with *him*. Had all three been together?

"Like I said."

Their light changed to green. Behind them, the honking of horns had instantly begun, a raucous symphony of impatience and anger.

Lily knew how they felt. Anger and impatience were not the half of it. Someone was toying with her, holding not only Greer over her head, but Cassie. The only reason she'd put up with this potentially risky charade was the possibility of getting some answers. Banning clearly knew something about Cassie. He also knew Greer had been on her trail. Might have even put her there.

And that was unnerving. She'd believed—for years—that she was the only one in the world looking for Cassie. Everyone else assumed Cassie was dead. But though Lily knew back then that Cassie left on purpose, she had no idea about what happened to her sister.

Now this detective's interest could only mean Cassie was still alive. Who had hired him to find her?

And his earlier question had hit a nerve. *Had* she wondered why Cassie hadn't looked for her? Daily. Lily had always pushed that awkward thought aside, but it was true, Cassie wouldn't have any difficulty finding her. Lily's face was on television and billboards and in magazine ads. Google Lily Atwood, and you'd get new entries every day. Not like Cassie, where the stories about her never changed or advanced. Online, Cassie Atwood was forever eighteen. If she were alive, she'd be around forty.

Lily'd believed, mostly believed, that Cassie must be dead.

Now Banning was looking for her. So was Greer. Smith had said he'd met with Greer at Lido. And now, Banning, too? Smith *and* Banning?

Smith *and* Banning?

"Was it just the two of you at Lido?"

"Just the two? Not sure what you—"

"Go," she said, pointing at the gas station. Smith *and*

Banning. "Now. I am not staying in this car one more second unless you tell me what the hell is going on."

Lily braced one hand on the dashboard as Banning veered the car into the gas station's entryway, one wheel jouncing over the curb, and brought it to a hard-braked stop, putting her beside a snake of red rubber hose looped around a hook on a rusty post topped by a battered metal sign reading AIR 25 CENTS. Banning had pivoted the car, backing into the marked spot, so they faced the street. He left the engine running. Buzzed down his window, letting in the hum of traffic on the street in front of them, the ping of the gas pumps, and the wafting fumes of oil and dust. The pounding bass of some heavy metal anthem came from inside the gas station's boxy glass-windowed office, its open front door revealing a rainbow of shelved snacks and wall-mounted reels of lottery tickets.

He turned to her. Peeled off his sunglasses.

But she spoke first.

"You're Smith." Lily heard herself saying the words, asking the question, almost before her mind had accepted the possibility. She tried to read his face, watching for bafflement, or denial, or amusement, or defeat. Or, maybe, victory. "You. Are. Smith."

Banning slid one hand into the inside of his jacket.

Lily flinched at his motion, her heart twisting. She'd gone too far. She should not have confronted him, not like that, not so directly, not trapped here in his car. She saw her door was unlocked. She unclicked her seat belt. Grabbed the door handle. Pulled it, opened it, felt the puff of warm air from outside.

Then heard the panel of her door bump up against the rusty post with the air sign. Her door would not open all the way. She eyed the available open space, gauging. Inches. Three maybe. Not enough room for her to get out. Even with the open door, she was still trapped.

"Lily? Going somewhere?" Banning, looking down, was scrolling through something on his cell. "I'll need to pull up, if you do."

He held up the phone, briefly, too quickly for Lily to see the screen. "So I guess you don't want to see the files and pictures I have?"

Lily drew in a breath, quieting her heart, assessing her choices. Pictures of what? Her? Greer? Rowen? Cassie? They were right out in public, a pony-tailed woman in front of them gassing up a sleek black convertible, and two gangly teenagers ambling toward the gas station's office wearing frayed cutoffs and Tevas. Any of those customers might recognize her, after all, she was Lily Atwood. All she'd have to do was yell and they'd come running, probably with cell phones recording everything.

"So the thing about conversations," Lily said. She kept her voice calmly reasonable, even friendly. It felt as if the car were getting smaller, this two-ton contraption of glass and steel that she'd entered with hesitation, and which now enclosed her without choice. She left her car door open and seat belt off, and wondered how it would feel to scream. What pictures did he have? But first things first. "The thing about conversations is that one person asks a question, and the other one answers. You're not keeping up your end of that, Banning. I asked if you were Smith."

She tilted her head, trying to look determined but pleasant at the same time.

Banning had put his phone into a cup holder on the car's center console, the screen facing him.

"From what I gather, there is no 'Smith,' " he said. "Isn't that a nickname?"

"You know what I mean." The car was too small for verbal jousting. And Greer had not checked in. "*You* called me from inside Lido, and from the sidewalk. And pretended to be Smith telling me to trust you? *That's* complicated. You know I protect sources. Why not just—"

"Because you wouldn't have believed me, would you?" Banning's face seemed to change, losing its veneer of wary sarcasm, as if some pretense had lifted. "If I had come into your office this morning and told you who I really was, you'd have been skeptical. Suspicious."

"Told me who you really were? You mean, told me you were Smith?" Weird though, "Smith" had called her this morning in her office, while Banning was there. Were there maybe *two* Smiths? "Or imagine, told me your real name? Why would I be skeptical? All you'd have to do was talk."

"I've watched you on TV," he said. "Everyone has. And I knew what you wanted—a perfect story. The spotlight. Success. So without you knowing who I was, I gave that to you. It's easy. I'm a detective. No big deal."

"Why, though?"

"Ma'am?"

Lily flinched at the voice outside her window, the rap on the passenger-side door. Turned to see a twentysomething wearing a gray shirt with a crimson horse stenciled on the front, the name *Erik* embroidered across the top of the pocket, and a ball cap turned backward. A scruff of attempted beard. The fragrance of motor oil and marijuana wafted into the car.

"Are you Lily Atwood?" he asked. He narrowed his eyes, looked at her. "You are, yeah, I see that now, too. Huh. Guy over there—" He pointed in the directon of the glass-fronted office. "Thought he recognized you. So what's up? You doing a story about this gas station?"

"Oh, thanks, Erik." Lily gave her best smile. This *guy*. *All* she needed. "So lovely to meet you. No, we're on the way to an appointment and my—"

"Friend," Banning broke in.

"Needed air for his tires," she finished.

Erik shook his head, disdainfully world-weary. "Right. I know how you guys work. You TV people. You're lying. You can't be here without permission. Just because you're TV, doesn't mean you can just—*hey*. Wait."

Lily saw his expression change from cynical to accusatory.

"Are you watching us or something?" He pointed a grimy forefinger at her. "Filming us? I have to call corporate, you can't take pictures here. Is that your cameraman? You have to leave. I'm gonna get nailed to the wall if you're taking pictures."

Lily tried the smile again. "No, truly, we're just chatting while we wait for our—"

A flash of light interrupted her explanation.

Erik had taken a photo of them. And now brandished his black phone at her. "I got the goods here," he said. "And I'm gonna send it to corporate if you try to pull anything. I have proof that I saw you, and told you to go away."

"It's a public place, Erik." Lily'd had it with this kid. This was insanity upon insanity, but no matter what, they had the right to be here. Plus Erik's dismissive "you're TV" annoyed her. "You can't tell us—"

Banning had shifted into drive. "Gotcha, buddy," he said, leaning across the console and speaking out Lily's window. "Don't want to get you in trouble. We're gone."

He inched the car forward, Lily barely managing to get her car door closed, then steered past the gas pumps and out toward the curb.

Lily twisted around to look over her shoulder and out the back window at Erik, who was still standing at the air pump, intently tapping the screen of his cell phone. She yanked her seat belt back on. His snapshot of her was probably about to be tweeted out to his who knew how many followers, maybe with some slacker-triumphant #screwthemedia tag, and his perceived victory over *the man*.

"Nice to be recognized," Banning said, pulling back into traffic. "Although—guess your undercover days are over."

"Yours, too," Lily said. "So. You're Smith. And I'm grateful for the stories. Now where the hell is Greer? And what do you know about my sister?"

BEFORE

CHAPTER 35

CASSIE

Cassie was one step from the bathroom. If she'd been one second faster, one second more confident, one second more decisive, she'd have been able to hide in the steamy privacy of the shower while Marianne handled Rajit. The resident assistants, freshmen were told on day one, were the dorm's absolute authority figures. And they could enforce the honor code rules, even to the point of recommending suspension, or worse. No men allowed except with permission and open doors, no alcohol, no loud music. Drugs of any kind meant instant expulsion, with no second chances. Rajit Rey, who might have been a supermodel in some other universe, now patrolled the hallways of Alcott Hall like she'd developed some personal radar that pinged on trouble. On hot plates. Cigarettes. Open booze.

Marianne, still clutching her philosophy book, now approached the RA as Cassie stood still, trapped by the opened door and Rajit's all-encompassing presence.

"Hey, you two." Rajit penned two firm check marks on her clipboard as if she'd accomplished some mission. "Meeting in the hallway. Like, now."

"What's wrong?" Marianne, sounding concerned, set her book on the bed and took a few steps closer to the opened door.

"I'm doing this one floor at a time," Rajit said. "By the elevators. Now."

They'd had a few of these meetings since school started two months ago. Someone's backpack had gone missing, and then forty-two dollars in cash from a desk drawer. Drugs had been confiscated, and everyone said it was roofies. A girl from someplace like Boston, who was even in Zachary Shaw's biology class, had "decided to go home" soon after. Had she known Jem, too? Cassie almost fainted now with that possibility.

Rajit pivoted on one black leather trainer and turned her back to them. "Put on shoes, Cass," she called over her shoulder.

Cassie wasn't the only one in a bathrobe as she and Marianne joined the murmuring huddle in the rectangle beside the three silver elevators. Friday night at Berwick, you could pretty much tell who was who at a moment like this, Cassie thought. The flannels and flip-flops and oversize pajama shirts of the stay-in studiers, the careful eyeliner and cleavage of the ones who planned a night prowling the bars of Mountville Street.

Not one of them, Cassie thought, carried the baggage she did. Of conscience, and a haunting decision. Mom always said if you told the truth and were sincerely sorry, then everything would be forgiven. Wrong.

She tied her robe belt tighter around her waist and tucked the lapels up under her neck, high as she could. Seventeen girls lived on Alcott Three now, since that Boston girl had bolted. They'd made a two-ringed semicircle around Rajit, who, clipboard in hand, stood in front of the shiny closed doors of the middle elevator.

"Ladies?" Rajit surveyed her charges, pointing her black pen at each of them, counting. "Good, seventeen. I need your full attention. In the back? Karen?

Hannah? You two want to hold your private conversation for later, please?"

With a murmur of sheepish assent, the students shifted positions in the too-small area, some with arms crossed, others with fingers absently twisting strands of hair. Third-floor Alcott was all freshmen, away from home for barely two months.

Cassie had chosen a spot farthest on the end, positioned herself behind Marianne. Cassie needed a barrier. Needed to hide her expression, if she had to. This meeting was probably about some new transgression, or new rule, or even about what happened at Wharton Hall, though the campus paper was reporting the police and the gas company had decided the explosion was an accident. Cassie yearned to be alone. To think about what—if anything—to do about Jem.

"So, ladies." Rajit tapped the edge of the clipboard against her chin. "Let me assure you, first, there's nothing to be afraid of."

"Afraid of?" a voice near the window almost yelped.

"Shh," someone else whispered. "Let her talk."

"Yikes." Marianne took a step back as if fear had pushed her into Cassie, who stumbled backward, off balance. "Oh, sorry, Cass," she said.

Cassie made herself even smaller.

"Berwick officials have asked me to inform you that—" Rajit consulted her clipboard, took a deep breath, then continued. "One of our community has been found unresponsive in their off-campus apartment. Law enforcement officials and campus authorities are now investigating the circumstances under which—"

"Raj? Was it drugs? Bad drugs?" The voice came from down the line, Cassie couldn't see who.

"Like an overdose?" someone added.

"If you'll let me finish, please." Rajit glared them

into silence. Checked her clipboard again. "Circumstances under which this student was found."

"Are they *dead*?"

"Dead?"

"Someone's dead? Who's dead?"

Their muddle of voices blossomed into a cloud of curiosity and concern. Cassie could almost feel the loops of fear tightening around her. *Dead?*

Rajit went on as if no one had interrupted. "Officials assure you that you are not in danger. You have no reason to be afraid. Elizabeth, you inquired, rather quickly, about bad drugs." The RA eyed the student who'd spoken up. "If you have any information about such things, I'd ask you to come to my office immediately after this session. You've signed an honor code, as you know, Elizabeth, and I find your question disturbing. If there's something you'd like to report—"

"No, no." Elizabeth waved both palms in front of her as if wiping away the subject. "I only wondered."

Rajit clicked her ballpoint, wrote something on the clipboard.

Cassie almost felt the weight of Rajit's gaze as it landed on her, for half a beat too long? This was Jem, it had to be about Jem, there was no way it wasn't. But she couldn't ask, couldn't even let it be known that she knew him. A flicker of hope tried to struggle to the surface. Maybe this was about someone else?

"So," Rajit went on. "I am asked by campus and law enforcement officials to let you know that if you have any information about a person named Jeremy Duggan—"

And there it was, there was no papering it over, no hiding from it, no hoping, no more bargaining with the universe. When Marianne turned to look at her, eyes wide, Cassie tried to return her surprised look in

kind, as if this were just as baffling or coincidental as
Marianne thought it was.

The murmurs again, the whispers.

"Wasn't he the one who—?"

"The guy in the explosion, right?"

"He's in the hospital, though, isn't he?"

Cassie's mind felt flat, like someone had erased the
whiteboard of her lies. What had she told Marianne
about Jem? Marianne, ditz though she appeared, had
a ridiculously good memory, even remembered Jem's
name from the newspaper, must have, because Cassie
was pretty sure she herself had never mentioned it.
It had been more than two hours since she'd left his
apartment. Whoever he'd asked to come help him—
that's who'd found him.

As Rajit hushed the students again, Cassie had taken
herself back to that apartment, tweed and leather, to
the darkening forest out the window, to the sound of
the tap water flowing into the nubby blue glass, to the
cool feel of the glass full of pink wine. To the baggies in
the cabinet. To Jem, talking on the phone to someone.

She'd worried that Jem had specifically told his
friend her name. That possibility, the frustratingly un-
knowable possibility, was the one thing that linked
her to him.

"Information about a person named Jeremy Duggan," Rajit repeated, her voice pitched over the
murmuring whispers, "or what he might have been
involved with in his apartment, or elsewhere, or if you
know anyone who might know something relevant—"
Rajit's eyes swept across the women who were listening, rapt, focused.

Cassie could almost hear her dorm-mates' thinking.
Did they know him? Did they know anyone who knew
him? She could totally hear Marianne's brain at work.

"You are asked to contact campus officials. Or come
to me. All discussions will stay confidential."

The elevator light pinged over Rajit's head again, and the familiar sound seemed to punctuate the realization that had just connected in Cassie's mind.

If Jem's friend, whoever that was, the one who'd come to take care of him and found him dead—he was dead, and no way to talk herself out of that—if Jem's friend knew she had been in that apartment, there would have been no "informational" meeting in this elevator hallway.

If Jem's friend knew her whole name, that she was Cassie Atwood, then the police would have come to find her.

But they hadn't.

Maybe she was free.

CHAPTER 36

LILY

Banning did not look at her. Keeping his eyes on the road ahead, he plucked his phone from the car's center console and handed it to her.

Lily accepted it, curious. "The screen is black," she said.

"Tap it," Banning instructed.

Lily touched the dark screen with one finger, and a photo appeared. Black and white, a screenshot from a newspaper. She used her thumb and forefinger to expand it, focusing on the block-lettered headline, though it was now so close up it only allowed her to read a few words at a time.

Local, she read. Detective. Fatal crash. She looked at Banning, who seemed to be hyper-focused on driving. She returned to the screen, scrolling down, skimming. Scrolled up again. "Local detective succumbs after fatal crash," she said out loud. "This is in the Berwick paper. About that detective, Kirkhalter." She stared at the screen, reading as she did. "Crash still under investigation, lead detective in the Cassie Atwood—'disappearance,' it calls it."

"Keep reading," Banning instructed.

"But I know this," she said. "I've read every article and every—"

"Humor me." Banning clicked on his turn signal and steered toward a stone-sided bridge over what Lily knew was a narrow estuary of the Charles River, today lined with redwood picnic tables, benches now empty, and with a lone figure holding a fishing pole, rubber boots ankle-deep in the water, poised at the bank's edge. The tips of slender marsh grass barely touched the surface, bobbing away as the breeze ruffled them, and a single green-headed mallard glided away, keeping his distance from the fisherman. A shield-shaped metal sign on a bright blue pole welcomed them to Watertown.

As they crossed the bridge, Lily focused back on the little screen, which had darkened again as she got her bearings. *Watertown,* she thought. *Why are we here?* Greer had been "gone" for three hours now. And Lily still didn't understand what "gone" meant. Plus, no officials had contacted her in search of her "missing" producer—no station management, no colleagues, no real Boston police detectives. But not Greer herself, either. Still, Banning hadn't answered any of her other questions, so she figured he wouldn't start now. She tapped the screen again.

"Retired from the force," she said, skimming as she read it out loud. "One sensational story in his thirty-some years on the job, the still-unsolved Cassie Atwood case. No apparent cause of the—listen. I know this, Banning."

He drifted through an octagonal stop sign and turned left onto an even narrower street. "Keep reading."

"Services, donations. Detective Kirkhalter leaves a wife, the former Sandra Wyzeck, and a son—"

"There you go," Banning interrupted.

Lily stopped. Stared at the screen. "Walter Banning Kirkhalter Jr." She read the name, then looked at Banning. Then back at the screen. "You're kidding me."

"Nope. Yup." Banning looked almost sheepish. "You can still call me Banning. My mother did, though it's really my middle name. To her, the only Walt was my dad. I was still a part-time student at the time he was a Berwick town cop."

Lily pursed her lips, trying to calculate.

"Are you saying—you were at Berwick College?" Lily waved his statement out the car window. "Come on."

"Not *with* your sister, if that's what you're thinking." Banning shook his head. "I always wanted to be a detective, too, but Dad told me . . ." He shrugged, seemed to be remembering. "Over his dead body. His words. We say things like that, you know, offhand. It's only an expression. Until it's reality."

Lily, eyes on Banning and watching his expression change, remembered what Cassie had said to her. Cassie had told her she loved her. That was reality. And it wasn't a dream.

When Cassie vanished, Lily had been about Rowen's age. Those sweet and formative years when every experience may be the one that changes you forever. Cassie had changed her, that was certain.

And Rowen. Her trusting and sensitive little girl, who at seven hadn't grown out of stuffed penguins and hair ribbons, and who still willingly snuggled with her under Gramma Lily's pastel crocheted afghan, and slept with Cassie's Penny. Rowen would become a teenager, in the blink of an eye, with intent, and passions, and what might happen to her? She'd be seventeen, eighteen, someday, and go off to college. And then what? Lily had not explained Cassie's story to Rowen—how could she, when she didn't understand it herself?

So Detective Kirkhalter was Banning's father. Lily's mind raced ahead. That's why he was here. He knew something about Cassie.

He seemed to be heading into the residential part of Watertown, a warren of twisty streets and well-kept houses. Many, she saw, with manicured forsythia bushes, the last of their yellow holding on in a losing battle against summer, and some with scatters of crocuses lining paved driveways.

Detective succumbs, Lily silently read the headline again. "I'm so sorry. I'd somehow gotten the impression that he'd died instantly," Lily said.

"No," Banning said. "Might as well have, though."

"I'm sorry," Lily had to say again.

"Yeah. Before he died, though, before the crash? He told me about your visit."

"He did?" Lily wondered what he might have said, whether he'd regretted how unpleasant he'd had been to her, how cynical and dismissive. Banning, *Smith,* she remembered, or whatever his name was, was lurching toward a point. And she did not want to derail his intentions. He knew about Greer. And Cassie.

"He felt bad about it," Banning went on. "He knew you were upset. It was hard for him to talk about that case. He'd initially been gung ho, he'd find the bad guy, get justice for Cassie, all the things cops say, and then at some point . . ." His voice trailed off. "My dad had his secrets, police business, he'd say, and we were taught to respect that, not ask questions. But I knew he looked—changed."

"By what?"

"But later," Banning went on, continuing to ignore her, "he told me that when he saw you, it all came back. His, I don't know, failure. He never said that word, but that's what everyone thought. Failure. He hated it. The scrutiny and the second-guessing. I used to go to the hardware store with him, places like that. Everyone knew him, and they'd always be offering him their theories. Where he should have looked, people he should have talked to. Small-town detective with a small-potatoes career, and then the one big case. And he blows it."

Lily took a deep breath. Stared at her feet. Reality still stung, no matter who was upset or disappointed. Kirkhalter had failed at his job, and she'd called him on it, and what's true was true. He should have found Cassie. A *good* detective would have found her. No point in saying that now.

"Hey," she said, looking up. Corner of Sycamore and Hamilton. "Where are we?"

Banning was steering the car into a carefully paved driveway, lined with the glossy leaves of what would soon be tulips. A modest white split-level on the corner, with a red door and closed white shutters, manicured lawn, and a twisty-branch Japanese maple in the farthest corner, its pale green leaves rearranging themselves in the afternoon's golden sun.

"My house," Banning said. He reached behind the visor, pulled out a garage door opener. When he clicked it, one side of the two-door garage began to clank open.

Banning's phone, she thought, remembering what was in her hand. She had Banning's phone. As he eased the car into the darkened garage, she tapped the screen again, making the newspaper article appear.

But as the car came to a halt, a shaft of light slashed through the gloomy garage. A door from inside the house had opened. And in the narrow doorway, a shadowed figure edged by an orange halo of incandescent lighting raised a hand in greeting.

Lily squinted.

The woman was coming toward her.

Waving.

Smiling.

BEFORE

CHAPTER 37

CASSIE

She'd thought it would be easier than this. Cassie zipped her black jacket closer around her neck, stuffed her gloved hands into her pockets, and kept her head down against the gathering December evening, crossing the snow-dusted quad on her way back to her dorm. She felt the safest out here, in public but alone, surrounded by classmates whose baggage consisted of nothing but textbooks and midterms and who'd gotten busted. She'd tried to participate, fit in, stay cool, but it was as if the universe were tormenting her. At every turn, someone or something—some fragrance or remark—twisted the knife in her conscience.

Marianne had a knife of her own. Her clingy roommate insisted on discussing Jem so endlessly that Cassie, plagued with nightmares about being chased and then trapped, had yearned to ask her to stop. But she couldn't. She had to make sure Marianne told her everything she heard. Marianne could provide another set of eyes and ears.

A few nights ago, they'd both gotten ready to sleep, and Marianne had propped herself on one elbow to face Cassie across the narrow braided rug between their matching twin beds, her pink-and-green comforter almost colorless in the late-night gloom. When they moved in that first day, Marianne had pushed to have their comforters match. *Super-cute,* she'd said, but super-cute was the last thing Cassie wanted. In the just-past-midnight dark, with the rumble of someone's CD playing down the hall, Marianne had brought up Jem once again.

"So, Cass? One more thing about Jem Duggan?" Marianne's voice was just louder than a whisper, as if that would be less annoying to someone who was trying to sleep.

Cassie had pulled her dark green blanket up to her nose, wishing she could get out of the conversation. But if Marianne had information, or was nosing around someone who did, Cassie couldn't afford not to hear about it. She closed her eyes, trying to keep a balance. Every time she did that, though, she saw Jem and his dark hair, and smelled that pink wine. When she opened her eyes, Marianne was staring at her.

"Cass? Are you asleep?"

Which had to be the stupidest question in the world.

"No." Cassie tried to keep the emotion out of her voice, needing Marianne to believe there was absolutely nothing wrong. Nothing like the emotional residue of a harrowing experience and the deep yearning for the dark safety of sleep. "What about him? Did you hear anything?"

"I don't mean to upset you, I really don't, but, like, you said you didn't have any kind of connection with him, Jem, I mean, I know that, but I was talking to Lyssa down the hall, and she said she'd seen you, that very day. She thought you didn't remember her name, but she knew yours. She was kinda pissed off, that's why she remembered. She even saw you talking to him. Jem. Like you were flirting with him."

"Flirting with—" Oh god, she had been. She thought about that moment and how annoyed she'd been that he was there. That bitch Lyssa. Had nothing better to do? But it all seemed so long ago now, and so pitiful.

"Oh, so funny. Flirting? That's so lame. I mean— yeah, he was there, at Wharton, that day. I guess I forgot about it. Did she say anything else? Lyssa?"

"No, I guess, just that you were talking to him. And she thought you two were hitting it off."

"Huh." Cassie gathered all her energy and propped her own head on her hand, looking back at Marianne as if she'd just had a revelation. "You think they had a thing? She was, like, *watching* him? And jealous?"

"Do *you*?"

Even in the gloom, Cassie could see Marianne's eyes widening. It was a random thing to say, but whatever.

"Oh, it's all so boring," Cassie replied. "So high school. Don't you think? Let's sleep."

She'd needed to keep her roommate close, too, to make sure she didn't inadvertently come across some tidbit of a lie that Cassie had woven and forgotten. Marianne loved to trip her up, to remind her of things she'd said offhandedly about herself, as if the girl were keeping some file of Cassie's history in her head, ready to correct her about her own life at a moment's notice. That was one good thing about having a roommate, about having no privacy. When you wanted to know about the other, it was easier if you were already joined at the hip.

Marianne, Cassie knew, wasn't hiding anything. Nothing worrisome was in her roomie's dresser drawers or under her mattress or in the pockets of the clothing hanging on her side of the closet. Nothing in her notebooks either, or in the diary stashed flat against the wall and then hidden by a row of Marianne's philosophy textbooks. What was in Marianne's head, though, that's what scared her. Why she had to stay vigilant.

Now, classes over for the day, she yanked open Alcott Hall's heavy wooden door, hoping Marianne was out with friends or studying somewhere and she could have more time by herself. Christmas vacation was coming, at least. She'd look at her calendar, and try to focus on studying. And try to plan.

But no. Marianne was sitting at her desk. Instead of having a book propped in front of her, she had a little swivel mirror.

"Oh, cool, perfect." Marianne didn't look up as Cassie entered, but focused on her own reflection as she drew a careful line along the edge of her eyelid with a streak of kohl. "There's a party. In—" She looked at the wooden clock radio on her nightstand. "Two hours. This girl's having it at her house. Her parents are in New York or something."

"Have fun," Cassie said. "Don't get caught, though. At her house? She's a townie? Isn't that kind of . . ." She let her voice trail off, letting Marianne fill in her own pejorative.

"She's cool. It'll be cool. Everyone's going. You have to come," Marianne said. "It'll be fun." She'd barely taken her eyes off her little makeup mirror, watching Cassie behind her and now applying mascara from a pink tube at the same time.

Plain-Jane Marianne had latched onto the idea of makeup from somewhere, maybe from Cassie herself, and now applied it with care and growing expertise. Transforming herself, Cassie thought. Almost as if she'd watched Cassie, learning from her, following her lead, creating a new version of herself in Cassie's image.

Marianne, mascara wand in midair, turned to face her. "Hey. Have you heard anything about Professor Shaw? Any news?"

And that was exactly the conversation she did not want to have, not even with herself, because no, she hadn't heard anything. Or even if he was still in the hospital, really. He hadn't been in class, and no one seemed to know where he was. No one said so, at least. Some new biology professor had shown up, and she'd just told them Professor Shaw was "on leave." When he returned, she'd have to make sure he remembered it was *his* idea that the two of them hang back. When the alarm bell rang that morning, he'd looked at her, significantly, telegraphing that he'd wanted her to wait for him. Something like that. She kind of remembered that. But she needed to keep that whole situation to herself.

"Huh?" Answering Marianne, she pretended she was trying to remember who Professor Shaw was. "Oh, yeah, no, I'm sure we'll hear when the time comes. But so, this party? The girl's parents are gone?"

So then she'd had to go to the thing, just to keep the subject changed. Wearing matching jeans and black puffer vests and dark hunter's plaid mufflers—Marianne had gotten hers about thirty seconds after she saw Cassie's and there was nothing she could do about it and it wasn't like she could stop wearing hers just because Marianne copied her—they'd traipsed across the snow-blanketed campus, across the "us and them" line of Concannon Street, which meant they were off campus and into the town of Berwick. Stars scattered across the inky sky, so vast and so distant, Cassie thought as they walked, and she wished she could be as far away as they were, as hard and safe as they were, and not haunted, every second, by who might know what and what might happen next.

She'd made a calendar of it, secretly, on the inside of her main notebook. Every day that passed after Jem—*after Jem*—she'd crossed it off, counting her days of freedom.

When she put an X on the day, as close to midnight as she could, she took a moment to thank whoever that she had survived yet again, with no sirens and no phone calls and no flinty-eyed detectives interrogating her about where she'd been and what she'd done. What she'd gotten away with. She didn't think of it that way, of course, because she hadn't actually done anything at Jem's. It would just look like she had.

That reporter at the hospital, though, Tosca something. Manukian. Cassie had read her stories in the *Berwick Journal* about the fire and the explosion and the investigation, but unless she'd missed it, Tosca hadn't interviewed anyone who'd mentioned Cassie. Maybe that whole thing was over? Maybe this Tosca was on to the next big story?

A chill rippled the back of Cassie's neck, and it wasn't the darkening night or the damp of the unexpectedly early snow. She remembered the day after Jem's death, how the story had made big headlines in the *U-News,* how she'd grabbed for it, folding the school newspaper in quarters to read it quickly and ducking into the bathroom so she could have some privacy as she skimmed the printed words for her name. The articles went on and on, all about how deeply sad it was, how ironic, that the person who'd been so valiant that he'd risked his life to go back into the building and apparently try to save Professor Shaw seemed to have succumbed as a result of the concussion he'd received as he failed in his "brave mission." It didn't mention family, and officials were only "offering their deepest sympathies."

But not one of the articles mentioned her.

Good, Cassie thought. But even as she'd been relieved, she'd also harbored one dark and ugly question. The one that kept torturing her. How did this reporter Tosca know Jem had gone in specifically to get Professor Shaw? Only she, Cassie, knew that. There had been just the two of them in that conversation. Jem was the only one who could have told someone his goals. And it would have been so easy for him to mention her name. There'd be no reason not to.

She imagined the interview, Tosca interrogating Jem, him still in his hospital bed, maybe medicated. *Why did you try to go back inside?* the reporter would have asked him. *To rescue Professor Shaw,* he'd said. Then the reporter—or nurse, or doctor, or relative—would ask, *Who told you he was still inside?*

And her name, Cassie Atwood, was the only answer.

What if that reporter started looking for Cassie Atwood? And then, of course, Tosca Manukian the reporter would recognize her as the same person who'd been in that hospital waiting room. And there would be the connection. Zachary Shaw, Jem Duggan, Cassie Atwood. All Cassie had wanted was to go to college, and have a cool, fun, popular college life, and now look. She was screwed, and it wasn't her fault. She walked, head down, hands jammed hard into her pockets, as if to keep herself earthbound.

And holy crap, she'd been sitting with Jem in the hospital waiting room. Talking with him. She'd even said something so loudly that people had looked at them! Shushed them! Anyone could have seen them, told someone, who then told someone, who then told someone else. And they'd put it all together and they'd come right after her.

Those tiny moments, those little things that don't mean anything at the time, or mean something else at the time, they all seemed to be tangling together into one big, horrible decision, and she was only eighteen, and how was she supposed to know any damn thing?

It felt like everyone in the world would soon be looking for her. Like that reporter. Tosca Manukian. What would happen when she found her?

"What's wrong?" Marianne asked.

Cassie brought herself back to the present, to the cold night, the silent streets, the sounds of their footsteps in the cracking glaze of hardening snow. "Wrong?"

"You kind of moaned," Marianne said.

"No, I didn't." Cassie had, maybe, made a tiny sound. Her stomach hurt, and everything hurt.

"Sure." Marianne stopped under a glowing streetlight, pulled a piece of notebook paper from her pocket, consulted it. "We're almost there, I think." She looked up from the directions. "Seriously. You okay?"

"Why wouldn't I be?"

"Geez," Marianne said. "You're fun."

Tosca Manukian. Cassie stared into the night. Reporters like her only wanted to ruin people's lives. To take things that weren't true and make them seem true, or seem to be on purpose, or write stories that were totally wrong, only to get headlines. At the hospital, Tosca Manukian had asked about Professor Shaw's condition, specifically, and then asked her, Cassie, if she'd been there at the time of the explosion.

"Cass?" Marianne's voice sounded accusatory. "Honestly. You made that sound again, and don't tell me you didn't."

"Sorry." Cassie wrapped her muffler more tightly around her neck. "I keep stepping on rocks or something."

Marianne must have been talking, and Cassie'd forgotten to listen. Circles of orange from the streetlights dotted the piles of shoveled snow that lined the narrow sidewalks, and she saw her own breath puff white as she spoke.

They'd reached an intersection, square-fronted homes with pointed snowcapped roofs, each with one triangular pine tree in the front yard. The street showed rutted tire tracks where brave drivers had persevered through unplowed streets. Cassie eyed the sky again, her stars now beginning to vanish randomly in the gathering clouds, their light erased by relentless dark. "Just thinking about how cold it is. Are we almost there?"

"It says 19 Ardella Street. This is Ardella." Marianne stopped, waved the paper she'd pulled from her pocket. She pointed to a green street sign, just readable in the streetlight glow. "You see nineteen?"

They both peered one way up the street, then the other.

"I can't see any numbers," Cassie said.

"Or kids, right?" Marianne tilted her head as if considering. "Kind of weird. You'd think . . . oh, crap, are we too early?" She looked at Cassie, eyes wide, hugging herself with flannel arms. "Are we like, lamely too early? Are we idiots?"

"It's after ten," Cassie said. "How can that be early?"

"I guess so." Marianne shrugged, acquiescing. She pointed to their right. "I see lights on down there. Let's try that."

Cassie heard a car slushing up behind them, its tires hissing in the icy mix on the pavement, headlights grazing the gray street.

Marianne stepped off the sidewalk.

The car was coming fast. In the dark, and the snow. And Marianne in that black vest and dark flannel. She grabbed her roommate's arm. Yanked it. Hard.

"Car!" she said. "Watch it!"

Marianne flinched, twisted, tried to take a step backward, but one booted foot slipped off the snowy curb. She landed, rear first, in the dank slush along the gutter.

"Ow!" she yelled, flailing her arms to regain her balance.

Cassie leaned down, offered a hand. "Oh, I am *so* sorry! You okay?"

"So stupid." Marianne waved her off. "My whole ass is wet. Now we can't even . . ."

"Girls?" The low voice came from the car. A man.

His car had stopped beside them, and as Cassie turned, she saw who was inside. She thought of the black marks she'd put on her calendar. Wondered if yesterday was the last day she'd make one.

Wondered if her time had run out.

"Girls?" The police officer had pulled his cruiser to a stop, hazard lights flashing, and aimed his flashlight at them through the open driver's-side window, its powerful beam alternating between Marianne and Cassie, who took a step backward, trying to put as much distance as she could between herself and this intruder.

The yellow beam landed on Marianne. "You all right, miss?"

"Yeah." Marianne puffed out a white breath. "Just tripped. All good."

The beam crossed the gloomy half-dark, landed on Cassie. She could almost feel the heat from the too-bright bulb, as if it were searing through her, then blinked, startled when the light shone on her face. She tried to look pleasant, and natural, but she couldn't help wincing in the glare. She put her fingers to her forehead, shielding her eyes.

The police officer lowered his light. Clicked open his door. There was not another vehicle on the road, not a sound in the snow-wrapped neighborhood, not a dog barking as the officer got out of his car. A squawk came from the radio inside the cruiser, muffled and garbled, words encased in static. Cassie saw flashing lights on the dashboard, tiny round ones, red and green and white, as the officer approached them.

"You Berwick students?" he demanded. He'd left his car door open and now stood in front of them, booted feet planted wide apart, looking down at them, no hat on his buzz-cut dark hair. A gold badge attached to a silver chain hung from his neck. He pulled a narrow spiral notebook from the pocket of his thick black bomber jacket. The streetlight glinted on the metal spiral, and he flipped the notebook open. Yanked a pen from a loop on his belt. "Names, please."

NOW

CHAPTER 38

LILY

Greer took the last step from the doorway into the garage and, in one quick motion, pulled open Lily's car door.

"Welcome," she said.

"Welcome? Greer? Welcome? What're you talking about?" Lily, searching Greer's face, felt like someone's mom, a mom who'd been terrified with fear that her daughter had vanished and there was nothing she could do about it, and now, seeing her safe, couldn't decide whether to be enraged or burst into tears of relieved joy. "Greer? Are you okay?"

Greer's smile vanished. "What d'you mean, okay? Of course I am. Why wouldn't I be?"

Banning had opened his car door and unclicked his seat belt. "Come on, you two," he said. "We can talk inside."

Lily didn't budge from the front seat and kept her eyes on Greer, hoping for answers. Looking for signs of coercion, or capture, or complicity. Banning's car door had closed, and she heard his footsteps coming around from behind, leaving her alone inside with her tote bag on her lap and her phone in her hand. She took off her seat belt. The car wasn't going anywhere without Banning in the driver's seat, and she was safer—whatever *safe* meant after all this—being on her own two feet.

"Talk? Inside?" She swiveled on the seat, planting her shoes on the concrete floor, twisting to glare at Banning as he came toward her. "What the hell is going on? I mean—you could have just, say, called me. Without all this drama. Greer?"

"Oh, I know. Yeah, all good." Greer was shaking her head like it was all water under the bridge. She backed toward the open door to the house, gesturing. "Yeah, let's go in. Apologize for all the subterfuge. But there were lots of moving parts."

Lily heard the clang and whir of some mechanism, and the garage door behind them began to lower, changing the light of the garage with every inch it descended. Shelves stacked with unlabeled cardboard boxes lined the garage walls, and the place smelled vaguely of damp and ash. The orange glow from the home's lighted interior seemed to grow brighter as the daylight vanished. How long had Greer been at Banning's house? Since last night?

She got to her feet, wary, slung her bag over her shoulder. Kept her phone in her hand. Kept her car door open, standing behind it like a makeshift barricade.

"Lily, it's fine." Banning now stood next to Greer. "Your producer made me show every damn piece of identification I—"

Lily's phone pinged with a message. Petra. Petra? Rowen was at school, still, at—she looked at the time. Two twenty-three. *You there?* the message said.

"Banning?" Greer said.

Lily still thought of him as Banning, even though she finally knew his real name.

"You need to get that?" Banning asked. "Call someone?"

She tapped a response to Petra. Rowen's class had

gone on a field trip to the aquarium this morning. *Penguins, Mumma!* Rowen had clapped her hands. She'd begged to take her stuffed Penny along. Why would Petra be texting?

Lily glanced at the two of them, then kept her eyes on the screen for Petra's reply. "Let me know when you want to include me in this. Since you abducted me, after all."

If something were really wrong, Petra would have called instead of texting. It had to be nothing. Still. If Lily didn't see an answer in ten seconds, she'd call her.

The garage door landed with a clank, metal on concrete. Lily flinched at the sound of it. Banning and Greer were being pleasant, for whatever that was worth, but there was no ignoring the reality that she was trapped here in this clammy, darkened garage with a guy who'd lied to her from the moment they'd met, and the one person in the world who she'd have predicted never would.

Nothing from Petra yet. "Listen, Smi—Banning," Lily said, "mightn't it have been easier to have the two of you come to the office this morning? Like regular people. Imagine how simple and painless that would have been."

"Did you tell her who you were?" Greer asked.

"After a complete charade outside Lido," Lily answered for him. "Dragging me there, pretending he was investigating your disappearance. When all the while he knew precisely where you were."

"Oh, no, no." Greer was shaking her head. "He didn't. I only texted him a while ago, saying I'd meet him here. What, Lil, you thought I'd been here all night or something?"

"Makes just as much sense as anything does." Lily risked a look up from her cell. "Which is none. I think you're both insane." Lily now stared at Greer and Banning, standing side by side. "And 'insane' is not hyperbole," she went on. "Tell me, right now—"

Lily's phone pinged again. Petra had typed one word. *Flowers.*

Flowers what? Lily typed back.

"Lily?" Banning interrupted her. "It's about Cassie."

"That's what I've been working on," Greer added. "See, I met with Smith—Banning—last night. He made me promise not to tell you."

"I'm sorry, Lily." Banning took over. "I told you in the car, I had to find out how you'd react. I was also trying to protect your sister, and I needed to know how much you'd confided in Greer. Turns out nothing. She knew nothing about Cassie. *I* told her about your sister. Right, Greer?"

"Right," Greer said. "So this morning I was—well, I am so, *so* sorry, but we had to keep it from you. In case it was all a big disappointment. But—"

"I think we can bring her home to you, Lily," Banning said. "If you decide you want that to happen."

"Lily?" Greer put her hand on Lily's arm for one brief moment. "I first thought we could surprise you with her. Do a live reunion show. But first, um, there are some things you need to know. Serious things."

"Cassie's alive?" In the thick gloom of the closed garage, something hissed and settled—an air conditioner kicking on, or water pipes refilling. Lily's world rearranged itself, too, making space for her sister.

"You know where she is?" Lily had to ask. Had to make sure. Had to believe it. "Alive? Where?"

More lilies arrived. Petra's words appeared on Lily's phone screen. *Same kind, from same place.*

It's fine, she typed back, trying to sound normal, trying to keep her brain from catching fire. And if Banning was Smith, sending flowers probably made as much sense as anything else he'd done. She narrowed her eyes, worrying. *Rowen OK?*

All is good.

Lily clicked off her phone, then looked at Banning, then Greer, then back again. They exchanged glances, but didn't answer her.

"Tell me. Now. Cassie's alive? Is that—true? So where is she?" And there was another question, another one that could change their worlds forever. Lily's. Rowen's, too. "And what 'serious things'?"

CHAPTER 39

CASSIE

"Did we do something wrong?" Marianne had answered the police officer before Cassie could decide what to say. Cassie felt herself shrinking away from this almost-menacing guy and his police car, longing to disappear into the snow and the night. She'd stay in the background and let Marianne talk, she decided. Long as Marianne didn't screw up. Why had she ever agreed to come to this party? The police were the last people she wanted to mess with. She pressed her lips together. *No.* If they'd wanted her, she was easy to find. They hadn't come looking for her.

"And where're you two headed?" the officer asked. "On this snowy night?"

The sound of the police car's idling engine, a low grumbling undercurrent, filled the space between them. Cassie couldn't decide if the cop looked suspicious or was genuinely concerned about Marianne's tumble into the slush. He was a real cop, no question about that, with the small shield-shaped Berwick decal on the side of his maybe gray car, hard to tell in the streetlights' glare. It had antennas on top. Plus, it wasn't like he was going to kidnap them, or hurt them, or something. He was just a cop who saw two girls on the street at night, and one of them had fallen. This was random, this was a coincidence.

But she felt so guilty, and she couldn't afford to let that show. Maybe she could distract him.

"My friend fell," Cassie said. "Because I guess she didn't see you coming. I worried you were about to hit her."

The cop raised his eyebrows, looked at them with some expression Cassie couldn't decode. "I saw her fine, miss." His voice was cold as the night. "And I saw you push her."

"What?" Cassie yelped. "No, I didn't!"

"Oh, no, no way, no, she's right, she totally didn't." Marianne's protest overlapped Cassie's. "She tried to help me up. She's my roommate, we're friends."

The police officer nodded slowly as if contemplating their denials. "Fine, then, young ladies. Shall we agree this was an unfortunate series of events, and go from there? I saw you, miss, beginning to cross the street. I was nowhere close to hitting you. But let's start our conversation over, shall we? Like I said, names. And destination."

"I'm Marianne Dawe," she said as if she couldn't acquiesce fast enough. "Alcott Hall."

"Alcott Hall is that way." The officer pointed his right forefinger across his chest. "Not the direction you two were headed." He turned his attention to Cassie. "And you?"

There was no way out of this, but she didn't have to make it easier. "Cassandra Blair Atwood."

"Thank you, Sandy," the officer said.

Cassie didn't correct him. She felt Marianne wanting to chime in, and needed to stop her. If the guy wanted to think of her as Sandy, all good. She kept talking.

"And we were kind of on the way to a friend's house." Cassie tried to look like a cliché of a college freshman, cute and a little baffled. A Berwick town cop, how on top of things could he even be? This was a coincidence. Nothing about Jem Duggan. "It's Friday, so no classes tomorrow, and we were just—"

"On the way to 19 Ardella?" He finished her sentence. "I fear your hostess is in a heap of trouble, young ladies. With us, and with her parents. You have one of the flyers they were handing out?" He held out his hand. "Let's have it."

"I, um." Marianne's hand went to her chest.

"I take that as a yes," the officer said. "You can just toss it when you get back to Alcott. But we arrived long ago and sent everyone home. You're late to the party, young ladies, but you got lucky this time. You weren't there, so it's not going on your record. If you cooperate. So count your blessings." He gestured to his car. "How'd you like a ride back to campus?"

"Cool," Marianne said. She patted one hand along her jeans. "I'm kind of wet, and now kinda cold."

Go back to the dorm in a police car? Cassie tried to decide whether that was a doable thing. But now that Marianne had said she was cold, she'd look like a jerk if she refused.

"Sure," Cassie said, drawing out the word, because she wasn't sure, not really. She didn't want to hang out with a police officer. But she didn't want this on her record. Her mother would kill her.

She and Marianne both slid into the back, coming in from opposite sides. Left the doors open. It felt weird, the hard black plastic seats, and heavy molded plastic mats on the floor. Now she saw there was a fine mesh screen between them and the front. She was sitting there, feeling like a prisoner in this strange car.

The officer was coming toward her open door. He reached out for it, looking right at her.

He closed the door with a jarring metallic thunk. She made herself as small as she could, almost curling up against the driver's-side door. She was invisible. Invisible. She had done nothing wrong.

"Officer?" Marianne had leaned forward, braced her hands against the front. Spoke through the mesh. "Did you work on the Jem Duggan case? Or on the explosion?"

"It's *Detective*," he said. His radio squawked, a blast of static. "And yes, in fact, I did."

Cassie saw his eyes go to his rearview mirror. Connect with Marianne's, then hers, then back to the road. She heard the cruiser's tires slushing on the pavement. Saw the lights of the Berwick campus visible in the far distance. There was no way to get Marianne to shut up.

"Why do you ask?" The detective had reached toward the dashboard, clicked the radio to black silence.

"Well, it was so scary," Marianne said. "Right? I mean, Cassie—"

Cassie closed her eyes. So much for being Sandy.

"—was actually there. In that building where the explosion happened. She was in Professor Shaw's office, even. She got out just in time. Right, Cass?"

This girl was an idiot. Why was she trying to make conversation? To ingratiate herself with the guy? Make sure this episode wasn't on her stupid record? Marianne was *such* an idiot. But what she'd said was true, and it didn't matter, in the real world that Cassie was creating, it didn't matter.

"Uh-huh," she said.

"And," Marianne went on, seemingly enraptured by her own story and super-obviously trying to show what a helpful person she was, "she talked to Jem, you know, right before he went back in to save Professor Shaw. Can you even believe it?"

"Lucky you," the detective said.

"Yeah," Cassie said. She desperately wanted to give Marianne some kind of shut-up signal, but there was no way to be sure this detective wouldn't notice. Seemed like half the time he was watching them instead of the road. "But I went out of the building when the alarms went off, like everyone else."

"So Professor Shaw was still in the building when you came out?"

The detective seemed to be driving more slowly than before.

"I guess so," she said. "I mean, I didn't—"

"Oh, no, Cassie, remember?" Marianne interrupted. She'd perched on the edge of her side of her seat, bracing herself to keep her face close to the mesh barrier as she talked. "You told me you had an appointment. And you came out, then Jem Duggan came out, and then you talked to Jem and you were the one who told him that the professor was still in the building. Remember? And *then* he went back in. To save him. You totally told me that. I totally remember that. It was even in the paper."

"Yeah. Sure." Might as well agree and cut this short. "It's all kind of a blur. I mean, I just happened to be there."

"It was so brave of him, right, Detective?" Marianne had plastered herself against the mesh screen as if it were normal to have such a conversation. She was really laying it on, all drama and performance. "And so incredibly sad now."

"You a particular friend of Jem Duggan?" the detective asked. He'd pulled to a stop sign, kept a foot on the brake, and twisted his head to look at them over his shoulder. "Either of you?"

"Not me," Marianne said. "I've never even—"

"No," Cassie said at the same time.

"But you were both in the building. Cassie? Talked to him, is that correct? Atwood, you said. Cassie Atwood."

"Yes, I guess so. Like, so were fifty other people, in the building, I mean, so I—"

"Of course." The detective took his foot off the brake. "No big deal." The car moved ahead through the almost-deserted neighborhood, where the blue lights of televisions glowed through translucent front curtains, and a lone woman in a long puffy coat followed a lumbering black Great Dane along the narrowly plowed sidewalk path.

The next right would put them back on Mountville, back in college territory. Maybe, Cassie figured, she could somehow get out of the car, say she'd planned to meet friends. Or something. Which would never work. Marianne would definitely not be nimble enough to improvise along with her, and that would make it worse. So far so good, anyway. The detective had asked his questions, they had answered them. She could gut it out until they got to the dorm.

They turned right on Mountville, where, despite the weather, the front doors of the Sand Bar and Outpost were wide open, orange lights radiant inside, and even far away, the fragments of live music escaped into the night. Thank all that's holy, she hadn't gone to the Post with Jem that night. That one wrong choice could have ruined her story. But then—might Jem not have died?

She thought about that for a beat, how every single thing we do, every single decision we make, opens one door and closes others. If they'd been in the restaurant, having burgers, would he have collapsed? And if he had, even if he had, they would have been surrounded by a million people and someone would have called 911 and no way she could have been blamed for any of it. She'd have been a victim, too. And brave. And sympathetic. And good.

Not like now.

She had made the wrong choice.

When would she even learn how the world worked? She was trying to do the right thing, but it never seemed to turn out right. There had to be some way to make up for what happened, to say she was sorry, because she was, she truly was, and she wished she could undo her decision, but she couldn't, but now she could never say so. The moment she explained, or even tried to, her world would crash around her, never to be repaired.

But now was now, and the doors to her past were closed, and if Cassie was going to get out and into the future, this was the time.

The police car continued through the town center, streetlights going by faster now, and then up the hill toward the campus gate, a lofty redbrick arch with curves of dark wrought iron cemented onto mortared stacks of fading smooth stones leading to the rocky cobbles of the main driveway. Closer and closer to Berwick. Closer to her dorm. Closer to freedom. Maybe she should fill the time, not let anyone else talk until they arrived at Alcott's front door. Then she would get out, say goodbye and thank you, and this would be over. Still, though, she'd have to figure out how to get Marianne to keep her mouth shut. Like, forever.

"Thinking about Mr. Duggan, though." The detective's voice from the front seat sounded infinitely casual. "How did you find out what happened to him?"

"Oh, our resident assistant had a big meeting," Marianne said. The car bumped through a pothole, and she lurched forward, one knee hitting the floor. "Ow. Remember, Cass?"

Remember was *all* she did. But Cassie needed to close the door on this. It didn't matter when they'd heard about Jem. This cop was just making conversation. Jem's death was an accident, and everyone agreed, because of his old concussion and then the new one. They said so in the paper.

"I forget," Cassie said. So yeah, forgetting about it was exactly what she would do now. Forget about the whole thing. *No,* she instructed herself. It never happened.

"Cass, come on, you do too remember." Marianne looked at her, wide-eyed. "By the elevators. Rajit made us all attend. Wasn't it, like, the day after they—he—right, Cassie? Or was it that day? The day he actually—"

"I said, I forget."

"Really?" The detective looked over his shoulder at her again, but she was too far into the corner to make eye contact, so she saw only his profile, radiating infinite skepticism. Or maybe just curiosity. "You forget?"

"Well, I guess it was—?" Cassie put a puzzled look on her face, even though he probably couldn't see it, but it was easier to pretend if you felt the part. And Marianne was staring at her. Definitely. "I'm trying to remember. We were all upset, because it seemed so scary."

Now it was her turn to find out stuff. "Officer—I mean, Detective—do you think there *is* something to be afraid of? I mean, like, that they're not telling us?"

"Cassie? No, wait. Seriously. You totally remember." Marianne talked over her again. "It was the same night. Like around, eight? Or nine? Totally. Rajit called us to the elevator, and you were about to take a shower. Because of all that alcohol smell. Remember? You'd just gotten home from the—"

Cassie felt the car's tires rumble over the lattice of snow-edged cobblestones, saw the golden warmth of Berwick's lighted archway. She saw Alcott Hall, so near, and yet, with Marianne's certain next word, so far away.

"Hospital," Marianne said.

NOW

CHAPTER 40

LILY

"Witness protection," Lily said.

Banning nodded. He and Greer sat next to each other on one long side of a rectangular dining room table, half of its glossy glass-topped mahogany covered with stacks of manila file folders. On the pale gray wall behind them, an oversize watercolor of a murky, dark forest, spiky pine trees slashed with a shaft of moonlight.

Lily, twisting a mug of green tea, sat opposite, staring at these unexpected allies, staring at the misty muddle of the watercolor, staring into her past and into her future. Equally muddled. The home—Banning's home, he'd told her, but it didn't feel like a detective's house—smelled of furniture polish and pencils and old paper; those files, she supposed, that appeared to be thick with clippings and papers. As they'd walked her to the dining room, she'd glimpsed a tweedy living room couch and an expanse of organized bookcases, then a burgundy-carpeted stairway to another floor.

Much as she'd protested, they'd pulled out a curved mahogany dining room chair with a jewel-tone upholstered seat and made her sit down. The bay window behind her, curtained with filmy gauze, softened the afternoon sun.

"You know this," Lily said. She felt the heaviness in her voice, the finality. " She's alive. In witness protection." She'd thought of those words in the past, from time to time, but always discarded them. And had never said them out loud. Alive. Witness protection. Protection from what?

"We think so," Banning said.

After an entire day of not answering one thing she'd asked him, Banning had come out with it, with hardly any fanfare, as they'd taken their seats. Lily had peppered him and Greer with demands, nonstop, as they led her into the house. But they'd obviously planned for how and when to tell her, and nothing she could do or say had deterred them.

She'd wondered—worried, actually—whether this was a trap of some kind, or a trick.

But now, here in this suburban dining room, there was nothing to trap or trick her about. These two knew about Cassie. Or said they did.

"I'm listening," she said.

"Well," Banning began.

"Because if she's in witness protection, protected from what? It means she had to be a witness to something. Or part of something illegal," Lily had to interrupt. "I mean, what would that even be? We'd know that, right? And there'd have been a whole investigation."

Lily's mind was going so fast, as if she were a reporter working on a story, that she needed to hurry to the end of whatever sentences Banning was about to say, faster than he could get there. Whatever Cassie had witnessed was not the point. The point was—she was alive. And possibly about to reenter Lily's life. "So whatever happened, you're saying, she's alive. Somewhere. Living as someone else. She could appear at any moment."

Banning nodded.

Greer nodded.

"Not in a cemetery, or a mental institution, or a hospital. Or in prison." All those things had plagued Lily as she'd searched, needing to know, needing to prepare for the worst, hideous bureaucratic dead beginnings or dead ends where no amount of being the famous and persuasive Lily Atwood would make a difference. And since Cassie had changed her name—which of course she had, because there were no Cassie Atwoods that could be her—then there was not even a place for Lily to start, let alone finish.

According to the Berwick police, she was a cold case. A missing person. Presumed dead.

"No," Banning said. "Not any of those places."

Lily spread her hands, entreating. "So then, where? Is there some reason you can't tell me?"

Lily heard a noise, like a thump, or a footstep, coming from—upstairs? Banning and Greer exchanged glances.

"Is she here? Is Cassie here?" Lily's heart fluttered, then pounded, as she almost came out of her seat.

"Oh, Lily, no," Greer said.

"That's my cat," Banning said. "I put her upstairs, but she's not happy."

This time, Lily did come to her feet, planted her palms on the mahogany. "Tell me right now." She used her quietest voice, demanding. "And Greer. What do you have to do with this?"

"Cards on the table," Banning interrupted. "I told you—as Smith—your sister was in danger, didn't I?"

Lily felt like bursting into tears. "Danger. From. What?"

"Let me show you this." Banning turned to the stack of file folders. Each shaped tab was labeled with a colored sticker, the writing on them faded and obscured.

Lily watched as he searched through them, then

tried to catch Greer's eye to see if she could get some
signal about what the hell was going on. But Greer
kept her eyes on Banning.

"Blue label." Greer pointed. "That one."

Banning already had the file open, and pulled out a
white business-size envelope. A name and address on
the front in blocky printing, a plain flag stamp. Ad-
dressed to Detective Walter Kirkhalter at an address
in Berwick, Pennsylvania. *Personal,* it said in bigger
block letters, and underlined. Lily tried to identify the
printing, tried to remember the last time she'd seen
something Cassie wrote, but only recalled a vague
memory of bold strokes and flourishes.

"You recognize this?" Banning held it up.

She shook her head. She wanted to, but she didn't.
Banning lifted the flap of the envelope and drew out
a piece of white paper, folded in thirds. The words on
it were typed, Lily could tell, but impossible to read.

"This is not signed," Banning said, gesturing with
the still-folded paper. "The postmark is generic. It's
from my father's correspondence."

"It is?" Lily frowned. She eyed the stacks of files,
remembering. "But your father told me—he told me
the files on Cassie were gone. Vanished, somehow, after he retired. Which I didn't believe, even then. When
I pushed him on it, he got angry. So you're saying
these are his files? So he lied to me. And what's that
paper?"

The thump came from upstairs again.

Banning's face darkened.

"Banning—" Greer began.

"It's okay." Banning took a deep breath, his dark
eyes flinty. "My father was a good cop, Lily. He was
honest, and reliable, but above all, wanted justice.
Even though sometimes it was his own brand."

"That's the cat, you promise." Lily felt frayed around
the edges, besieged. The possibility that Cassie was up-

stairs made her knees unsteady. That Cassie might come down those carpeted steps made her brain go thin.

"Yes," Banning said. "Cassie's not here. Like I said. But if she were—"

"But she's not."

"She's not. But if she were—well, there's no one else but you who'd recognize her, that's the thing. Corroborate her identity. Especially if she wanted to hide it. No one else who might know things that only Cassie would know. If we ask her, and she denies it, there's no way to prove it."

"We?" Lily searched their faces, but both were looking at her without expression. "Who's we? And *if*? So you're not sure."

"Everyone else who knew her as Cassie is long gone or dead," Banning went on. "Your mother. Your grandmother. The few people she knew in college—they can't help."

"She's been gone for more than twenty years, Lily," Greer said. "She was at Berwick for—not for very long."

Lily pressed her lips together, thinking of family, and loss, and how the only reason families stayed families, stayed in touch, was that they wanted to. If they didn't, the bonds were easily broken, relationships ignored, memories forgotten. Family became a random coincidence of genetics, mutated by time and distance and desire.

"Eighty-three days," Lily said. She envisioned Cassie's calendar in that spiral notebook. The crossed-off days. She and her mom had counted them and calculated with them, wondering what Cassie was waiting for. "She had a calen—never mind. So why do you think she's in witness protection? What's the letter? And *are* those your father's files, Banning? Why did he tell me they were gone?"

"I know what he told you," Banning said. "He

explained it to me—your visit, and your questions, and your persistence. But I, like everyone else, thought your sister's case defeated him. And when his files went missing—"

"Did he think someone was interfering with the investigation?" Lily interrupted.

"He never spoke of it again. Where she was. Why he'd stopped looking. No matter how often I asked. But I had to find out exactly what happened to her. Kind of why I became a detective. Then after my father died, this letter arrived."

He held it up again.

"We were all distracted, and the unopened mail piled up, and my mother—" He handed it to her. "We didn't find it until later."

Lily flapped open the top, then the bottom. No date, no signature. The words were typed in the middle of the page.

Thank you so much, the letter said. *You have given me a perfect life. And I am grateful for it every day. But I want to be me again. And I miss my little sister. Watching her is not enough. Is it finally safe now? Let me know. I want to come home.*

CHAPTER 41

CASSIE

Cassie stared at her own hands, fingers interlaced, clenched in front of her on a long rectangular table. She sat, alone, in a metal folding chair in a window-less room at the Berwick police station, her puffer vest draped around her. It was too chilly in here to take it off, but too stifling with it on. Strips of fluorescent lights buzzed above her, and an empty chair waited across the table. Someone had tried to soften the room, unsuccessfully, by sticking a tilty plastic ficus in one corner. She'd taken a chance coming here, understanding it was risky, understanding the stakes. And now there was no turning back.

Hospital. Marianne had said that word just as they'd turned onto Berwick's cobblestoned driveway. Cassie hadn't responded. Neither had the detective. Cassie thought she'd seen the detective's shoulders stiffen as he steered them farther into the campus. But he'd said nothing, not a word in response, and driven in silence up to the front doors of Alcott Hall. Maybe he didn't hear her say it, Cassie had hoped. Or didn't care. Maybe it didn't matter. Maybe she'd worried about nothing, and she'd get out of the back seat and never see this person again.

The detective had stopped the car, kept the engine running, shifted into park.

"Thank you," Marianne had said, "so much. It's incredibly cold, and I'd probably have gotten the flu or something if . . ." She'd rattled at the handle of her door. It didn't open.

Cassie did the same thing. Her door didn't work either. She kept her hand on the molded plastic.

"I control the back doors." The detective had sounded congenial, even amused. "Don't want the bad guys getting away, right?"

Something clicked, and Marianne's door unlocked. Cassie's didn't.

"Can you un—" Cassie began.

"Ms. Atwood will join you in a moment," the detective told Marianne. He pushed something, and the grated screen between them purred down, leaving the space between the front and back seats open. "I have a question or two for Cassie."

He twisted his body to look at her, one jacketed elbow bent over the curve of the front. A blast of cold hit Cassie from Marianne's open door, and the distance of sidewalk between her and her dorm's front entryway seemed as far as the moon.

Hospital, Marianne had said. Cassie could almost hear the dominoes falling.

"Cool." Marianne turned, bent her head back inside of the cruiser. "Questions because she was at the explosion thing, right? And knew Professor Shaw?"

"Something like that." The detective pointed at Marianne. "Can you close that, please? Getting chilly in here. The heater can't compete."

Cassie tried her door again, expecting nothing, got nothing, and winced as Marianne's door slammed closed. She watched her roommate stride up the front walk, then turn, smiling in the lamplight, to give her a last finger-flutter of a wave before she went inside to innocent safety. Cassie, heart sinking, had given up on the door handle, and sat as deep into the corner of the back seat as she could. This would be a turning point, she knew it. That one word, *hospital,* had given everything away. There would be no more cross-outs on her calendar. She'd been free, but that was all over.

She'd been in the freezing back seat of a police car, with a detective who was only pretending to be nice. She'd seen drugs. She'd left a man, unconscious, without even calling for help. He'd died, and she could have saved him. But she hadn't. She'd had her chance, been smart, and made herself pretty, and worked hard to get where she was. And now—after that one tiny word from her oblivious roommate—it would all come out. She'd destroyed her own life along with Jem's.

She wondered if there'd be a trial. How she'd pay for a lawyer. She wondered what jail was like. Her mother would pretend to be sympathetic, but no matter what Cassie said, or how she tried to explain, Mumma would never truly believe her. And Lily. Lily, little innocent Lillow, would grow up with a sister in prison.

"My name is Walt Kirkhalter," the detective had introduced himself in the car. "Detective Kirkhalter."

"Hi," she'd said, ridiculously. She was eighteen, so she guessed he could talk to her without her parents and ask her stuff. There must be rules, but she didn't know them.

Kirkhalter shifted in his seat, apparently trying to see her. He unclicked his seat belt. Turned to face her. "It's difficult to talk like this, Ms. Atwood, with you over on that side. And no need to cringe away from me. You can leave the car at any time. Would you like to go inside the dorm? I'm happy to come back. Stop by and see you at your convenience."

"That's okay." Come *back*? The *police*? To her *dorm*? No, thank you. She undid her own seat belt and scooted over to the middle of the back seat, compromising. Put a cooperative look on her face. "You said you had questions?"

The rumble of the engine and the whir of the heater filled the space between them. Kirkhalter buzzed down his window, just a crack, letting in a sliver of the night. Through her own window, Cassie saw dark shadows move across the campus paths, silhouettes of students in pairs or packs, randomly illuminated by the ranks of gaslights lining the walkways. Cassie heard a peal of laughter. It felt like she would never laugh again.

"We would have found you, you know." Kirkhalter broke their silence. "I'll give it to you straight. Jeremy Duggan's building has a pretty suspicious super, lives on the ground floor. And this guy, well . . ." Kirkhalter shook his head as if amused. "Some people, you know? Don't have enough to do. Anyway. He does a lot of watching. He saw you go in with Mr. Duggan. The Friday he died. And then he saw you come out. Alone."

"He saw me?" Cassie, frowning, tried to envision it, remembered a wrought iron fence with—maybe—basement windows below. She didn't remember windows. But she didn't remember no windows. Now it was almost too late to deny it. "Um, it was Jem's apartment, so he lived there, so of course he wouldn't come out. Wait. How did he know it was *me,* though?"

Kirkhalter scratched the side of his forehead with one finger. "He didn't actually, Ms. Atwood. But you just confirmed it."

Cassie's cheeks burned, she felt the heat in her face, and somehow a chill at the same time. "You just lied to me?"

"That's called being a detective, Ms. Atwood. If I'd asked whether you'd been with Jeremy Duggan that night, what would you have told me?"

"I would have told you the truth." Cassie lifted her chin. This had to be unfair. "I always tell the truth."

"Good. That makes things a lot easier. I appreciate it."

Cassie mentally edited her story, changed it, shortened it. Reimagined it, the way it needed to have happened. She'd met Jem on Mountville Street, just randomly, everyone was on Mountville on Fridays. She'd seen his bandage, asked about it, like anyone would, he'd been in the school paper, after all, and she'd walked him home like anyone would have, dropped him off, left. Some stupid super couldn't know how long she'd been there. Unless he kept some kind of timetable, which no one would.

"And your roommate confirmed you'd been at the hospital."

The hospital thing. He *had* heard Marianne, and that made it more complicated. What if—

"Just so you don't have to decide what to say," Kirkhalter went on. "We'd checked the hospital to see if Professor Shaw had any visitors while he was there. Do you remember a receptionist, name of Sarita?"

If she remembered the receptionist, then she'd been there. "Why?" she asked.

"So much for the truth." Kirkhalter reached out, turned a dial on the dashboard. The radio's row of pin dot lights cycled on again, flashing a row of white, then red, then green. A squawk of static announced a successful connection.

"So, Ms. Atwood. Your decision here. You can get out." He'd pointed toward the dorm. "You can do what you want, pull your story together, call your parents, whatever. You could try to run, which I highly discourage. Trust me, you would not get far on your own, and it'd merely make matters worse when we found you and brought you back. Nothing says guilty like running away. So here are your choices. You can talk to me, here in the back of this cold, uncomfortable police car in plain sight of everyone. Or we can go back to the station."

Cassie knew what to say, knew it from *Law & Order* and from everything. "Do I need a lawyer?"

"Do you?" He lifted an eyebrow.

Crap, maybe she had put that wrong. Now she had to say she didn't. And what if that wasn't true? What if she did need a lawyer? He was twisting her words, and it wasn't fair. Cassie winced at a sound, startled, but it was the campus clock tower bells chiming the hour. They'd ring ten times, she knew. She almost laughed. *For Whom the Bell Tolls,* they were reading that in English class now. "It tolls for thee," the poem said.

"Look, Ms.—Cassie." He smiled, and Cassie couldn't tell what he was thinking. He wasn't that old, but, like, early forties. And she guessed he seemed nice enough, in a someone's older-brother kind of way.

"I know you're worried about what happened to your friend Jem Duggan."

"He wasn't my—"

"And you were in Zachary Shaw's biology class. I know that."

"So were about a million other—"

"Cassie?"

The bells kept ringing, low and relentless and unstoppable, and it felt like her life, like the bells were saying, *Wrong, wrong, wrong,* and there was nothing she could ever do to make it right again.

"Yeah?" Whatever he was about to say, there was no way she could stop that either.

She saw the detective's chest rise and fall, saw an expression cross his face as if he were making some kind of a decision.

"Maybe we should talk at the station." He'd waited. Watched her. "It'll be more private there. I promise you can leave whenever you want. I'll even drive you back in an unmarked car."

She'd been alone in this room for fifteen minutes now. The door to the windowless room opened, and she flinched at the sound. Detective Kirkhalter, now wearing a black sweater and gold badge hanging from a dark cord around his neck, carried a card-board tray with two lidded paper cups.

"This might take a while," he said. "Milk and sugar, like you said. Can't guarantee the quality of—"

"Why am I here?" Cassie had to interrupt. This was like some terrible movie where everyone was trying to hide something and no one knew what the other one knew, but she was not the good guy—she knew that much, at least—and all she wanted was to have this be over, but it would never be over.

She watched Kirkhalter put the coffee onto the pit-ted wooden table. He removed one cup and put it in front of her. A heater kicked on somewhere, whirring more stale air into the ugly room. *Mumma will be so mad,* the silly thought went through her mind.

Kirkhalter pulled out the metal chair opposite her, and with a sigh, sat down.

"I need your help," he said.

NOW

CHAPTER 42

LILY

The tears came to Lily's eyes now, she could not stop them. The words on the paper in front of her blurred, misting into a vague and unformed picture of the person who typed them, and where she was, and what she—*Cassie*—must have been thinking when she did. Cassie had touched this paper, too. She dug in her tote bag for a tissue, blinking fast to stop the tears. She'd wondered if this day would ever come, and now that it seemed imminent, her heart felt too full to believe it. Full of love. And fear. And uncertainty.

"You're saying she's been in hiding for all these years. With help from law enforcement. And now, what, she wants out?" Lily sniffed, dabbed at her eyes. She looked at the words her sister—was it?—had typed. *Watching her is not enough.* Cassie had been watching her. Like she always said she would. And then, *But I want to be me again. And I miss my little sister. Is it finally safe now?*

Let me know.

"She must believe she's not in danger anymore," Greer said, more to Banning than to Lily. "That they've forgotten about her."

"Which is wrong," Banning added. "They never forget."

"They who?" Lily wondered what she'd missed, what Banning could have discovered that she hadn't. She still thought of him as Smith, which was unsettling. "I mean, I did all those DNA things, ancestry tracing, but there was never a match. Everything was a dead end. I guess I thought—if she wanted me, she could find me."

"This is about her, Lily. Not about you." Greer's admonition was gentle, a tentative therapist cautious with fragile emotions. "And about Banning, too, actually. He only found this because his father died. It's difficult for everyone."

"I know, I know." Lily felt the heat come to her face. Greer was right. Her sister—her *sister*—had spent all those years hiding something. That the whole story about her disappearance wasn't true? "But the police made a big deal about *searching* for—"

"Lily?" Banning interrupted. "You just told us your sister had attended Berwick for eighty-three days. That's so specific. How did you know that?"

Lily knew, exactly, how she'd calculated. The dates on Cassie's calendar were etched in her memory. She told them the story of the black composition book and the hand-drawn calendar. The crossed-off days. How often she and her mother had examined them. Counted them. Tried to decipher what Cassie was looking forward to.

Banning leaned across the table. Steepled his fingers to his lips. "Do you still have that calendar?"

"No," Lily said. "I think the police took it, in fact. Eventually. Your father, I guess." She shrugged. "I suppose it was in those files."

"Well, it's not there now. And your memory doesn't prove anything. Still. Can you remember what day she marked first? The date?"

Lily pictured it, its fading ink, its uncertain pencil lines. It looked as if Cassie had used a too-short ruler to make the grid, with each line falling off at the end. "November 10," she said. "We used to talk about that, why that day was so important to her. She was obviously waiting for something—but what? Was she *planning* to vanish, and counting the days until she'd never see us again?"

Banning and Greer exchanged looks.

"What?" Lily said.

"Tell her," Greer said. "Lil, you have to listen for a sec. Just let Banning talk."

"I—" Lily started to interrupt, then stopped. "Okay."

"So when Cassie was at Berwick," Banning said, and his voice went low and patient as if he were about to tell a story to a restless child, "there was a lot going on at the school. Petty theft, some not so petty, the usual drunk kids, and a few emotional meltdowns. There were also—drugs."

With a quick motion, Banning pulled several manila file folders from the middle of the stack in front of him. Greer put her hand on top of the rest, stopping the ones underneath from slipping onto the carpeted floor.

"My father worked those cases, too."

"Drugs?" Lily asked.

"Diet pills. Ecstasy. Cocaine. Roofies. You know, it was the '90s."

"She doesn't," Greer said. "She was seven."

"You're telling me Cassie sold drugs." Lily had to make them say it.

Banning chose a red-labeled manila file from between the others. Opened it. And slid the open file across the table.

"Lily? Read this."

He indicated a line midpoint on what was clearly a letter, two horizontal indentations showing it had once been folded into an envelope. The edges of the once-white stationery had yellowed, and someone had put a tiny black check mark in the upper right.

Lily saw the stationery's bright blue letterhead, the words *District Attorney,* the state seal of Pennsylvania. The capital letters: PLEA AGREEMENT. Lily read the two words by Banning's forefinger.

"Cooperating witness?" she said out loud.

"You can read the rest," Banning said. "But bottom line. This is a letter from the Berwick County district attorney confirming that someone—someone not named—had agreed to offer incriminating information about something."

"And you think that was my sister. This cooperating witness." Lily touched the words on the letter. Playing out what they must mean. For Cassie. And, inevitably, for her. "That she was an informant. That your father put her into witness protection. Which means she was involved in the drug dealing. My sister."

"I'm afraid so," Banning said. "That's the only logical explanation."

"I know that's awful for you, Lily." Greer reached across the table. "Now I'm not sure how to keep it from the public. That's why we wanted to talk to you."

Lily put her elbows on the table and covered her face with her palms, trying to shut everything out. Trying to replay the last two minutes of this disturbing conversation, trying to combine Banning's words and this letter into an understandable story. And trying to understand why Greer and Banning seemed so in league. But more important—her sister, Cassie. Rowen's Aunt Cassie—the person she'd trained Rowen to love and admire and see as a special person who lived far away—was a drug-dealing informant and possibly involved in a murder, who was in so deep she'd traded her freedom to avoid going to prison. How would she ever tell Rowen that? She was struggling to believe it herself.

But maybe—she took her hands from her eyes, put them to her lips as if in prayer, and did what any good reporter would do. Looked for another explanation. And there was an easy one. One that was way more likely. She used one finger to tap on the words again, *cooperating witness*.

"Wait. Cooperating. What does that even mean? It was the '90s, like you say. Little fish, college kids, caught up in things, and zealous cops rounding up anyone who might be even peripherally involved. Ruining their lives." Lily smoothed the letter from her sister over and over and over. Thought of all the times she'd searched strangers' faces for Cassie's. "Banning? Cooperating about what?"

"A known drug dealer, a man named Jeremy Duggan, was found unresponsive in an off-campus apartment that day. Police later announced his death."

"That day? What day?"

"November 10," Greer said. "The date on your sister's calendar. She wasn't waiting for something to happen. She was marking the time *since* something happened. Since Duggan's death."

Lily's brain struggled to come up from underwater. She hadn't seen anything about a death—or a murder—in her research. She would have noticed. But sometimes newspapers glossed over drug gang deaths as if the victims were not worthy of sympathy or column inches.

"It's awful, Lily," Greer went on. "Your life has been so perfect. Up 'til now."

Lily felt her shoulders sink. Her sister was a criminal who'd made deals with the police and was in hiding. A nightmare. And not just for Cassie. *Thank you for a perfect life,* her letter had said. Her letter pleading with the now-dead Detective Kirkhalter to set her free.

"You don't think she killed . . ." Lily took a tentative step into that possibility. *I've done a bad thing,* her sister had told her. So bad that an apology would not be enough.

"Killed, witnessed, participated." Banning sighed. "Doesn't matter now, means to an end. Any cop will tell you that. Indisputably, though, she must have been involved."

"It might have been—a coincidence." *There must be an explanation,* Lily thought. Cassie was smart. But eighteen. Vulnerable. Only a freshman in college.

"I'm afraid not a coincidence," Banning said. "She must have known about the drugs. And Jeremy Duggan's death. She must have traded that information for her freedom. Or as much freedom as she could have."

"But why didn't your father explain that to me when I came to see him?"

"Witness protection—that's not how it works, Lily. There are no goodbyes. He wouldn't have been allowed to tell you."

Lily shook her head, eyes downcast, trying to understand. Her phone, screen up on the table beside her, pinged with a message from Petra. *Going to pick up Rowen.* At least something was working the way it should. Then, with a start, she sat up straight.

"Wait. Wait, wait, wait."

"Wait what?" Greer said. "Who messaged? That's Petra's ping. Is it about Rowen?"

Lily put up her palms as if waving away the space in front of her. "Not about that. About Cassie. So you're saying she didn't 'disappear'? Or she did, but it was just a story? A police cover-up? And that's why the files are missing? And your father, Banning, told everyone, told my *mother*—"

"Don't kill the messenger, Lily, I'm just trying to untangle—"

"Told *everyone*." Lily heard the tension in her own voice, the anger. "They put it in the newspaper, in big headlines, that Cassie had *vanished,* and the police were working oh so hard to solve the case, and it was awful, and her poor roommate was terrified . . ."

"Lily, it's all in the past now." Greer had come around the table and sat down beside her, put one hand on her shoulder. "We only thought you'd want to know. And decide what to do. I know it's devastating, but I'm here to help. Really. Banning, too."

Lily wrenched herself away. "People were gossiping. And whispering. And scared. My family's life was ruined. My mother *died* over it. And it simply— wasn't true?"

BEFORE

CHAPTER 43

CASSIE

"You need my help? Help with what?" Cassie curled her hands around the blue paper cup, the coffee inside warming her still-freezing fingertips. This detective's statement—that he needed her help—was far from what she'd predicted. She'd expected him to grill her about Jem. About what happened after the explosion, and then in Jem's apartment. Not to mention the hospital. What could she have that would help the police?

"Tell me what happened with Jeremy Duggan," Kirkhalter said.

See, she knew it. She pressed her lips together, staring at the milky coffee as if it were the last thing she'd ever see. He didn't mean *help* like help them solve something. He meant *help* like confess.

And maybe he already knew what happened, maybe that guy, the super, had—oh, she had no idea and the whole thing was a mess and now she was in the police station, and all she wanted to do was cry and go home and then cry some more, but it wouldn't undo anything.

She was a good person, she *was*. She was eighteen, and her life was over. What happened wasn't going to change, that was over and indelible. The only thing that could change was herself. Maybe she could prove she was good.

She willed away her tears. She should tell the truth.

"I went to see Professor Shaw at the hospital. Because I'm his student."

"Understandable." The detective took a sip of his coffee. "By yourself?"

"Uh-huh." Cassie nodded.

"Not with any other of Shaw's girls?"

"Girls?"

"Oh, I apologize," Kirkhalter said. "Police shorthand. Not girls. Women. The other women students who Professor Shaw—knew."

Cassie frowned, trying to understand. "I'm not sure what you mean."

"Did you have a special relationship with Professor Shaw?"

Cassie felt herself blush, even now. Of course she didn't, but thinking about it made her nervous. "No," she whispered.

"Go on," the detective said.

She told him about Jem's arrival, and their discussion as the Wharton alarm bells rang, and how she'd seen him go back into the building to rescue their professor. Then that Friday at the hospital, how they'd met by chance, and he'd asked her to walk back to his dorm with him.

"At least I thought it was his dorm. But it was an apartment, off campus." She half laughed, rueful. "Well, you know that. So we went upstairs." She watched for a look of disapproval, but there was none.

"He *said* he was going back inside to rescue Shaw? The day of the explosion?"

Cassie blew out a breath, looked at the ceiling. Square beige tiles, water stained with splotches of dingy yellow. One was warped and sat loose in its tan metal frame. "I guess . . ." She tried to remember. "I think I just assumed it. But why else?"

"And that night in his apartment, did he talk about Professor Shaw?"

She shook her head.

"Did he offer you drugs? Were you selling drugs with him? Using? Buying?"

"What?" No one could prove what she'd seen. Could they? "No, of course not."

"Then what?"

"Well, I was scared, because I didn't really know him, but I felt kind of guilty, because he wouldn't have gone back into Wharton that day if not for me—"

"*That* wasn't your fault, Ms. Atwood," the detective interrupted her. "But go on."

She told him about the wine he'd given her. About Jem's collapse. Even about the water she'd brought to him. Not about the drugs in the cabinet.

"We knew someone was there, Cassie. There were fingerprints everywhere, and we can easily see if they match yours. Blue jean fibers in the carpet, not Mr. Duggan's. He apparently called someone to stay with him? You heard that call?"

Cassie nodded. The phone call she'd obsessed over. It wouldn't matter now. "Sort of."

"But his friend only knew a woman had been there, Jem hadn't said a name. So all we knew was female, young, wearing jeans. Not much to go on."

Cassie thought of the crossed-off days on her calendar. After all that anxiety, it wasn't *Jem's* friend who'd mattered. It was her own friend. She needn't have worried. Until Marianne said the word *hospital*.

"Did he come on to you, Cassie? Or try to force drugs on you?" Kirkhalter leaned closer, his voice almost a whisper as if wanting her to confide in him.

"Did you push him away, and that's why he fell? Did he hit his head, and you got scared, and that's why you ran when you saw he was dead?"

"I didn't push him."

"Here's the thing, Ms. Atwood. Under some circumstances, that might be considered negligent homicide." Kirkhalter scratched behind one ear, as if considering. "Maybe involuntary manslaughter. Hard to know what a district attorney might decide. They're pretty tough. And they're not gonna like that you left him there. You cleaned up, didn't you? You ran. And covered up. We'd asked everyone for information, any information. And you never came forward."

Cassie saw a concerned look cross his face.

"But—you—because." She had to make him understand. "I thought he was *fine*." The room seemed to be getting smaller and smaller, Kirkhalter using all the oxygen. "I just happened to be there, and even the paper said it was his second concussion, and natural causes, they said, and—I didn't know what to do. I mean, how was I supposed to know?"

"I understand, Cassie, I do." Kirkhalter looked at her with what seemed like sympathy. "But you're eighteen. Supposedly an adult. You made a pretty bad decision. And I hate to tell you . . ." He took another sip of coffee. "The medical examiner can overturn a natural-causes opinion. Just like that." He snapped his fingers.

She flinched at the sharp sound. It seemed to bounce off the grungy walls and the shabby ceiling and her unforgiving metal chair, and echo back at her, taunting her. *Just like that.*

He shook his head, eyeing her. "Cassie? A jury is not gonna like you. Have you heard the term 'consciousness of guilt'? Basically, it means if you do things that a guilty person would do, a jury can use that to decide you actually are guilty."

"But—"

"Picture your jury, Cassie." The detective turned to the blank wall to his right. Made a broad gesture as if presenting a huge image. "Picture the twelve men and women sitting in those uncomfortable blue chairs in the jury box, looking at you. The people who've heard your story. Are you seeing them?" He looked at her, an assessing glance.

She nodded. She could see them perfectly. They were all frowning at her.

"They're hearing from the police, and I'm afraid that would include me, that your fingerprints were there, your jean fibers were in the carpet, the building super saw you, and you never came forward to tell us you'd been there. Even though you were asked specifically. You lied and covered up and then lied some more. You left a man to die. Your lawyer would never allow you to testify—I mean, what could you do but deny it again? Why would anyone believe you? They already know you're a liar."

Cassie gasped, she didn't mean to, but she did, and she could really see those jurors. They'd hate her.

"Smart girl." Kirkhalter nodded, looked at her square on, narrowing his eyes. "Now you understand. How would *you* vote?"

"But it's not true. I didn't mean to—I didn't know—I thought he was fine," Cassie said again. Her voice sounded like it was coming from another person, like she didn't exist anymore, like she was powerless and small and fragile as milkweed.

Kirkhalter looked at his watch. Almost eleven, Cassie saw. Was time running out in some way?

"Detective? What can I do?" she said.

He tapped his forefingers on the battered surface of the table. Blew out a breath.

"Cassie? Listen. I believe you."

"Oh." Her hands flew to her chest as if to hold in her heart. "Thank you."

"But no one else will."

She stared at him.

"And, Cassie? Your Jeremy Duggan was a stone-cold drug dealer. Big time. We know that. And the world is better off without him."

Her eyes widened.

"Still." He sighed. "The law doesn't care how bad the guy is you kill. Murder is murder."

He swirled his coffee, and she thought she was going to die. Which might make this all easier.

"On the other hand, I do. Care. And if you're willing to help us catch Duggan's supplier, the big fish, the one who's providing coke and meth and X to college kids, giving roofies, right? To your own friends, probably? We might be able to work a deal. You'd have to testify against him, or at least give a grand jury enough information to send him away. I could help you with what to say."

"Well—"

"But if anyone ever knew it was you, your life would be in danger. The bigger suppliers are not gonna be happy with you. When they are not happy, they retaliate. Welcome to the real world. And *that* threat, that *promise,* would never go away."

Her brain was about to explode.

"So you'd have to disappear," Kirkhalter went on. "We'll help you."

"What? No. That's crazy. Disappear? You mean like witness protection? No way. Why would I do that?"

"You don't have to." Kirkhalter shrugged. Drained the last of his coffee.

"What if I don't?"

"Well . . ." Kirkhalter turned to the jury wall again, made the same gesture. "Then you'll face your jury. And roll the dice on going to prison for life."

NOW

CHAPTER 44

LILY

The afternoon had shifted behind them, the sun moving across the springtime sky, its light playing through the gauze curtain and onto the framed watercolors of the painted forest. At one point, a fragile pin spot of sunlight hit the topmost branches of one of the pines, and Lily saw a tiny bird that had been hidden in the changing shadows.

"Well, I suppose what you say is true, Lily," Banning said. "Yeah. The 'Cassie has disappeared and probably planned it herself' story was, yeah, a fabrication. Ends and means, like I said. But it's not like *I* had anything to do with it. I still wondered—but at some point, I have to admit, I gave up on hearing about Cassie Atwood again. Until the letter."

He tilted his head back, looked at the ceiling. Then back at her. "I apologize. I gave you those stories as Smith so you'd trust me when I told you about your sister. Now I guess that was a dumb idea. I thought you'd be relieved. Happy to see her."

Greer nodded. "We thought you'd be overjoyed."

"I am," Lily whispered. "Of course. It's just a shock." How was she going to handle this? She'd look like a monster if she told the truth. Banning and Greer were only trying to help, and had offered her, in fact, the answer to a question she'd been asking for so many years. How could she explain it was the answer she did not want to hear?

"Aren't you happy to know she loves you?" Lily recognized Greer's persuasive voice, the one she used to try to convince a reluctant victim to do an on-camera interview. "And misses you?"

"You told us you had no idea where she was." Banning sounded disappointed. "Did you look for her?"

"Of course I looked." Lily walked the line carefully. She had searched for her sister, sure. But not to bring her home. She'd wanted to make sure she stayed away.

Cassie had done something bad. She'd said so herself. Bad enough that an apology would not make it right. Little-girl Lily had not believed it.

But grown-up Lily knew it must be true. And grown-up Lily could not afford "something bad" in her life. The longer Cassie was—gone, vanished, un-accounted for, and presumed dead—the safer Lily's life and career would be. And now, even worse. If bad guys were after her, that put Rowen in danger. She hadn't protected her daughter for all these years just to have it all fall apart because the mysterious and shadowy Cassie decided to reappear. And bring her toxic history with her.

She pressed her lips together, appalled at herself. Harsh and horrible and sad. Protecting perfection had a price. And she was paying it, this heartbreaking minute, in this suburban dining room.

She could not allow Cassie to come home. But how could she refuse her own sister?

Greer had put her arm across Lily's shoulders, and it was all Lily could do not to shrug it off in frus-tration and anger. How would Lily explain this to Rowen? How do you tell a child their aunt is a—whatever she was? How do you tell the world? How do you keep the social media mob from descending? But it was her own sister. Her only sister. Lily closed her eyes, suddenly weary.

She was one phone call, one text, one knock at the door away from having her life fall apart.

Greer had leaned in even closer. Her arm lay heavy on Lily's back. "Lily?" she said. "It's just a question of getting out in front of it. Embracing her. Giving her another chance. You'd be—an angel of mercy. The good sister." She scratched the back of her neck with one finger. "But I gotta say. From that note, it seems like it's your decision. She won't appear unless you tell her to."

"Right. If you keep quiet, maybe she'll stay away." Banning took the cooperating witness letter and slid it back into the red-tabbed file. "I mean, I *suppose* she will. You're not hard to find. If she changes her mind and decides to appear on her own—there's nothing stopping her."

"Who knows how she'd handle it, Lily," Greer added. "On her own. How public she'd go. It'd be out of your—our—control."

It felt like the wheels were in unstoppable motion. And who knew what Cassie Atwood—or whoever she was now—might say. Maybe she wanted money or power or control. Or revenge. Cassie—or whoever—had made new rules.

"Why didn't she just show up?" Lily said. "Why all the drama?"

"It's hardly drama," Banning said. "More like reality. I assume the letter meant she wanted my father to promise she'd be safe. Since we don't know who she was being protected *from,* we can't help with that. But 'they' know, whoever 'they' are, and when she reveals herself, she might be in danger. But, Lily?" Banning spread his hands as if he were imagining a scene. "Here's a thought. You could tell her that. You could actually *protect* her."

"Exactly." Greer nodded. "She obviously trusts you. Maybe she'll trust you enough to listen when you tell her to stay away. Maybe Banning could meet with her, too, explain about his father."

"Meet?" Lily said.

"Right?" Greer went on, looked at Banning. "If Lily can figure out how to contact Cassie, we'll choose a private place to meet. It'll have to be fast, but she'll be safe. You both will. And Lily? If it goes wrong somehow, Banning could be there to protect you."

Banning tilted back in his chair, then thunked it back onto the carpet and stood, gesturing toward the kitchen. "Anyone want water?"

"Sure," Greer said.

"No, thanks." Lily wished she were home, with Petra bringing Rowen from school, with things the way they were before. Before Cassie wanted to come back.

Greer turned to her as Banning left the room. "I didn't know he was going to make such a big production of this." Greer kept her voice low, talking close to Lily's ear. "That's why I called you, right? At the station? That was me. He'd told me not to let you in on it, but I didn't want you to worry. So I pretended to be Smith. To let you know Banning was legit. As for me, I was meeting a friend, and it's complicated. But I only want to protect you. And you love Cassie, I know that. You have that photo on your bulletin board. That's her, isn't it? You wouldn't have kept that if you didn't care. And she loves you, too, Lily. Imagine how she must have missed you."

Was that true? Lily wondered.

"We'll get through this, Lily." Greer kept talking, her tone persuasive. "You're juggling so many things. You must feel so off balance. But I'm here."

They sat in silence for a beat, then another, the inevitability of the future looming. Cassie was coming. Cassie. Who wanted her life back and who might ruin Lily's as a consequence.

"She told me to remember she loved me," Lily whispered. She could hardly focus on what Greer had said; her mind was too full of Cassie. "And that she'd always know where I was."

Greer laughed. One short, sharp sound. "Oh, forgive me," she said, touching her fingers to her lips. "I know this is serious. But duh, everyone knows where you are."

Lily widened her eyes, realizing how true that was. And how easy it was to know. She pulled her phone from her blazer pocket, opened her Instagram page. Fifty-eight thousand followers. The good news and the bad news.

"Here." Banning placed a sleek green glass of ice water on the table.

Lily held up her phone. "Fifty-eight thousand Instagram followers," she said. "I bet Cassie is one of them. It's like—maybe she means more than 'watch me' on TV. Maybe she's watching my feed."

"*Probably* is," Banning agreed.

"Lily?" Greer leaned forward. "Try to contact her on Insta. Think of a way. Tell her you want to see her. Then when you meet, explain why she needs to go back into hiding. Yes?"

"Maybe." Lily pushed back her chair. The world had tilted off its axis, and she struggled for equilibrium. "But think about it. She's got a new identity. She could be anyone. A friend, a new nanny, a neighbor. If the bad guys are watching me—well, I meet people all the time. And she's not trying to hurt me, because she's even asking my permission."

"I should have thought of that." Banning toasted Lily with his water. "So simple."

"And I was saying, you could be there, Banning."

Greer pointed to him, then to herself. "And me, too. Just in case. But Cassie needs to see the files. And hear about your father." She winced. "I'm sorry. But she wrote the letter to *him*. Which means when she wrote it, she didn't know about the accident. And why it might still be dangerous for her to come out."

"Good point." Lily nodded. "But thank you, Banning, for bringing this to me. Even though I would have listened to you without your whole Smith charade."

"Maybe," he said. "Maybe not. It wasn't just about *you* trusting *me*. I had to know whether *I* could trust *you*."

"Now we have to decide what to say on Insta. Can't hurt to try that." Lily had to move ahead. Banning's methods didn't matter. The result was the same. "This *is* good. My sister is alive. You can understand—it's a lot. I'll see her, and we'll both decide. And thank you, Greer."

"You know I'd do anything for you, Lily," Greer said.

CHAPTER 45

GREER

Who'd have thought perfect Lily had so many secrets? I'd watched her in that dining room, the sunlight bestowing its glow on her as if it understood who was important, watched her process this news of her sister. Watched her—I know her well enough to grasp how she views things—calculate how the arrival of this not-so-perfect sister would affect her. Not affect her *sister*, for crap's sake, the one who had hidden and covered up and lived in cowering fear for all those years, but how it would affect *her*. I'd put my arm across the back of her chair, trying to connect, but I could actually feel the animosity radiating from her. Thank god I hadn't pushed for the live family reunion thing. That would have been a disaster. For Lily, at least. Not for me or the ratings.

And besides the secret sister, the secret boyfriend. The secret *married* boyfriend, father of her out-of-wedlock (I know, not PC) daughter from the past who she'd manipulated and threatened and stonewalled. And deprived of a father.

Poor guy, just wanted to see his own daughter. I couldn't get over that. Little Rowen, turns out, was just another pawn in Lily's path to perfection.

Talk about perfection. The elegant Sam Prescott

hadn't seemed like a bad father candidate this morning when I first saw him at the aquarium. Quite the opposite, in fact, striding toward me on the wide sidewalk wearing an expensive-looking charcoal cotton sweater, perfect for the salty spring breeze coming off Boston Harbor. Graying hair and crinkly laugh lines, I saw, as he held out a hand to shake mine. In his other, he carried two lidded paper cups in a cardboard container. I could see why Lily'd been attracted to him. Even though he was married.

"Cream and sugar?" he'd asked, holding out the tray. "That's the one closer to you."

"Perfect," I said. I was still wondering how Banning knew the Graydon School had a field trip this morning, but that was not my department. He was a private detective; his job was to find things.

"Wait," I said, realizing. "You were at Lido. The maître d'."

"You thought so, maybe." He actually twinkled at me. "I had to see what you looked like, didn't I? How else would I have recognized you this morning? But I left after Banning reassured me it would work. You remember that."

"Yeah." I took my coffee, unsettled. Banning had brought him to the restaurant. He'd shown me to the private room. He'd opened the door while we were talking, and I'd thought he was a waiter. "We're fine," Banning had told him. I'd thought he was talking about the wine.

Sam Prescott and I sat on a slatted wooden bench outside the glass-walled aquarium, coffees in hand, waiting for the Graydon bus to arrive. He'd told me, as if we were old pals, that he'd been shocked when Lily threatened to ruin his life if he tried to get joint custody of Rowen. He leaned toward me, confiding, as the harbor drifted its briny fragrance over us. He'd been devastated, he'd said, when Lily refused to even let him *see* Rowen, let alone get to know her.

He hadn't set eyes on his own daughter in seven years. I couldn't imagine what that would feel like. I missed my father every day. Poor Rowen—I keep calling her *poor Rowen*—had that unique bond taken from her. By Lily. Her own mother.

"Her whole attitude, her insistence. Her selfishness. It wasn't like the Lily I thought I knew," he'd said, looking out over the water, talking to the sky. Two seagulls dived and looped across a swath of cloudless blue, screeching at each other. "We'd had an amazing time together. You know how it is. I thought we'd had something. Even with . . . everything."

He'd looked at me with those green eyes—green eyes, I'd seen them instantly, wondered if that proved anything—and searched my face. "I know it was wrong. But have you ever fallen madly in love with someone? At first sight?"

"Sure," I lied. Weird question to ask a stranger, but maybe he was nervous. I agreed, because that's what one does. "Amazing."

"Yeah." He took a sip of his black coffee, then stared into the paper cup, seeing whatever he saw. "I suppose I fell for who I thought she was. She already had that Lily persona. Still, she told me everything. That weekend. And after that."

I nodded, watching for the Graydon bus. Wondered what "everything" meant.

"She was such a star in the making," he went on. "She'd come to Aspen that first weekend to—" He stopped, glanced at me. His eyes were darker than Rowen's, but green was green. "Sorry. I'm babbling. I'm nervous."

I risked it. "Did she tell you about her sister?"

"Cassie," he said. "Yes."

I nodded. "What'd she say? Did she have any idea what happened?"

"What's Rowen like, anyway?"

He'd ignored my question. Understandable. I felt so bad for him, this vulnerable man who should be happy and proud of his little girl, watching her grow up, hugs and balloons, but had to settle for sneaking pretense. It broke my heart.

"She has your eyes," I'd said.

Now, in Banning's dining room, Lily's past was descending on her. I watched her fiddle with her phone while Banning messed with his files. I'd trusted him as Smith, more than Lily had. And it seemed like Banning and I still worked pretty well together. If Cassie went away again, things would be back to status quo, but Lily and I might have a deeper bond. Maybe she'd treat me with more respect.

And she'd never know I was also helping keep her secret lover at bay. Cracks in our Lily's façade. And I'm here to plaster them over. #PerfectLily continues unblemished, all because of me.

"I need to call Petra," Lily said, raising her cell phone. "Where can I—"

"Kitchen," Banning said. "And there's a bathroom just past the fridge. If you need."

Lily was already tapping her phone as she walked toward the kitchen. That phone call made me nervous. If she talked to Rowen after she talked with Petra, and if Rowen mentioned seeing me and my "friend" . . . I should've dropped that tidbit into the conversation earlier. But too late now.

The sound came from upstairs again.

"I gotta check the cat," Banning said, gesturing toward the sound. "Be right back."

"Right," I said.

It had worked perfectly, the aquarium thing.

"That's them," I'd said finally, pointing to the yellow bus that had pulled up in front of the aquarium's main entrance this morning. *The Graydon School* was painted on the side. A little face peered out from each open window—pigtails and curls, glasses and headbands.

"Do you see her?" Prescott had come to his feet, then sat down again. We'd chosen our bench strategically, predicting the bus would have to pull up to the front, so we didn't even have to move to get the best view of the girls clambering down the bus's front steps.

"Not yet, " I said.

One leg at a time, each in flapped-over white socks and white running shoes, followed by a plaid skirt and white shirt. The Graydon girls dutifully lined up like ducklings, one behind the other, fidgeting and pointing and whispering.

"Is—?" He pointed.

"No," I said.

Rowen was not quite the last one off the bus, but as soon as she emerged from the shadows inside, Prescott stood, still holding his coffee, staring.

"Yup," I'd said, but he wasn't paying attention to me at all. "That's her stuffed penguin, I guess. Lily says it's her thing."

It was more interesting to watch Prescott than it was to watch Rowen. His face softened, and I don't think I was imagining the emotion in his eyes. His chest rose and fell, and he did not take his eyes off her.

"Now what?" he asked. "Do we—you—we—just—"

"Hi, Rowey!" I called out, putting my coffee on the slatted bench. I cocked my head for Prescott to follow as I strode toward her. Banning had assured me it was all taken care of, whatever that meant. But if it was supposed to be a coincidence, I had to behave as if it were a coincidence. "So fun to see you!"

I approached her in line, arms open to give her a

hug. In two steps, a woman in a crisp white shirt, black blazer and skirt and serious red lipstick placed herself between us.

"Excuse me?" she said. "May I help you?"

"This is my auntie Greer, Ms. Glover," Rowen explained. Her eyes widened as she stepped out of the row of her classmates and made the grown-up-sounding introductions. "She works with my mom at the TV station. Aunt Greer, this is Ms. Glover, the headmistress at my school."

"What a coincidence to see you, honey," I said. I felt Sam Prescott behind me. Felt him taking a step closer. "Ms. Glover, I'm Greer Whitfield. Rowen's emergency contact, in fact, after nanny Petra. You can see that in Rowen's files. I'm Lily's producer."

"Ah. Of course." She looked me up and down, assessing. Her gold earrings glinted in the sun. "Ms. Whitfield."

I saw the headmistress's attitude instantly shift. Lily's name always did that, for better or for worse. Glover also eyed Prescott, and I had to wonder how much she knew. But this would be over soon.

"Mind if we catch up for five minutes?" I asked. "It's such a beautiful day, and I promise to bring Rowen right in. I know Penny the penguin wants to see his relatives."

"*Her* relatives," Rowen said. "And yay, I can show you my new poems."

I heard Prescott spool out a breath. He was so close I could smell the coffee he still held. His adorable daughter, wide green eyes, bangs perfectly cut, a model of politeness, and she wrote poetry, too. Rowen had glanced at him, maybe wondering why I hadn't introduced him, maybe bored with grown-ups. Maybe just a happy kid.

The row of students, once perfectly straight, was beginning to lose its shape in the blue sky and sunshine, the lure of the harbor and the sailboats and the ice cream trucks tempting the girls to stray from their once-disciplined line. Two other adults, a fifty-something woman with long gray dreads and a much younger one in a flowered Lilly Pulitzer dress, tried to shepherd their charges back into place. The older woman waved to Glover, pointed toward the front entrance, and then her watch.

Now or never.

"Five minutes," I said.

"I'd like to, Ms. Glover," Rowen said.

"Of course." Ms. Glover glowed cordiality. "Here's her ticket," she said, handing me a printout. "When you're finished chatting, just take her to the front desk. I'll tell the attendant to bring her to us."

Now pacing again, I checked out Banning's living room, looking at the books on the shelves. Old-fashioned *Reader's Digest* anthologies, striped covers lined up precisely, looked as if no one had ever touched them. He'd told me he'd rented the place, an Airbnb or something, once he'd learned Cassie wanted to re-enter the world. Said he should be here with Lily when it happened. Which seemed like a smart move—he was the only one who knew what had happened, and he had his father's files.

He'd lied to Lily about that. He'd told me his father had only pretended the files were lost. He was probably embarrassed that his father had lied to Cassie's family and to the public in such a destructive and devastating way and didn't want to make him look bad in front of Lily. Of course, it didn't matter what *I* thought. I wasn't Lily.

"So back then, they pretended she was missing," I'd said. "Even implied she was dead."

"Yup." Banning had nodded. "They couldn't reveal she was in witness protection; that's the whole point. So they had to create some sort of explanation.

And if she's dead, she's safe. No one's going to be looking for her, so from Cassie's point of view, it was a prudent decision."

"Not so great for Lily and her family, though," I had to say.

"Look. What can I tell you? After he died, we found the files."

"Is there anything that says where she is?" I'd asked. "I know you didn't tell Lily, but—"

"Nope." Banning had shaken his head. "That's why I'm here."

Lily came back into the dining room, holding up her phone.

"All set," she called out. "Rowen's still at school, all good, Petra was just touching base. Where's Banning?"

"He went to check on the cat," I said, standing at the archway at the bottom of the stairs. I pointed up.

"It's really a cat?" Lily ran one finger over the curved back of her chair. Picked her tote bag from the rug and hoisted it over her shoulder. "Huh. I just realized I'll need a ride home. Could you . . . ? Petra can take me to the station tomorrow."

"Of course," I told her as I gathered my own bag from under my chair. "And why say it's a cat if you don't have a cat?"

She pursed her still-glossed lips at me, and I swore her hair was still perfect and her blazer wrinkle-free. She'd had a crazy unsettling morning, heard that her long-lost sister—as we'd say in TV—was asking for permission to see her, and yet she looked absolutely camera ready. But, as I continued to learn, Lily was capable of hiding quite a bit. I'd never look at her the same way, now that I knew that under that veneer of perfection lay a few ugly secrets. Very Dorian Gray, without the portrait. I felt powerful somehow. And she didn't even realize how much I knew, which was another tasty emotion.

"You promise it's not Cassie?" She looked at me, like I was an unreliable little kid. "You and I are friends. I count on you."

"I promise," I said. Friends. Sure, when it's convenient.

Footsteps coming down the stairs. One person.

"What's the plan?" Banning asked.

"How's the cat?" Lily asked. "What kind of a cat?"

Banning raised one eyebrow. I wondered how this was going to play out.

"Cassie's upstairs, isn't she?" Lily said.

"I told her she wasn't," I said, though I supposed I didn't really know.

Banning crossed his arms in front of him. Rolled his eyes, amused. "That's why you get the big reporter bucks, Lily. Why would I go to all the trouble of . . . whatever. I get you've had your share of news for the day. So, no, not Cassie. Yes, a cat."

"I told you—" I began. Thinking to reassure her.

"And also a guy who's a client of mine," Banning interrupted. "From out of town. Staying here. But you don't need to be concerned about that. He had a big day sightseeing, and he loved what he saw. He can't wait to do it again. As soon as possible, he just told me."

"That's full service," Lily said.

They say when you're caught in a lie, every element of your body reacts. That's why polygraphs work. Your heartbeat, your breathing. Your nervous system gets jumpy, no matter how Zen you are, and every single one of your muscles contracts. I would have failed a lie detector right then. Miserably. I pretended I was having trouble finding my car keys, which made it reasonable to hide my face in my bag. *He can't wait to do it again,* Banning said. *Loved what he saw.* That was no chitchat. That was a message. One chance meeting is explainable. Two chance meetings is a conspiracy. I would absolutely refuse. He could get himself another flunky.

"So what's your plan?" Banning asked Lily. Because of course *I* didn't matter. "You think about what to say to contact your sister? And we should decide where we're all going to meet, just in case it happens quickly."

"Ah," Lily said. "I was thinking about here, actually, neutral territory. But seems like you have a full house. So maybe at the station?"

"The aquarium is nice," Banning said. "Outside, pretty, kinda public. You could bring Rowen."

I looked for my keys even more diligently. The aquarium. *Seriously?*

Lily shook her head. "That's where she was today, funnily enough. But inside's better, I think. More private."

"Well, here's fine with me," Banning said. "If it works for you."

"Sure," Lily said. "Your files are here, too."

He handed her a white business card, looked like the same one he'd given me at Lido. "Here's my number. Call me the moment you hear from your sister."

"If I do."

"If you do."

The two of them were talking so fast, a game of ping-pong, that I felt invisible. Banning must have been taunting me about sightseeing, but why? And Lily had no idea that the client upstairs, and possibly able to hear every word we'd said must be—*must be*—Sam Prescott. Her secret lover. The man with designs on her daughter.

CHAPTER 46

LILY

The landscaping of the neighborhood's elegant homes showed off springtime, Lily saw from the front seat of Greer's white Audi. Multicolored rows of tulips and the last of the daffodils, dogwoods in white-petaled bloom. Five o'clock, and the sunlight had softened as if reluctant to let the day go. Lily herself would be happy to say goodbye to it. But then, tomorrow would come. And, possibly, Cassie. She tried to imagine how her sister might look. The pretty one, she'd been. The smart one. For a while, at least.

"Turn here," Lily said, pointing to her left.

"I know." Greer tapped the brakes, keeping her eyes on the road.

They'd already gotten caught behind a school bus delivering batches of kids onto the sidewalks, and two had dashed across the street, oblivious to the scatter of traffic. Rowen would be safely inside by now, Lily thought, probably playing in the backyard with Petra and Val. Talk about oblivious. Their lives were about to change, and there was nothing Lily could do to stop it.

She fussed with her seat belt and gathered her stuff, impatient and confused and trying to figure out how else to feel. For all these years, Cassie was someone who'd only been real when Lily was a child. But all the while, Cassie had been living a new reality. And now wanted to draw Lily back into it.

Greer, driving with back straight and eyes darting between her mirrors, hadn't interrupted her thoughts. Lily'd been grateful her producer wasn't more inquisitive. Maybe Greer was as exhausted as she was. Banning arriving, then Lido, and finally the house on the corner. Those files. And the letter from Cassie. With its message to Lily. This day had lasted for weeks.

She closed her eyes, leaned her head against the back of the seat. *I'll try to know where you are,* Cassie had told her that night, and Lily knew it wasn't a dream, no matter what that detective had later tried to browbeat her into believing.

Smith—Banning—was Detective Kirkhalter's son. She'd always predicted Smith had ulterior motives, and she'd been right. But there was only so much information a brain could hold.

And now here he was, dumping Lily's past into their lives. Which meant she'd have to tell Rowen about Cassie. She could not afford to have her daughter hear about it from somewhere else. To Rowen, Cassie was only a picture of a little girl with a dog. Making her a person—a flesh and blood fortysomething woman who was suddenly her real-life aunt—would have to be handled step by careful step.

Lily saw the graceful willow in the corner of her yard, then the front of her house came into view. She was absurdly relieved every time she saw the white-painted siding and navy-blue door. Somehow she always worried it might not be here when she arrived. Burned to the ground. Or surrounded by police cars, red lights flashing disaster. The world was relentlessly unreliable.

"Thanks so much," Lily said as Greer steered into the driveway. "Want to come in?"

Greer shifted into park, but left the car running. "No thanks. Gotta head home to the . . ." She shrugged. "TV, I guess. What're you gonna do, though? Are you Instagramming your sister? I hope—" Greer looked at her, apologetic. "Lily? I hope this wasn't too awful for you. I know it was a lot to take in, and I truly thought you'd be happy."

"Did you know Banning told me you were missing? Like—*missing*?"

Greer's eyes widened. "That's elaborate."

"Right? Thing is . . ." Lily pursed her lips, trying to grasp an escaping thought. "During all that time at the station, he had to know you wouldn't arrive. Or call me. How did he know that? Why'd he even get you involved?"

Greer shifted into reverse, kept her foot on the brake. "Yeah, I asked him that. He told me he needed to gauge your reaction firsthand. Without me. Again, Lily, I'm so sorry. But I'm new to the Cassie thing, so I wasn't sure what to do. If I chose wrong, all I can say is I'm sorry."

"It's okay. It's not you." Lily had to let her off the hook. She'd never heard Greer sound so apologetic, so insecure. And she'd have been involved, one way or the other, if Cassie had just shown up. "And yes, about contacting her? I have some ideas. I mean, it's a gamble. But that letter said I should let her know, and . . ." She sighed, heavy with the weight of it. "I have to warn her. If she's in danger? Whatever Cassie did, someone was not happy with it."

"Can I help at all?" Greer shifted back into park.

"Her choice," Lily said. Maybe it came out sounding harsher than she'd meant it. But Cassie, out of nowhere, had taken over her life, and Rowen's, too.

"But like you said, she doesn't have to be Cassie. She can be a girlfriend. A new nanny. A book club member."

"Maybe."

"You gonna tell Rowen about her? Because—"

"You think there was really a cat?" Lily interrupted. "And can you believe Banning had a client there? I wonder what the deal is. Maybe he made up the client story, when actually he and some guy upstairs are secret lovers." Lily didn't want to discuss Rowen with Greer and was pretty obviously trying to change the subject, but she was baffled by Greer's instant reaction to the cat question. "Whoa. Do you hate cats or something? You look terrified."

"Oh, no." Greer shook her head quickly, dismissing. "I was only thinking. I completely keep forgetting to tell you I saw Rowen today. At the aquarium. That's why it was so coincidental that Banning mentioned it. But I didn't want to say anything about Rowen in front of him. Silly, I guess."

"Thanks. Happy to keep her out of the spotlight." Lily clicked open her car door, then frowned. "But wait. At the aquarium? I thought you were—what did you say you were doing this morning? My brain is a little fried."

"So. Weirdest thing," Greer said. "I was meeting a source—it'll probably be nothing, but we need to get something on the air this month, and the source, this guy I'd known off and on for a few years, suggested meeting at the aquarium, so I'm like, fine, it's a pretty day. And no sooner were we there than the Graydon bus drives up, and out pops Rowen, carrying a stuffed penguin."

"Oh." Lily nodded, imagining that. "Right when you were there."

"Told you it was weird," Greer said. "So we chatted briefly, and that's that. She was very polite, I must say. Her headmistress was with her, and—"

"How fun," Lily said. She had a headache now,

full-on, and she had to get inside. "Your phone's ring-ing. Thanks for the ride, Greer. I'll see you tomorrow."

Lily had her house keys out before she reached the front door. She glanced at the mailbox, empty, and the white bench underneath it. Empty. She pursed her lips as she unlocked the door, remembering. There'd been a package there last night when she went to Wil-laby's. But she hadn't brought it in, and when she got home, she'd forgotten about it.

"Huh," she said out loud as the door clicked open. "I'm home," she called out.

Val and Rowen bounded out of the kitchen and down the hallway, Rowen's white tennis shoes squeaking, Val's claws skittering across the entry-way's hardwood floor. Rowe threw her arms around Lily's waist, burying her head in Lily's chest.

"Mumma?" She looked up, still holding on. "I got to see real penguins. At the aquarium. And we got these shirts." She stepped back, pointed to the logo on her short-sleeved tee.

"You and penguins." Lily shook her head. "You took Penny, honey. I thought we talked about that." Val snuffled at Lily's feet. Maybe smelling Banning's cat, Lily thought.

"How did you know?" Rowen pooched out her bottom lip. "I'm sorry, Mumma. I know you told me to use my own judgment, which means that I'm not supposed to do it, but I really wanted to, and—oh, did Greer tell you? I saw Greer!"

"Good subject change, bug," Lily said. She hung her tote bag over the stairway newel. "Yup, she told me. You can't escape the eagle eye of your mom, kiddo. Remember that. But I'll forgive you. Did you have fun, anyway? Let's go see what Petra's planning for dinner."

"It was so pretty, and the penguins were so funny—they're called rockhoppers. They have orange feet!"

"Uh-huh," Lily said. Where was that package?

"And, Mumma, does Auntie Greer have a boyfriend?"

Lily stopped just at the archway to the kitchen. "A what?"

Rowen shrugged, her thin shoulders almost hitting her ears. "She was really nice to him, and they talked to Headmistress Glover. I saw them on a bench. When I was on the bus."

"Who?"

Petra came out of the kitchen, wrapped in a too-big apron. "Hamburgers," she said. "Sound good?"

"And french fries!"

"Who, honey?" Lily asked. Greer had said she was meeting a source, so it all fit together. But odd that Rowen would label him a boyfriend. "Who did you see on the bench?"

"Aunt Greer and the man," Rowen said. She took Lily's hand. "Come on, hamburgers."

Lily laughed, shook her head. "Great. Petra? Did you see that box that was on the porch yesterday? Just a regular brown box?"

"Yes," Petra said. "I put it in your office upstairs. Haven't you seen—"

"Oh, right." Lily nodded. That made sense. "I haven't been up there since whenever." She stopped, drew in a deep breath. Looked at the coffee table in the living room. "Can you go check it for me, Rowesy? Make sure it's in my office? You can leave it there if it is. I just want to know."

"If you don't be mad at me about Penny."

"This is not a negotiation, Rowen." Lily pointed up the stairs.

Rowen dashed away, Val clambering after her.

Lily walked toward the third vase of pink-and-white lilies. "Petra? I know the package is fine. I just wanted to—you called me about these."

Petra nodded. "More lilies. I was worrying. Do you want me to get rid of them?"

Lily shook her head slowly, wondering. "It's fine. I'll see you in a minute. You have hamburgers to consider."

As Petra left for the kitchen, Lily walked toward the elaborate arrangement, the amber-tipped stamens, the curving white petals lined with fragile stripes of burgundy. The fragrance, as she got closer, was almost intoxicating. A two-pronged green plastic stick poked up from between two voluptuous flowers. In between the prongs, a tiny envelope.

Lily knew, without opening it, what it would say. And when she did, she was right.

She knew, without one further thought, what she was meant to do.

CHAPTER 47

GREER

I backed out of Lily's driveway, almost relieved. I'd never seen Lily look so wary, so overloaded. It was a lot, as I'd tried to reassure her, to grasp the actual evidence that her sister was a drug dealer and potential murderer. And I couldn't imagine what she'd do if she found out that the other half of her secret life had been ten feet away from her, in the very same house.

But she'd never know, and at least that part of the story would soon be wrapped up. Sam Prescott had been tender and careful with Rowen at the aquarium. And he'd done a good job of sounding politely interested in her without seeming suspiciously interested. Happily, Rowen hadn't asked his name, and I hadn't offered it.

"I see you brought your penguin," he'd said to her. I'd told Rowen he was an old friend, in town for a couple of days, and that I was working with him on a story. If she tried to recount that relationship to Lily, it would sound perfectly plausible. I'd worked at several other TV stations, and keeping connections was part of the job.

"Her name is Penny," Rowen had explained, holding her stuffed toy between both hands as if politely introducing them, too.

Prescott had laughed. "She looks like she's had some tough battles with the other penguins and maybe lost a few. Or maybe the winters are tough in the Arctic?"

"Antarctic," Rowen corrected him. "She belonged to my Aunt Cassie," she went on. "So she's older than me."

That had been a moment, I remembered, as I braked at a stop sign. I kept my eyes on the road as the evening rush hour traffic passed, but in my imagination, I was reliving this morning.

"That's so nice," I'd said. "Where did your aunt give you Penny? Did she come to your house?"

Rowen plopped the well-worn plush toy onto her lap and wrapped both arms around it. "No. She gave Penny to my mom, and my mom gave her to me. She keeps me company if Mumma has to work in the night."

"Mumma," Prescott had said. I could watch him tasting the word. It must have made it more poignantly real, I thought, knowing who "Mumma" was, and what she had done to him. And his daughter.

"What does your . . . Mumma . . . do?" Prescott asked. I supposed he was pretending he had no idea who Lily was, which was understandable. But knowing what I knew from Lido, I'd needed to find one more thing. At least one more thing.

"Rowe? When did she give Penny to your mom?" I asked. I was embarrassed with myself for interrogating a seven-year-old, but this might be valuable information. "And where does your aunt live?" I tried to balance the likelihood that Rowen would report this conversation to Lily, and how a little girl might present it. At Lido, Banning had told me Cassie had been in witness protection for the past twenty-plus years. And had not connected with Lily at all. If she'd given Penny to Lily recently, that meant Lily knew way more than Banning thought. And way more than she'd told him.

"I don't know." Rowen shook her head. "Just far away somewhere."

"About your Penny. Have you always had her?" Prescott crafted a more careful question.

"How long is 'always'?" Rowen asked.

So that wasn't going anywhere. For the next ten minutes, we'd chatted, or more precisely, *they'd* chatted, about fish, and birthday cake, and school, and Rowen's poetry. Prescott had recited the beginning of "Jabberwocky" with much enthusiasm, and Rowen had giggled as he did.

"Those are silly words," she'd said. "Mumma reads that to me."

Father and daughter, I'd thought, watching them. After seven years, instantly on the same wavelength. I could feel the emotion from Prescott, the longing and the restraint. I wondered if this one brief meeting would make it worse for him. Why was Lily determined to keep them apart? My animosity toward her solidified. For her selfishness and her denying Rowen such a critical part of her development.

"So unfair," I said out loud.

A car came up behind me, beeped. I waved an embarrassed *sorry* at the driver behind and pulled out of the intersection. After we'd walked Rowen to the glass entrance of the aquarium, Rowen had hugged me goodbye and solemnly shaken hands with the man she did not know—and maybe never would know—was her father. Prescott, those green eyes softened with sorrow, had gone back toward the nearby Long Wharf hotel. Where I, dumb me, thought he'd been staying. I'd driven to Banning's house as instructed.

I'd felt honored, really, to bring those two together. It was heartbreaking, the idea that maybe they'd never see each other again. It's possible, I thought, trying to give Lily the benefit of the doubt, that Lily had been waiting for the right time to tell Rowen about her father. It'd be silly to keep it from her, and I was actually surprised that Rowen hadn't already asked. But maybe she had. How would I know? Lily never talked to me about anything but work. I smiled, realizing how much the world had changed. Never talked to me until now.

Still, why should Lily have more right to tell her daughter about her parentage than the child's father? Seemed like that should be equal. And even after an acrimonious split, it wasn't like Sam Prescott was a serial killer. He was just already married. Lily was just as much at fault—if there was a fault—as he was.

"Come on in," Banning had said when I arrived at the house on the corner after leaving the aquarium. As promised, he'd shown me the stack of files, explained where they came from, and let me read the printed-out newspaper clippings in one of them. The ones that reported the death of Jeremy Duggan. I hadn't seen any of those in my fast search of *Cassie Atwood Pennsylvania police investigation* because Cassie's name hadn't been mentioned in those articles.

As I drove back to my apartment, I almost forgot to look at the highway. My mind was full of those clippings. As a journalist, I notice bylines. And the articles from the local paper about Duggan were all written by the same person. A reporter called Tosca Manukian.

I pulled off at an exit and into the parking lot of a fast-food place. I could almost smell the french fries. I hadn't eaten the entire day. Fries or research? I sighed. If I had low blood sugar, I wouldn't be able to think. I took my phone with me as I yanked open the door of the restaurant, the fragrance of oil and salt reassuring me I'd made the right decision.

I ordered, got a hamburger, too, and a chocolate

shake, and leaned against the window, tapping my phone. As Smith, Banning had always told us the straight scoop. No reason to think he'd change now that we knew who he really was.

Google took forever to open. I watched the thing on the screen spin like some jackpot was waiting to appear and the universe was trying to keep me in suspense. Finally the search screen appeared. *Tosca*, I typed.

"Burger and fries? Ma'am?" a reedy voice called out. I looked up. "Shake?"

The orange-shirted counter girl slid an orange plastic tray onto the tiled surface in front of her. I stashed the phone in my pocket.

CHAPTER 48

LILY

Lily took the silver letter opener from the pencil-filled ceramic coffee mug on her desk. She'd thought the opener was useless, old-fashioned, one of those thank-you-for-your-speech commemorative mementos that seemed to accumulate around her house. She felt bad throwing them away—plaques and coffee mugs, vases and paperweights—because the people meant well, but it was just so much clutter. Now this particular clutter was exactly what she needed. She poised the sharp point over the paper tape that sealed the brown cardboard box, ready to slice it open. Then paused.

As she'd noted the day before, there weren't any of the expected store logos or markings on it, and the label was typed. It was not so long ago—well, it was, actually, more than ten years ago, when she was a rookie in a Denver newsroom—that they were all ordered never to open a package or letter if they didn't know who'd sent it.

Which was a tough call for a reporter, whose entire journalistic life might be hinged on an anonymous tip. As Lily knew all too well these days. This box was light, but something was in it. She shook it carefully. Listened. Nothing.

She puffed out a breath. This was not going to be a

bomb or anthrax or the severed head of a horse. Stabbing the point through the top of the tape, she drew the letter opener slowly down, the ripping the only noise in her private upstairs study. Petra had turned on her music in the kitchen; Lily felt the faint bass vibrate through the floor. Petra and Rowen sometimes danced as they cooked and set the table, and Rowen seemed to be developing very particular tastes about music. Mercifully, she was past her "Baby Shark" days.

Lily stuck a hand through the opening of the box. Ripped open one side, then the other. Several layers of thin white tissue paper lay underneath, pristine and evenly creased. She lifted the first layer. Saw a hint of something black underneath.

Lifted the second layer. And tears came to her eyes.

She closed the door to her study, her knees suddenly unreliable, and walked back to the box. The tissue paper lay open as if revealing her past. And possibly her future. A fuzzy black-and-white stuffed penguin was nestled inside, tags still attached. On one webbed foot, the printed tag gave the penguin's name.

Lily lifted the new Penny from her box, and it was all she could do not to hug it to her chest. She felt like a child again, a child in the darkness, with her big sister, her revered older sister, the beautiful one, the smart one, whispering confusing secrets to her in the night.

Lily remembered their unsettlingly quiet house afterward. Their mother, even quieter, and Gramma Lily arriving. The police had first promised answers, and after none came, the police went away. Mom had died, and then Gramma, too. And Lily, on her own at nineteen, had struggled and managed and worked and tried to forget.

And in that journey, what lingered most, what haunted her most, was "I've done a bad thing."

Now Lily finally knew what the bad thing was. Her sister was a drug dealer and maybe a murderer.

The penguin lay there, staring at her. This was unquestionably a gift from her sister. Besides Cassie, no one alive—no one but Lily herself—knew where and how the original Penny had been bestowed.

"What are you trying to say, Penny?" Lily whispered. Because what she could not comprehend—if Cassie was truly a killer and a drug informant, and had stayed successfully hidden for all these years, why would she want to reveal herself?

Unless. Lily sat at her desk, moved the keyboard away from in front of her, and set the penguin in its place. She stared at it.

I'll try to know where you are, Cassie had told her. So she must know Lily was a reporter. A reporter who prided herself on finding the truth. Was that what Cassie was asking for?

"Mumma!" Rowen's voice came up the stairs, muffled by Lily's closed door.

She opened it and called down, "What, honey?"

"Petra says ten minutes."

"Tell Petra thank you, I'll be right there."

Ten minutes. Dinnertime was sacred when she was home. She had ten minutes.

She tapped open Google, trying to decide what one search she could manage successfully but quickly. What had Banning told her that she could use? She'd already searched for anything about Cassie Atwood, and there was nothing. Kirkhalter. She'd researched that, too. Berwick? November 10 at Berwick? That could work.

She typed, *Berwick College, November 10,* and the year. Google instantly presented football, homecoming, professors, fundraisers, fall festival . . . ah. Too much to search. Six minutes. She closed her eyes and pursed her lips, trying to retrieve the name.

Jim. John. Jen. Jeremy. Jeremy. Duncan? Duggan. Jeremy Duggan.

Jeremy Duggan Berwick, she typed. *Murder.* Then deleted that word. *Dead,* she typed.

The headline appeared instantly. *Man Found Unresponsive in Off-Campus Housing.*

She clicked. Scanned. Scanned first for Cassie's name, but of course it wasn't there, or she would have found it long ago. No pictures in this one, not that it mattered, but in describing Duggan—*no family,* it said, *police searching for any next of kin*—it seemed there'd been some sort of fire at the college in a place called Wharton Hall. Duggan had apparently tried to rescue a Berwick professor called Zachary Shaw, who for some reason had not heeded the fire alarms in the building. Then Duggan had been *found dead,* it went on, with no real details given, in his apartment. There was no mention of drugs. Or murder. It only said police were investigating the cause of death.

Good old Berwick police. Always investigating.

"Mumma!"

"Coming, honey!"

Penny watched her from the tissue paper nest. *When you see her, she'll remind you of me,* Cassie had told her. And if she had opened the package yesterday, when it arrived, might she have deciphered the message—if it was a message, but didn't it have to be—sooner? But she'd been on the trail of the lily bouquets.

Lily tapped her fingers together, thinking.

But why would Cassie send flowers *and* a penguin?

"Mum-*ma*!"

"Two minutes, sweetheart!" She closed the flaps of the cardboard box and stashed it under her desk. "Sorry, Penny," she said. "It's only for a little while."

Back to the search. She typed, *Zachary Shaw Professor Berwick.* And stared at the results. A drug "kingpin," the first story called him, and admired biology professor had been charged—blah blah—Lily had to skim, she needed to know this, but could not be late for her dinner with Rowen—with selling Ecstasy, Rohypnol, and methamphetamine to his students. *Nice,* Lily thought. She read on, quickly as she could. The charges stemmed from wreckage discovered in the fire; apparently, he'd kept his stash in a vacant basement office, and officials "speculated" that's why he'd stayed behind. To retrieve them. Or make sure they were destroyed.

Lovely. Talk about a college education. Shaw had been facing a hefty prison term.

"Good riddance," Lily said out loud. One more Google entry for the charming professor. She clicked it open.

Zachary Shaw. No trial, case closed, pled guilty. So there must have been enough evidence that his lawyers decided there was no percentage in facing a judge and jury. Someone must have given prosecutors the inside scoop on his activities.

"Oh, Cassie," Lily whispered to herself. "How did you know Zachary Shaw?"

She stared at the article. Then went back to the one about Jeremy Duggan.

Both were written by the same reporter.

Lily looked up *Fire Wharton Berwick* and the date. The articles about the "tragedy in a century-old building that ruined a revered and irreplaceable amount of artwork and history" were also written by the same local reporter.

How many Tosca Manukians could there be? If she was alive, Lily could find her and get some answers. Or at least a few more facts.

She sensed Rowen's presence in the office doorway. The little girl's fists were planted on her hips, and she wore an exasperated expression Lily remembered all too well. Sam Prescott had looked at her that way more than once. He'd seemed so perfect, Lily remembered. Seemed to know exactly what Lily needed to hear, and when. Sam Prescott always got what he wanted. He'd told her that, *I always get what I want*, and at first, it was luscious and romantic. And then it wasn't. His life had changed, too, since then. But it could not include Rowen.

"Dinner, Petra says."

"I know, I'm all ready," Lily said. "Just trying to finish something so we can have time together tonight."

"What was in the box?" Rowen craned her neck looking for it. "Something for me?"

"Nope," Lily told her. "Work stuff."

She collapsed her screen. Zachary Shaw. Jeremy Duggan. And her sister, Cassie.

Cassie, who was out there, somewhere close, waiting for Lily to decide what to do.

CHAPTER 49

GREER

The first french fry is always the best, I thought, savoring the oil and salt and crunch and the splash of ketchup that had dripped onto my fingers. I instantly felt better, my brain getting back into gear with the carbs and promise of protein. I took a hit of milkshake, the cold sweetness hitting the back of my mouth. Small pleasures, I sighed, but you took them where you could. I put my phone on the white vinyl table in front of me, the waning afternoon light streaking soft and gray through the wide restaurant windows.

So where was I? Tosca Manukian. I tapped my phone back to life, and the search was still there. *Manu,* I typed. And then the phone rang. I rolled my eyes at the universe and took another bite of french fry as I waited for the caller ID.

Wireless caller unknown, the readout said.

"Damn it," I muttered.

"Yes?" I answered. No need to give away anything. If I don't know who they are, I don't have to tell them who I am.

"It's Banning," the voice in my ear said. "Did Lily tell you what she was going to do?"

"I'm fine, and you?" I said. What was I, his lackey,

messenger, spy? Caller unknown, huh? The detective probably had an endless supply of burner phones.

"What did she say on the way home? D'you think she knows where her sister is?" Banning had completely stopped using his Smith voice. "Did Lily decide how to contact her?"

I contemplated turning my phone off, pretending I was out of batteries, pretending I was in a cell phone dead zone. Was I Lily's babysitter now? The restaurant door kept opening and closing, letting in the late afternoon along with batches of chattering students and cranky children and exasperated moms.

"She wasn't very talkative," I said.

"Understandable. And?"

"And nothing." I tried to see if I could unwrap my hamburger and surreptitiously eat it while he was talking. A pickle fell onto the tabletop. "That was it. She went inside. I left. Her nanny will bring her to the station tomorrow. That's all I know."

Silence.

I contemplated eating the pickle anyway.

"Did you ever know—" I'd been about to ask Banning about Tosca Manukian, but maybe I'd keep that to myself. "Uh, anything about the actual case where Cassie was the informant?"

Silence.

"What about it?"

"You said this Jeremy Duggan was involved, and he was found dead. You mean murdered?"

"The police never confirmed that."

"Didn't his family want to know what happened? I mean, this guy was dead, and then Cassie disappeared. Wasn't that like, two plus two? Seems like?"

"My dad said they weren't connected," Banning said. "And apparently, the victim had no family."

"Lucky for the Berwick cops," I said. Then remembered. "Oh. Hang on." I took a sip of milkshake, stalling, embarrassed at my own sarcasm. Banning's father had recently died, and here I was dissing him. I needed to change the subject. "So. Sam Prescott. Is he headed back to . . ." I didn't know where. "Wherever?"

"That's why I called, in fact. He said you were terrific with Rowen."

"Yeah, great." I stabbed my straw in to the milkshake, pulled it squeakily up and down though the crosshatch in the plastic lid. "I only helped him because it seemed like a sad story, and—"

"And because my client made it clear that if you didn't, he had no bones about telling the 'not-so-perfect-Lily' story to whoever would listen. Which would be everyone." I heard a soft chuckle through the phone. "That Lily, she's got some baggage."

The restaurant was filling with the dinnertime crowd, and I was taking up a whole booth. I noticed a family giving me the stink eye as they crowded around a table.

"Be that as it may," I said, agreeing without throwing her under the bus. Party girl with an illegitimate daughter from a married boyfriend and a drug-dealing murderer sister. Not a good look. Not a good outcome for me, either. "So that's over at least, and we can all move on to the Cassie part of the equation. I'm sure—"

"Yeah, well, no," Banning interrupted.

I'd finished the fries without realizing it, I saw with annoyance. I didn't even get to enjoy them.

" 'Yeah, well, no,' what?" I crumpled the paper wrapper, irritated.

"My client wants to see Rowen again," Banning said.

I felt my mouth drop open. "Not a chance." I shook my head, even though he couldn't see me. "Not with me involved, at least. I'm done with that. We had a deal. No. In case that's not clear, I said, 'Not a chance.' "

"I hear you," he said.

"Good."

"So. Should I get Headmistress Glover involved again?" That little chuckle again. "She's very cooperative, if the price is right. You know how she is about . . . fundraising. And my client doesn't really care about the cost. Problem is, I'm not so sure about Glover's, shall we say, discretion. That's the thing here. Your call, of course. But I do know Lily can rely on you. That's why I'm giving you first choice."

"This is—"

"This is an offer, is all," Banning said. "But. I also wonder if the garrulous headmistress might be tempted to tell our Lily that she saw you and my client waiting on that bench as the Graydon bus drove up, saw you pointing at said bus, and making a beeline for my client's daughter. I'm not saying she definitely would do that. But she might. Since she already told *me* that. Since I had asked her to watch for you."

I almost choked on the milkshake. "What?"

"Didn't you think it was odd? That she didn't find it unusual that you were there? That she allowed you to take Lily Atwood's daughter away? Or did you think that was a result of your persuasive charm?"

The hubbub of the restaurant faded into a blur, the clinking of ice cubes and some guy pushing a wet mop across the floor, a roar of laughter from a row of kids as a dad made two orange straws into fangs.

I had gotten myself into this, with good intentions. To protect Lily. To help Rowen's poor father. And even the Cassie thing. It broke my heart for Lily, and for once, I felt like she trusted me. Relied on me. Noticed me.

But if Lily knew, or even suspected, that I had escorted her reviled ex-whatever-he-was to see the daughter she'd tried to keep from him, that'd be the end of—of everything for me.

Lily would hate me. She would get me fired. She would prevent me from ever working anywhere again.

I had no choice.

CHAPTER 50

LILY

Lily tried to listen to Petra and Rowen's dinner table debate about ketchup on hamburgers, but her mind was on that penguin. And she needed to find Tosca Manukian—*try* to find her, at least—and see what she knew about Jeremy Duggan. Banning had implied that Cassie had something to do with his death. More than implied. But there'd been nothing in the newspaper articles on the web that said anything about murder.

She stabbed her fork into her burger, wishing hamburger buns were free of carbs. Someday, she thought, she wouldn't have to care about being thin. She and Rowen could just do whatever they wanted. She chewed, pretending to listen to Rowen and Petra. Her mind was actually on a college campus, long ago and far away.

Maybe Cassie hadn't actually killed Jeremy Duggan. Maybe she'd just known what happened to him. Which got her in trouble with whoever had killed him. It hit her with a jolt, fork midway to her mouth, that maybe soon she'd be able to ask her sister in person.

"Mummacita," Rowen said.

"Hmm?" Lily yanked herself back to the reality of the dinner table.

"Could that be *Mumma* in Spanish? We're learning Spanish."

"Sure," Lily said. "I love it. And you're Rowencita?"

"That's funny!" Rowen laughed. "Funny like 'Jabberwocky,' Mumma."

"Whoa, you're going too fast for me." Lily had to smile. Rowen's attention span was sometimes about zero. "Did you and Petra read 'Jabberwocky'?"

Petra shook her head, rearranging the tomatoes on her mayonnaise-coated, sesame-seeded bun. Petra could eat anything. "I leave that to you, Lily. English is difficult enough for me, let alone funny English."

"No, the *man* knew it," Rowen said. "Aunt Greer's boyfriend."

Lily took a sip of wine. "You told him about 'Jabberwocky'?"

"No, Mumma." Rowen wore her Sam expression again, eyes rolling. "When Auntie Greer told him about my poems, he said it. To me."

"Auntie Greer's boyfriend," Lily repeated. Hadn't Greer said she was meeting a source? Might this guy have been Banning? Her eyes widened, picturing it. Imagining it. With *Rowen*? "Did this boyfriend say his name?"

Rowen shook her head. "I don't think so. And then pretty fast, I had to go inside. Auntie Greer took me. And Penny loved—" Rowen stopped. Looked down at her ketchup-streaked plate. "I'm sorry again, Mumma," she said to the plate.

"I didn't know she was taking her, Lily." Petra grimaced at Lily, then pointed a finger at Rowen. "What if you had lost her, Rowey?"

"But I didn't," Rowen said. She frowned. "I wouldn't lose something I *loved*. That would be terrible."

Lily put down her fork, smoothed her white cloth napkin. She wasn't hungry anymore. Her darling Rowen had no idea how often, as she grew up, she would have to grapple with losing something she loved. But what was lost, sometimes, could be recovered. Cassie must be hoping for that.

And Lily was on the other end of those hopes. There was no way to do anything but face it. And deal with it. If Cassie had some secret nefarious motivation, blackmail or extortion or whatever it might be, Lily would have to find out. But she couldn't start investigating until she got back upstairs. And she'd flat-out ask Greer if she'd introduced Rowen to Banning. That would be completely unacceptable.

"Delicious, Petra, thank you." She scooted her chair away from the table and smiled at Rowen. "May I be excused? I have lots of work things to do. And then— you come get me when it's time for bath?"

Once upstairs, she pulled the penguin box from under her desk, flapped open the sides again. She stood the penguin on its black webbed feet and leaned it against the side of the box to keep it upright. The white tissue paper opened on either side like an extra pair of wings. Lily pulled out her phone, clicked to camera, snapped a photo. Took another one, a close-up of the Penny tag.

If she posted it on her Instagram page, Cassie might see it. Or she might not. But in the absence of any other instruction, at least it was a step. She stood, staring at the penguin, trying to compose an Instagram message. Maybe—*Call me?*

She laughed, a rueful, weary laugh. Like the Bat-Signal in the comics she used to read. Still, the person who needed to know what it meant would know what it meant.

But maybe she should make it more specific. She lowered herself into her desk chair, swiveling it left to right and back. *Look at this wonderful penguin,* she could say. *I'd love to thank the person who sent it.*

Which would bring out every weirdo in the world.

Maybe: *My sister and I used to* . . . No, nothing about sister. Because if Cassie could see the post, so could everyone else. How about, *How wonderful to receive this, dear one. I cannot wait to see you. Message me!*

That could work. She shrugged, having a discussion with herself. Couldn't hurt. No one else knew about the penguin.

She opened her photos to make sure her pictures were in focus and usable. And as she scrolled the photo grid, she saw the selfies those college students, Iris-Colleen and Soraya, had taken of them outside Lido this very morning. Which seemed like a lifetime ago. Lily smiling, with the two young women grinning on either side of her. And behind them on the sidewalk, the image of Walt Banning, focused on his phone, unaware he was in the shot.

Leaning back in her desk chair now, she used her thumb and forefinger to expand his face. If someone knew who he was, he'd be completely recognizable. He'd told her he was Detective Walter Kirkhalter's son, and was trying to help Cassie by letting her know her letter hadn't been received by the person who she'd hoped could guide her back to the life she'd had to leave behind. Banning had shown Lily an obituary, a perfectly authentic-looking obituary, and seemed to know a lot about the investigation.

But, she thought, what if he was lying?

What if coming back was the worst thing Cassie could do?

Lily clicked off the photo, clicked off her phone. Put her elbows on her desk and her head in her hands.

CHAPTER 51

CASSIE

Sasha Forrestal checked her Instagram yet again. Unlike her friends—well, not friends so much as colleagues—who worked with her at the Pemberton Grille, she followed only one person's page on this social media.

Her sister. Lily Atwood.

But Lily had posted nothing today. Still, it was early, before 6:00 a.m., so early that no one else was in the restaurant yet. Alone in the industrial-size kitchen, she could cook and check Instagram and wonder if her life was about to change.

But nothing yet.

Sasha tucked her phone in her back pocket, picked up a wooden spoon, and touched the edge of it to the bouillabaisse she was making for tonight's special. Tasted it. The fennel and saffron were emerging nicely. She'd put Mozart on the old boom box they still used. First one in chose the music, that was the rule, but she'd let her staff change it as the day wore on.

When she'd first "disappeared," hiding in an apartment Kirkhalter had found for her in upstate New York, she'd watched news conferences where the detective had insisted they were looking for her. She'd wondered how the hell he'd gotten away with that charade, but no one seemed to push them.

The detective had told her that day to choose a new name that would be easy for her to remember—and difficult for someone to guess. And to keep it secret, even from him. So she'd picked Sasha, for the mysterious character in the Virginia Woolf novel they'd been reading in English class, and Forrestal, like her actual last name, Atwood. Kirkhalter—or whoever was in charge of the whole thing, she'd never been totally sure—had sent her a blank Social Security application to fill out, with a new number already on it. Every month, money from a trust account went into her numbered bank account. Enough to keep her in food and shelter and reasonable security. And anonymity.

At eighteen, there wasn't much backstory they needed to concoct.

Becoming Sasha Forrestal, she'd chopped her hair and bleached it, changed her eyebrows and her attitude. No one from nowhere, an orphan without a history. She had no choice; she was not only protecting herself but her family. She could never relax. Never feel free. Never escape that someone might be looking for her. And looking to kill her.

She'd become a waitress, then a line cook, and then a sous chef, saving tips and salary and as much as she could of Kirkhalter's stipend. Saving for what, she wasn't sure. She could cook, she could make people happy and nurture them. As long as they didn't ask any questions. She'd learned how to defend herself, just in case.

She'd buried herself in books. She'd missed school, feared for her education and so devoured the classics, books on the syllabus lists she'd never be assigned to read. She moved to historical fiction and mysteries, and romances, allowing herself to live someone else's life and deal with someone else's problems. Making narrow escapes and wrong decisions and still ending up happy or at least enlightened. *The Prisoner of*

Zenda, she'd read, and *Les Misérables,* anything that had to do with loneliness and separation and the isolation that came with guilt and remorse. *Crime and Punishment.* She'd read it dozens of times.

When her mother died, she took her life in her hands—so Detective Kirkhalter had warned her—swathed herself in a black shawl and headscarf, and hovered just past the small ring of mourners who'd come to say goodbye to Cecile Blair Atwood. Dad was long gone, and Gramma Lily. The very memory brought more tears to her eyes.

She'd seen Lily, too, at the funeral, not seven years old anymore but eighteen, the same age as she herself had been when she'd spent her last day as Cassie.

On the ten-year anniversary, she'd read the almost-nostalgic coverage of her disappearance. So last century, it had faded into history.

But even as Sasha, she was still Lily's sister. Felt a stronger bond with her, even, since they were the only two left. She'd followed Lily's career like a secret special fan, not difficult to do with a sister who thrived on social media. And when Lily seemed to settle in Boston, Sasha had left her job in the anonymous crowds of New York City—where part-time restaurant jobs were easy to get—and moved what few belongings she had up here to New Hampshire. Close enough to see Lily on cable, far enough that they'd never cross paths in real life.

Now, after all these years, after she'd been Sasha longer than she'd been Cassie, she'd decided, *What the hell.* She'd find her sister. Risk it. Go for it.

Lily would recognize her, of that she was certain. Sure, a part of her had been hesitant. Terrified, really. To undo the infinite caution that more than twenty years of hiding had taught her. What if they—whoever *they* were—were watching Lily, to see if a Cassie-possibility tried to contact her? Lily had a daughter now, too, and that broke her heart. Cassie might have been an aunt, *was* an aunt, not that her niece had ever known her.

She'd researched the prison sentences for people convicted of manslaughter. Turned out, because she hadn't *planned* to murder Jem Duggan, it wasn't first-degree murder. The maximum sentence for man-slaughter, she'd learned, was twenty years. She'd served that. More than that.

She remembered closing that internet search, feeling a weightless sense of freedom as she passed judgment on herself. She'd paid her dues. She could set herself free. She was sick of it, of looking over her shoulder every minute of the day, Kirkhalter's "people" be damned.

But after she'd never heard back from the detective—and later read he'd died—she was stuck. Without guid-ance from the one person who knew her real story, it was impossible to know whether it was safe to contact her sister. Or if anything was safe, or would ever be safe again.

What would Kirkhalter have advised her to do? She'd never know. She was on her own. As always.

Her first plan was simply to show up in Lily's office. But that hadn't seemed fair to Lily, to dump such an ugly history on her unsuspecting sister. She'd warned little Lily, that late final night in her bedroom, that she'd done something bad. But who knew if Lily even remembered. She'd been so young, and so sleepy, and the whole thing was so impossible.

The second idea, the bouquets of lilies, clearly hadn't worked. Cassie decided, stirring the soup, that it must have been too obscure.

Lily was a TV star. Maybe she got anonymous flowers all the time. That's why Cassie had actually had them sign the second bouquet. And the third one, too. *From Cassie,* trying to make it clearer. She didn't know Lily at all, so how was she supposed to get her a secret message? Much less let Lily know how to respond.

Sometimes, walking with her rescue dog Pooch through the foothills of the White Mountains, she'd allow herself to think of it, alone with nature, where no one would judge her or question her or push her about her past. All those questions people asked without a second thought—*Where'd you grow up? Where'd you go to college? Do you have family?*—she'd shut them down. And as a result, shut down any chance at relationships. She was a murderer. How was she supposed to tell someone that bit of biography?

And, tramping through slick fallen leaves and tangled underbrush, seeing the occasional blue jay or a skittering rabbit, she always decided, in the end, if she had to give up her life in return for taking someone else's, the fact that every day was a punishment was what she probably deserved.

The bouillabaisse simmered, bubbling with promise. Soon, the morning staff would begin to arrive, trickling in with paper cups of coffee and earbuds in to pick up their white Pemberton Grill coats and assignments for the day. They'd stopped asking her to join them restaurant-hopping or going to the movies or celebrating birthdays. She wished she could be their friend, wished there were a way to explain it, but again, there wasn't. She wondered if they whispered about her, or speculated, or decided she was socially inept. "The reclusive Sasha Forrestal," so said the article about her cooking in the local paper, because of course she couldn't do an interview. She'd concocted an elaborate, sad story about being shy and private. About letting her food speak for her.

She knew if they published her photo, she'd have to leave.

Back at eighteen, anything seemed possible. She'd

thought it would be easy, or at least not so difficult. As she got older, the gaps in her life, the losses, became more like crevasses, splitting wider and wider, trying to separate her from who she was.

Now she wore her past like an invisible burden. She deserved it, she had no doubt about that. She mourned Jem Duggan every day. She could have saved him, but she hadn't, and now she was no one.

At least the contemptible Zachary Shaw and some of his drug-dealing crew were sent to prison back then—and she'd helped with that, no question, telling the detective and the grand jury what she'd seen in Jem's cabinet in exchange for her freedom and new identity, agreeing to trial testimony that in the end, after Shaw's plea agreement, she never had to give.

But Kirkhalter had warned her on that very last day she was Cassie. "The memories of those people are long," he'd said. "And they know who your family is, and they're waiting for the minute you relax." So she'd never relaxed.

Zachary Shaw was dead now, had never been freed. And that was her one good thing. Still, the threat of retaliation—by someone thinking she'd not only ratted out the drug dealers but also killed Jem Duggan—kept her hidden. She stayed in a prison of her own making.

The bouillabaisse needed more lemon, she could tell from the fragrance, and she pulled open the kitchen's imposing stainless steel fridge to select a perfect one. The pungent citrus bloomed around her, and she blinked, startled, when juice from the first slice landed in her eye. She wiped it away with one finger, like a tear.

She'd cried so much.

She stirred the fishy soup, watching the oil rise to the top, and the bursts of chopped herbs ebb and flow with each movement of the wooden spoon. How many times had she replayed that last moment with Jem? If she had only . . .

Her notifications pinged. She took out her phone. Lily had posted on Instagram.

And it was a message to *her*. Had to be.

CHAPTER 52

LILY

Lily had been right. There were not that many Tosca Manukians. Two, in fact, and one of them was ninety-three years old. Possible, but not the better candidate for the reporter who'd covered the Jeremy Duggan death, the Berwick explosion, and the arrest of Zachary Shaw. The reporter, she knew from her own experience, who must know far more than she'd ever put into her articles back then. Now, if the woman only remembered.

She rolled over in bed, the early light from the dawn peeking through her white bedroom shutters. Six in the morning, way earlier than she usually woke up, but she'd basically stayed up all night, unable to sleep, unable to turn off her brain, willing the time away until she could call London, where this Tosca Manukian wrote for a boutique literary magazine. Five hours ahead, she calculated, so when she'd finally nailed down her quarry, it was the middle of the night in the UK. Lily ached to call her, yearned to email, but it was ridiculous to do such a thing. Tosca Manukian, crossing fingers she was the right Tosca, would not have been inclined to be helpful if awakened at 3:00 a.m. So Lily waited.

At six in Boston, though, overseas it was eleven

on Thursday morning. She'd tried to talk herself into calling at five, but that still seemed impolite.

She tapped in the phone number she'd found. She heard nothing, then something, then nothing again as the phone signal somehow traveled three thousand miles. A crackle, then the unmistakable sound of someone completing the connection.

"Yes?" A woman's voice.

"I'm a reporter calling from the United States," Lily began. She knew, also from experience, that an unfamiliar voice asking someone's name was sometimes off-putting—conjuring bill collectors or salespeople or police. "My name is Lily Atwood, and I'm the younger sister of—" Lily, nervous, had strayed from her own script. "Is this Tosca Manukian, who used to write for the *Berwick Journal*? Years ago? Twenty-some years ago?"

"I'm sorry?" the voice said.

Lily's heart sank. Maybe this was the wrong Tosca. She'd stayed up all night, wrapped in her hopes. "Oh, I apologize for—"

"Yes, this is Tosca Manukian," the voice said. "And yes, I worked for the *Journal*. You said your name was—"

"Lily Atwood." The relief washed over Lily like a door had opened into her future, or something had been released.

"Atwood?" Manukian's voice changed. "As in Cassie Atwood? Was she found? What happened?"

Five minutes later, Lily and Tosca Manukian were face-to-virtual-face on Zoom. Manukian, pushing a sophisticated sixty, Lily calculated, or older, with elegant cheekbones and gray-streaked hair slicked back in a chic bun. A white shirt and pearls and a navy blazer, Lily saw, almost a copy of what Lily often wore. Now, crack of dawn in Boston, Lily just wore a white tee and sweatpants, although Manukian couldn't see the sweatpants.

After Manukian had agreed everything was off the record—*Call me Tosca,* she'd said—Lily had bullet-pointed the story for her, including the witness protection deal.

"And that's all I know now," Lily finished. It had crossed her mind, in the middle of the night, that maybe Tosca Manukian had known Cassie was in witness protection and helped in the cover-up. But reading her articles, she'd seemed like a solid journalist, and Lily doubted she'd been in the pockets of the cops. Lily'd decided to chance it. "So—Zachary Shaw, Jeremy Duggan, Cassie Atwood. Detective Kirkhalter. You remember?"

"Of course," Tosca said. "I looked you up before our call, and saw you in Boston on your channel's website. Lily Atwood, huh? And you were just a little girl. Hard to believe."

Lily had to agree, but there it was. She couldn't imagine Rowen dealing with that, with the disappearance of a sister, unexplained and mysterious, like a dark fairy tale that turned out to be real. Did Rowen think of her father like that? Someone who'd vanished? The unsettling thought crossed Lily's mind, but she dismissed it. You can't miss something you never had.

Sam Prescott had called Lily, two years ago. Said his new wife was willing to ignore his past. To embrace Rowen. Was Lily interested? he'd asked. In altering the custody agreement? *Over my dead body,* Lily'd said. *Forget it.* She'd hung up and collapsed into tears. That was the end of that.

Sam had made his decision once. Left Rowen. She could not allow Rowen to risk another one-eighty. Sam Prescott could not be in charge of their lives.

So far, this morning, not a hint of the others in her house awakening. For now, on this transatlantic call, Lily had privacy and opportunity. Now if she could only get answers.

"Yes, I agree, hard to believe. It's been a long time. But, Tosca? Can you remember if anyone ever speculated that Cassie Atwood had been sent away? Or was in hiding somewhere?"

Silence on the other end. "Wow, no," Tosca finally said. "I mean—that would be—no. I mean, we all know about college girls. It's difficult, Lily, but sometimes people, especially headstrong young women, simply vanish on their own. They're good at it."

"Why'd everyone give up on her, then?" Lily winced inwardly at the harshness in her own tone. Saw the surprised look on Tosca's face on the monitor. "Sorry," she said. "That came out wrong."

Tosca was shaking her head. "You know journalism. There's one story, and then there's another one. Dogs bark, and the caravan moves on. Happy to tell you whatever I remember."

"Thanks. So much. So—anything?"

Tosca looked away from the camera, pursed her lips.

Lily could almost see her thinking.

Tosca looked up. Touched her pearls. "I was at the hospital one day, when Zachary Shaw—he turned out to be a drug dealer, you know about that, right?—was recovering from the explosion. Trying to see if I could get any information. And there was a young woman in the waiting room, who, I kind of—oh, right. I heard her ask the receptionist about Shaw." She gave a soft laugh. "This is the stuff I remember. Haven't thought about it for years."

"Was it Cassie?"

"She never said her name, I'm fairly sure. And I

remember she was very pretty, in a '90s kind of way. But . . ."

Lily watched Tosca look up at the ceiling. Tosca's apartment had a flowery Liberty of London–looking wallpaper, and she sat on a plump, dark green armchair. A languid white cat, sleeping, stretched across the back behind her.

"She was talking to another kid there. I thought a student, at the time. He had one arm bandaged, and . . ." She squinted at Lily as if trying to see into the past again. "Maybe a bandage on his face."

"And who was that?" Lily wondered why that was important.

"It's just—it might have been Jem Duggan. Word on campus was . . ." Tosca tilted her head, as if a memory was eluding her. "Some student, a chatty freshman girl, told me she'd heard from her roommate that he'd gone into the fire to save Zachary Shaw. Who knows."

"Jem?"

"Jeremy. They called him *Jem*. Duggan, they discovered, was never enrolled. Just hung out on campus. And the thing is, it was later that same night that he was found dead."

They stared at each other across an entire ocean. Tosca, Lily thought, must be making the same connection she was.

"They didn't put his photo in the papers," Tosca went on. "Turned out he was a drug dealer, too, like Shaw. In league with him. College big shots probably wanted it to go away. But from the one photo the cops showed me afterward—yes. Might have been Jem Duggan."

"So, um." Lily had to ask, had to, and the answer she got would change her life and Cassie's life. And Rowen's, too. "So do you—did you—do you think she, Cassie, um." She was having a hard time getting the words out. "Could Cassie be connected to Jem Duggan's death?"

Tosca smoothed one shaped eyebrow, and the cat behind her stretched out two white front legs and tucked them under her again.

"Your cat is so elegant," Lily said.

"Her name is Lillian." Tosca laughed. "For Lillian Hellman. Small world. And, yes, I did think of it—the explosion, and Duggan, and then the missing Cassie. I asked the police about a connection, but . . ." She lifted both palms. "They acted like I was crazy. Kirkhalter. I mean, yeah, I know cops lie." She shook her head, and Lily could see her remembering. "But they totally waved me off."

"That's why she was sent away, is what Walt Banning told me," Lily said. "The cops—Detective Kirkhalter himself, apparently—*arranged* it. Got her to inform on Zachary Shaw. And then faked the 'missing' thing to give her a cover."

"Wow," Tosca said. "That's either brilliant or horrific." She let out a long breath. "If that's how they nailed that Zachary Shaw, though. Wow. He was a big fish."

"But not the biggest," Lily said. "The biggest fish might still be unhappy. And still waiting for Cassie to emerge. Or—not. But you knew Detective Kirkhalter? You know he died?"

"Sure, yes." Tosca shrugged. "I talked to him a lot back then. And later. Cassie was the case who got away, he told me. Wow. You're saying that's a complete fabrication?"

A door opened behind Tosca. Lily caught a brief glimpse of a man, then the door closed.

"My husband," Tosca said. "We're headed out of town in ten minutes."

"One more thing," Lily said. "Really, really quickly. I'm going to text you a photo."

"Of who?"

"That's what I want you to tell me," Lily said.

CASSIE

"Can you take over the bouill?" Sasha tried to keep her voice sounding normal as she handed the long wooden spoon to Maree, the first arrival of the morning. The kitchen would soon fill with the bustle and clank of a lunch service in progress, and Sasha had to be alone with this message, even for five minutes. Two minutes. The Instagram post from Lily seemed like a live thing in her hand, a lifeline or a doorway, or maybe a noose. She couldn't decide, not here, not with fish soup fumes in her face and the overhead fans rattling and the imminent arrival of a chattering crew.

"You okay, chef?" Maree, a star student with real culinary skills, eyed her up and down as she accepted the spoon. "Zora says to give you a kiss from her. She's latched onto you somehow. And you're so patient with her. Now she wants to be a chef, too."

"Love to have her," Sasha said.

Maree had seemed to be a friend possibility, too, but that would never happen. Maree's daughter Zora was seven, and sometimes, seeing her, Cassie thought her heart would break for what she'd missed. She saw the trust in Zora's eyes, her reliance on her mother, their bond. That would never happen in her own life.

She'd deserted Lily—though she'd had no choice—
and set her life on a lonely path. Lonelier, because no
one here could ever know who she really was. Sometimes it felt as if she wasn't really anyone. But no one
would know that either. And so the cycle continued.

"And give her a hug back." Sasha smiled, oh so casually, though it was all she could do not to bolt out
of the room. "I'm just gonna get some fresh air before
the lunch chaos starts. Check for pepper."

And before Maree could answer her, Sasha was
out the back door and into the parking lot and leaning against the back of her Jeep, staring at the screen
of her cell phone.

She'd gotten a message from the past, and an approval of a future. Now she needed to make a decision.

She used two fingers to look at the photo again,
close up, a photo she'd seen so often in the past and
then forgotten, the reality of it hitting her like the day
so many summers ago when her father had snapped it
with that boxy little camera. Lily—she guessed Lily—
had cropped the photo a bit, leaving out the front
of their white painted house, with its redbrick chim-
ney and spider plants in curvy metal holders dangling
from hooks on the porch ceiling. She'd kept only the
bottom edge of Cassie's skirt, and the little socks with
white lace edging, and the shiny black Mary Janes
that had been her favorite. And the dog. Pooch.

Who else had a cute dog like this? Lily had asked
in the post. She'd added puppy emojis, and hearts,
and a smiley face. *Love to talk to you about it!* To
anyone else, adorable dog-loving Lily. To Cassie, it
was a message. Had to be.

Cassie stared at the sky, past dawn now, the edges
of the last of the morning pink vanishing around the
edges. A new day. Lily had kept that photo. She hadn't
forgotten her. Didn't want to forget.

She stared at her phone screen.

But this message must mean—*must* mean—someone had seen the letter she'd written to Kirkhalter. Maybe a fellow police officer or someone who'd worked on her case with him. This message from Lily proved it was safe for her to come out. Made sense that there was a backup plan, and the backup person must have found Lily and told her.

And this was Lily's signal, saying yes, I want to see you. And no one but Cassie would be able to decipher it. Without even using the flowers she'd sent, or the Penny.

"Smart," Sasha said out loud, and felt more like Cassie than she had in years. She was looking at her real self. This photo of her with Pooch proved she existed, proved there was another life that she'd lived, where she'd dreamed of the future, and bossed her kid sister around, and swanned off to college with high hopes and lofty dreams. And now here she was, no one, and a murderer.

But with this one photo, Lily had told her everything was all right now. The past was over. And she could have her family back, what was left of it, and that was enough. More than enough. She could never be Cassie Atwood again, of course. But she could have her Lillow and her niece. Rowen, she'd read somewhere. She could know Rowen.

All she had to do was answer this post.

CHAPTER 54

GREER

You take a step and take another step and think you're doing the right thing, then all of a sudden, you aren't. I stared out the front bay window of my apartment, watching the street come to life; someone running, a guy in sweatpants pushing a jogging stroller, a yellow Lab trotting beside them. People with normal lives, on a regular Thursday, who hadn't made a deal with the—well, not necessarily the devil, but with someone who'd promised to ruin my life if I didn't betray Lily.

I shook my head, sighed, wrapped my arms around myself, shivering even though the May morning was gloriously sunny with the promise of summertime to come.

How in the world, I'd asked Banning yesterday, was I supposed to have a second "coincidental" meeting with "my friend from out of town" and Rowen Atwood? Rowen was a child, sure, but she wasn't an idiot, and the first thing she'd do would be to tell Lily. And after that, there'd be no explanation.

Work it out, he'd finally told me. *I'm sure you can think of something. You just tell me where to tell him to be, and when. And it has to be tomorrow.* Which was, now, today.

I'd driven home from the fast-food place, panicked and terrified. Taken a slug of bourbon, maybe two, and fallen asleep. But morning had come, and now I put my hands over my face, covering my eyes, wishing there were an escape.

When my cell phone rang, I almost leaped out of my skin. *Lily.* What had Rowen told her? Did it not even matter what I thought, or what I worried about? Maybe Rowen had described Sam to Lily, said he had green eyes like hers or something, and Lily was calling me now, about to go crazy, in rage or tears or however it would be. As the phone rang a second time, I thought about my bank account and how long I could survive without a job.

I could change my name, it crossed my mind, start over as someone else. Put myself in witness protection. Ha ha.

The phone rang a third time, and I considered letting it go to voice mail, pretending I'd been in the shower—it was seven in the morning after all—and then see what message she left and then see where to go from there.

"Hey, Lily," I answered the phone, making my voice sound sleepy, as if that's why I'd delayed in answering.

"Listen, Greer? I know it's early."

I tried to decode her attitude.

"Hi," I said.

Silence.

"Lily?"

"Yeah," she said. "Yesterday at the aquarium. When you just happened to be there when Rowen was there."

"Yeah, I was meeting a source, actually an old pal, and—"

"Yeah." Now there was definite ice in her tone. "So

you said. But I have to ask you, Greer, and it's important. It's fine, whatever it is, but I have to know."

"Sure." Now that she was about to ask me, I had to figure out what I would say, how I would explain it, and maybe the truth would be best, but what was the truth, even? That I thought Lily was being unfair? That I felt sorry for the man who—

"Was that Banning? I'd told you Rowen was going to be at the aquarium, hadn't I?"

I'm sure Lily was surprised at the sharp pitch of my laughter. She couldn't have known the relief it contained.

"Oh my gosh, Lily, of course not. One hundred percent no, absolutely not. I mean, how could that even—" I stopped. Waited to see if she believed me. And why not? It was the blessed damn truth. "He was with you."

"Oh," she said. "Right." I heard a sigh, maybe a yawn. "Look. I didn't get much sleep last night. Moving on. I sent a message to Cassie. Who knows whether she'll get it, or understand it. A long shot, I suppose."

I could look on Insta. I could look at Lily's page, see what she'd posted. What she decided might mean something to her sister. But she must have thought of that, realized that I could easily see the page. Banning, too. But we'd discussed it, so all fine.

"Great," I said. "Wow."

"But here's the thing," she went on. "Something's wrong with Petra's car, whatever, and she can't take Rowen to school and can't drive me to the station, and I know it's early, but—I mean, I could put her in an Uber, or both of us in an Uber, but—yeah, I'll do that. I should have thought of that before. Never mind. I'm too tired. I'll take an Uber to the station, too. Unless—well, Cassie. But I wanted to know about Banning. That's why I had to call."

"No, no." I tried to calculate, fast as I could, to see if there was a way to make this work for me. "Here's the thing. That friend from out of town is on his way here right now, and we're going out for a quick breakfast before I have to get to the station, and I was actually going to take him out your way, to that fun diner in Newton?" I was making this up as fast as I could and hoping it didn't sound too unlikely. "Then he's leaving town. So I'll bring him with me, and pick up Rowen and drop her off. All good. It's not even out of the way."

Silence. I decided to take that as agreement. This might be the solution, except—ah, it hit me what I'd forgotten. If I picked up Rowen at Lily's, I'd have to keep Lily from seeing that Sam Prescott was in the car. Which was impossible. And bang, game over. Damn. Dumb, dumb, *dumb* idea.

"Or not," I said. It'd be fine either way. I could just say the guy made other plans. I shook my head. Lie upon lie.

"She doesn't need to be there until eight thirty," Lily said. "Let me see what happens with Cassie. If anything."

"Works for me." I tried to keep the relief out of my voice.

Silence.

"Lily? You still there?"

"Yeah." Her voice was soft, barely a whisper. "I just checked my Insta. I have a message from Cassie."

CHAPTER 55

LILY

Cassie was an hour away. Lily sat, feeling separated from reality, in her living room. How was it to message with a ghost? Five hours ago, Lily had clicked off an Instagram exchange with Cassie, or whatever her name was now, she hadn't said, and that's exactly what it seemed like. The aura of the not-quite-conversation—typed, not spoken—still haunted her.

First the connection with Tosca. Then this. The past was coming back to life.

Cassie had messaged her on Instagram from an address called @Zendagirl. *Pooch,* the message had said. *Right?*

Rowen and Petra had still been upstairs, and Lily, still at her desk, had pictured that photo of Pooch. She'd cropped it to keep out Cassie's face and the façade of their house, and then imagined it flying through the ether to wherever Cassie was. Somewhere exotically far away? Next door? It didn't matter; it would land where it landed, and then the real journey might begin.

Pooch. Lily stared at the letters in the message, heart clenched and a faint buzzing in her brain like the first rumbles of an advancing thunderstorm or the shudder of an impending earthquake. After one long breath, one inhale, one exhale, she'd answered.

Yes, she typed.

No phone, the answer came back immediately. Lily wondered where her sister might be; in a Manhattan penthouse, in a rustic cabin in the wilds of Michigan, on a beach in Bali. What did Cassie do? How did she live? What might she look like, still gorgeous and willowy—Willow and Lillow, their father had called them—or tough and hardened? *I can be to you by two this afternoon.*

The maps in Lily's head began to rearrange. She could almost see the circumference of distance five hours might entail. Five hours away. Long Island, Maine, upstate New York.

Yes, Lily had typed back. She and Banning and Greer had decided they could meet at Banning's house. Banning had the files. They would prove who he was and reassure Cassie that he wasn't a threat, but actually an emissary from his deceased father. Because there was no other way he could have known about this.

Remember hornet tree? Lily typed. *Kind it was?*

Cassie typed back an emoji of a bumblebee. *One sting,* she'd typed. *Yes.*

And the name of our drugstore? The idea had come to Lily's exhausted brain around three in the morning. That was her reporter self at work, planning for things that might not happen. But might.

Yes. I remember.

Intersection in Watertown. Corner house. That was the riskiest part. But there was no code for Watertown, and if Cassie had been worried her Insta was monitored, she never would have answered.

Two PM, Cassie had typed.

Yes, Lily answered.

See you soon.

And then the typing stopped.

Lily had somehow made it through the morning, fueled by coffee and uncertainty. Rowen went to school, accompanied by Petra, via Uber. Greer was at Channel 6, after Lily informed her she wanted to stay home by herself in case Cassie responded. A lie, but she didn't feel comfortable telling Greer anything.

Banning, she supposed, was in the house at the corner of Sycamore and Hamilton. Lily had almost called him, too, but stopped. Worried there was something she'd overlooked. Or couldn't know. That the gamble she was taking used loaded dice.

But she could not allow Cassie to arrive and not be there to meet her. That die was cast, loaded or not. She'd tell Banning, and Greer, when the time came.

Her own Uber had taken her to Channel 6, where she'd picked up her car and headed for Watertown.

When she turned the final corner onto Hamilton Street, she saw the garage doors were closed. But lights were on, upstairs and down. Banning must be home.

She buzzed down her car window, letting in the afternoon, foot barely on the accelerator, putting off the inevitable. The moment Banning looked outside, he'd see her, and the secret would begin to come out. These were her last minutes in this part of her life, she knew that. No matter what happened next, from now on it would be different.

The neighborhood was peaceful this time of afternoon, a lone lawn mower buzzing somewhere in the distance, a cardinal twittering *pretty pretty pretty*. There were no sounds of approaching cars, driving slowly, checking street signs for their destination.

And what would she do, in that moment when some car door opened and there was Cassie? And she'd recognize her, of that Lily had no doubt. Was she supposed to throw her arms around her, burst into tears? She'd been seven the last time they'd talked, Lily a tousled bed-headed kid, groggy and bleared with sleep. Now she was Lily Atwood, fifty-eight thousand followers, three Emmys, and an unsullied reputation for perfection. Relatable, admirable, aspirational. With a sister, now, who was a murderer.

CHAPTER 56

GREER

"What the hell, Greer? Do you know anything about this?" Banning's voice, hard and sharpened, hissed into my ear.

"About what?"

I'd leaped out of my skin when my cell phone rang, swiveled my desk chair away from my computer screen as if I'd been caught goofing off. I'd completely ignored my Channel 6 work for the past few days, as had Lily, I was sure, and soon that would catch up with us. Lily could skate, uncriticized, but it was my responsibility to find our next story. Still, the mysterious Tosca Manukian tempted me. She was out there, had to be, somewhere, with answers. I'd thought I'd found her this morning, but the phone in London I'd decided was hers went to voice mail. Lily was home, waiting for Cassie's reply.

Somehow, I had to get Sam Prescott to see Rowen again, *today*, and no matter what scheme I tried to concoct, it was completely impossible. Any connection I could make with Rowen would of necessity include Lily, and that was a deal-breaker. No question she'd recognize Prescott. And even if, as in one scenario I'd gamed out, I insisted to Lily I had no idea who Sam

Prescott was, that would be received as laughably ridiculous.

I'd told Banning that, several times, when I finally called him back.

"So *you* think of something, Banning." I'd been driving to Channel 6 yesterday, racking my brains, and finally decided to put the ball in his court. It had crossed my mind to keep driving, on and on and away. Maybe Cassie had a good idea. Escaping and disappearing was sounding pretty tempting. "There's no way I can do that, and you know it."

"My client is leaving town today," Banning told me, his voice crackling through the car's Bluetooth. "If he doesn't see Rowen, I don't get paid."

"I don't see how that's my problem," I said.

"Perhaps." He'd given that mirthless chuckle. "It'll be Lily's problem."

And if Lily had a problem, he didn't need to say, so did I.

Now he was back on the phone. Smith, our benefactor, still held my future in his hands. As Banning. And asking if I knew about something.

"Banning? I asked you—about what?"

"About *what*? About our precious Lily." Now Banning's every word seethed with irritation. "She's in her car. Sitting in my driveway."

"Why?" I squinted as if somehow I could see all the way to Watertown.

"How the hell do I know?" I'd never heard Banning sound so bitter. "Did she tell you anything?"

Oh, dear heaven, I thought. What the hell was I supposed to say?

"About what?" Pitiful, and repetitive, but maybe he'd tell me.

"About Cassie. Damn it, Greer. Did Lily hear from Cassie?"

I opened my mouth, but nothing came out. That

wasn't my information to give. I had already betrayed Lily, already done something despicably inappropriate, and somehow this, being asked to tell her final secret—I couldn't do it.

"I have no idea," I told him.

"Have you talked to her today?"

"I'm at Channel 6. She's not here, is all I know. But you know that, too. Look. Banning. I have nothing. Nothing to tell you. If Lily's in your driveway, then why don't you go ask her why?"

"Look. Greer. I'll deal with Lily. You'll get a call to go pick up Rowen at Graydon. Then you'll both come to my house."

"What?" My answer came out a yelp, and I was glad no one was around to hear it.

"Apparently, Headmistress Glover has been trying to reach Lily all morning, but Lily's phone has been turned off."

"No, it hasn't."

"Oh dear. Tell the headmistress that when you see her. But apparently Rowen's class is being dismissed early today, teachers' meetings or some such, and poor Petra's car is in the shop, where she is, too. Funny how that happens, today of all days. And you are next on the Graydon call list, are you not? Rowen needs to be picked up now and brought here. Because here is where Lily is, and she cannot be left home alone."

"That's the stupidest story I've ever heard," I said.

"And yet, all true." Banning's voice was velvet. "And if you refuse, then our Lily will hear the whole saga of your little aquarium jaunt. If you agree, Rowen will have a lovely note of explanation, which she can happily present to her mother, in the headmistress's own handwriting on her own personal stationery. Ms. Glover will simply cash the nice check. She trusts you to take care of Rowen. Isn't that perfect?"

I closed my eyes, just for a beat. "What do you really want?"

"I want Rowen to be safe. I want my client to be able to go home happy. I want Lily to be reunited with her sister. I want you both to keep your jobs. Isn't that exactly what you want, too?"

I hated him. Hated him with all my being. But maybe it was shooting the messenger. Lily had an impossible secret past, and that past existed whether Banning told us about it or whether we found out the hard way. Sometimes there are no good choices, just necessary ones.

"Where will Rowen meet me?"

"In front of the school. Fifteen minutes?"

"Twenty," I said. "And then I'm done, Banning."

"See you soon," he said.

CHAPTER 57

LILY

Maybe Cassie wasn't coming. Lily's ears almost ached with listening for an arriving car. She'd thought about going inside Banning's house, telling him about the Instagram connection, about their plans. He'd grill her, she figured, but she had no specifics, only that it was Cassie, *definitely* Cassie, alive, and somewhere five hours away, and with a cell phone and an Instagram account. Lily had checked it, of course, @Zendagirl, and saw she had nothing posted, no followers, and was only following one person. Lily Atwood.

Lily, waiting in the driveway, had scrolled through her own Instagram photos, imagining her life through Cassie's eyes. Cassie, a drug-dealing killer, examining Lily's affluent, privileged, perfect life. Cassie would know of the Emmys and her TV investigations, of Lily's glittering appearances at charity balls and celebrity bike rides and her perfectly lighted promo shots at the news desk. She'd know about Rowen, the BG with penguin ribbons. Lily took a deep breath, wondering how that made Cassie feel. Seeing how different their two lives had been. How different their choices had been.

Cassie had taken her eighteen-year-old self and created some kind of a life. Lily would recognize her, she was confident of that. You could not disguise a sister.

She opened the car door, steeling herself to tell Banning what had happened. *My sister is*—could she even say those words, *my sister*?

Closing the car door behind her, she leaned against the warm metal, arms crossed in front of her. She was stalling, but there was no reason to go inside. Spring had blessed her with a perfect day, as if nature approved of what was about to happen. She lifted her face to the sun, knowing Cassie felt the same sun, wondering if Cassie had ever been happy again. How could she, if she'd killed someone?

A drug dealer, though. Who'd probably destroyed countless lives. She was only eighteen. Lily felt tears in her eyes. Her sister—her beautiful, smart sister— had made a horrendous decision that ruined her life. She'd asked Lily—not in so many words but the reality remained—she'd asked Lily to forgive her. *I want to come home,* she'd written. But there was no home but Lily. And Rowen.

No car engines yet.

Banning must not have seen her, or he'd have come out. He was as eager to hear about Cassie as she was. And he could only think, by Lily's unannounced arrival, that they'd connected.

Those files, that's what haunted her. She needed those, needed Cassie to see them to understand how risky it was. Only Banning's father truly knew whether it was safe for Cassie to reemerge. Even this meeting, Lily knew, was risky. And Lily had allowed it to happen.

No. *Cassie* had allowed it to happen. And she'd have to leave. Ignoring it wouldn't make the danger go away. Cassie had ruined her own life. All these years later, Lily could not let her ruin hers, too. Hers and Rowen's.

Harsh. And horrible. And heartbreaking.

Still no car engines. Banning's street was serene and suburban, on one of those days where the wind carried birdsong through the trees and urged the clouds in their journey across the blue. A collection of pudgy robins occupied the lawn next door, pecking and poking the ground with focused determination.

Lily looked up, startled, as Banning's garage door clanked and whirred. The white metal hesitated, then lurched, sending the robins next door into a flurry of motion as the segmented sections began to rise.

Shoes appeared first, then legs, legs wearing jeans, then hands, then a plaid shirt, broad shoulders, a face in shadow.

Lily straightened, smoothed her hair, tried to decide what she would say to Banning. It half crossed her mind, in a flash of a second, that she'd message Cassie to stay away. Tell her that she'd be in contact again, that she couldn't make it, that it wouldn't work. A flurry of excuses paraded through her mind, anything to stop the world and stop this upheaval of her life. But no. She had to assess Cassie's true motives before Cassie herself took control.

The figure stood, motionless, at the shadowed edge of the garage. But it was not Banning. He was shorter than the lanky detective. Broader. Bigger. And there were no cars in the darkened garage behind him. Who was this?

Lily clutched at her chest, took a step back, put her hand on the door handle, her mind racing. If this was someone from Cassie's past, the "they" Banning and Greer seemed to be sure were still threatening her, Lily had to run. Banning had obviously fled or escaped or been taken away. Lily's plan—fragile and risky from the outset—had just fallen apart. Lily opened her car door, ready to get away as fast as she could. She'd message her sister to turn around. Warn her. *Go back wherever you came from.* But how had they found out?

"Lily?" The man spoke, and his voice stopped her, froze her, as if someone had pressed the pause button on the video of her existence.

She turned toward the garage, toward the voice, keeping the car door between her and the man in the plaid shirt. Hearing that one word, hearing her own name, in a voice she'd never thought she'd hear again.

The man stood, then took one step into the sunshine.

"Sam," she said.

CHAPTER 58

CASSIE

Did she think of herself as Cassie? Or as Sasha? She checked the rearview yet again, looking for something or someone she wouldn't recognize if she saw. She'd connected with Lily, and if anyone had somehow noticed, and somehow found who was connected with her Instagram name—might they be following her? She patted her purse on the seat beside her. She was used to it, the fear. She'd prepared for it.

The stretch of highway into Massachusetts was infinitely boring, stretches of scrub interrupted by cookie-cutter fast-food places and alien-looking expanses of solar farms, menaced by breakneck drivers. Cassie drove, steadily, eyes on the road, her mind in the past and in the future.

It was Maree's little daughter, Zora, that did it, that first day they'd met in the kitchen. Zora holding a plush panda, and the black and white of the stuffed toy, even the way Zora's thin arm wrapped around her lovey as if they were inseparable. *We outgrow our toys,* Sasha thought, *but we're not supposed to outgrow our need for comfort and affection. Or the knowledge that we're not alone.*

Your fault. Her mind would not let go of that blame, like some annoying song you can't get out of your head. She turned on the radio, thinking to drown out her relentless conscience. But the classical station she chose wanted her to buy flowers for Mother's Day, so she switched to Oldies 108. Instantly, she was back on Mountville Street, clueless, full of her self-centered dreams, as if having a hamburger with Jem Duggan—or not—would change her life.

"But it did, didn't it?" She heard the bitterness in her voice as she snapped off the radio. Because she had gone to his apartment, because she had left him to die, because she had seen all those pills. Now he was dead, and she was no one.

Two more exits until the turnoff for Watertown. It had been a snap to google the street corner Lily had designated to her in code. Lily had kept that photograph of her, Cassie thought of that, yet again. It was what had tipped her to make the final decision. Not only that Lily had understood the instructions, but that she'd kept the photo.

She'd stay Cassie, though. She couldn't risk using her real name—her new name, she corrected herself, not real—until she was sure it was safe.

The threat will never go away. Kirkhalter's warning words were clear in her mind. But he was dead, and that was the problem. Who had told Lily about the letter she'd sent? It had to be someone who knew what happened. And who knew enough to convince Lily that it was safe for Cassie to emerge.

She had to trust that.

CHAPTER 59

LILY

With the car door between them, Lily had two choices. One, get into the car, rev the engine, and back out as fast as she could.

Or. See what the hell Sam Prescott was doing in Banning's garage. Why he was here, rather than with his new wife in wherever the hell they lived. Lily was having a hard time coming up with proper nouns.

"Sam?" she asked again. That one she knew. *Rowen*, she thought. But she was safely at school where, at least, nothing could harm her. Lily closed the car door behind her, making her choice to stay. Cassie was on the way. She'd be here in fifteen minutes, if she hadn't changed her mind. Sam knew about her sister, she'd told him the whole story, as much as she knew back then, along with everything else about her life. Their time together, she almost smiled remembering it, their world for that crystalline moment in time. And then the moment had shattered. But she could not allow Sam to see Cassie. Cassie had to stay separate. Away. Not be connected to her.

"Yeah."

He hadn't moved except to jam his hands into his back pockets, again a move that transported her. That stance of his, that sometimes undecipherable

combination of shy and cocky, that shift of hip and
set of jaw. All he'd said was *Yeah,* and years vanished. She had not made a mistake, no matter how
many times she'd replayed it. If she had the chance,
she'd have made the same decisions, because Rowen
was the result. Plus, she trusted her own judgment.
Sam had been honest, and so had she, and there
were things that felt—at the time—meant to be.
They were Lily-and-Sam once. Once.

Twentysomething Lily had let her heart win, just
for that twenty-seven days.

"What are you doing here?" She frowned, calculating all the connections that had to be made for this
moment to happen. "And I mean—here. How did you
find out I'd be here?"

Sam's eyes widened, that green she would never
forget. Even ten feet away from him, she could feel
the pull between them, whether it was loss or need or
memory. Or her imagination.

"How'd *you* find out?" he said. "I hope you're
not"—he shrugged—"too angry. I'd hoped you'd never
know, I have to admit. But when the offer was made, it
was impossible to say no." He took a step toward her.
"I've thought about us, Lily, so much, and Rowen, and
I know I was a total jerk at the beginning, but back
then, my wife—"

She put up her palms, double stop signs. "Just stop
talking," she said. And she couldn't help it, she scanned
the strip of Sycamore Street behind her for Cassie. Just
a matter of minutes now before a car would turn the
corner and bring Cassie back into her world. The two
dangerous secrets in her life, time bombs that were
never far from her thoughts, were now on a collision
course. And there was nothing she could do to stop it.

But not yet. No cars, no buzzing lawnmowers, or
barking dogs, or strolling letter carriers. Just the last
two people in the universe she'd ever thought would

be standing together on a street corner in Watertown, Massachusetts.

"And wait. How'd *I* find *out*?" Lily risked a step closer. Whyever he was here, it was not to physically hurt her. "Offer?"

Sam followed her scan of the street. "Banning's doing some errand. I told him on the phone I'd seen you. When I saw the car, I thought—" He stopped, sentence hanging in midair. "But I guess *you* came instead of—"

"Sam. Right now, in freaking English, and with finished damn sentences, tell me what you're talking about."

As he told her what happened, they might have been standing on Mars for all the sense Sam's story was making. Banning's approach. His promise. Graydon. Fire alarm. Seeing Rowen coming outside with her classmates. Watching her.

"Maryrose Glover?" Lily repeated in disbelief. "Did that for you? She would *never*—"

"What can I say." Sam shook his head. "It was all I could do to stay in my car in the Graydon parking lot. And then you arrived. And I saw you, too."

But in the end, the wolf was there, Lily thought.

Sam kept talking, and Lily heard the words, some kind of words, about Rowen, and how he had felt, more and more, that he needed to be part of her life. And he'd hired Banning to help him.

"And that was you. At the aquarium." The movie in Lily's mind, wide-screen and Technicolor and taunting, played the image of it. "Greer," she whispered. "Greer let this happen. Made this happen."

"That's why I thought you were here," he said. He'd taken another step closer. "Because you knew."

"Don't. Even come near me." Lily had always done the best she could. Tried to make the best decisions, tried to protect Rowen, tried to have a life.

"You incredible asshole. You incredible asshole. You hideous, terrifying creep of a stalking—I should have you arrested for, for, I can't even find a word." She tipped her head back, looked to heaven, tried to understand. Failed. "I thought you were at least human."

She grabbed her cell phone, ready to call, but stopped. She had no safe place. Not Greer, not Graydon. Not anyone. And Rowen was—

"But that's why I'm here, Lily, don't you see? I *am* human."

"You're an assh—"

"So you said. But every time I tried to do it the right way, you kept me from her. You said, 'No, never.' You said, 'Over my dead body,' if I remember. You said, 'Forget it.' " He threw up his hands, turned away from her, then pivoted back. "Could *you* forget our daughter? Look, I have a new life, and so do you. And it's all good. But we—*we*—have Rowen, and it's not—"

"Fair, you're gonna say," Lily interrupted. Couldn't help rolling her eyes at the cliché.

"Roll your eyes, fine. Exactly what I'm going to say. Because it's true. I miss her, and even from the damn parking lot, I could tell she was lovely, and like you, and I wish you could—for one moment, just *one*—understand that I can't turn that off. No more than you could."

"Turn it off? Off?" Lily could barely look at him, but she could barely not. "You didn't care about her when she was born. You didn't care when she took her first steps. Said her first word. You didn't care for seven *years*. You don't get to care now."

"I always cared! You never let me. Hate me, blame *me*. Do it. I don't care. But Rowen should not bear the weight of it."

"Oh, right, so you thought the solution was to buy off my producer and my daughter's—"

"*Our* daughter's—"

"—headmistress, and hire some detective to—"

"You weren't supposed to know."

The air seethed between them. A single airplane streaked overhead, a white contrail slashing the blue.

"Sam. Listen."

He cocked his head. "To what? I don't hear anything."

"No, I mean—to me. Listen to me. Banning lured me away from my office yesterday morning so Greer could take you to Cassie. And he told me Greer was 'missing' so I wouldn't wonder why she wasn't calling. I thought it was a bullshit story when I heard it—" She shook her head. "It might have been true. And I couldn't risk Greer being in danger." She realized now how she'd reacted to protect Greer, but Greer had reacted to harm Lily.

"But none of that," she finally went on, "was about Rowen."

He frowned. And seemed honestly perplexed. "So—"

Now it was her turn for the bullet-pointed words. Cassie. Confidential informant. Witness protection. Drug dealing. "Cassie sent a message to Banning's father," Lily continued, "asking whether it was safe for her to come home. Not a word about Rowen, or you. And that's why I'm here. About *Cassie*. Not you and the perfidious Greer, who'll never work in Boston or anywhere else again, believe me."

"Cassie," he said.

"Yeah. So what are the odds, d'you think," Lily went on, "that the son of the detective who put my sister in witness protection just *happens* to be the same guy you hired to spy on my daughter?"

From far away, a car horn honked. Both of them went silent, waiting. But no car came around the corner. The neighborhood was in afternoon limbo, too early for rush hour or the dismissal of school. No kids playing, or delivery trucks grumbling by. It was as if the whole neighborhood was holding its breath.

Sam shook his head. "But that's not how it worked, Lil. Lily." He took one step closer. "Listen. I didn't go hire him. Banning came to *me*."

CHAPTER 60

GREER

I felt like a kidnapper, there was no other way to put it. If some thuggy cop had pulled up alongside us on Watertown Street, lights flashing and siren keening, I would not have been surprised. *No, Officer, this child strapped into the back seat of my Audi is not my daughter,* I'd admit. *No, I don't have her mother's permission to have her with me. Yes, I am doing it at the instruction of someone else.*

At least there'd be no one to miss me while I spent the rest of my life behind bars.

"It's like a snow day with no snow, right, Greer?" Rowen's ponytail sported her usual penguin ribbon, and she held a glossy book about Antarctica on her lap. She'd buzzed her back window up and down as we drove.

"Like a snow day with no snow. It sure is," I lied. Lying to a seven-year-old, that's as classy as it comes. This was Lily's fault, though, and if I hadn't been trying so hard to protect her, I would never have agreed to this. I was, like, committing a Class A felony so she wouldn't be humiliated and canceled by her murderous sister. Nice reality, perfect Lily. I hoped she wasn't ruining mine as I was trying to save hers. And sure, save my job and reputation, too.

"What happened to Petra's car?" I was making conversation now, how civilized of me, watching Rowen through the rearview mirror. But in the back of my mind was the potential collision that was in progress. If Sam Prescott was at Banning's house, and Banning had seen Lily in his driveway, then either Banning had to get Prescott out of there, or we'd be witnessing a confrontation worthy of a soap opera. We lurched over the patched asphalt of the stone-sided Watertown Bridge. It was bad enough—

"Ducks! Look!" Rowen crowed, pointing to the Charles River. "And a man is fishing. Think you could catch a duck? And Petra's car had a broken thing." She shrugged. "The tow truck came."

"Interesting," I said, using my all-purpose filler word for when I was thinking about something else. It was bad enough that Banning had strong-armed me into bringing Sam Prescott's daughter to see him—though I still felt sorry for him—but then Banning had amped the consequences to make me the victim. Me! That not only would Lily—and I—be trashed by the publicity surrounding the notorious Cassie, but I would face devastating consequences when Lily discovered my betrayal.

Just one happy family. But in the end, and in the beginning, it was Lily's fault. I wasn't the one with the slutty life-baggage.

"So your mom will meet us at a friend's house," I said as we drove closer, "and then you and your mom can spend the rest of the day together. Maybe you can ask her to take you to see the ducks."

"Ducks *and* ice cream," Rowen said.

"You drive a hard bargain, Rowey." I offered her an over-the-shoulder smile I didn't feel. But Banning was waiting at the house on the corner. He'd seen Lily in the driveway. He knew Rowen and I were on the way. Why hadn't he called to stop me?

Lily in the driveway.

We stopped at a red light, and Rowen buzzed down her window. A waft of spring air washed into the car, fragrant of green and damp earth. Outside on the river, ducks quacked in insistent conversation; and a fisherman, all floppy hip waders and short-sleeved shirt, sloshed farther into the water.

Lily in the driveway.

If she knew I was bringing Rowen there to meet with Prescott, it meant she was there waiting. For *me*. Like a sitting duck in a shooting gallery. Once we arrived, there'd be no way to explain it.

CHAPTER 61
LILY

"Banning came to *you*? Is that how detectives work?" Lily squinted at Sam as if trying to squeeze some logic out of what he had just told her. "What did he say? Maybe, 'Hello, sir, just inquiring at random if there's any detectivey thing I can do for you'? Please. Spare me."

Sam leaned against the chassis of Lily's car, almost at the headlights, his legs out in front of him, showing battered cordovan loafers with no socks. "Nice to see you, too," he said. "Been a while."

"Come on, Sam. Just tell me the deal."

Sam shifted position, steadying himself on the white hood of the car. "He called me. In Denver. He said he had information that Rowen might be in danger."

"What?" Her voice went up, fueled by fear and panic. "Danger of—"

"Lil. Hang on. He said your career was in trouble, and asked if we'd kept in touch, and if I knew where your sister was. He said Cassie was about to come out of witness protection, that she was hell-bent on blackmailing you. That she was dealing drugs, had murdered someone, and was about to ruin your life. With something that had to do with Rowen. He said if I cared about you, about Rowen, that I should come get my daughter and take her far away. He told me if I knew where Cassie was, or thought *you* knew, I should tell him. And that he'd help you deal with Cassie."

Lily's chest twisted with the possibility that might be true—she'd worried about that, a version of it, herself. The dark side of Cassie's return. The destructive side. Ridiculous of her, as she let this looming disaster sink in, that she'd allowed herself even one vision of a happy ending.

"Why didn't he talk to me, then?" That was the question. "Mightn't that have been easier? His father was the cop who sent Cassie away. Seems like I'm the one he should've come to."

"Honey—" He clamped his lips together. "Sorry. Lily. But he *did* come to you. And to answer your question, I don't have any idea. All I heard was that Rowen might be in danger, and you, and what else could I do?"

"What does your new wife think of that?" Lily asked it, her tone arch and unnecessary, before she could stop herself. Standing here in someone's driveway, in the middle of suburbia, she almost couldn't decide if she was fighting for fighting's sake. Or if she really wanted to know.

"My wife—Isabel—wants me to be happy. I told you that when I called that time. She's great, we're fine, but she knows how I feel about Rowen and about your decisions. We all made choices back then, Lil. But she says now, this one is between you and me. She'll be happy if I'm happy."

Happy, Lily thought. That word again. As if that were a word that had meaning these days. Now she had an impossible choice.

She had signaled Cassie to meet her. Which might have been the worst thing she had ever done. Now she had to decide whether to stay and face Cassie—no matter what was about to happen—or leave to protect Rowen.

"Danger from what? I need to go get Rowen at school. But I can't because—wait. So why are you here?"

"I might ask you the same thing." Sam looked at his watch.

The one she gave him, Lily saw. So many years ago. Without engraving, without connection, without evidence. But she recognized the chunky metal band, still sitting perfectly against his wrist.

"You're waiting for someone." Lily scanned the second-floor windows of the house behind her. Empty, not a flutter of a curtain, or motion of a shadow. *A cat,* went through her mind. There was no damn cat. "Who?"

"It's almost two." Sam lifted his arm, and the watch crystal flashed in the sun. "Yeah. I always liked it."

"Sam," Lily said. There was no way out of this. "Listen. Cassie is on the way, and she'll be here any minute. But I have to go get Rowen. What if what Banning told you is right? What if Cassie is planning to—"

"I'll be here, too," Sam said. "With you. We'll handle it together."

The rumble of a car engine murmured into the silence between them. Lily moved to the center of the driveway where she could see both ways. Sam stepped beside her. There'd be no way for her to recognize Cassie's car, but she imagined it'd be moving slowly, trolling for the white house on the corner. She'd see Lily before Lily saw her.

"That's an Audi," Sam said. "Does Cassie have an Audi?"

"No idea," Lily said. The car came closer. Lily took a step toward the street, and then another. "Kidding me?"

Sam joined her. "What?"

The car came closer. Slowed. Slowed even more.

The back seat passenger window buzzed down. A thin, white-shirted arm waved out of it at them, followed by a smiling face and a flutter of penguin ribbons.

"Mumma!" Rowen called out. "I see you!"

CHAPTER 62

GREER

I'm not sure what choice words would have come out of my mouth if Rowen hadn't been in the seat behind me.

And I'm also not sure what I thought I could delay by driving more slowly, because the endgame was staring me in the face, and there was no way to escape it. Like an "at home with the stars" photo from a glossy magazine: the tousle-haired Lily, wearing sleek black pants and a black blazer, standing with the craggy Sam Prescott, in blue jeans and a plaid shirt. Standing side by side. Clearly waiting. For us.

"Mumma!" Rowen's voice, joyful and innocent, made it all the more horrific. Yes, she had her hand-written note from the headmistress, but I didn't have much faith in its persuasive power. And the inescapable fact that Lily's loathed Sam Prescott was standing right next to her meant my days were numbered. Even if he hadn't told her what happened, Rowen would recognize him, and no amount of zigging and zagging could cook up a reason why Prescott was at this house. My "coincidence" story was shot to freaking smithereens, and so was the rest of my life.

It crossed my mind to gun the engine, and bat-out-of-hell it away, but that would probably be kidnapping. Literally, federal offense kidnapping. Even more than it already was. I hadn't participated in concocting Banning's plan, but I was part of it. And a reporter and a lawyer were witnessing it.

Banning. Where was he anyway? He'd clearly been here when he called—he said Lily was in the driveway. And that he'd get rid of her before we got there. Or take care of her. Or whatever he'd said. That obviously hadn't happened. I was on death row right now, the only way to describe it. And no way to avoid the consequences.

Rowen unclicked her seat belt, and had clambered out almost before I'd pushed off the ignition. Again, it was tempting to slam it into drive and head for the hills. But it wasn't as if I could disappear. Unlike Cassie, I had no detective to help me. I would stick with the headmistress story, I decided. Banning would back me up, and the headmistress would, too. Last thing she'd want would be for Lily to get wind that she'd been paid off. Maybe Maryrose Glover and I could run off together, all Thelma and Louise.

"Mumma! Look, Aunt Greer, it's Jabberwocky man!" Rowen ran to Lily for a hug, and now her ponytail whipped back and forth as she looked at each of us. I stayed as far from them as I could. "Mumma, this is the man who—is he a friend of yours, too? How come you didn't tell me? And why is he here now? Does he live here? Remember me?" She held out her hand for him to shake it. "I'm Rowen. We met yesterday. At the—"

"I know, honey." Lily's voice was as measured as I'd ever heard. She looked me square in the eye, with the same expression I'd seen so many times when she had trapped a white-collar bad guy in his lying tracks. Stronger folks than I had collapsed under its laser focus. "I know all about it. All. About. It."

She blinked twice. "Why do you have my daughter now?" she asked me. "If I may be so bold."

"There was a thing at Graydon," I began the agreed-upon explanation. "Your phone didn't work, the headmistress said, and Petra was at the car place, and my name is next on the contacts list."

"Right," Lily said. "The headmistress."

"Of course I remember you," Sam was saying. He'd crouched next to Rowen, and they were now almost eye to emerald eye. I'd always thought she was a miniature Lily, but seeing them together, she was as much Sam Prescott as she was Lily Atwood. "My name is Sam."

"Sam. Do you know my mother?" Rowen, infinitely polite in social situations.

"I do," Sam said. "In fact—"

"Mr. Prescott and I are old friends," Lily said. As if she were providing lines in a script. "And we haven't seen each other for years. Many years. He lives very far away. We—"

"That's exactly what I was going to say," Sam said. He stood, eye to eye with Lily now. "I'll be leaving town soon, though. And probably won't be back."

I could watch them, communicating. Understanding each other. As if I were invisible. I wondered how much Sam had told her. Not that it mattered; toast was toast. I also wondered where Banning was. Why he hadn't come out to join in the fun party. *Coward*.

"Good," Lily replied. "Rowen and I will say goodbye, then. Rowey? Say goodbye to Mr. Prescott."

Lily's phone buzzed in her hand. A text. She looked at it, a puzzled expression on her face. She pushed at the screen several times as if there might be more. Cassie, I predicted. *Oh*. Was Cassie on the way?

"Where's Banning?" I asked Sam. After all, Rowen thought we were pals, and Lily probably wondered the same thing. Might as well do her research for her yet again.

"Doing some errand, he told me," he said. "He's been gone a couple of hours. Three, at least. He should be back any minute."

"No." I shook my head. "But he was here, like, an hour ago. He called me to say he'd seen Lily in the drive—" Oh, crap. I stopped. I was on death row, and giving myself the lethal injection.

"I called him to tell him she was here," he said. "Surprised me, too."

"Greer?" Lily had put her arm around Rowen, drawing her closer. She was still staring at her phone. "I'm going to need your car keys."

I reached into the zipper pocket of my bag, then stopped. She was taking my keys? "For what?"

"Sam, I need you to . . ." She took a deep breath, and I saw something change, a decision, or a moment of clarity, I had no way to decode it. "If you'll do me a favor, I need you to take Rowen and do something fun for a while. Would you like that, Rowen?"

So Lily was going to kill me, here in Banning's driveway, and she was getting rid of the witnesses. Probably not, but that's what it felt like.

"Yes, please!" Rowen's face glowed with delight. "If it's fine with you, Sam, and it's fine with Mumma. We're having a snow day without the snow. That means we can do a fun thing. Sam, do you like ducks?"

"Ducks are the best," Sam said. "Can't wait to see them. Lily?"

"That sounds perfect. If you can give me and Greer about an hour, we have one thing to clear up. But you two should go have fun."

I handed over the key fob. "GPS Watertown Street," I said. Fun. Ducks. Lily sending her daughter off with her hated ex-lover. I was in the Twilight Zone. "You'll see the Charles River."

"Rowen knows my phone number, Sam," Lily was saying. "Don't you, Rowey?"

"It's 617 . . ." She recited Lily's number.

"Good, sweetheart. Now, Mr. Prescott is a very trusted friend, Rowen, so you take good care of him, okay? And Sam? Thank you."

Sam clicked open the doors of my car. I was about to be stranded here, with an enraged Lily and an enraged Banning—whenever he showed up—and who knew what else.

"Sam?" Lily called after him.

He and Rowen were halfway to the car. Sam stopped, turned, looked at her.

"We'll deal with . . . the rest of it later, you know?" she said.

"Together," he said.

"Together," Lily said.

CHAPTER 63

LILY

Lily watched her daughter walk away with her father, a duo she'd never imagined she'd see. The engine of Greer's car purred into life. Rowen, strapped into the back seat, waved as the car pulled away, and Lily felt as if the invisible string connecting them was being stretched to its limits. But knowing what she knew now—Cassie on the way—it was her only choice to get her daughter to safety.

Banning had lied to them all from moment one, she now knew. That story he'd told Sam about Cassie's motives—it might be true, and it might not be. Either way, he'd lied to one of them. Or maybe even to both of them. She could only imagine what he'd said to Greer. Standing here in the sunshine, the poor woman looked like she was about to faint with humiliation. As well she should. But at least Greer wasn't about to ruin her life, the way Cassie might be planning to.

"Is there something you'd like to tell me, Greer?" Lily tried to keep the fury out of her voice, facing the woman she'd worked with for almost two years, and who she now realized she hardly knew. "Hardly knew" was how Lily liked to keep it with work colleagues. Maybe, with Greer, she should have dug a little deeper for the stuff they don't include on résumés. Like honor.

"I'm so sorry, Lily." Greer nudged a loose clump of dirt at the edge of the lawn with the toe of a black running shoe. As always, she wore jeans and some random tee, today with a thin black blazer. "I can explain, if you'd let me."

"All ears," Lily said. Two fifteen now. Cassie was late. Either she had misjudged the traffic—from where, Lily didn't know—or was lost, or wasn't coming. What happened next would dictate the rest of Lily's life. The tightrope of her career, the publicity and the spotlight, and the daily, even hourly knowledge that everyone was always looking at her, judging her. It was the life she'd chosen, she knew that. The volatile life of a "public figure," as the lawyers called her. The "talent," as she was in television. #PerfectLily on social media. And once that crashed into smithereens, all the king's horses would be, as always, worthless.

Greer cleared her throat. "Well, when Smith called to meet at Lido—Banning now, we know—he first told me he'd been hired by a 'client'—Sam Prescott, we now know—who wanted to—"

A car came around the corner. Not slowly, not stopping for the stop sign, not trolling for house numbers. The car, the same beige four-door Banning had driven yesterday to Lido, and to the gas station, and finally to this very house.

"Banning," Lily said. She slipped her hand into her jacket pocket, needing the reassurance her cell phone was there.

The car had barely stopped as Banning got out and slammed his door. Ray-Bans hanging from the collar of his black tee, and black ball cap still on, he strode up to her and Greer.

Lily saw him assess the open garage door. Then the second-floor windows.

"Was I expecting you?" He looked at Lily, then

looked at Greer. Then at Lily's car. "You came here together?"

"Well," Greer began.

Lily silenced her with a look. That answer would require too much explaining. "I knocked, but no one answered. I guess your client left. I came to tell you Cassie's on the way."

Banning narrowed his eyes. "When?"

"When?" Greer said.

"Two o'clock." Lily held up her watch. "She's late."

"Good. Glad I got here. You should have called me. Where'd she say she was coming from?" Banning squinted into the sun, jabbed on his sunglasses.

"She didn't," Lily said.

"Did she tell you the name she's using now?"

"She didn't," Lily repeated. "But, Banning, is there something you forgot to tell me about her?"

"Like what?"

"Like about her motivations."

"How would I know her motivations?" Banning almost snorted the word, waved off her question. "You know I haven't been in touch with her."

"Right," she said. "Just making sure." She looked at her watch again. Not even a minute had gone by. What Banning had told Sam couldn't be true—if Banning had been in touch with Cassie enough to know her intent, he knew a lot more than he was telling Lily now. And her money was on Sam's truth. She'd trusted him from the beginning, seven years ago. Yes, they'd made some terrible decisions. And after that, she had, too, along the way. Maybe. But this Sam was still her Sam, she could tell. And she not only trusted him, she trusted herself. And her own instincts. She'd better be right. He had Rowen now.

"Maybe Cassie's not coming," Lily said.

"You think?" Greer said.

"She'll be here," Banning said.

"Maybe you two should go inside." Lily pointed to the front door. When Cassie showed up, Lily needed to talk with her alone. And she didn't want Cassie to panic when she turned that corner and saw three people watching for her in the driveway. "Yeah. Go in. I'll wave at you to come out when the time comes." She held up her phone. "Or I'll call you, Greer."

"You sure you're okay?" Greer asked.

"Is that what you care about?" Lily kept her voice calm, but knew Greer understood her fury. And disappointment.

"We'll be watching," Banning said. "In case you need us."

"Sure," Lily said.

Maybe the whole thing was ridiculous, she thought as she watched them go in the front door. Standing here in a dumb driveway for the last half hour, waiting for the thing she'd been sure for most of her life would never happen. Cassie's last words to her, her parting words on that long ago night, had been *I love you*.

But no. That was wrong. Cassie's last words to her were in this morning's text. And they'd been *See you soon*.

CHAPTER 64

CASSIE

She was late, but not that late. Cassie fretted at the interminable stoplight before what the GPS map called the Watertown Bridge, drumming the steering wheel with her fingers. The Charles River was in front of her, an estuary or an offshoot or whatever they called them, so serene and sparkling in the afternoon sunlight. A man in a plaid shirt walked with a little girl along the shore, the girl—his daughter?—pointing at the green-necked mallards and their dowdier spouses. The man and child looked so connected, Cassie thought, then laughed silently at her own vivid imagination.

The light turned green. And then another one, and another one, and at 2:17 by her Jeep's dashboard clock, she turned at the corner of Hamilton and Sycamore and saw the woman standing in the driveway.

How long is twenty-five years? Long enough for a little girl to become a successful journalist, with a career and a daughter. Long enough for some memories to fade and vanish forever and others to rise to the surface, gilded and permanent, Christmas tree mornings and shared peppermint sticks. A new puppy, flop-eared and skittery and beloved. A wide-eyed seven-year-old watching her too-confident big sister pack up for college, a final hushed goodbye in a sleep-scented bedroom, all calico quilt and whispered useless apologies. Not long enough, though, to erase the guilt of what had happened, Cassie's stumble into a dark and dangerous world, where she'd made an inescapable decision. She had lived, at least, but in constant fear. Was twenty-five years long enough to erase fear?

The woman in the driveway was turned to her, watching her arrival, her outline familiar and unfamiliar. Lily touched her hair, and Cassie was close enough now to see her take a deep breath and take a step toward the street.

With a crunch of loose gravel, Cassie eased her Jeep to the curb and parked behind a tan four-door. And she didn't think, didn't wait, didn't wonder, didn't assess. She clicked open the door, and in an instant, they were in each other's arms, Cassie's shoulder bag sandwiched between them.

And then Cassie pulled away, had to, adjusted her shoulder bag and took a step back, looked her younger sister square in the eyes.

"I can't believe it," she said. "You *are* perfect."

"Oh, please, Cassie, *I* can't believe—are you okay?"

Cassie saw the tears in her sister's eyes, and they were in her own, too. "You kept the photo of Pooch and me."

"Of course," Lily said. "But where have you been? I can't believe—"

"Is this where you live?" Cassie gestured at the split-level home, the empty garage. "And sure, I'm fine. I'll tell you the whole thing, it's—"

"Listen, Cassie." Lily had grabbed Cassie's forearms, her grip tight over the long sleeves of her white tee. "I know this is insane, standing in the driveway of someone's house—not where I live, no—and if there were any easier way to do this, I would. But I have to ask you. Just—listen for two seconds. I know it's crazy. I'll tell you the whole thing in a minute, I promise, but back then, at Berwick, was that Detective Kirkhalter going to charge you with killing Jeremy Duggan?"

Cassie's answer spilled out of her, and she realized it probably didn't make much sense. "It was because I left him in that apartment, I didn't know he was dead, but he did die, and Kirkhalter told me a jury would never believe it was an accident. Not really an accident, I guess, but just—coincidence. There was all kinds of evidence, I know there was, but it wasn't my fault that he died, not really, and Kirkhalter told me—wait." She stopped, wondering about the missing link. "Lily? How did you know to contact me? I know Kirkhalter is dead, so—"

Lily had reached into her jacket pocket, pulled out her phone. Seemed to be reading something. Closed her eyes briefly, put it back.

"We have to hurry," Lily told her. "I've seen the confidential informant letter, and it's only about Zachary Shaw. Do you remember—"

"Dead." Nothing could diminish that memory. "In prison."

"Okay." Lily pressed her hands together, as if in prayer. "And you didn't sell drugs, did you?"

"Of course not," Cassie whispered. "I was a kid, a dumb kid, but all I wanted was to—I was a only freshman in college. But I knew if I didn't take Kirkhalter's offer, I'd be behind bars. I told you Lily, that night, that I'd done something bad. And I had. But it's more what I didn't do. I left him to die, and he died. And no matter what our mother used to say, no apology would make up for that."

"I know," Lily said.

"Who's that?" Cassie had seen the front door open. And now two people were coming out. First a woman, someone she didn't recognize. And behind her, close behind her, a man in sunglasses and a ball cap.

LILY

"Don't say anything, Cassie," Lily whispered as she moved closer to her sister. Greer and Banning, damn it, *damn it*, were emerging from the front door. Why? She'd told them to stay inside. *Damn.* Her sister—her sister—had the aura of a forgotten woman, pale skin, random hair, soft but tired eyes. The arms beneath her T-shirt had been muscled, and Cassie seemed wiry and strong. It was her eyes, though, twenty-five years older with the joy extinguished—that twisted Lily's heart. She expected Cassie to look different, of course, but in her mind, she still pictured Cassie's vibrance, everything about her glowing and confident. All that had vanished.

"Okay, I won't, but who is that?" Cassie whispered back. She'd retreated a step or two, Lily saw. Good.

Greer and Banning were walking toward them, Banning behind Greer, not beside her.

"I'm sorry, Lily." Greer's voice, though Lily had never heard it sound that way.

"Sorry?"

Lily felt Cassie retreating even farther.

"Stop right there, Miss Atwood."

"What're you talking about, Banning?"

"Not you, Lily. Your sister. Cassie. Stop right there."

Lily linked her arm through her sister's. "Banning?"

"Cassie Atwood, I'm Detective Walter Banning Kirkhalter from the Berwick Police Department. As you know, there is no statute of limitations on murder. And we now have an informant who will testify against you for the murder of Jeremy Duggan. You'll have to come with me."

"What? No! Lily?" Cassie had moved away from Lily, and backed up, closer to her car. "Lily? You lured me here? You *knew*? This was—oh my god, I can't believe it. I trusted you! I answered you! You're my sister!"

In a flash, Cassie turned and sprinted to her Jeep. Opened the driver's-side door. Stood with the car between her and the three in the driveway.

"No, no, no, Cassie, I didn't, I didn't." Lily had to make her understand. Banning had tricked her. And he was not a cop, no way. He'd lied to them from the beginning. What the hell was he doing? "I swear—"

But with one harsh motion, Banning had shoved Greer to her knees. Pointed his gun at Greer's head. Behind his sunglasses, Lily could tell his eyes were on Cassie.

"If you run, Cassie, I'll kill this woman," he said. "She's your darling sister's only friend. And then I'll kill Lily herself. Happily. And you'll be responsible for two more deaths."

"What? No, Cassie—Greer—how did—?" No real cop would ever do this. Lily had no idea what to do, no idea, but she knew this was wrong, wrong in every way, and impossible. Why did no one drive by, where were the neighbors, how could this place be so empty? This was not how this was supposed to unfold.

"Officer. Stop." Cassie's voice, demanding and decisive.

Cassie walked, one slow step at a time, from behind her car. Lily started to approach her, hand in her pocket.

"Lily. Stop." Banning's voice left no room for argument. "Don't even think about calling 911."

"Cassie," Lily said. "Listen to me. This man is lying. No cop would use an innocent person as a hostage."

"I'll come with you." Cassie's voice cut like ice through the spring afternoon. "If you put the gun down."

Lily watched her walk toward Banning, one palm in the air, one slow step at a time, surrendering. To what, though? Banning was no cop. What was she doing?

"Cassie. I'm sorry." Greer, on her knees on the asphalt, wiped tears from her eyes with both hands. Her voice almost a wail. "I didn't know. I didn't."

Banning kept the gun pointed hard at Greer. There were three of them, Lily knew, but it was too risky to try to overcome him. His gun changed the equation.

"Only if you put the gun down." Cassie had stopped walking. Yanked up the strap of her shoulder bag. "That's the deal."

"There's no deal," Banning said.

"Look," Lily said. "Banning. Whoever you are. You're in a nice little neighborhood in Watertown. Broad daylight. Every one of these houses probably has surveillance, state-of-the-art cameras rolling, all around us. People are probably watching you right now. And the minute there's a gunshot—I mean the *second*—some of the people in these nice little homes are gonna be on the phone." In an instant, she took her own phone from her pocket and held it at eye level so he could see she wasn't dialing. Then stashed it back. "So. Do as Cassie says."

"I'll come with you," Cassie said again. "If you put the gun down. And I mean—*down*."

Banning inched the gun away from Greer's head.

"Cassie?" he said. "And *I* mean—now."

"My sister told you to put it down first," Lily said. "On the driveway."

"Or else I'm not going with you," Cassie said. "Go ahead, kill anyone you like. It'll be the last time you see daylight. Like my sister said. You're right here in public. And there'll be two of us left to stop you."

Greer's eyes had widened, her tears flowing, unstopped.

Lily wanted to cry, too, but knew she couldn't. She had to see this through. She had a weapon of her own, but she would not take it out of her pocket until the right time.

Maybe four feet between Cassie and Banning. They stared at each other. Eye to eye.

"Put it down," Lily said. "And, Greer, you stand up. And kick the gun over by my car."

"Now," Cassie said. "If you want me? *Do it*. Last and only chance."

The metal scraped over the asphalt, and the gun stopped in the shadows beside Lily's car.

"Cassie? Remember the person your pal Duggan called back then while you were snooping in the kitchen?" Banning asked. His sunglasses glinted. "Yeah. I see you do. Well, he's told us everything. And if I don't report in, it's over for you, Cassie. And you, too, Lily, for hiding a fugitive. So Cassie? You're done. There's no one to help you this time."

"I know." Cassie's voice sounded weary. "It was worth it to be with you, Lily, even for this long. I wish I could have seen Rowen."

Lily reached into her pocket. Greer skittered away. Banning grabbed Cassie's arm.

"Don't even try it, Lily," Banning said.

Lily pulled out her phone. "It's just a phone," she said. "If you're a real cop and telling the truth and have a warrant for her arrest—"

"I don't need a warrant." Banning's voice stayed

confident. "She's coming of her own free will. Because she knows she killed Jeremy Duggan."

Lily held up her phone screen, took two steps forward, glanced at Greer, and waved the phone in Banning's face, hoping to distract him. "Look. Don't you want to see the pictures I have?"

"It's a black screen," he said.

"Don't move," Greer said. She had grabbed the gun and held it, pointed at Banning. "You know I'll shoot you. My turn now. Let Cassie go."

"Bitch." He swore under his breath as Cassie stepped away.

"Oh, did I not hit the right button?" Lily tapped her phone. "I got a text from a woman named Tosca Manukian a few minutes ago. She's a reporter. From Berwick. And I'd sent her a photo—from outside Lido, remember? The selfies with the college students you were so annoyed about?"

Cassie, now behind Banning, was reaching into her purse. Lily held Banning's eyes.

"So the hell what?" Banning said.

"And turns out—this Tosca Manukian knows Walt Kirkhalter's son is a dentist in Erie."

"That's bull—"

"But she did recognize *you*," Lily went on. "She says you're Jeremy Duggan."

CHAPTER 66

LILY

Lily watched Cassie's face change. Realizing.

In an instant, Cassie took a step forward. Lily saw her take a gun out of her bag. Stab it into Banning's ribs. With the other hand, Cassie ripped off his sunglasses and his hat and tossed them aside. They landed upside down on the asphalt. Cassie had opened her mouth. But nothing came out. Her gun stayed tight against Banning's side.

Greer kept the other gun pointed at Banning, too. "Jeremy Duggan? But he's—"

"Whoever you are." Lily came closer, savored each word. "You can't be arresting my sister for the murder of Jeremy Duggan. Because Jeremy Duggan is *you*. And you're alive. And now I'm calling the real police."

"That's ridi—"

"Shut. The hell. Up," Cassie said, every word precise. Paced. Ominous. "*You*. I spent the last. Freaking. Twenty-five years. Living in constant fear. Now hold up your freaking hands."

Cassie pushed her gun harder into Banning's ribs. He obeyed, palms toward Cassie, eyes burning, face white with anger. Lily saw Greer's arms trembling, but keeping two steps away, she continued to hold Banning's own gun pointed directly at his chest.

"Every second of every day." Cassie's voice, rock and steel, did not waver. "I've prepared for this moment. Wondered if I'd ever have to use this thing. Getting ready. Practicing. Worrying about what nameless stranger would show up to retaliate for what I'd told the DA. And now I realize it isn't some nameless stranger. And I'm a good shot. Asshole."

"I'm calling 91—" Lily began.

"And here's more good news," Cassie interrupted. She tilted her head, the center of attention.

Lily could almost hear herself breathing. Even the next-door robins stopped their grubby pursuits.

"The world thinks you're already dead," Cassie went on, "so now I can kill you for real. And it won't even count."

With a flap of wings, the robins fluttered away.

"Cassie." Lily took a careful step, approaching. "Honey. Don't."

"Why not?" Cassie widened her eyes, all innocence. "Who'd have killed him? Cassie Atwood? That poor girl is long gone. Years and years ago. Presumed dead. Right, *Jem*?"

"They'll track you down in thirty fricking seconds," Banning said.

"Oh, you think?" Cassie's pale eyebrows went up. "Track me *down*? Good luck with that, asshole. You and your goons haven't found me for twenty-five years. You don't even know my name."

Even Lily saw Banning look at Cassie's car.

"No license plate," Cassie said. "That's why I was late. I stopped to take it off."

"It wasn't my idea," Banning began, his voice wheedling and persuasive. "Kirkhalter told me it was the only way to—if I got caught, he'd get caught."

"Kirkhalter was *dirty*? In on it? A drug dealer?" Cassie's eyes narrowed.

Lily could almost see her sister's mind at work.

"Kirkhalter—pretended you were dead?" Cassie went on. "How did he even—oh my god, how does *anyone*—he stole my life. And my family's. Blamed me. To save his disgusting drug-dealing lying self. And to save *you*."

Lily understood, too. They'd used Cassie. Manipulated her. Erased her. No wonder Kirkhalter had been so harsh and dismissive when Lily had gone to see him. Lily was the reminder that the aging cop had trashed the justice he'd once vowed to uphold. That he was a drug dealer and a criminal and a relentless liar. Every word Lily said that afternoon, every tear she'd cried, had twisted the knife.

"You *left* me in that apartment, you incredible bitch," Banning retorted. "You left me to *die*. And then *I* had to disappear, too! I've waited and waited, *waited* for the moment I could make you pay for ruining my life. Don't you see how—"

"Shut. Up. Ruin *your* life? *Yours?* You two hideous self-serving creeps decided to sacrifice me—sacrifice *me*—"

Lily saw her sister's shoulders straighten. Her chin went up.

"Well, now it's your turn, isn't it?" Cassie said. "What goes around—"

"Honey?" Lily kept her voice quiet as if soothing an angry child. "It's okay. Don't shoot him. We'll work it all out. You're home now. And you, Banning. Duggan. Whoever. Don't move."

"Lily's always right," Greer said. She and her gun inched closer to Banning. "Everyone knows that."

"Don't. Anyone. Move." Lily tapped at her phone. "This is over. Cops are on the way."

CHAPTER 67

LILY

"That's her. Sitting at the picnic table." Lily pointed across the grassy riverbank, past the cattails and the long grass, past the gently flowing iridescent water, where Rowen and Sam Prescott sat side by side, looking at a book. Sam had called while she and Cassie and Greer watched the three police cars drive away, and he'd agreed to hang out with Rowen a bit longer. They'd found Watertown Bookshop, he'd said, and told Lily they'd be fine and reading by the Charles whenever she got there.

Cassie stood next to her on the still spring-muddy shoreline, shading her eyes from the last of the afternoon sun. "What a cutie. Rowen, I mean."

Lily had known the minute she read the text from Tosca Manukian this afternoon that Banning was a fraud. And that meant Sam Prescott had been used by him, too. They'd all been part of his scheme to lure Cassie from hiding. To put Cassie back into Banning's—Jem Duggan's—sights.

It had taken the police less than two minutes to arrive.

"None of you move!" The first cop had arrived, approaching cautiously, weapon drawn.

Lily imagined what he must have thought, two

women holding guns on a guy in the middle of a sub-urban driveway. Her clutching a phone.

"I'm Li—" she began.

"Miss Atwood!" The cop had planted himself in front of her. Weapon pointed at the threesome in front of him. "Get behind that Jeep. Are you okay?"

"That man threatened to kill us," Lily said over the officer's shoulder. "And to kidnap the woman on the left. She's my sister, and she's holding a licensed registered weapon. The other woman has *his* own gun. He had it to her head, but we—"

"She was about to kill me!" Banning cocked his head at Cassie.

"No, I wasn't," Cassie said. "Why would I do that?"

"Tell us about it at the station, sir," the officer said. A second officer and then a third had arrived, cars screeching to the curb, doors slamming, cops running. "Ms. Atwood, are you okay?" one asked. "You and your friends?"

"Yes, of course, thank you so much." She read his name tag. "Officer Nguyen. And for coming so quickly. It's all because of a big story I've been working on. This is my producer. And like I said, my sister."

"Hey! Officers. These bitches are lying." Banning's face had gone dark with anger. "Why don't you arrest *them*?"

"Because this is Lily Atwood," Officer Nguyen said.

Lily could still hear the sound of the handcuffs clicking onto Banning's wrist.

"Why didn't you kill me in the first place, Jem? At Berwick?" Cassie had put her gun back into her tote bag and stood, seething, focused on Banning. "Why didn't you just come after me then? You knew I'd seen your—"

"Damn Kirkhalter told me he already had." Banning almost spit out the words. "He said, 'I've dealt with her.' That he'd 'handled' you. And then you were gone.

What else was I supposed to think? I thought you were long dead. And good riddance."

"Kirkhalter?" Cassie frowned. "Detective *Kirkhalter* said that?"

"Let's go." Officer Nguyen held Banning, one hand on his shoulder, one on the handcuffs behind his back.

"Can we hear this, Officer? Please?" Lily knew this was the only moment they might be able to get the real story.

"Who do you think I called that day in the apartment?" Banning said. "I knew you'd seen the stuff, and thanks for not calling for help, by the way. You being such a coward was the only thing that made this work. Kirkhalter and I got me the hell out of there and announced I was dead. Kirkhalter told me he'd blame you for it, Cassie, and get rid of you, too. So I thought you were no threat. But then he got that letter. And told me. As soon as I read it, I knew you were still a problem. What a damn moron. What a freaking *wimp*. And he refused to tell me where you were."

"But Kirkhalter died in a—" Lily began.

"Problem was, after that, I had no way to find you, Cassie," Banning said. "But I could find *you,* couldn't I, Lily? I could use you as bait and help your beloved *sister* find *you.* And I'd be here when she did. I figured Cassie would recognize me the minute she saw me. But whatever. She wouldn't have much time to think about it. You either. And the person who killed you both? Well, that was no one who existed. Case closed."

"We have to take him now, ma'am," Officer Nguyen said. "We'll be in touch. We know where to contact you, of course."

"You should have stayed gone, Cassie." Banning— *Jem Duggan*—spat the words as he was escorted into the back seat of the cruiser. "You're such a—"

But whatever he said was slammed away by the closing door.

"I'm so sorry, Cass, I feel horrible about this," Lily said now as they walked toward the picnic bench.

"You couldn't have known." Cassie touched her shoulder. "That's fame, I guess, Lily. It's great until it isn't."

Their strides matched in the newly green grass and scatter of dandelions.

"D'you think Banning—I mean Duggan—killed Kirkhalter?" Cassie asked. "Caused the crash somehow?"

"We'll probably never find out," Lily said. "But Kirkhalter was part of the drug thing. And the apparently-dispensable Zachary Shaw, too, who they got *you* to throw under the bus. Wonder how many real deaths those three were responsible for."

"Yeah. And it has to be true," Cassie said. "Like I told you in the car, I did hear Jem—Jeremy—calling someone that day. The only other person who could have known that was the person he called. *Kirkhalter.* A dirty cop." She drew in a breath. "Oh. D'you think he paid for me, all these years, with drug money?"

They took a few more steps, side by side, along the riverbank.

"*You* paid," Lily finally said. "You spent your life hiding. After he made you feel guilty for a murder that never happened."

Cassie stopped at the water's edge, turned to her. "Yeah," she said. "But you've saved me from that now, little Lillow."

"Mumma!" Rowen's voice carried across the water.

CHAPTER 68

GREER

Everyone has something now, I thought as I stashed the last of my notebooks into the brown cardboard box I'd taken from the Channel 6 mail room. *Everyone has their happy ending. Lily, Sam, Cassie, Rowen. Everyone but me.*

I'd write my resignation letter, keep it brief and unspecific. New job opportunities elsewhere, I'd say. Television was a nomadic business. No one would care.

Especially not Lily.

For her, I'd left a sealed envelope with a note inside. *I'm sorry,* I'd written. I had no idea what else to say.

I spooled out a breath, looking at my now-empty bulletin board, the scatter of paper clips on my desk. My black WE CAN DO IT mug taunted me from inside that cardboard box and rolled onto its side as I hefted my possessions. Then I put the box down again.

And sat in Lily's chair.

My knees still hurt from that driveway.

Because of Lily.

From when I'd had a gun held to my head. From when I'd almost been killed. I could still feel that circle of metal on my scalp, still feel the hot breath of that—person, who'd found my one vulnerability; that

I understood my job, and would do it no matter what. To keep Lily perfect, to protect her—and look, I'm not saying I wasn't trying to protect my own career, too, I'll own that—but everything I'd done, *everything,* was to protect Lily. Perfect Lily.

I'd saved her damn toxic sister. I'd risked my life, *my* damn life, for that woman.

Lily wasn't so perfect when I'd arrived in Boston, was she? Had I ever taken any credit? No. Not one moment of applause, not one sparkly watt of spotlight was aimed at me, and that was fine. I was her producer, and I'd produced her perfect life. And now where was I?

Alone in some crappy office in a crappy local TV station, as if *that* was the pinnacle of success. There were a million Lily Atwoods out there, a million Lilys who only wanted to be perfect and famous and have someone do all the work while they took all the credit.

How many of them, I thought as I stared at my cardboard box, how many of them had a producer who was devoted enough to almost get killed for them?

And as if it were such a hideous betrayal to help a little girl see her own *father.* I'd only tried to make poor Rowen's life perfect, too, but oh, *no,* all I got was that Lily *look* as she turned her back on me.

She should have thanked me. But, of course, why start now?

Someone else would thank me, though. I could so easily find someone else's life to produce. Some Lily-to-be in some other city. Someone who'd be grateful for my wisdom. Lily wouldn't dare say a word against me.

I stood, and with both hands, took the container with the white orchid from Lily's desk. I walked out the office door and down the corridor, silent and alone, deliberate as a bride carrying her bouquet. Then, in one motion, I dumped the orchid into the big blue wastebasket at the end of the hall. Heard the whump as the ceramic container hit the bottom.

Back at the threshold to our—her—office, I surveyed the room one last time.

That white envelope on Lily's desk, my apology, almost mocked me.

I'm sorry, I'd written. What a lie. Lily's the one who should be sorry.

I picked up the envelope and tore it in half. And then tore it again and again and again and again.

I tossed the tiny pieces into the air like so much confetti. The bits of paper floated, silent, to the floor, a puzzle of paper that could never be reconstructed.

And I walked away.

CHAPTER 69

LILY

"That's Val," Lily explained as she and Cassie came into the entryway. The dog was snuffling around Cassie as if she had a dog treat in every pocket. "And this is Petra, who helps me with Rowen and everything else in the world, and who won't, at least, jump on you like the silly dog. *Down,* Val. Petra, this is my sister, Cassie."

"Val's just excited, Aunt Cassie," Rowen said. "I kind of know how she feels. Mumma, is Aunt Cassie staying with us?"

"Nice to meet you," Petra said.

"You, too," Cassie said. She scratched behind Val's ears. "Good pooch."

"Can we handle two more for dinner, Pet? Or we can all get takeout." Lily peeked out her front window, saw what must be Sam's Uber pull up to the curb. He'd gone back to the house on the corner to get his belongings, a police officer with him to make sure nothing else was touched. Or dangerous.

Police were keeping Jeremy Duggan in custody, Officer Nguyen called her to report. They'd discovered where he'd been this morning. Shopping.

"In his car, we found bags with clothing for a little

girl," Nguyen told her. "Dresses, underwear, pajamas. And a pink suitcase. He'd bought each thing at a different store."

Lily had felt the blood drain from her face.

"Did he have plans to travel with a child? If you know?" Nguyen asked.

"My daughter—he'd arranged for her to . . ." Lily's knees had almost failed her. Banning—she still thought of him as Banning—had maneuvered Greer to deliver Rowen straight to his door. Would he have used her as a pawn? To force Lily to choose between handing over her sister and saving her daughter?

They were all chess pieces to him—Lily, Rowen, Sam, Greer—to manipulate however he needed to get to Cassie. Get back at her. If Lily hadn't arrived first, he might have traumatized a little girl.

And in the end, the wolf was there.

"You're not letting him out, are you?" Lily asked.

"Not a chance," Nguyen had said. "Assault with a deadly weapon. Possession of a loaded firearm. Attempted murder, in my book. Stalking, too. Admitted he's watched your house. Something about seeing a flower delivery?" Officer Nguyen had said. Lily'd heard the mockery in his voice. "He'll stay behind bars all weekend, done deal. After that? Well, once *you* testify, he's in for good. Like I said. You're Lily Atwood. We'll need to talk with you, of course, but not until Monday. You and your sister okay, ma'am?"

"Lily?" Petra was saying. "*Two* more?"

Lily pointed out the window. "My friend Sam just arrived."

"No problem." Petra saluted her with a wooden spoon. "I made enough lasagna for weeks."

"Yay." Rowen clapped her hands. "This has been such a perfect day, Mumma," she said. "We had a snow day with no snow, and Aunt Cassie is here, and I got to meet Sam, and see ducks, and now we have lasagna. Awesome."

She'd retrieved her school backpack and Antarctica book from Greer's car. "I'm taking my stuff up to my room. Can Sam finish reading me the Antarctica book? Pleeeease? C'mon, Val."

"It depends." Lily understood how much those two words might mean, how much depended on what happened next. She looked out the window again. The sun was beginning to set, and she saw Sam standing on her flagstone front walk, suitcase in hand, staring at the front of her house. She knew what he was seeing; the tender-leafed weeping willow, the yellow tulips, the white fence around the backyard. A home. He had one of his own, too, a happy one, out in Colorado. And he'd have to leave here soon. "We'll have to ask Sam."

"You were just like that," Cassie said to Lily as the little girl and her dog trotted upstairs. "Always so enthusiastic. You loved everything." She took a deep breath, let it out as she looked around. "Oh, the lilies. I was worried I got the wrong address from my web search. You *did* get them."

Lily thought about Smith, how disturbed she'd been about those flowers when they first arrived. "Thank you," Lily said. "Long story about those. And oh— the stuffed Penny. Thank you. You made me cry, Cass. Rowen still has the original. It's her most precious thing."

The two sisters stood in the entryway, the music from the kitchen behind them, footsteps of girl and dog upstairs, and Lily wondered if time could ever stop, or slow, or moments be preserved forever. How families ebbed and flowed, but somehow, if they were lucky and patient—well, maybe that's what a perfect life truly required. Time and patience. And understanding.

"I'm so sorry about what happened to you," Lily began. She caught a glimpse of herself in the hallway mirror—makeup long gone, mascara cried away, hair in disarray, a streak of dirt on her jacket, and it didn't matter. "I looked and looked for you—" She heard how inadequate that was. And how, although once true, she could never let Cassie know how much she'd once hoped her sister would stay away.

"You're—okay, Cass? Happy?" Whatever happiness meant. It was impossible to know what to say. Impossible to understand the decisions her sister had made. And what had been done to her. "Have you ever thought about suing—someone? Sam's a lawyer; he could help. And I'm definitely calling Tosca Manukian. *I* can't do a story about this, but she can. It's outrageous."

"It is what it is, Lily." Cassie's smile was rueful and accepting. "Tosca Manukian. How well I remember. Listen, we can talk about it all later. From what you told me in the car—you've got something more urgent to deal with."

Lily saw Sam through the screen door, opened it before he knocked.

"Hey," she said. Again the air was heavy between them, some ridiculous force field.

"Hey," Sam said.

"We have lasagna." Lily felt like a fourteen-year-old.

"Does that mean I'm invited?" He stashed a battered brown leather suitcase under the hall table. "Hi, Cassie. Quite a day."

"Got that right," Cassie said. "Listen, I'm gonna go see how Petra's doing. Maybe she could use a second cook."

"Petra?" Sam asked as Cassie left them.

"Nanny," Lily said. "Come in. Sit."

The music from the kitchen wafted in, and a scent of cheese and oregano and tomato mixed with the fragrance of the lilies. Lily sat in the far corner of the couch. Sam took the big chair, diagonal.

There was silence, thick silence, and Lily wanted to fill it, needed to fill it, could not think of what to say. Sam was—still Sam. Still, ridiculously, married. But this time, happily.

"You were horrible at the beginning," Lily said, and then regretted it instantly, what a stupid, *stupid* way to start a conversation.

Sam leaned toward her, forearms on blue-jeaned knees. "Guilty," he said. "My wife was—enraged. Crazed. Convinced me you had ruined my life, and hers, and never, ever, not for one moment, let me forget it. That was hardly the place to bring Rowen. I had to keep her away."

"You didn't seem too upset about it." Lily remembered it so clearly. Sam's dismissal, the emotional doors slamming shut.

"I—what can I say?" He stood, turned away from her, then back. "She's gone, my life has changed, and so has yours. You have all this now." His gesture swept the room. "And a perfect daughter. Who I've missed every day."

"She's upstairs." Lily pointed. "And she wants you to keep reading the Antarctica book to her."

"How do you feel about that?"

"I feel like . . ." Lily paused, assessing. "I feel like I'm keeping a secret from her."

The silence again, then laughter and barking from upstairs.

"Should we tell her together?" Sam asked. "And then figure it out? Isabel will be—thrilled. And I know Rowen will live here. With you. It's fine. It's better. My plane is tonight, the Uber is coming back for me. I just—I don't want to lose her."

Lily stood, and they were face-to-face, and she didn't know, couldn't decide, how could she, whether to hug him or shake hands or burst into tears.

The Jeep's driver's-side door was open. Cassie on one side of it on Lily's driveway, Lily on the other. Rowen, holding the old Penny, stood on the front steps, still in her jammies, watching. *Give us a moment,* Lily had told her.

"We could still come see you, though, couldn't we?" Lily pleaded. Friday morning. Cars crisscrossed her street, a school bus chugged by. Lily'd let Rowen stay home today while she decided what to do about the betrayal of Maryrose Glover. School cafeteria inspections, fire drills. Probably Glover had fed Smith both those stories, maybe he'd even paid her for those, too. Maybe public school *was* safer. At least the headmistresses didn't take bribes. "Please. Tell me where you live. What you do."

Cassie shook her head. "Everyone will know who you are. It's too dangerous," she said. "Duggan—he was just a tiny part of the—the thing. Even if he's out of the picture, I still did what I did. I testified against them all, and as far as they're concerned, no matter what happens, I'll never be safe."

"But Banning—Duggan—is *not* dead!" Lily needed to convince her. "Kirkhalter had nothing on you—it was—it was—and it was such a long time ago!" Lily got angrier every time she thought of it. Greer was so wrong. Cassie—her sister—was a victim. And long ago and far away, Lily had been in love with an unhappily married man. If her audience didn't like Lily as a result—that was *their* problem. But she predicted they'd love her even more.

She and Cassie had talked about it all night, arguing, explaining, cajoling, entreating.

"After Jem Duggan's trial, it'll all come out anyway,"

Lily said. "And it wasn't even *about* your drug testi-mony, right? It was Duggan's *personal* revenge."

But Cassie had stayed firm, no matter how Lily tried to persuade her.

"I can never feel safe," she said.

"Cassie, listen," Lily said now, unwilling to let her sister leave again. "I can do a big story about it. What-ever. I'll quit, if I have to, to write it. It doesn't matter what people think. You're more important. Justice is more important."

"Thank you, honey." Cassie reached out, touched her arm. "But the world isn't perfect, Lily. Even you can't make it be. And the more you try to force it, the more it laughs at you."

"But—"

"And I love you, Lily, and our Rowen—but I won't ever feel safe. Not ever. Not for me, not for you, not for her. You're probably right, but I have to go. I'm better *out* of the spotlight. You're better in it."

"But I don't even know how to find you."

"And that's how it has to be. For now, at least. And I do know where to find you, baby sis. Maybe I will."

Cassie reached for her and enveloped her, and she was that little girl again for that brief moment, loved and protected and safe.

"Remember me, okay, little Lillow?" Cassie whis-pered. And then she let go.

The car door slammed, and the Jeep pulled away.

Lily walked through the grass, the green of the morning blurred through her tears.

"Mumma?"

Lily saw the concern on Rowen's face as she ap-proached the front porch.

"Are you sad that Aunt Cassie is going?"

"I am, honey," she said.

"Do you want to hold Penny?"

Lily took the plush black-and-white toy. And watched the Jeep disappear.

"I'm happy about Sam, Mumma. And Val is, too, and Penny is, too. Aren't you, too?"

"I am," Lily said.

"And, Mumma?"

Lily looked down at her daughter. Cassie had tied her penguin ribbons this morning in perfect bows. Rowen's life was about to change in ways the little girl couldn't have imagined. Or maybe she could.

"Know what would be perfect?" Rowen asked. "If I could be just like Aunt Cassie when I grow up."

"I hope you *will* be, honey." Lily handed Penny back to her rightful owner and draped her arm across her daughter's shoulders. "They say you can't choose your family," she told her. "But if we could, we would still choose Cassie."

ACKNOWLEDGMENTS

Acknowledgments are the opportunity for the author to thank everyone who helped make the book possible. But for this book, there's so much more to acknowledge.

On March 12, 2020, I was sitting in seat C3, flying to Palm Beach, typing this book madly on my laptop, and feeling gloriously happy. *I love this book*, I was thinking, as I typed. I was on my way to a big book event to celebrate *The First to Lie*, and I thought— *wow, what a perfect life. I love being an author.* The next day, homeward bound, I sat on the return flight, laptop closed, terrified. What would happen to us all?

I came home so relieved to see my husband, knowing our lives would never be the same. The next day I decided deadlines were deadlines, and I went back to my manuscript. I stared at my computer, but I couldn't write. My beautiful, fabulous book seemed so . . . unnecessary. *Entertainment?* I thought. *Storytelling?*

And then I realized, more powerfully than ever, that I had decided to be an author, with agency and intent, and that writing this novel would be the very best thing I could do. It's always safe inside a book, I decided, and I powered forward.

And here's what brings tears to my eyes. So many

people in my book world did that, too. My incredible editor, Kristin Sevick, home with her family and homeschooling her kids, rearranged her life to make room for me and this book with grace, brilliance, and her usual genius. My incredible and brave agent, Lisa Gallagher, almost trapped in London, persevered throughout and never broke our connection. My brilliant and talented family at Forge Books also pivoted, regrouped, and powered forward: Our invincible chairman, Tom Doherty, the man who started it all. Fritz Foy at the helm. Thank you: Linda Quinton, Lucille Rettino, Eileen Lawrence, Jenn Gonzales, Brian Heller, Christine Jaeger, Brad Wood, Laura Pennock, AJ Murphy, Talia Sherer, Alexis Saarela, Libby Collins, and Laura Etzkorn. *All of you* transformed into superpeople and kept the fires burning. When it came time for a cover, the brilliant Katie Klimowicz created this luminously gorgeous one. From home. I am in awe of this team.

At Jungle Red Writers, we made the same decision. My sister bloggers—for eleven years now!—Rhys Bowen, Deborah Crombie, Hallie Ephron, Jenn McKinlay, Lucy Burdette, Julia Spencer-Fleming, and I leaped onto email—should we stop? Did blogs matter anymore? Yes, we decided. They matter more than ever. And we came through this together, with endless ups and downs, and with each other.

My gang at Career Authors, too, renewed our intent to share our experiences with those who want to make a career of being an author. I am grateful every day to Brian Andrews, Dana Isaacson, Paula Munier, and Jessica Strawser (and tech whiz Jon Stone). I treasure our Monday mornings at 10 when we laugh and plan and commiserate on Zoom.

And I am joyful to acknowledge the amazing Hannah Mary McKinnon. Our friendship bloomed during the pandemic, as I joined her on her groundbreaking

First Chapter Fun, which she created to help writers in this horrible time, and which she and I have now grown to incredible success. I would not have been involved without the pandemic. Would not have known her. They are strange thoughts.

The brilliant Karen Dionne and I came up with The Back Room, another way to handle the woes of pandemic writers. We are so proud of our Zoom up close and personal events, inviting authors and readers to share in our interactive panels. This never would've happened without the hideous pandemic, and Karen and our Back Room crew are such shining stars.

Think of how we have all grown during this! Andrea Peskind Katz at Great Thoughts. Pamela Klinger-Horn. Ann Garvin and the glorious Tall Poppy Writers, dear friends and crusaders and so talented! Ann-Marie Nieves. Suzanne Leopold. A Mighty Blaze, still blazing with Jenna Blum and Caroline Leavitt.

Bookstores, too, had to figure out how the heck to handle the pandemic. The Poisoned Pen, Wellesley Books, Brookline Booksmith, Murder on the Beach Mystery Bookstore, and Page 158 Books all sprang into action, helping readers stay connected with the books they devoured. Congratulations, you rock stars, and thank you for everything.

With infinite gratitude, too, to the brilliance of Dick Haley at Haley Booksellers. Kym Havens at An Unlikely Story Bookstore and Café. Book Club with Style, Jamie's Grab You a Book, Tattered Page, A Novel Bee, and Annie McDonnell at The Write Review, and oh, the incredible *Friends & Fiction* podcast!

For Robin Agnew, Janet Rudolph, Lisa Unger, Erin Mitchell, Kristopher Zgorski, Dru Ann Love, Laura Rossi, Barbara Peters, Lisa Scottoline, and James Patterson.

For the skill and talent (and patience) of Mary Zanor, Maddee James, Mary-Liz Murray, Nina Zagorscak,

Marie Ricci, Mary Lou Andre, and Charles Anctil. For my darling producer, Mary Schwager, and my dear sister, Nancy Landman. For my neighbors Amy Saltonstall, Maureen McKibben, and Rene Augesen—we all navigated the River Street pandemic together.

And oh, the West Newton post office! What a lifesaver.

I have to acknowledge you the most, dear readers. We are getting through this together, through horribleness and fear and incredible uncertainty—and I truly would not be here without you.

And Jonathan, Jonathan, Jonathan.

As always, I am so happy with our traditions: some of the names in the book are from generous auction donations, but I will let you all guess. I have tweaked some geography to protect the innocent. And thank you—I love it when people read the acknowledgments.

Read on for a preview of

THE HOUSE GUEST

Hank Phillippi Ryan

Available in Winter 2023
from Tom Doherty Associates

A FORGE HARDCOVER

CHAPTER 1
FRIDAY

Alyssa swirled the icy olives in her martini, thinking about division. She stared through her chilled glass to the mirrored shelves of multicolored bottles in front of her at the hotel bar. Division, as in divorce. Not only the physical division, hers from Bill, but what would happen after the lawyers finished. They'd already created a ledger of their lives together, then started the Macallens's financial division. Which would be followed by the devastating subtraction.

Bill had subtracted her from his life; that was easy math. With a lift of his chin and a slam of the front door and a squeal of Mercedes brakes. She'd asked him why he was leaving her, *begged* to know, yearned to understand. But Bill Macallen always got what he wanted, no explanation offered or obligatory. She had done nothing wrong. Zero. That's what baffled her. Terrified her.

She jiggled the fragments of disappearing ice. *Division*. The Weston house. The Osterville cottage. The jewelry. *Her* jewelry. The first editions. The important paintings. Club membership. The silver. Money. The lawyers, human calculators who cared nothing about her, would discuss and divide, and then Bill would win. Bill always won.

All *she'd* done for the past eight years was addition. She'd added to their lives, added to their social sphere, organizing and planning as "Bill's wife," fulfilling her job to make him comfortable and enviable and the image of benevolent success. She'd more than accepted it, she'd embraced it, and all that came with it. And then, this.

I need a break, he'd told her that day. She pictured that moment now, a month ago, could almost smell him, a seductive mixture of leathery orange-green aftershave and his personal power. Bill talking down to her, literally and figuratively, wearing one of his pale blue shirts, expensive yellow tie, all loose and careless, khaki pants, and loafers. A *break*! As if his life with her was a video he could casually put on pause while he did more important things. *What things?*

Alyssa felt her shoulders sag, assessing the other parts of her life grouped on Bill's side of the ledger. She understood, she did, it was difficult when a couple split. Allegiances were tested. Loyalties strained. She jabbed at the closest green olive with the little plastic stick. But Bill had taken the friends. She'd have thought some of them, at least, would've stuck with *her.*

But they'd all sided with Bill. Every single one of them. And now—at the club, at the gym, at the mall— all Alyssa got was pitying glances. Fingertip-hidden whispers. Unanswered calls. As if they, in their hothouse world of affluence and connection, understood something she didn't.

The music from the speakers in each corner of the Vermilion Hotel's earnestly chic, dark-paneled bar floated down over her, some unrecognizable tune, all piano and promises, muffling conversations and filling the silences. A couple sat at one end of the bar, knee to knee. On vacation, on business, clandestine. Impossible to tell. At the other end, a sport-coated man, tie loosened, used one finger to fish the maraschino cherry out of his brown drink, popped it into his mouth, and licked his fingers before he went back to scrolling on the phone in front of him. Alyssa was in the middle. Alone. She drew in a deep breath, all peaty scotch and lemons and strangers and elusive perfume. Alone.

When she and Bill first met, that night at the charity event, they both had big plans. Now only *he* had them. When she wasn't Bill's wife anymore, who was she? And did she have the power to change that?

Her phone lay face up on the zinc bar, its glowing screen taunting her with the proof. No matter how many times she looked at it, her calendar messaged her new reality.

You have no events. No. Events. Only blank days, one after the other, calendared out in front of her. She scrolled back through her past, the listings grayed out now, ghosts of occasions. Charity balls, gala dinners, speeches by successful entrepreneurs, justice-for-all somethings, and a fundraiser where they'd auctioned off A Day with Bill that went for thousands. Everybody loved Bill, and somehow, calculating again, Alyssa was the beloved plus-one. Now, in the excruciating math of marriage—addition, division—she was the minus.

Nothing had changed for *him*. Bill was always jetting off, to New York, or Chicago, or someplace exotic. She reached into the shoulder bag hanging from the curved back of her bar stool, slid her hand into a side pocket, and pulled out a postcard of sunlit palm trees, like they used to see in Saint Bart's. Bill sent them just often enough to be manipulative; unsigned picture postcards showing lush flowers and blue skies. *Here's where you aren't,* he seemed to say. *Here's where you will never be again.* Here in Weston, where she *was,* she had slush. Slush, punctuated by crocuses. Spring in Massachusetts.

She imagined Bill walking in and seeing her, alone

on a Saturday night, on this well-worn stool at a suburban hotel bar. Brown roots showing. Manicure
failing. And courtesy of the doomed-to-divorce diet,
gone almost scrawny at five pounds thinner. If Bill had
caught her here—which he wouldn't, she'd picked
this place because it was out of their orbit—he'd
have sneered that dismissive sneer at her vodka with
three, now two, olives. Alyssa Westland Macallen,
almost-divorced at thirty-five. She swirled the ice again.
Childless, friendless, pitiful. Her husband, fifteen years
older, was off having all the fun. That didn't seem
fair.

"May I get you another, ma'am?" The bartender,
high cheekbones and frowning his concern, paused,
wiping out a champagne flute with a blue-striped
towel.

Ma'am, she thought. Might as well have *cliché*
stamped on her forehead.

She looked at her watch, pretending. "Oh no," she
said. "How did it get to be so late? Everyone will be
expecting me."

"Ah." The bartender held the flute up to the row
of tiny lights twinkling above us. "Of course." Alyssa
watched as he checked the glass for spots, then, turning away from her, slid it into place on a thin wooden
rack.

Bill. William Drew Macallen. *Where are you? And
with who?* There could be no other reason but that he
was tired of her. And prowling for wife number two.

She stared at the pale place on her finger where,
for eight years, three months, and twenty-seven days,
her wedding ring had been. A piece of jewelry the universe prescribes that means one is married, and happy,
and off-limits. There was no piece of jewelry denoting
sorrow, or confusion, or disequilibrium. And now her
once-welcoming, once-glamorous home was empty,
and when the nights got dark and long, it terrified her.

As if Bill were lurking. Watching. Waiting. Even when Bill was gone he was there. Present in every shadow. She hated being alone in that house. Hated it.

She'd rather be in a random bar alone than be by herself in that house. Maybe she'd simply drive around. Forever.

"Just the check," she said to the bartender.

"But it's early."

The voice beside her—inquiring, hesitant—startled her. She hadn't noticed anyone walking up behind her, and had deliberately left the black padded barstools on either side vacant, a barricade against intrusion or discussion. Or introduction. Alyssa was not here to find companionship or conversation. In fact, the last thing she wanted was to talk to anyone. What would she even say? Even the simplest of questions—*how are you?*—could send her to tears.

The newcomer's fingernails were bitten and nubby, and her pilling sweater just the wrong shade of blue and uneven across the shoulders. She slung a raveled canvas tote bag over the back of her stool. Her curly-wild hairstyle had been an unfortunate decision, as was her hair's not-quite-auburn color.

What was this, the misfit convention? But that was . . . mean. And the world wasn't all about Alyssa Westland Macallen. It felt like it right now, but this woman was proof it wasn't. To this newcomer, the world was about *her*. That was just as valid. Alyssa should at least be civil.

"Early? Oh, well, maybe, but I have to get home," Alyssa said. No reason to take out her personal bitterness on a complete stranger. "Tough day," she added, explaining.

"Tell me about it." The woman shot her one glance, then looked back down at the polished metal bar.

Not a chance, Alyssa thought. She poked at her last olive. The well of her loss could not be filled with chitchat. But the weight of—something—seemed to be almost visible on this woman's thin shoulders. She'd made herself as small as she could, elbows close to her body, bare legs twisted around each other, one chunky heel of her scuffed black shoe hooked in the rung of her bar stool.

Alyssa fingered her right-hand diamond, embarrassed at its extravagance. Her birthstone, a gift from Bill during the first April they'd known each other, and not even her seething annoyance with him would convince her to take that off. She turned her hand palm up, hiding the ring. Opposite of flaunting.

"I'm sorry," Alyssa said. "Better days are ahead, I'm sure."

"Huh," the woman replied, more a huff than a word. She shrugged, one pilled blue shoulder briefly raised. "Have a nice night."

She'd hardly looked up, which gave Alyssa a chance to look at the newcomer in the expanse of mirror across from them. Dancers, the skilled ones, can express themselves with simply a gesture, or a posture, becoming a dying swan or an ill-fated fairy. *Poor thing.* The words came to Alyssa's mind at this woman's body language. She almost made Alyssa feel lucky. She swiveled her stool toward the stranger. Just a fraction. Not an invitation, simply an acknowledgment of humanity.

"You okay?" Alyssa had to ask. The music from the dining room behind them drifted in, silkier now, an encircling shimmer.

"Sure," she said. This time her demeanor seemed different. Something like defeat, Alyssa decided. Or fear.

"Get you something, miss?" Even the bartender's voice had softened.

"My treat," Alyssa said, surprising herself. She hadn't meant to say anything.

"Oh, I—"

"I insist." Alyssa felt her shoulders square, and a glimmer of empathy push its way through. Even the background music had shifted to a major key, optimistic. This was good. This was positive. This was progress. If she could help this poor woman, it might be a step in the right direction for herself as well. Maybe if she heard someone else's troubles, it would diminish her own. It couldn't make them worse.

CHAPTER 2

Alyssa smiled, for the first time in she didn't know how long. "Everything I start to say comes out wrong," she confessed. "Like a bad movie."

The bartender had placed a square, red-bordered napkin on the bar in front of the newcomer, and a dark globe of burgundy on top of it. He slid a tiny bowl filled with salted brown and orange bits—nuts and crispy things—next to it. "Enjoy," he said.

"How about—what's your sign?" The woman took a sip of wine, signaled her approval to the bartender, and angled her body toward Alyssa's. Offered a brief glimmer of a smile at the banality. "Or your major in college?"

"That was a long time ago." Alyssa smiled, then risked a quick assessment. "Longer ago than for you, I guess. How about—new in town? What brings you here? We can try all the classics."

"I'm thirty-two," the woman said. "New in town, that's an easy one. Yes. What brings me? That's more complicated."

And then silence. The couple down the bar had ordered onion rings, and the salty pungent fragrance wafted close to them. Black leather booths along the back wall were filling, Alyssa saw in the bar mirror. The gathering layers of conversation wove a murmuring soundtrack.

"Complicated?" Alyssa hadn't meant to pry, and her first instinct had been to leave the woman to her own life and concerns. But then she'd gone full Good Samaritan, and now she was stuck with it. For a few minutes at least. This woman's hair reminded her of her high school friend Kiereen, who'd walked out of sophomore French class one day and never returned. Madame Lemaire had explained to them, in French, some story about a sudden illness. We were *friends,* Alyssa remembered sobbing to her mother. She didn't tell me *anything.*

"Friends," her mother had sneered, stabbing out the charred end of a cigarette. "There are true friends, and false friends. Kiereen's family is rich, and they are not like us." Alyssa, who'd confided in Kiereen, and trusted her, hadn't understood that back then. Now she did. She also understood feigned sincerity, and the adjustable life span of friendship. Friendship based on expediency, necessity, opportunity. Money. The friends Bill brought to the marriage had left it, along with him. Or he had taken them.

This woman's eyes seemed unhappy, like Kiereen's once had, and she now stared into her burgundy as if she were seeing something Alyssa couldn't.

"I didn't mean to guilt you into talking to me." The woman's voice held no accent, no history. "When you said you were leaving, and I said it's early—it was simply an observation." She shook her head, a fleeting moment. Lifted her full wineglass. "I'm fine. And you're very generous. But I'm fine."

"You keep saying that," Alyssa said. "My mother used to say that. *I'm fine.* It meant—leave me alone."

"Oh, and now I've offended you." The woman's

eyes welled, and she faced Alyssa full-on. "I didn't mean it that way, I was just—letting you off the hook. I'm Bree."

"I'm not *on* the hook—Bree?"

"Embry," she said. "Bree. Lorrance."

"Alyssa—" She paused, martini glass raised, wondering if this was the opportunity to go back to her maiden name. She could be Westland, starting now. It wasn't like this encounter was going to be any longer than the length of a martini. It was after ten, pushing ten thirty, and Alyssa was eager to be done with this day. "Westland. Alyssa Westland."

"Nice to meet you." Bree clinked the edge of her wine glass, the red liquid sloshing, then finding its balance.

Three tones chimed from inside Bree's canvas tote bag. Bree startled, flinched, and a splash of burgundy spattered the white napkin.

"Oh, I am so—did any get on you? That beautiful white shirt? Oh I am so—"

The phone chimed again. Bree pulled a black cell phone from her bag, peered at the screen.

"No, not at all. Look. Not a drop." Alyssa waved off her concern. "You need to get that?"

The woman's face darkened as the phone chimed again. She closed her eyes, just a beat, then opened them again. *Poor thing,* Alyssa thought again.

"I should just turn it off, I know that," Bree said. "I just worry it's—it doesn't matter. But it's never anything, it's always—" She grimaced as the phone rang again, and scratched her forehead with what was left of her fingernails. A red welt appeared above her left eye.

The phone rang again. Then went silent. The silence seemed louder than the ring.

"Finally." Bree jammed the phone back into her bag. "He'll stop now."

The onion ring couple, arms thrown across each

other's shoulders, walked behind them, laughing. Alyssa watched their progress in the mirror, saw the woman wobble in her heels, saw the man catch her, steady her, and pull her closer. Saw the woman kiss his cheek.

"Why don't you refuse the call?" Alyssa asked. "When you see it's a person you don't want to talk to? Sorry, and I'm being pushy, but I mean, hit the button that says not now, or whatever it says?"

"Because then he knows I know he's called," Bree said. "And I've responded. And that means he knows I have my phone, and I'm looking at it, and he's *making* me react. I refuse to engage. I refuse to—"

Looking at Bree's face, hardening, and seeing Bree's hands curl into fists, Alyssa wondered if anyone in the world was happy. Besides Bill, of course. Any *woman*, maybe, a better question. Which she knew was her own bitterness again, and not reality. Alyssa had once been happy, and needed to remember everything in life was ephemeral. Even the bad things.

"Men," Alyssa offered, a one-word indictment.

"So true."

The bartender approached, a white towel tucked into the strings of his striped apron. Pointed to Bree, then Alyssa, inquiring.

Alyssa put her hand on top of her now-empty martini glass. "Driving."

"Sure," Bree said. She lifted her glass. "I'll put it on my room."

"Oh," Alyssa regrouped as the bartender turned away. Edited her imaginary biography of this woman. "You're staying here?"

"'Til the money runs out. Which might be soon." Bree puffed out a breath. "Or until . . ."

Alyssa waited. The woman was not finishing her sentences, as if she'd run out of steam or intent, or simply words of explanation. It was just bar chat, anyway, where social graces were not as stringent. And unanswered questions the norm.

"Until?" Alyssa finally prodded her, weary of the suspense but nonetheless curious. She couldn't figure this woman out, a thirtysomething from out of town? Staying in a hotel, at least, for some reason. Alone? Unhappy about something, and wanting to talk but not wanting to. Alyssa's one year at New England Law—which she'd loved until she loved Bill more—had taught her that every story had a secret, and every storyteller had a motive. Maybe this woman had left her—husband? Boyfriend? She'd seemed to agree with Alyssa's indictment.

"Or until what?" Alyssa asked again.

Bree's second glass of wine arrived. She looked at it, down through it, then picked it up, swirling the deep-red liquid.

"Or until he finds me," she said.

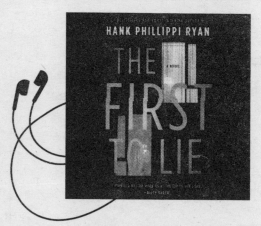